WHAT LIVES IN THE DARK

What Lives in the Dark

Edits & Proofreading by Jessica Johnson

Cover Design by rebecacovers

My Writing Playlist:

- willow – Taylor Swift
- not like you - stripped – Nightly
- Like Real People Do – Hozier
- pov – Ariana Grande
- ivy – Taylor Swift
- Wildest Dreams – Duomo
- brokenhearted - sunset – joan
- How To Move On – The Wldlfe
- Something To Hold On To – The Band CAMINO
- Delicate - Taylor Swift

To you, the person reading this. You are the only reason I want to write in the first place. Thank you.

Chapter One

SOMETHING WAS WRONG, AND I KNEW IT.
Stella would have told me if something completely crazy was going on, though… right?

The day was dragging on. I tried to focus on the blur of syllabus after syllabus, but usually ended up zoning out. Stella slipped back into her relative silence. My brother, Seth, barely spoke, though that happened often when he was around Stella.

What a great way to start off senior year—with everyone acting like it was the end of the world or something.

They'd both been acting weird all day, and I'd given up trying to figure out why by the time lunch came around. I just needed to get through the day, which seemed to be a harder task than I thought it would be. I felt strangely weak, and I had a headache that threatened to turn into a migraine every time I worried about what was going on with Seth and Stella. So, I decided to make that a worry for later.

When the last bell finally rang, Stella turned to me with some of that usual sparkle back in her eyes. It took some of the heaviness off my heart, but there was still that pit settling in my stomach that I couldn't quite ignore.

"Hey, do you think I could come over and hang out for a little bit? I need to sort out our reading list for AP Lit, and I'm pretty sure calculus is going to be the bane of my existence if I don't start memorizing this syllabus, like, yesterday."

I was a little startled at the intensity that came with her question, her dark eyes sparkling. Her curls were braided back away from her face, but the ends were floating wildly on the breeze running through the classroom. That wasn't what I was expecting her to say.

"Of course, you can come over, Stel!" My voice came out a little choked, but I was worried clearing it would draw attention to the nervous edge in the air, and I wasn't sure I was ready to talk about it. Stella seemed satisfied, at least, and her smile looked genuine as she turned away from me to walk towards my car.

Stella was my best friend, and I could probably count on my fingers the number of days I had ever spent away from her— barring those weeks of family vacation in the summers. In fact, just trying to think of a specific day I spent without her had me coming up empty. Trying to think of anything besides what was happening right in front of me seemed a little harder than I thought it should be, and my head began to hurt with the strain of it. I'd woken up that day with my head feeling heavy, like it was full of stuffing, and the feeling hadn't really worn off.

Stella even asking to come over was more of a formal habit at this point, but it was something that she'd done before. Some time, I was sure.

I shook off my bad feelings of the day as we walked to the parking lot to my car, trying my hardest not to let myself think about anything but the steps I was taking, but…

Everyone was staring at me.

Okay, so it wasn't *everyone*… But there was a core group of people that were definitely staring at me. They were staggered, almost as if they were not trying to be obvious in that they were together. I only assumed they were a part of a group because they had the same glazed, black eyes and hair that was slicked back. I surveyed my surroundings, silently and quickly counting them. There were fifteen in total, at least from what I could see: eight boys and seven girls. They were dressed in what looked like school uniforms, which stood out, since they weren't required at our school. The girls each had their hair pulled back into tight ponytails. Similarly, the boys' hair was either cropped short or gelled back away from their foreheads. Everything about them was a little too… perfect. Maybe eerie was a better word.

I pulled my attention back to Stella, who seemed to be rambling quickly about something now, her eyes seeming to dart back and forth without stopping on one thing for too long.

"Anyway, and then they forgot to bring me my fries and so I sent them back to get them. But guess what? When they brought them out, they were cold! Cold. Can you believe it? And Seth was all, 'Just eat them, it'll be fine,' and I was like, 'Are you kidding? I'm not paying for cold fries!'"

She was definitely panic-rambling, which set my pulse racing. The fact that I was so absorbed in my own thoughts that I hadn't even known she was speaking until now also worried me a little bit, but it seemed like I often got lost in my own thoughts.

I let her continue talking as I mulled over what to do next. The eyes surrounding us followed me all the way down the hallway. When we reached my locker, I grabbed her arm, dragging her to a stop with me.

"Stella," I started, looking her directly in the eyes, "what is going on? Is everything okay?"

She looked taken aback at my question, as if there was absolutely nothing going on and *I* was the one acting weird. Maybe I was.

Her eyebrows furrowed slightly, her eyes going wide and innocent.

"What are you talking about?"

She genuinely looked confused. Maybe I was overreacting. *Or she's a better actor than you thought she was*, my mind said, and I shook my head a little bit. My thoughts were so clouded today.

"Lyss?" She grabbed my hand, her brown skin a stark contrast to the paleness of mine. "Is everything okay with *you*?"

Her eyes were so open and honest, I had no reason to believe that she would lie to me. I couldn't think of a time she had ever lied to me before, not once, in the last fifteen years of friendship. Though she did avoid the question, and that didn't escape my notice. I shook my head a little again to try and clear the doubt, telling myself I was just being silly.

"Yeah, no, I'm good," I reassured her. "I don't know, maybe it's because it's the first day of school, but I'm getting bad vibes from those people over there." I tilted my head in the direction of a couple of the dark eyes that still held me in their gaze. "Do you see them?"

Stella's eyes swept over the crowd of students, landing lightly on one of the girls. She nodded.

"Do they look like..." I suddenly felt self-conscious with the question. "Are they staring at us?"

I watched Stella's face only as she turned her gaze back to me. She smiled but there was a tightening around her eyes. I knew her too well for her to be able to lie to me.

"Vying to be the center of attention, much?" She laughed but I didn't like the way it sounded. She grabbed my arm again, just like she'd done on the way into school that morning and pulled me with her as she continued to walk down the hallway.

Maybe I was just going insane? I thought I could live with that explanation.

Chapter Two

SETH WAS ALREADY AT THE CAR WHEN we arrived, of course, and he was practically bouncing up and down. How did he always have so much energy, even after eight hours of classes?

"What's all the excitement about?" I asked when we got close enough for Seth to hear me.

He was still bouncing on the balls of his feet, his golden hair swooping dramatically to one side. He wore glasses today, I realized. When had he gotten glasses? Instead of answering, he looked from my face to Stella's. I thought maybe I saw something pass between them, and I could have sworn I saw Stella's head shake once, almost infinitesimally. Before I could open my mouth to say something, Stella launched into what was almost a convincing retelling of making eye contact with someone named Carter Matthews. I don't know why this guy was all of the sudden so important to her, when I'd never heard of him until now. Stella had never spoken about Carter before, and I was confused by her sudden enthusiasm and insistence that he was staring at her first, and that he must be wanting to ask her to go out this weekend, but she was going to have to turn him down because she wasn't interested and also already had plans. What was even stranger was that, as we pulled out of the parking lot, Seth began adding to the conversation. He was saying something about how Carter would be fun to add to the group of us who were already going. Was I hearing this correctly? Seth and Stella were usually either fighting or ignoring each other, not making small talk. I had let myself look past the other strange things that had happened that day, but this was sending me over the edge. Seth and Stella were speaking about something that I had no context for, that seemed relatively unimportant, and he wasn't even making fun of her.

I *knew* something was going on.

I remained silent as I drove us home, listening to the rambling pair continue to talk about something I didn't quite comprehend. My brain was so fuzzy—all I could focus on was the road in front of me. Their voices blended into the background like white noise.

I would ask Stella about it as soon as I could corner her in my room. She may not say anything with Seth there, but if I could get her alone, I was sure I could coax the information out of her. Just like the time I found my broken iPod in the back of her closet, and I coaxed the information out of her little by little until she finally broke and told me everything. And got me a new iPod for my birthday.

I was convinced she knew something was going on today. Maybe it was something with their family? But, judging by the way he was acting, Seth was definitely involved somehow. His sudden enthusiasm was one of the things that was bothering me the most.

The whole drive home I planned out exactly how I was going to get Stella alone to question her, but when we got through the front door, something even more strange happened. Stella followed Seth into the kitchen, the two of them still jabbering about nothing, and she sat on one of the bar stools as he went to the fridge for a snack.

Fine, I thought to myself. *If they want to play that game, I'll play right along.*

I resigned myself to sit at a stool next to Stella as Seth brought over a tray full of unused ingredients that I was sure were going to be ruined within twenty minutes. I took out my notebook to at least pretend and do something other than decipher the conversation going on around me (They were talking about different types of Italian dishes now?), and the strangest afternoon of my life continued like that for about two hours. I was losing my mind by the time Seth had burnt his fourth try at garlic bread and his phone rang.

He took it out of his pocket and glanced at the caller ID. With a quick, darting glance at Stella, and then at me, he said, "I have to take this."

With what seemed like reluctance, he answered the phone and pressed it to his ear, making his way to the living room with a "Hey man, what's up?"

This was my chance. I turned to Stella and opened my mouth to ask her if I was going crazy or if the rest of the world was, but she beat me to it.

"This has been such a weird day, huh Lyss? I thought senior year would feel different."

I looked at her, a little miffed that she had still not let me speak. My mouth was opened from my getting ready to say something, and I closed it with an audible pop.

Stella also thought the day had been strange? If she was talking about how weird people had been acting today, then surely, I was just making something out of nothing when it came to her and Seth? Maybe something big was going on and Stella just wasn't ready to tell me yet. I felt a small wave of guilt as I thought about that possibility. I was so focused on how I was feeling, but what if something was going on with my friend? Maybe I was just nervous about my last year of high school and my mind was playing tricks on me.

I smiled at Stella, trying my best to keep those racing thoughts at bay. "It was definitely a weird day. I thought I was the only one who was feeling it! I keep thinking you and Seth are trying to hide something from me."

I chuckled and so did Stella. And I almost believed her. But when you've known someone for as long as I've known Stella, you know when something isn't right.

I tried again.

"Stel—", I began, just as Seth burst back into the room.

"So," he breathed, "what did I miss?"

Did he look at Stella when he asked that?

"Nothing!" Stella practically sang, spinning around on the stool. She cleared her throat. "But if I'm going to have to watch you turn more ingredients into lumps of coal, I'm gonna need some pizza. Anyone else?"

"Hurtful. But yes, I am definitely always down for pizza," replied Seth.

Stella and Seth dove into an argument about whether or not we should get mushrooms or jalapenos or pineapples on the pizza. Thin crust or hand-tossed? I stopped listening.

"What do you think, Lyss?" They turned to me and asked for my opinion.

"I'm not really hungry," I said, and they turned back to their discussion about pizza toppings, almost as if I hadn't spoken, and as though pizza toppings were the most important thing that anyone had ever taken time to discuss. I tried not to glare at them, but I knew they would be getting a death stare from me if they ever happened to look in my direction, which they didn't.

Finally, after the pizza was ordered, we moved the party into the living room and the discussion had moved from the riveting topic of food and onto the tantalizing question of which movie we were going to watch.

I'd officially had enough.

"Okay." I slammed my hand down on the coffee table. Seth and Stella both sat on the couch as I was in the chair just to Stella's left. They both stopped whatever they were arguing about this time and looked at me. Stella's eyebrows knitted together, the way they always do when she's trying to convince me she's innocent. I remembered that look from the iPod incident. I also knew from experience that I could break her eventually, if she wouldn't willingly give up the information, of course.

"What's wrong, Lyss?" She sounded so sweet and naive; I almost stopped my next sentence.

Almost.

But it had been a long day and I was tired of being left in the dark.

"What's going on here?" I asked her, and I looked at Seth too, for good measure. They were in on this together, I knew it. At that moment, I didn't really care if whatever was going on was something that either of them didn't want to talk about. I was tired of them ignoring me, and my head felt like it was going to explode.

"What do you—" Stella began. But I cut her off with the raise of my hand.

"Don't pretend like nothing is going on because I know something is. You were acting weird at school all day, and then you've been acting strange all afternoon too. You too, Seth." I pointed at him, feeling a little bit like a mom.

Seth gulped. Like, he actually gulped. The way you see cartoon characters or over actors in movies do.

He and Stella looked at each other then, and I saw something once again pass between them. Since when were they close enough to have conversations without even speaking? I couldn't think of a time when they had hung out enough, just the two of them, for this kind of relationship to bloom without my knowing. I was sure they were going to find yet another way out of telling me the truth when Seth sighed and gestured to me while still looking at Stella, like he was telling her to go ahead and let me in on the secret. Stella looked uncomfortable, and I couldn't imagine why. We didn't have any secrets from each other. At least, that's the reality I lived in until that day. I didn't remember a time she was ever uncomfortable around me or nervous to tell me anything about her life. She was always an open book. But right then, she was having a hard time finding the words to tell me whatever it was she was going to say.

"Okay, um, Lyss, I want you to know that, um, I didn't know, I mean, I didn't mean for you to, um…" She trailed off and looked at Seth for help.

Seth rolled his eyes, leaned forward, and said, "We're dating."

I couldn't understand what I was hearing.

"Who's dating?" I said, stupidly.

Seth rolled his eyes again and grabbed Stella's hand. Her eyes widened a little and her mouth fell open slightly, but her fingers looped through his like they belonged there. Whatever shock she'd felt was short-lived and by the time she turned her gaze to me her expression was blank, careful.

I was still confused.

Seth tried again. "Alyssa, Stella and I are dating. We have been for two months now. Secretly, obviously, and I thought we were doing a pretty good job of it until today."

He looked pleased with himself, and I turned to Stella's red face. She was glaring at Seth but when she turned to me, she looked… scared. Of me? I realized my mouth was open and I closed it quickly.

I'm not sure how long I sat there, frozen, shocked, and confused. Stella cleared her throat and said, "Lyss? Um, say something?"

She said it like a question, like she was trying to push me to give her my reaction without actually trying to push her luck in the moment. I was speechless, and I wasn't sure what else I felt.

The biggest question running through my mind was: Did I believe them? I thought it could explain a lot of the stuff that went on that day, but there was a heaviness in my gut that was making me second-guess everything around me.

But this was Stella. My best friend. And Seth, my brother. There was no way they would lie to me about something like this.

Stop, I thought to myself. *You're being dramatic.*

And I was being dramatic, I knew that, but I also had the feeling that nothing was going to be the same after that day. I had the feeling that Stella and Seth being together was only the beginning.

I was also confused because Seth and Stella dating only fit one piece into the puzzle. It didn't explain who those people at school were, and I didn't even think it really explained their behavior today. But what could I say? It was definitely news, and I knew my imagination could easily get away from me if I let it. Again, I was back to the thought that I was just going crazy. And, again, I thought that was a plausible explanation.

I drew my eyes away from their intertwined hands and up to Stella's face. It was still red, but she'd erased most of the emotion from her features. She didn't look scared or angry anymore, she actually looked kind of bored. I realized she and Seth were both waiting for me to say something.

"Oh. Uh…" I mumbled. As usual, when I was trying to process my thoughts, my brain couldn't form complete sentences. It didn't help that I had a pounding headache and was still finding it hard to focus on anything at all.

"Um, that's… great? Well, maybe great's not the right word. I'm still processing." I gave Stella a smile, but her expression didn't change. It was still blank, and a little eerily so. I continued. "But it's okay. I wish you guys told me sooner, I felt like there was some kind of conspiracy against me going on today with how strange you guys were being."

I was having a hard time meeting Seth's gaze for some reason. If you're an older sibling, even if that younger sibling is only one year younger than you are, you kind of feel responsible for them growing up. I still saw Seth as the kid I needed to protect, not the teenager who was now dating my best friend. It was weird, and I had to admit that to myself. As much as I was going to pretend to be unbothered by this, I was a little bit bothered. I think any normal person would be.

Stella visibly relaxed at my words, and that made me feel both better and worse. At least she wasn't feeling bad about it now, but then… had she been so afraid to tell me that my bumbling reply was even better than whatever she thought I was going to say?

"Oh my gosh, I'm so relieved. Thank you! I've been so worried these past few weeks; I've barely been myself! I'm so glad you've been busy with your college stuff. I just didn't know how to tell you what was going on! I didn't know how you would react. I mean… it's *Seth*." She gestured to him with her free hand, and her voice had a tinge of disgust that I didn't really understand. "I'm just as surprised as you are."

Had I really been that busy the past few weeks that I didn't notice this was happening? My brain wasn't letting me look back enough to determine how I felt about that as my headache grew with every passing moment. What had I even spent my whole summer doing?

"You wound me," Seth said in response to Stella, putting his hand over his heart. I was also analyzing his behavior, but he seemed pretty normal. The smile on his face was smug as he looked at me.

"I really doubt that," I mumbled. He looked anything but wounded.

Stella pursed her lips. If I was really trying to make them feel like I was fine with their newfound romance, I didn't think I was doing that great of a job. I noticed Seth making circles on the back of her hand with his thumb. My stomach did a flip and I put the smile back on my face.

"It's fine, I promise. I was just surprised!" I put that smile back on my face and I felt like a phony. "Don't worry about me, I'm happy for you guys. And I think I might starve if we don't move on from this conversation and order pizza!" Truthfully, I wasn't feeling hungry at all. I just couldn't think of anything else to say. That heaviness was still settled in the pit of my stomach, and my headache wasn't making me feel any better.

Stella smiled, small and tentative, but I thought it was real. It was a smile of relief. She really *had* been afraid to tell me about this. I could almost see the weight lift off her shoulders as she settled back into the couch, and I felt unease twist my stomach for some reason.

Seth smiled one of his goofy grins that told me he was never really worried about my reaction (or he didn't care what it would be), and that he was only keeping this a secret because Stella asked him to.

As Seth walked out of the living room, he took out his phone to order the pizza. That left Stella and I sitting in the room together, alone.

It felt like the buffer that allowed me to hide my feelings from Stella was gone. I was looking anywhere but her face, and the few glances I allowed myself in her direction told me she was doing the same thing to me, pretending to be fully engrossed with something on her phone. I really didn't care much that they were dating. That I could deal with. What I was worried about then was the nagging voice in the back of my head that was telling me this wasn't the whole story. My anxiety was focusing on that point in my chest again, and I felt it growing hotter. I breathed into that feeling in an attempt to keep it at bay and I hoped Stella didn't notice. Whatever she was thinking of she didn't even try to talk to me.

Seth couldn't have been gone for more than two minutes, but it felt like an eternity. Stella and I hadn't spoken while he was gone, and I knew he would be able to feel the tension hanging in the air as soon as he walked back into the room. With the pizza ordered and the three of us settled in with a movie, the silence felt a little more comfortable, but it was still a silence that hadn't been there before. I barely registered what was on the screen as my thoughts continued to race. Something still wasn't adding up but trying to think through it had started to make me feel sick.

I couldn't help but feel like I wasn't getting the whole story. Stella and Seth should have known that I wasn't going to react super negatively to their news, and I couldn't imagine Stella being that scared to tell me anything, let alone that she was dating someone. Even if that someone was my brother.

I had a sinking feeling that something else was going on. But, just like earlier in the day, I pushed those thoughts away and resigned myself to a night watching Bella and Edward stare and sigh at each other on the screen. But I could still feel their nagging pull at the back of my mind. There was something going on that they didn't want me to know about, something big enough to scare Stella into silence rather than chancing my finding out.

I looked over at the couch where she and Seth sat, curled up under a blanket. Stella laid her head on his shoulder, and he had his arm around her. Weird, but I'd seen them in similar positions before in the past fifteen years, before they were ever a "thing". Still, my gut told me something was going on. It also told me I wasn't going to get any information from Stella and Seth.

I couldn't explain how I knew, but I knew.

After the vampire and human had been reunited, Stella had gone home, and Seth had declared he was staying up to watch some documentary on the living room TV, I was finally in bed. I wished for sleep, but my mind could not stop racing. I thought about the weirdness of the day, the explanation that it was all due to Stella and Seth getting together and being afraid to tell me about it, and the more I thought about that the less sense it made. They had never acted like this before.

Then, I thought about the strange students I had seen at school. The ones with the perfect, slicked-back hair and the dead eyes. I had never seen them before today. Who were they? And why did I have such an eerie feeling when it came to the look in their eyes? I had thought they were staring at me as I walked down the hallway, though Stella had carefully avoided those concerns and simply steered me in another direction to change the subject. Which was another weird thing.

I tossed and turned for hours, but eventually sleep found me. I dreamed of dark figures chasing me as I tried to run, but my limbs moved like they were underwater. I saw Seth and Stella there, too, watching me try to escape the demons as I screamed to them for help.

It wasn't the most restful night I'd ever had.

All too soon, my alarm rang, and it was time to start another day.

I groaned as I silenced the alarm after the third snooze and dragged myself out of bed. My brain was still so full of questions that no one had bothered to answer for me yesterday— answers I knew they had but they were hiding things from me for some reason. My brain still felt groggy today, but at least the pounding in my head had muffled into a dull roar at my temples.

I dressed quickly, now late thanks to my snoozing habits, and rushed down the stairs. My dad was already gone, and instead of smelling Seth burning something in the kitchen, there was a box of donuts with a sticky note on top.

"Early call with a client, thought I would save your stomach today. Love, Dad," it read.

I smiled. At least my dad was still acting normal, though I hadn't seen him in what felt like a while. It couldn't have been more than a day or two, right?

Donuts were his go-to to save the day. He especially bought them when he'd been working at the office more often. I didn't remember him arriving home the night before, and that felt weird to me.

"I wonder if *he* knows about Seth and Stella," I mumbled to myself a little grumpily as I grabbed a strawberry cake donut. I still didn't feel hungry, but my mouth was almost watering from the smell.

"Talking to yourself again?"

I whipped around so fast I nearly dropped my donut. The voice I heard was male, but it was not from my brother or my dad. There was a stranger in my house, and he was standing right behind me.

Chapter Three

"WHO ARE YOU?" I SHOUTED AT THE stranger, who was casually leaning against the door frame in my kitchen. He was examining a black dagger as if it were the most interesting thing he'd ever seen, and I watched as he used the tip to clean the fingernail on his right thumb.

He laughed, and the sound was soft.

This boy had the darkest hair I had ever seen, so dark it was almost blue. It was cropped short at the sides, but the top was longer with a few shiny curls that fell over his forehead and almost into his eyes. His eyes, I noticed, were also dark. They didn't look black, but I couldn't tell exactly what their color was from the way the shadows from his hair fell over them. It was a stark contrast to the pallor of his skin, and I found myself staring like an idiot.

As if he could feel my gaze, he looked up from his knife and directly into my eyes.

"Alyssa, did your family really not tell you I was coming?"

His voice was extremely nonchalant, as if he didn't have a care in the world. It looked like he was laughing at some private joke as he smirked at me from across the room.

"My… my family? What do they have to do with you?" My voice shook, and I took a second to clear my throat. "Which, might I remind you, I still have no idea who you are and why you're in my house? With a *dagger*?"

My voice rose at the end of my sentences, making them questions rather than the firm statements I intended them to be. My uncertainty and obvious lack of understanding of the situation made my intruder smile even wider. His smile wasn't menacing or terrifying in any way. Actually, it was completely infuriating.

I forgot about the dagger and the fact that this man was a stranger who somehow knew my name, and I stood with my hands on my hips and my jaw set, looking him directly in the eyes and willing him to answer my questions. I also forgot I was holding a donut, which probably made me look even more stupid.

He chuckled again and jammed his dagger into a sheath at his side. My eyes followed his movement, and when I raised them back up to his face, he was staring into mine again. There was a twinkle in his eye that hinted at some emotion I wasn't sure about.

"I'm sorry," he said smoothly, stepping farther into the kitchen. "I'm being rude. I guess I shouldn't have assumed they told you anything. Dr. Gold gave me orders to come collect you, not that you would have any idea why."

He had a slight accent that I couldn't place. It didn't seem to be from anywhere in particular, but it was smooth and lilting, almost lulling me forward.

He continued speaking as my mind was racing.

"My name is Seely Evanson. It's a pleasure to finally see you, Alyssa Gold."

He stuck a pale and calloused hand out toward me, but I was again frozen at the sound of my name coming from his mouth.

"I… How do you know my name?" This question wasn't the one I thought was the most pressing, but it was the first thing that came into my mind and out of my mouth.

He nodded at the question, that same infuriating smile crossing his lips, and dropped his hand back to his side.

"Right. I'm sorry to burst in on you like this. I'm sure it must be a shock to find a stranger standing in your kitchen—and one with a dazzling smile at that."

On cue, he flashed his smile wider and wagged his eyebrows at me. I narrowed my eyes, and he sighed in response, his smile only dropping slightly.

"Uh, right. Well, anyway, like I said, I'm here to collect you. Shall we?"

He snapped his fingers, and another boy came in, younger than either of us. The boy looked maybe fourteen, whereas the intruder, Seely, looked like he could be anywhere from eighteen to twenty. The younger boy stumbled through the doorway and stood at attention at Seely's side, much like a soldier awaiting orders. Seely turned to him, and the boy's shoulder stiffened. My brows raised in surprise. Whoever Seely was, he seemed to demand authority and was obviously granted it, at least by this boy, Simon.

The other stranger in my kitchen.

"Simon, please gather Miss Gold's things. Her trunks are at the foot of the stairs, and I expect everything to be packed and in the car in fifteen minutes."

Simon gave one sharp nod and scurried off into the living room. Seely turned his attention back to me, that smile playing on his lips, and lifted his eyebrows.

"Well, then. Are you ready to go? I thought I would brief you in the car."

My head was absolutely spinning at this point. I had been awake for all of thirty minutes and there was one stranger in my kitchen with a dagger at his hip and at least one more on his way to my room to, apparently, pack it up and move it to a still unknown location. I felt like I was floating, like this was a dream or something. That center point of my chest was on fire again, and I practiced my breathing. As my anxiety escalated, so did the racing thoughts. But I needed to focus.

"Wait," I said, looking at Seely. "I… I don't know what's going on! I woke up this morning running late for school, I came into the kitchen to get some breakfast and instead found some stranger with a knife leaning in my doorway, and now a boy is packing up my stuff to take me somewhere else? Where? And what do you mean 'your family didn't tell you?' Tell me *what*?"

I couldn't stop my mouth from spilling out my every thought. I was growing shriller and more panicked as I continued on.

"And another thing! I don't even know who you are! Seely? What kind of a name is that? And just because you tell me your name does not mean I know who you are. Where are you trying to take me? Either way, it doesn't matter. I'm not going anywhere with you. I have AP English Lit in fifteen minutes."

I made a move to step forward, but before I could Seely was there. He grabbed my forearm and held me in place—his grasp firm and unyielding. The smile was completely gone from his face now.

"Ouch."

The word came out as more of a whimper than I intended it to. Truthfully, he wasn't really hurting me. His grip was uncomfortable, but my reaction was sprung from surprise rather than actual pain.

At that quiet word, though, Seely immediately dropped my arm.

"My apologies," he said, clearing his throat. "It's been a long day already and we're only just getting started. My nerves are a little fried at the moment." His eyes darted from my face to the clock on the wall and back again. He truly seemed uncomfortable now. "Are you all right?"

I rubbed at my forearm where he had grabbed it. "I'm fine. I was just… a little surprised. I wasn't expecting you to do that, and I didn't even see you move. It's probably just information overload. Or the lack thereof, I guess."

Seely looked at me like he was only just realizing I was there. His mouth was pulled to the side in a smirk that almost looked like he was trying to hold back a wider smile.

"What?"

Seely only stared at me, and I was getting angry again. I remembered that he had still not given me any answers and that I still didn't really know who he was, and it also was not lost on me that my only attempt at leaving the room had been swiftly and deftly thwarted. Seely seemed nice enough, but I could still feel his grip on my arm, and I thought about how easily he'd stepped in to stop me just then. I knew in my bones he could be dangerous if he chose to be.

Just then, the boy, Simon, cantered back into the room.

"Everything is packed and ready, sir. The trunks are in the car and Dexter is waiting for you right outside."

Seely nodded toward the boy without taking his eyes from my face. Simon gave a sharp jerk of his head that I assumed was meant to be an imitation of Seely's own and disappeared back into the living room.

"Again," Seely held his hand out to me another time, "are you ready to go? Your things are in the car."

I opened my mouth to protest, but, before I could get any words out, he used the hand that was already outstretched and gestured for me to stop.

"I know you have questions." He sounded exhausted, and I had the feeling he was a little annoyed with me but was trying to be patient—like I was a child he was having to explain obvious things to.

"But here is not the place to debrief you on them," he continued on. "Your father called us last week to collect you. Something happened and we're trying to figure it out, but until then I need you to come with me. That is all I can tell you here."

He was still holding out his hand, now in a gesture of welcome. I knew he wanted me to take hold of his outstretched hand, and he looked at my face expectantly. As if the information he just gave me was the only thing I needed to hear in order to go who knew where with at least two strangers.

Three. I remembered Simon mentioning someone named Dexter waiting for us outside.

I shook my head.

"I'm not going with you."

Seely's face fell. He dropped his hand back to his side and straightened up.

"Alyssa," the way he said my name, like he knew secrets about me that I didn't even know yet, made a chill crawl up my spine. "I'm afraid I have strict orders that I am not allowed to take *no* for an answer."

He snapped his fingers again and two different boys, older than Simon, it seemed, appeared in the doorway. They had the same stern expressions and looked to Seely expectantly for their next instructions.

I felt the blood drain from my face. They were not going to let me go.

I braced myself to run as my mind continued to race, thinking about the different exit routes, and calculating how far I could get depending on which direction I went. My mind was still racing as I looked at Seely's face. He shook his head infinitesimally, his eyes sad and his smirk gone.

"I wouldn't try it, Alyssa. We're everywhere around the house and down the block. They told me there was a risk of you attempting to escape, but I guess I just assumed your father would have told you *something*. And your brother? I don't know why they didn't tell you, but I'm sorry. It's unfortunate that this is your first impression of me." He took a deep breath. "However, I do have my orders."

Seely nodded his head toward me, and the two new boys reached me in a matter of seconds. They each gripped one of my arms, firm and unmoving. I couldn't see clearly.

"Alyssa, please. I promise everything will make sense, or at least more sense, soon. I intend to explain it all to you once it's safe to speak."

I felt something wet drop onto my shirt and realized my blurry vision was due to the tears now flowing freely from my eyes. Seely looked genuinely concerned for my well-being, but as I looked at his face, I felt the world closing in on itself. The edges of my vision went from blurred to black, and I felt like I was looking at his face through a tunnel.

"Steady, she's going under," Seely sighed. It was less than a whisper to my ears.

That's the last thing I heard before the world went completely black.

Chapter Four

THE FIRST THING I RECOGNIZED AS I woke up was the smell. Wherever I was, it smelled like fresh coffee beans. My brain perked up at the scent and I started to hear the sound of someone speaking softly on either side of me. It was very warm, wherever I was, and I realized I had a heavy blanket covering me.

When I opened my eyes, I realized why everything was so dark and muffled—my head was huddled under the blanket that covered my whole body. The other people in the room must have realized I was awake because they'd stopped speaking. It was silent except for the hum of something—an engine, I realized. We were in a car.

I sat up quickly, too quickly, and my head started spinning. Slowly, I lowered myself back onto my elbows. I realized I was in a very large town car, maybe even a limo. The car was shaded, and I couldn't tell if it was because the sun had gone down or if the windows were just extremely tinted. I took in the feel of the black leather under my forearms and noticed that most of the roof of the car was a moonroof. Its cover was pulled over the opening, which didn't help me determine the time of day or how long I'd been out.

I was lying on the seat that was on the left side of the car, my head facing toward the driver. Directly in my line of sight, on the back seat, sat a boy I hadn't seen yet.

This boy had medium brown skin and a shock of freckles that covered his face. His hair was a dark brown too, though it was a normal dark brown, not like Seely's.

"No offense, but your hair looks like something's made a nest in it."

With a start, I turned my head towards the seat across from me. Of course, the comment had come from Seely. He was lounging in the seat with his legs spread out almost straight in front of him, looking at me with that same smirk on his face as before. I had barely known him for a couple of hours, but already I felt like this smirk was just a part of who he was as a person. Actually, when I thought about it, I had lost all sense of what time of day it was.

"Alyssa? Are you okay? I only half meant what I said about your hair."

The smirk hadn't really left his face, but I thought his concern sounded real. I ignored the part about my hair. It looked like a mess on its best day, and I could only imagine what it would be like after everything I'd gone through already.

"I'm… fine? I think." I answered him, my throat dry. "How long have I been out?"

As if he could read my thoughts, Seely handed me a bottle of water. I mumbled a thank you and proceeded to down the entire bottle. He handed me another one and took the empty trash from my hand.

"Um, thanks," I said, feeling a little embarrassed but not really caring enough to stop myself from taking a big swig of the new bottle. "You didn't answer my question, though. How long have I been asleep?"

"About four hours," he said, fiddling with the empty bottle he had taken from me.

Four hours? That meant it was close to noon. I guessed that meant, then, that the windows were extremely tinted rather than it being night out.

"Four hours. Okay. Where are we, exactly?"

My voice sounded weak and tired. And I guess I had a pretty good reason for that. My day had started out like any other, even though I was running late, and it ended up with me sitting in a strange car headed for who knows where. To top it all off, I hadn't even gotten to eat one of the donuts my dad left, and I was starving as well as dehydrated.

I remembered that I had asked Seely a question, and I looked up from my mental reverie back to Seely's face. It was now nearly free of a smirk at all, which I knew probably meant I was about to find out the information I wanted to know the most. Unfortunately, it also seemed like this information was not going to be fun for me.

"Just tell me, please."

"Alyssa," Seely said my name very slowly. Or was my brain still working in slow motion? "I promised that I would answer your questions, and I will. But are you sure you are ready to hear this right now? Have you eaten anything yet?

"I don't need food. I need answers." I could feel the panic that threatened me in the kitchen this morning creeping back up my throat. I swallowed another drink of water, forcing it down before I continued. "I believe you don't have intentions of hurting me, really I do. But that doesn't mean I trust you. I just need you to tell me the truth. Please."

Seely looked at me for a moment and then nodded, that smirk threatening his face again. He held my empty bottle by the cap end and lightly tapped the other end against his thigh.

"For the record," he fully smiled now, "I don't believe that you aren't hungry. We interrupted your breakfast this morning and you've been out like the dead ever since."

He was right, of course. I felt like he had an annoying habit of being right most of the time.

"But I'll make a deal with you. I'll answer a couple of questions now, and I'll answer the rest after you've had some food." He pointed the end of the bottle at me. "You're a lot more fun when you're awake, and I know you probably don't want to spend another four hours passed out either."

He had a point, and I conceded to his conditions with a nod. I would get my answers, maybe not all at once like I would like, but I would get them. I don't know why, but I was pretty sure Seely was a man of his word. Even though I had just told him I didn't trust him, a little piece of me was beginning to. His eyes were piercing as they stared into mine, and I realized that the color I hadn't been able to place before was a deep green color. *You're being ridiculous*, a piece of me whispered, *focus on the questions, not the eyes.*

Seely smiled at me and raised his eyebrows. "Don't you have some questions?"

"Oh, right." I felt my cheeks heat and I knew my face was red, which I resented. I had a weird feeling that Seely knew exactly what I had been thinking as I stared at him.

Seely chuckled and I sat up fully on the seat, moving my legs over until my feet were planted on the floor of the car. My head still felt a little fuzzy, but the water had definitely done its job and the car was no longer spinning. But then I was faced with the dilemma of what question should I ask first. I had so many unknowns swirling around in my brain that I wasn't sure which one to pluck out and ask.

Seely waited patiently while I sifted through my muddled thoughts. The only thing that gave him away as remotely annoyed or irritated was the way he continued to fiddle with the water bottle. I got the feeling that he was used to being composed with people, almost like a kindergarten teacher. Which, I guessed, would make me the five-year-old in that situation.

I looked Seely square in the eyes as I asked my question. "You said you thought my family would have told me something about what is going on. What did you mean by that?"

He leaned forward at the waist, his arms resting on his knees, lightly tapping the water bottle on his left hand.

"That's the first question you ask me?" His lips went up at the corners a little. "There's a lot of information that goes along with that, we might have to start somewhere smaller."

I nodded. I thought that may be the case. I mean, I still didn't know who this man was or who he was associated with.

"Okay, fair enough." I took another drink of my water. "Let's start with who you work for."

Seely's position didn't move but his smirk widened.

"I work for myself. Next question?"

"That literally didn't give me any information."

He leaned back, then.

"But I did answer your question. Next."

"Fine. How is my father involved in whatever it is that you're involved in?"

I remembered Seely saying my dad had called them to come and 'collect' me. I guessed that meant the semi-kidnapping that had occurred that morning, but I still didn't know why. My dad had never acted like he was hiding anything from me, at least that I could remember. The possibility that these boys who had invaded my house this morning had less than honorable intentions was still pretty high. I hoped the answer to this question could at least ease some of that tension.

"Dr. Gold is a founding member of the Association Against the Undead. The AAUD, for short."

He said the initials of the organization in a way that sounded like "odd".

"The... Association Against the Undead?" I repeated, blandly.

"The AAUD."

Seely was still smirking, seeming to enjoy my very evident confusion.

"Okay, the AAUD," I continued, choosing my words carefully and slowly. "And what exactly is it that you guys… do?"

"Alyssa, what I'm about to tell you may be hard for you to process. Are you sure you don't want something to eat first?" At that question, Seely nodded toward the other boy, whom I had already forgotten was there, not even waiting for me to answer. That boy took out a cell phone and seemed to be sending a message to someone.

"I'm so sorry, I didn't even ask your name."

My conversation with Seely temporarily forgotten, I turned to the other boy. He smiled at my sudden burst of interest in him, looking a little bit sheepish, but he answered in kind.

"My name is Dexter, ma'am."

A bell rang in my head, and I remembered the other boy that was in my kitchen, Simon, saying there was someone named Dexter waiting for Seely and me outside. Dexter's accent was purely British, and its smoothness reminded me of Seely's, though the accenting was different. Dexter smiled politely at me, not a smirk to be found on his face.

"Please, call me Alyssa."

I stuck out my hand towards him and he reached his back to me without hesitation, shaking my hand.

"I believe I will stick with the formalities at this time, ma'am. While I appreciate the offer, I wouldn't want to step on… anyone's toes. Especially, uh," his eyes darted to my left for the briefest second, "your father." His smile turned a little more joking, but I wondered if I saw some other emotion in his eyes. "He signs the checks, you know."

No, I didn't really know. and I wasn't sure why my father would ever be upset at someone calling me

Alyssa, but I returned his smile and nodded, removing my hand from his. I had other questions that needed to be answered.

Looking back at Seely, I realized that he was probably right about the food. I couldn't fully even concentrate on what he was saying to me, let alone pretend to understand where the conversation was going. Though my stomach felt like lead, I thought I probably did need some food. I remembered that I'd also barely eaten the night before. And this conversation would be hard enough to follow under normal circumstances. The AAUD? It sounded more like something my brain was making up rather than a real answer to my question.

"You might be right about the food thing." I told him. "I'm feeling a little lightheaded, and I think I'm going to need all the help I can get to follow this conversation."

Seely looked satisfied. "I had a feeling you would say that. Dexter already notified the driver; we'll be stopping shortly. But I'm glad to know you'll eat willingly. I was beginning to wonder if you were going to need to be force-fed."

He smiled at me, crookedly and in a way that made me wonder at all the secrets he was still hiding behind that expression. I thought he was probably really good at getting out of tough situations and telling the truth a lot with a smile like that. That thought made me shiver, and he reached across the aisle between us to pull the blanket back up to my shoulders.

"Th-thanks," I responded, my teeth chattering.

His eyes narrowed at me. "You're not going to go into shock on me, are you?"

Seely placed a hand on each of my arms and began rubbing them gently to create some heat through friction. I had started shaking worse now, and I thought that maybe I *was* going into shock. I hated feeling weak and incompetent in front of Seely, and even Dexter, who was purposefully not looking in my direction. He was instead focused on Seely, as if he could give important instructions to him at any moment. Again, I realized that Seely was a very important person somehow. He demanded respect from everyone in every space I had seen him in up to that point, even from me. I mean, after knowing him for just a few hours (most of which I had been unconscious for), I was worried about what he thought of this outburst of emotion. I felt like I couldn't control myself, which was terrifying in itself, so obviously I chose that moment to ask another question.

"Pl-please tell m-me m-more about the A-A-AAUD."

Seely was still trying to warm me up, and he looked at me skeptically.

"You want me to dump more on you when you're falling apart like this? I don't think that's such a good idea, Gold."

"If I can suggest something, Seely?" Dexter spoke up for the first time.

Seely turned his head until he was facing the boy, but his hands were still on my arms. He gave a short nod, which I was beginning to recognize as his usual symbol of acknowledgement to those who seemed to be working under him.

"I don't think you could make it any worse," Dexter continued on. "If she really is going into shock, it might be best to distract her."

The car slowed and eased to a stop. Dexter's phone beeped and he glanced at the screen.

"I'll return shortly," he turned to me when he said the next part of his sentence, "with some food for the lady."

I smiled at him with gratitude as best I could, my teeth still chattering. Seely watched Dexter leave, and I thought his eyes tightened slightly as he watched him go. I wasn't sure if he liked Dexter much, but I couldn't find an obvious reason why. I just felt some kind of tension between them that I had no context for, and I couldn't place.

Seely turned his attention back to me, and I was acutely aware that his hands were still holding my arms as if he was afraid I was about to literally fall apart, and he had to hold together the pieces.

"I'll tell you about the AAUD, but you have to promise to pay attention to your breathing. One breath in your nose and release it out your mouth, like this."

He demonstrated a steady breath, helping me find a soothing pace. I held on to that rhythm as I concentrated on keeping myself together. Seely didn't know that I spent a lot of time breathing into my chest like this. I could feel the heat gathering there, and I breathed into it like I always did when I felt myself spiraling. I was not going to completely fall apart for the second time in front of this virtual stranger, and I was not about to let myself pass out again.

"You okay?"

I nodded, and Seely moved from where he knelt on the ground to the seat beside me.

"I'm going to take your wrist and monitor your pulse. Do you mind?"

I shook my head weakly, my breathing already calming down the shaking.

Seely grabbed my wrist gently and pressed to the point I was sure he could feel my pulse. I was also sure that it was racing, but I could feel myself calming down even as we sat there in silence.

"The Association Against the Undead was founded in the 1980s," Seely began. He spoke softly and calmly. I felt safe, and also interested in what he was going to say next, and I let his voice soothe me as I continued breathing.

"Your father, Dr. Gold, and my father began the AAUD together. You see, they were both Harvard boys, and their fathers before them had been a part of a similar organization that had since been dissolved. Their fathers were friends and told them of their old organization when the boys came of age, which happens at thirteen as far as the AAUD is concerned."

Seely was still pressing down on my wrist with his left hand, and with his right, he was holding my hand in place. He was also tracing absent-minded circles on the back of my hand with his thumb. It seemed like some kind of soothing gesture, and it was working. His hands were even colder than my clammy ones, and my skin tingled where he touched it. I looked up from his hands on mine and into his face. He was focused on a point across the car, looking like he was trying to remember the story exactly so as to not leave anything out for my benefit. His eyes had flecks of gold around the middle of the irises, within that strange shade of green.

Breathing. Right. I had lost my rhythm a little.

He seemed to be unaware of the growing effect his proximity was having on my ability to concentrate on my breathing, but he continued with his story.

"The AAUD came about because our fathers knew the story of the creatures who are ultimately dead," he smiled a little, "and they were the first to recognize that these creatures had come back. Our grandfathers dissolved their organization because they thought the problem had been eradicated." He sighed and shook his head like he couldn't believe how naive our ancestors had been. "Or that's the reason they gave. The whole situation surrounding the dissolving of the AAUD the first time is pretty shady, but that's what's on paper. Obviously, as our fathers found out very quickly, that was not true. The Undead very much still exist."

"Wait." I interrupted him. "What are the 'Undead'? What does that mean?" I used my free hand to make air quotes around "Undead". He wasn't making any sense. And yet... I felt like I'd heard this somewhere before.

Seely looked at me like he couldn't believe he had to explain this, or maybe it was that he wished he didn't have to. Like I should already know what he was talking about. But, to his credit, he took a breath and at least tried to help me make sense of it.

"I assume you've heard the term 'undead' before, yes?"

I blushed, thinking about my slight *Twilight* addiction. He furrowed his brows a little at my embarrassment, not knowing where it stemmed from. And I was not going to tell him.

"Um, yes. Like vampires?"

He nodded.

"Yes, vampires, zombies, spirits," he said, shrugging like that was no big deal, "things like that." Seely smirked a little. "But just a little different from *Twilight*, though."

My mouth almost fell open as he shook with quiet laughter. How had he guessed what was going through my mind? I rationalized that a lot of people would probably go there when talking about vampires, so it wasn't that strange, but something about it made me feel uncomfortable.

I waited for him to continue and clarify what he meant a little bit more, but he just stared at me. He also still held my hand (a fact I was acutely aware of).

"You're trying to tell me that the AAUD is some kind of organization that fights against... zombies and vampires? Do you think I'm stupid?"

He opened his mouth to answer, but something about his face made me hold my hand up to stop him.

"Don't answer that," I said. "But really, you can tell me the truth."

"Alyssa, I'm being dead serious." He smiled. "No pun intended."

"Seely, I know that those things aren't real, they're just scary stories that stem from legends people made up a long time ago."

"Maybe you're right, but every legend has at least one leg in the truth."

The hair on the back of my neck stood up. I had the sinking feeling that Seely was being serious. But vampires and zombies and other undead things? My head was starting to swim again, my sight blurring, and Seely tightened his grip on my hand. He took his free hand and placed it on my back.

"Lean forward and place your head between your knees before you throw up!"

It was a command as much as it was a plea to avoid cleaning up a mess. Though I still hadn't eaten anything so I wasn't sure what kind of mess there would even be. However, I did what he asked, and my head started to clear almost immediately. Seely stroked my back in a circular motion, and I tried to focus on my breathing again.

"The creatures we hunt aren't vampires and zombies exactly," Seely continued with his explanation. "They *are* where the legends come from. But they aren't anything mortals really have a name for."

He paused for a second, but I needed the distraction.

"Keep going, please."

My voice came out like a squeak, but I guess he heard me fine because he barely missed a beat before continuing.

"These creatures are much like you and me. Except, of course, they're dead." I could hear the smile in his voice. "In order to become an Undead, you have to be drained of all the blood in your body, then filled with at least a few drops of blood from an Undead. After that, you have to be buried in the ground, in a grave."

He paused for a moment but continued to stroke my back. I knew I could ask another question or break the silence in some way, but I didn't think there was any harm in letting him continue on for a little longer. I was enjoying the human contact, actually.

"I'm very surprised Dr. Gold didn't tell you any of this before I came," he said gently. "He could have told you about... some of this stuff at least."

When Seely said that, a lightbulb went off in my brain. I sat up quickly. Too quickly, as it turned out, because the back of my head collided directly with Seely's nose.

"Oh my gosh, I am so sorry! Are you okay?"

He was rubbing his nose with tears in his eyes, but he laughed and said, "I think I'll survive."

"I'm so sorry," I said, but the giggle in the middle of the sentence kind of diminished the effect. Seely shot me a look that, combined with his red nose and watery eyes, made me laugh even harder for a second. I cleared my throat before continuing.

"Really, I am sorry. But when you said that I remembered that my dad actually did tell me something about this."

Seely's eyebrows quirked up at that in surprise, and what looked like a question, but I continued before he could say anything.

"I remember him telling me bedtime stories about the world between the living and the dead. He used to tell me about the people who lived in that in-between world; about how they could go between the worlds because they were a part of both of them. They were human and something more, at the same time."

I remembered my dad telling me these stories, but it didn't click until Seely had told me similar things that he claimed weren't just fairy tales. My dad had told this stuff to me as stories to help me fall asleep as a child, but what he hadn't told me was that any of it was real. At least, I didn't remember him telling me that. But, as always, thoughts of my past came with a headache, so I shied away from the thoughts.

"Why would my dad not tell me any of this? Why would he call you to come get me without telling me anything about the AAUD or Undead or *you* and where you're taking me?"

I was feeling that heat inside my chest, and a fiery sensation that almost felt like ice racing through my veins. I could feel it spreading from the center point of my chest and down to the tips of my fingers.

Seely was looking at me, his eyes wide and pitiful. He was feeling sorry for me, I realized. I wondered if that should make me feel ashamed or angry, but honestly it just made me feel *seen* in that moment.

"I don't know why he didn't tell you, Alyssa. I wish he'd at least given you a heads up before I snuck in and kidnapped you." That crooked smile spread across his face again. "But he didn't, and now we're here."

He was right. He was over-simplifying things and speaking more matter-of-factly than I would, but he was right. I was here now, and my dad had already made the decision to not tell me about any of this, and now I had to face it. I felt so tired, my arms feeling like lead as that icy fire retreated back into my chest and disappeared altogether.

I hadn't realized I was crying until I felt a hand touch my cheek, wiping a tear that was running down my face. I had cried so much today, and I hadn't even had lunch.

"Please don't cry," he said, his voice was almost pleading. "I will try to answer any questions you have, but I'm afraid it might be too much for you all at once. Especially when you still don't have any food in your system. Where is Dexter, anyway?" He mumbled the last part to himself, glancing at the door.

I noticed he hadn't removed his hand from my face, and I turned slightly to look at him. He looked at me with something I couldn't place, crossing his features. He moved his hand from my cheek and tucked a stray piece of hair behind my ear. I caught my breath as his hands grazed my ear, his touch leaving a strange warmth in its wake. I thought it might have even raised some goosebumps on my skin.

Seely had a hand on either side of my face now. The rough skin of his palms scraped against my skin and sent a shiver down my spine. I was looking into his eyes, and I was stuck there, hypnotized, frozen, powerless.

Something in the air thickened and I forgot to breathe again.

I leaned in and breathed in the scent of him. He opened his mouth slightly and I caught a whiff of something sweet and spicy, like a cinnamon candy. I leaned in farther until our noses were millimeters from touching.

I thought I heard Seely whisper something like, "Do you remember?"

"Uh-hem."

Someone cleared their throat, and I snapped my head around to the door quicker than I thought possible. Seely's hands were left in the air where my head had been only seconds before, and they hung there for a second before he dropped them swiftly back onto the car seat.

Dexter was standing in the open car door, looking oddly like there was some expression he was trying to keep out of his face. His mouth was twitching a little, like he was fighting with himself to keep a smile at bay. I felt my face flush hotly, but then I saw what he had in his hands, and I couldn't think about anything else.

He was holding a beautiful, glorious, greasy bag with a large drink.

"This is for you, Miss Gold," he said as he held out the food to me. "There was a line, or I would have been here sooner."

His eyes darted towards Seely, and the smile still played on his lips. He was probably thinking about how he was grateful he wasn't here sooner. Seely already looked like he was ready to strangle someone, and I watched as he narrowed his eyes at Dexter and shook his head slightly. Dexter laughed quietly as he sat down, carefully averting his eyes to something that seemed very interesting on his phone.

The whole thing was so strange, but I guessed that was the theme of the day. I wanted to ask questions, but I wanted the food more, and I really didn't want to risk pushing Seely over the edge. He was still glaring at Dexter, his eyes narrowed and his chest rising and falling slowly. He was practicing his breathing, which was probably not a great sign.

Instead, I turned to Dexter, who had put down the phone and was holding out my food to me with a smile on his lips.

"Thank you so much, Dexter."

I reached out and grabbed the food, gratefully. I could smell the food now that I held it in my hands and my stomach rumbled. Taking out the greasy burger, I tried not to notice Seely standing up softly and moving back to his seat across from me. I also tried not to think about how he hadn't said a word since Dexter came in. I *also* tried not to think about what he *had* said: "*Do you remember?*"

Some part of my brain pricked at the words, and I got a very sinister feeling that maybe there was something important I had forgotten. But I hadn't met Seely until that day, and there was no secret we had together. Whatever he said, it hadn't been what I thought.

Right?

Chapter Five

I DOWNED THE BURGER TOO QUICKLY and, though it tasted good, it fell into my stomach like a rock. I didn't feel satisfied, and I wondered whether that was because of the stress of the last day or just because I was still hungry. Either way, it was a weird feeling.

I realized, happily, that the drink Dexter provided me was Diet Coke, which was my favorite. Well, except for hot tea, but I didn't think many fast-food places probably had that as an option.

I had an absent thought that it may be more than a coincidence. These people seemed to know more about me than normal strangers ever should. Maybe even more than I knew about myself, at least where

Seely was concerned. I pushed that feeling away, though, because I didn't have time for another spiral that afternoon. Two, maybe three at this point, was enough for anyone for one day.

I also tried not to notice that Seely still hadn't spoken a word since Dexter interrupted our conversation approximately 20 minutes earlier. We'd started driving again almost as soon as Dexter had handed my food over, and I kept the time on a small analog clock that was located just above the partition between us and whoever was driving us to wherever we were going. I almost laughed at the thought that I still barely knew anything about my situation; I didn't know where I was going or really who was taking me there. I knew nothing about Seely or Dexter, even though I was beginning to trust that they didn't want to harm me at least. I mean, they'd fed me and Seely had kept me from spiraling and throwing up, so I assumed he wasn't planning on murdering me. I still didn't know if I believed Seely about the "Undead" he tried to tell me about. I mean, it was just all too much. We lived in a world where these things didn't exist—*shouldn't* exist, and I couldn't wrap my mind about any of it being real. These things were scary stories my dad used to tell me, not anything I should have to worry about in real life.

I stole a glance at Seely then, my eyes swiftly surveying that he was sitting very still, his eyes gazing pointedly out the window, past my head. It was obvious he was lost in his own mind, staring just to fix his eyes on a specific point, and I wondered what could have possibly soured his mood so quickly. One minute he was comforting me, wiping my tears, and telling me everything was okay, and the next...

"Do you remember?"

Seely's eyes cut over to mine in an instant. It was like he could hear my thoughts, yet again. If the Undead were real, then maybe mind readers were too. I gasped and looked down quickly, taking another drink of my soda.

Had I imagined the strangeness emanating from him? I probably hadn't even heard him right. And people are bound to notice you staring at them if you do it for long enough. Maybe he was just tired or thinking about what he had to do on this mission or wondering what he should tell me next. There was a rational explanation for everything (except maybe all the talk about vampires and zombies), and I was blowing things out of proportion, just as I'd been doing the day before. I thought Seth and Stella were hiding something big from me when all it had been was that they were dating. I almost called them out for something when they hadn't really done anything wrong. Though I still had a strange feeling about that whole situation.

I decided I was going to suppress what my subconscious was telling me and give Seely and his team the benefit of the doubt. My gut, obviously, could not be trusted.

"Finished, Miss Gold?"

I jumped slightly as Dexter reached out to take the empty bag and Coke I had downed like an animal. I handed them to him, a somewhat embarrassed grin on my face, and he stuffed them into a bin on the side of one of the control panels that I would not have taken for a trash can.

"If you need to freshen up or anything at all, we can make a stop. We still have a few hours to go," he said, smiling at me once again. There was something nice about his smile, and also a little familiar. I felt comfortable around him.

"I'm fine, thank you," I assured him, smiling back. I was truly grateful for his kindness, and the grin that spread across my face was just a natural response.

"Alyssa probably needs to rest. She won't have much time for that once we reach Headquarters, and I'm fairly certain she will have many questions for her father when she sees him again."

It was the first time Seely had spoken in (I checked the clock quickly) twenty-two minutes. He was looking at Dexter as he said it, though, and carefully avoided glancing in my direction. His voice was rough and low, like he was trying to conceal whatever emotion had overtaken his mood. I had my money on anger, but I didn't know him well enough to truly guess.

"Of-of course, Seely," Dexter stammered. He seemed nervous. Maybe even a little bit scared. This was a change from the teasing grin he'd had on when he first came back into the car. Maybe he'd thought better about the way he'd responded to walking in on us after Seely's mood had gone so obviously sour.

Again, I wondered about Seely and who he really was. He seemed harmless with me, but there was still a level of dangerousness creeping beneath the surface of the few conversations we'd had. Ever since Dexter had walked in on... well, whatever had been happening between us, something had shifted in Seely. I didn't want to see anything else. Actually, after my meal, I was feeling even more tired. I was also very thirsty, though at that point I'd had two waters and an entire Diet Coke. Maybe I just needed to sleep it off.

"I think I'll take a nap, actually."

My voice came out squeakier than I was prepared for, and I cleared my throat. Seely didn't even glance at me, he just nodded and continued staring out the window. I studied his face for a moment, trying to decipher his expression. He must have felt my gaze because he looked at me and caught my eyes with his for an excruciating couple of seconds. I couldn't break away as his eyes searched mine. I didn't know what he was hoping to find there, but his gaze was so intense on mine I couldn't look away. Luckily, he smiled and said, "Try and get some sleep, Alyssa. We'll be driving for a couple of hours."

The smile was wrong and didn't fully make its way up to his eyes, but the weight in my chest eased up a little bit. At least he was trying to be amiable. Maybe he would take it easy on Dexter.

I snuggled back into my blanket and faced away from Seely, my forehead resting on the seat in front of me as I curled into a ball. I wasn't expecting to fall asleep so quickly after being out for four hours earlier, but I guess fainting isn't the same as getting restful sleep, and my body was still recovering from nearly losing it to shock just half an hour before. So, as I focused on relaxing my shoulders, my arms, my legs, then my fingers and toes, I drifted off into sleep.

Somewhere in between being asleep and awake, there is a space of consciousness where everything you're hearing in the real world feels like something that is happening in your dream. It's that phenomenon where you're performing on stage in your dream as your alarm is going off in the real world. That's the state I found myself in sometime later.

I don't know how long I had been asleep, but my mind was beginning to wake up before my body. I could hear hushed voices around me. I recognized the voices in my subconscious, and I maintained steady breathing so they wouldn't know I was close to waking up. Dexter and Seely were speaking softly around me, and my semi-conscious ears zeroed in on their conversation.

"I'm sorry, Seely. If I'd known that was happening, I never would have—"

"I know. It's fine."

Seely's voice was clipped but reserved. And he didn't sound like he was particularly angry at Dexter. I was relieved, realizing I had been more worried for the other boy's well-being than I realized.

"I just… if I may ask…" Dexter was clearly uncomfortable, but I was willing him to finish the question. Now I was curious.

"Just out with it," Seely sighed, probably resigned to the fact that he wasn't going to like Dexter's question.

"When I opened the door, it looked like," he paused. "She doesn't remember, right? I thought our orders specifically said—"

"No," Seely interrupted, his voice only a whisper. "She doesn't remember anything."

"I see."

They were silent for a moment, and I could feel the tension in the air.

"I'm sorry, Seely," Dexter said after a moment of silence. "I shouldn't have asked. It just seemed like—"

"I *know* what it seemed like," Seely snapped at Dexter. I heard him take a breath to steady his quick anger. "I know what it seemed like because I thought the same thing. I guess I just *hoped* that she would remember *something*. That she would remember anything about me. But she doesn't remember, and she won't remember. I knew that coming into this, and I can't change it now. We have a job to do."

I heard Dexter mumble something that I couldn't quite make out and slip back into silence. Soon the lull of the moving car put me into a deeper sleep again.

Chapter Six

I DREAMED I WAS UNDER SOME SORT OF weight. It wasn't exactly water, but I couldn't breathe, and I was clawing my way to the surface. In my hand, I held a dagger with a crystal-clear hilt, and I could see that the inside of the hilt was filled with deep red rose petals and gold flakes of something. It was beautiful, but the dagger couldn't help me when I was buried so far under the ground. I was screaming, or at least I was trying to, but the blackness just suffocated the sound and filled my lungs as they tried to fill with nonexistent air. It was too thick, and I couldn't find the surface. I clawed at the black, trying to find even a little bit of light but knowing it was already too late and I was going to die. I dropped the dagger and used my left hand to dig through the darkness as well, but my lungs were filled with no hope of fitting any air inside, even if I could find any. My eyes had gone dark, and the world faded away into nothing.

I woke up with a start, coughing and gasping for air. Seely was already there, pounding on my back and yelling something I couldn't hear over the sound of my hacking. Dexter held a bucket under my mouth, and I coughed something up; something black and murky. Just like in my dream.

I couldn't catch my breath, and more and more of the filth came out, embarrassing me a little bit but terrifying me even more. I heard Seely say something to Dexter and Dexter jumped out the open door. I realized absently that we had stopped, and I wondered if we had made it to our destination.

My coughing had subsided slightly, and I was taking in sharp, ragged breaths. My throat felt raw and shredded from the muck, and my mind was racing like never before. So much had happened to me in one day, and I was sure I would go into shock again.

Seely was there, rubbing my back now instead of pounding on it, and asking me if I was okay.

"I'm fine," I said as I coughed a couple more times.

"*That* was not *fine*." His words came out like a growl.

I looked at Seely and he was seething with barely controlled rage. Was he angry with me? I couldn't understand why he would be, but it kind of felt that way.

Dexter looked between us and opened the door to leave. I hadn't noticed we stopped, and I wondered if we were at our destination.

"I'm going to let them know we're here," Dexter said, shooting Seely a look. I thought it could be classified as pity.

Seely only nodded without looking at him, and he stepped out the open door and was gone before I knew it.

I turned my attention back to Seely and saw that he was still staring at me.

"I'm so s-sorry, I d-don't know what happened —," I practically whimpered. I was trying to breathe through the scratchiness at the back of my throat, but I started coughing anyway. My lungs were burning like they were on fire.

"I am not angry with you, Alyssa," Seely was rubbing my back in those soothing circles he'd been doing earlier, and I felt a wave of relief that he wasn't upset with me. "I promise if you try to apologize for this, I will become even angrier than I am now."

I looked at him, still clutching the ice bucket Dexter gave to me. His eyes were blazing, and I couldn't fathom why he was angry at all if it wasn't directed towards me. Annoyed, I would understand. Terrified or worried? Absolutely. But angry…?

"Do you know what's happening to me?" I rasped, my voice barely a whisper.

My heart was still thundering in my chest, but the panic of not being able to get any air subsided as I took excruciating breaths, in and out, in and out. That fear was being replaced by an icy terror that I didn't want to let take hold. I could tell that if I let that feeling sink its claws into my mind, I would never sleep again. I pushed against the ice in my veins, focusing on the heat that was growing at the center of my chest and breathing into that feeling like I always did. I couldn't let it in.

Seely looked at me then, I mean *really* looked at me, probably for the first time since we were interrupted by Dexter. There was something in his eyes I couldn't place, some pain I couldn't decipher, but it was the kind of pain I knew I didn't ever want to feel. He opened his mouth as if to say something, but nothing came out. He closed his mouth and stared at me with that unfathomable expression.

The air between us thickened again and I felt like something was about to change, even more than it already had that day. I sat the bucket down and wiped Seely's curls from where they had fallen onto his eyebrows. I wasn't sure what possessed me to do that, but I couldn't stop myself from reaching out to him. I didn't know why he was angry, and I didn't know what was happening to me, but I had the feeling he knew more than he was willing to tell me. And I couldn't stand that look in his eyes. I wanted to wrap my arms around him and comfort him, as though I'd known him for years instead of days. As if he was the one who was just throwing up black sludge out of nowhere.

Seely closed his eyes at my touch and captured my hand in his, trapping my palm against his cheek. His eyes remained closed as he took a deep breath in, and then let it out again. I sat perfectly still as he brought my hand from his cheek and kissed the inside of my palm. The action was so intimate, and yet it felt perfectly right. My brain was feeling so foggy, I couldn't make sense of any of this.

"I can't."

Seely placed my hand in my lap and got up. Before I could blink twice, he was out the door, shutting it behind him a little too aggressively to be construed as casual.

I sat there, the car door's slam ringing in my ears, feeling a little bit stung for some reason. What had gotten into me? I didn't usually go around brushing strangers' hair out of their eyes. Nor was I usually concerned with what they were going through. But there was something about Seely, and even though I had gone through several traumatic things throughout that day, I felt like I needed to help him somehow.

"Stupid," I muttered to myself. I overstepped and he walked out, just like any normal person would. I should have paid closer attention to boundaries. I should have just left it alone. But truthfully, I didn't know what I should have done. And he'd kissed my hand, I told myself. He overstepped too. Though, I definitely wasn't storming out of the car because of it. In fact, I liked the way the skin of my hand was still tingling from the touch of his lips.

My brain was so muddled. What was wrong with me? I guess being woken up from a nightmare by choking on actual black sludge was not the most restful or soothing experience, but it didn't explain the feelings that were threatening to arise the more time I spent with Seely—which absolutely made no sense because I didn't know this guy. I shouldn't be feeling *anything* for him, especially since he'd basically just kidnapped me.

My mind continued to race as I fought to make sense of everything. What had just happened? What was that dream all about and why did it turn into something very real? I rubbed my neck. It was sore and throbbing, and the pain was like sandpaper in my throat. I hadn't imagined it. That wasn't something that was going on in my subconscious mind, that was real. The fear in both Dexter's and Seely's eyes was palpable. And so was Seely's anger. As much as I wanted to pretend it had all been a figment of my imagination, I knew it wasn't.

After sitting in the car alone for what seemed like forever, someone rapped on the window of the car door. It opened, and there was… Dexter. I felt a little bad that my heart sank as the face I'd hoped for didn't appear.

"Excuse me, Alyssa, could you come with me, please?"

He held out his hand to me, his impeccable manners unwavering. I guess after he'd just witnessed that scene, he finally thought it was okay to call me by my first name. I sat for just a second too long, but he gave me a reassuring smile. He'd had a front row seat to what just happened to me, and I was grateful for his silent encouragement. I returned the smile as best I could, though I'm sure it was really a grimace, and I accepted his hand. I tried not to gag as I could feel the grit between my teeth, and I let him lead me to the door.

Dexter helped me onto the ground, and I blinked at the sunlight. We had been driving for so long that the sun was setting, but the contrast between the light through tinted car windows and the actual sun still took my eyes a few seconds to adjust to. My legs felt stiff from laying and sitting for so long in a relatively cramped space, so I stretched them out one leg at a time.

When most of the spots had disappeared from my vision, I turned to Dexter. He was still holding onto my arm, making sure I was steady before letting me go.

"Thank you, Dexter."

I smiled at him, and I genuinely felt it. I felt terrible in general, and I was still fighting against the burning in my chest, but even after the events of the day, Dexter was treating me with kindness. It was such a pleasant light in the dimness of everything that had happened.

Hurriedly, he let me go, like he didn't want to be caught holding on to me for too long.

"You're very welcome, Alyssa. Right this way, please."

I shook my head as he turned. These guys were acting so strange, and I couldn't figure out what they were all about. I set my pace to follow his, but when I finally looked up to see where I was, I stopped in my tracks.

We were in front of a mansion. I mean, a *huge* mansion. It was a soft gray stone exterior with giant stained-glass windows that existed on every floor. My eyes wandered up the surface, seeing that there were three floors in total. The building had three parts and we were standing in the courtyard directly in front of the main entrance. There was another wing of the building on either side of us and we were surrounded by the massive structure. I immediately thought of pictures I had seen of Notre Dame and of Trinity College in Dublin: gothic infrastructure in all its glory.

This building was a mixture of both, and it was beautiful. I couldn't imagine where we could be in the United States for a building like this to exist. It looked like something out of a gothic novel; something that could only really exist somewhere in Europe.

The fog of the day clung around the corners of the manor like spider webs. The air was heavy with rain, but a cool breeze blew my hair and the fog around in a way that made my skin crawl. It was too slow, too ominous, too… Well, I wasn't exactly sure.

The creepiness that accompanied the beauty made me feel something an awful lot like dread.

But it *was* beautiful. I couldn't help when my mouth fell open in shock and I let out an audible gasp.

Dexter turned to me; his eyebrows drawn with concern. He stared at me for a moment and then turned back towards the mansion, seeming to follow my gaze. His face smoothed out into an understanding smile.

"I felt that way at first, too. I came here with my family when I was ten and I remember thinking it looked like England."

I turned my attention to him, closing my mouth. "You've been here since you were ten?"

Dexter nodded.

"Yes, and I'm nineteen now so I've lived at the AAUD for almost half of my life." He shrugged lightly and turned back towards the entrance.

He may have been nonchalant about it, but I couldn't stop myself from thinking about what he'd said. What must it have been like to grow up here? I had my home and my dad and Seth, and it was wonderful. But there was nothing like this place where I'd grown up, nor anywhere near there. I could imagine running through this castle-like structure as a child, finding and exploring every nook and cranny of the place. My imagination would have gone completely wild in there, and I was a little bit afraid it might still.

The sun was setting, but the clouds were dark and racing. I'd felt the humidity in the air, and it looked like a storm was coming. Dexter looked back at me again when I didn't seem like I was going to move forward, and he gestured toward the grand entrance in front of us.

"We should probably get inside before it starts to rain." Dexter smiled at me again. "Your father would not be too happy with me if I let you stand out in the rain. Nor would Seely, for that matter."

I ignored the last part; I couldn't think about Seely anymore right now. Instead, I focused on the beginning of his sentence. My dad was here. I was ready for some sense of normalcy, and, hopefully, for some answers. Seely had answered several of my questions, but there were things I needed to ask my dad. I still couldn't believe he would keep anything this crucial from me. And from Seth. Oh no, where was Seth? What was I going to tell him? And Stella too? Strapped with a new need to get these questions answered, I followed Dexter through the double doors.

The inside was even more beautiful than the outside. We entered a foyer that had to be bigger than my entire house. The floor was wooden, interlaid with a diamond pattern of different shades of brown. To my left, there was a dark, wooden staircase that led to the second floor. It was polished to a shining state. Directly in front of me, across the massive room, there was a fireplace. The fire was set and blazing, and the inside of the foyer was toasty and comfortable.

The doors closed behind us with a loud, reverberating *bang*. I whipped around to see two men standing on either side of the doors. They looked like butlers or something, and I realized that that may exactly be the case. I didn't know people really had butlers anymore. Dexter looked at one of them, the one on the right.

"Carlton, could you show Miss Gold to her rooms, please?"

I began to protest, not sure how I felt about being alone with yet another stranger today, but Dexter stopped me with the raise of his hand.

"I would take you myself, but I have to report to Seely and the commanders." He smiled, looking apologetic. "Carlton will take you to your room where your things should have already been dropped off. Take some time, get settled, maybe even rest some more. It's been a long day." *And you look like a mess.* He didn't say the last part, obviously, because he was a gentleman, but I knew he had to be thinking it. Seely had even made fun of my hair earlier. I couldn't have looked great, even before I was throwing up black sludge.   I winced at the thought, having almost forgotten about that incident completely as I was staring at the massive mansion that surrounded me now.

Dexter was right, and even though I wasn't thrilled about being left behind again, I had been kept safe so far. I also didn't think I really had a choice. I nodded and attempted a smile. Dexter grabbed the top of my arm and squeezed it encouragingly. It was such a warm, brotherly gesture that my mind instantly went to Seth. I missed him, and I wondered where he was and what his role was in all of this.

"Carlton, if you please."

Dexter tilted his head toward me as he turned and walked through the foyer towards the burning fireplace across the way. Carlton made his way over to me. His hair was white, and his face lined with evidence that he liked to smile, which made me feel a little bit better about being left alone with this man.

"Right this way, ma'am." He drawled the words out in a striking southern accent. I hadn't been expecting it.

I smiled at Carlton and followed him up the stairs of the mansion. I traced the wooden banister lightly with my fingers as I climbed a step behind Carlton. He began filling the silence with information about the mansion, when it was built (1921), how long he had been at the mansion (since 1950, and his father and mother worked here before he was ever born). He also talked about my father, explaining how good of a leader he was for the AAUD and all the good he had done in the years since he and Seely's father had taken over the task.

"Mr. Evanson is an… interesting man. And he's good at what he does, but there is something about your father that brings a special element to the job." We were still walking towards my room, and I realized it must be a part of the east wing of the mansion. I was again struck by the enormity of the building, and I began to wonder how I would ever find my way back to the entrance again.

"Your father," Carlton continued, "he has compassion. Even for those who don't deserve it."

I was listening intently to his comments about my father, very interested to learn anything about this part of his life that I had no knowledge of.

But Carlton didn't say much more as we came to a door, nearly as heavy and big as those at the entrance. He stopped and turned to face me. I must have had my 'lost in my head' face on—which my dad always says either makes me look angry or terrified—because a look of concern flashed across his face.

"Oh, these are just the ramblings of an old man. Please, dear, don't listen to me— except about the banister on the kitchen stairwell of course, that thing is a death trap waiting to happen. I'm sure your father will tell you everything you want to know."

I attempted a smile for what seemed like the millionth time that day, and Carlton turned and unlocked the door with an extravagant-looking skeleton key. The door creaked open, heavy on its hinges, and Carlton stepped to the side, holding out his hand in a gesture inviting me to enter. I walked in and felt my mouth fall open yet again. This house was amazing, and I thought I would stop being surprised by its extravagance, but the room was more beautiful than I could have imagined.

"I'll, uh, leave you to it then, Miss."

I just nodded, still taking in the room. I offered him a small smile, but there was no denying that I was distracted.

Carlton chuckled quietly. "The bathroom is the door to the right; the left is the closet. Your trunk is there, at the foot of the bed. I'll let your father know you've arrived, but he is in a meeting with Mr. Evanson and Mr. Seely. I'm sure he'll give you some time to rest and freshen up."

I stood there, staring at the four-poster bed donned with a fluffy comforter that was a dusty-pink color. The bed was covered by a canopy with gold flowers embroidered into the fabric. I heard the squeak of the door hinges as Carlton began to close them, and I turned.

"Thank you." I smiled at him, and I hoped it told him I was truly grateful for his kindness. When you've had a day as I had, any act of kindness is appreciated. This man tried his best to make me feel safe and comfortable, and I was so thankful for that.

Carlton just nodded in assent and closed the door the rest of the way. I walked over to the ornate thing and ran my hand across the engravings. They were depictions of battles. People fighting distorted figures, their swords slicing and chopping through the bodies of whatever it was they were up against. It was a gruesome sight for a carving, and I dropped my hand, feeling sick to my stomach. The pictures were in stark contrast to the beauty of the rest of the room. I was going to try my best not to look at those much while I was here.

Turning away from the door, I made my way over to the end of the bed where the ancient trunk sat, supposedly filled with my clothes. I remembered Simon in my kitchen this morning, and I figured this was the trunk he had been talking about when he told Seely they were collecting my things from my room. I heaved the lid of the trunk up and began rifling through my options. It seemed like almost my whole wardrobe was in there, which was a pretty big feat considering how much of a clothes hoarder I had always been. I picked an outfit blindly, whatever seemed comfortable and practical (and really whatever my hands touched first), and I got up to find the bathroom.

Something hit the floor with a thud, and I gasped, jumping a little bit. My nerves were officially shot, and my stomach was still churning. I also felt the start of a headache coming on. I knew my body wasn't going to be able to take much more before I completely crashed.

What hit the floor wasn't sinister, though—it was a picture. I bent down to pick it up and I held back the tears as a lump climbed its way up my throat. It was a picture of Seth, my dad, and me from our vacation last summer. We went on a cruise to Cozumel and swam with dolphins. In the picture, Seth is completely freaking out and my dad and I are laughing at him while the dolphins swim around us in a pool.

I smiled and walked the picture over to the stand beside my bed. This picture used to sit on my desk, and it was one of my favorites. Simon must have packed this too, and I smiled again at the random act of kindness. I couldn't explain where the feeling came from, but I suddenly knew I was going to be okay. I didn't know where I was or what I was about to find out about my family. I was feeling hurt that my father had hidden this big part of himself from me for this long. I was worried about Seth. I didn't know what was going on with Seely or why I cared so much. I just had a feeling that I was on a path that was out of my hands. I had a feeling that everything was going to work out the way it was supposed to. I was feeling hopeful for some reason, and I tried my best to hold on to it.

With my change of clothes in hand, I made my way to the bathroom to wash away the grime of this very long day, and I had a little extra spring in my step that hadn't been there before.

I made a mental note to tell Simon thank you the next time I saw him.

Chapter Seven

BANG BANG BANG

I woke up with a start and looked around, disoriented. It was dark in my room, and I couldn't remember where I was for a second.

BANG BANG BANG

Whoever was at my door was getting impatient, and I was getting annoyed. My money was on Seth, trying to be funny. I pushed my wet hair out of my way and leaned over to turn on the lamp beside my bed. I switched it on, but it took me longer than it should have to realize that I was not actually in my own home and in my own bed. I was at the AAUD headquarters in the giant pink bed they had laid out for me. I groaned as I turned onto my back from my stomach. Looking up, I could see that the underside of the canopy was the same pink as the comforter with gold roses embroidered across the expanse of it. I couldn't deny its beauty. I thought it might be something I'd choose for myself if I'd gotten the opportunity to decorate.

What time was it, anyway? I didn't see a clock on the nightstand, but I really hadn't looked around the rest of the room. After my shower, I very literally fell into bed and was asleep before my head hit the pillow. There was something about the hot water of the shower that had loosened all my muscles and made my eyes droop. It took everything in me not to curl up into a ball under the hot water and sleep right there.

I was happy to find everything I needed in the shower, like shampoo and body wash—moreover, I was excited to see the toothbrush on the vanity. I'd brushed my teeth thoroughly (twice) and tried to ignore the grittiness that reminded me of the black sludge from earlier. I rinsed my mouth and spit until there was no longer a trace of black.

I wasn't really looking forward to explaining that dream to my dad later, especially since I had no idea what had happened, and I wasn't sure what I would even say. I was sure Seely had already told him and that I wouldn't have a choice in the matter.

I didn't know how long I slept, but it couldn't have been all night, considering it was still dark. We'd arrived sometime after noon, though, so I'd been asleep for a good several hours. I still felt exhausted, and I wondered if I would ever feel fully awake again. If these past couple of days were any indication, the answer was no.

I rubbed my eyes and tried to concentrate on what I was supposed to be doing. Why was I awake again?

BANG BANG BANG

"Oh, right," I muttered, turning my head towards the door. "Who is it?"

I called out the last part just loud enough so that I hoped whoever it was at the door would hear me and tell me what they wanted so I wouldn't have to get up. Or that they would go away.

Rather than hear footsteps retreating or someone answering my question, I heard a scratching sound. To my horror, I realized that someone was unlocking the door.

I jumped up, but it was too quick for my heavy head to handle. I stumbled and fell just as the door opened, and I landed right in Seely's arms.

"I believe this is at least the second time I've caught you today. Well, I guess the first time I had my men catch you." I felt him shrug. "Still counts."

I didn't have to see his face to know he was smirking at me.

I looked up at him and scowled, my mood automatically turning sour.

"I would have been fine."

"You would have also been bruised. But that's okay, I accept the magnanimous praise I'm sure you're feeling right now."

I was suddenly furious. Who was this man to tell me how I felt? Whatever fuzzy feelings I'd felt in the car were definitely gone now. I squirmed under his grip, trying to break free.

"Let. Me. Go," I growled through clenched teeth.

The words were clipped, and I knew he would be able to tell I was angry. He made sure I was steady on my feet before letting me go and stepping back with his hands up in a mock signal of surrender. He raised his eyebrows and smirked, mockingly. I hated him for that.

"What are you doing here?" I asked him, crossing my arms tightly across my chest. My hair was still wet, and the room was colder than I thought it would be. Seely noticed that I was shivering, and he snapped his fingers at whoever was outside the door. Simon walked in and stood at attention in front of Seely.

"Miss Gold is cold. Please fetch her a robe or a jacket or something."

Simon, like the good soldier he seemed to be, immediately walked to the closet. I hadn't explored that section of the room yet, and I didn't imagine there would already be clothes in there for me. I wondered whose they were, because as far as I could tell most of my things were safely tucked away in the trunk Simon had packed for me.

Simon returned from the closet with a white robe, and he handed it out to me ceremoniously. He practically bowed, and I had to hold back a giggle.

I gladly accepted it, grateful to have something to warm me up. I slipped my arms in and wrapped it around myself tightly.

"Thank you, Simon," I said, giving him what I hoped was an appreciative smile. "And thank you for my picture, also. That was very thoughtful of you."

I swear I saw Simon blush, and as I gestured to the picture Seely's head turned slowly to study it. His jaw tightened. I looked from Seely back to Simon and saw that he was looking at Seely, warily.

"Um, yes. Of course. I just grabbed whatever I could, but I'm glad it happened to be something that brought you comfort." He wiped his palms on his pants like they might be sweaty.

Simon answered without looking at me, his eyes still locked on Seely, who was still looking at the picture.

"Sir, if we are all set here, I will gladly escort you to the meeting hall now."

Seely turned to the boy.

"Please."

Seely's tone was clipped, but I was relieved that he didn't seem to be aiming hostility towards Simon. I didn't understand why he seemed so upset at the fact that Simon had thought to grab my picture. He didn't make any sense, ever. At least not at any moment I had been with him today. But, if I was being completely honest, my reactions toward him didn't make much sense either. He infuriated me, and I was pretty sure I hated him. I thought about earlier in the car and the air thickening between us. I remembered my need to comfort him and the uncontrollable urge to push his hair back.

"Alyssa? Are you okay?"

I snapped out of my daydream quickly. I realized I had been staring at him, and I felt my face flush as I turned toward the door.

"Of course. Let's go if we're going."

I thought I heard Seely laugh softly, and I turned to glare at him. He had his hand over his mouth to hide his smile and I felt the inside of my chest begin to heat.

He gestured to the door. "Simon will lead the way, *Miss Gold.*"

Yup. I hated him. The warm and fuzzies in the car could be chalked up to shock, hunger, dehydration, and sleep deprivation. This man was not someone I was interested in getting to know more about.

I followed Simon out the door, resolutely not looking at Seely, who had fallen into stride directly beside me. He had to be purposely trying to annoy me at this point. No one was speaking and the only sound through the long corridor was the muffled taps of our feet hitting the floor. I was grateful for the robe Simon had found for me, and I snuggled it in closer to my face, taking in the scent. It smelled like my home, like the laundry detergent we used. That was a weird coincidence, but not very concerning. I'm sure plenty of people used the same laundry detergent. It brought me a little bit of comfort, and I welcomed the feeling of safety that accompanied it.

"How are you feeling?"

The question came from Seely. I felt his gaze on my face, but I didn't look over to him. He wasn't much taller than me, maybe a few inches. I was about five-foot-eight, so he was probably still over six feet tall. I hadn't been able to tell any of this in the car, and I hadn't been conscious for long when I first met him at my house. I ignored the satisfaction I felt that he was a little taller than me. That didn't matter, and I was being stupid.

I didn't want to answer him. I thought I might just keep walking and remain silent until we got to wherever we were going. But then I also thought about how, in that scenario, I would look like the petulant child, and he would look like someone who was being shunned for simply being concerned for my well-being. I took another whiff of the smell of my robe and stared straight ahead.

"I'm fine, thank you." I tried to stop there; I really did. "I would have probably been even better if I had been woken up by anyone else, if that someone didn't bang on my door and then break into my room, and also if said person didn't try to completely infuriate me at every turn." I took a deep breath, willing my voice to stay even. "But yes, I'm completely, perfectly, and incandescently happy."

Seely said nothing, and I sneaked a glance in his direction. His lips were pulled into a tight line, and I was pretty sure he was holding in a laugh. The corners of his mouth were twitching slightly.

We continued walking and Seely still said nothing, which was almost worse than him making fun of me. It was worse because I knew that he had to be thinking of a million things to say that would make me angrier, but at least I didn't have to hear his voice. A win, I thought.

We continued down the long corridor that I had taken earlier with Carlton, and then down the stairs toward the foyer. This time, we turned left and made our way toward the fireplace where Dexter had disappeared when we first arrived. As we rounded the corner, I saw what looked like a dining room table, with massive, wing-backed chairs donned in red velvet with a gold rope around the seams. I didn't realize everyone had stopped walking until I felt someone grab my arm and pull me to a stop. I looked over to see Seely looking back at me, his arm gripping mine at the top.

"I should probably know better than to further anger a woman who has already quoted *Pride and Prejudice* to me—"

"It was from the movie, not the book," I interrupted.

He continued, unfazed. "But I should tell you that, unless you wish to make a bad impression with my father, you should wait to be introduced before waltzing into the middle of the meeting which is currently in session."

I looked over toward the table and this time I noticed the hands draped over the armrests and the glasses sitting in front of three of the red chairs. I didn't appreciate being manhandled, but I could see that Seely had saved me from at least one wave of embarrassment I really didn't need to deal with that night.

"Fine."

I jerked my arm free from his, fully aware the move was reminiscent of a toddler's fit. Seely leaned down, close to my ear.

"Alyssa, you may want to work on your manners before you speak with the— OOF!"

I elbowed him in the ribs, hard. I didn't know who he thought he was, constantly invading my space like that, but I was just about over it.

"Seely, I think you'd better take a step away from that one. She's got a wicked right hook, too, I've seen her use it on her brother."

Hearing his voice, I almost started to cry. I turned my head to him, forgetting all about my anger towards Seely for a moment.

"Daddy!" I yelled, not caring that I was supposed to be introduced or whatever Seely was talking about, and I ran to him. He laughed and wrapped me in a hug, and it was all I could do to swallow the lump in my throat that threatened to become a sob. I was so relieved to see someone who I knew was safe, to know that I was truly safe here. It was a great feeling for about five seconds. Then, I remembered that my father was hiding things from me. I remembered that the reason I was brought here like this was that my dad hadn't been honest with me. I remembered that I had a million questions to ask him, and I remembered that I felt just a little bit betrayed.

I pulled away to look at his face. It was crinkled with the smile he still wore but watched it fall slightly as he took in my expression. He ducked his head slightly, looking a little bit embarrassed. Or maybe even ashamed.

"I'm sorry, Lyss. I know you must have a ton of questions. Please, have a seat." He gestured to Seely and Simon behind me.

My throat went dry, and my stomach did a flip. I *really* wanted some tea. I needed to ask my dad about the dream too, but I wasn't sure it was something I could put into words. I was still trying to process it myself.

My dad gently took my arm and brought me to a chair beside his. He pulled it out for me, and the formality of the whole situation was strange to me. Seely, to my annoyance, sat in the seat directly across from me. He made me uncomfortable, looking at me like he wanted to tell me a secret. I tried to avoid his eyes, but that's kind of hard to do when someone is directly staring at you for an extended period of time. So, instead, I looked up at him and stared right back. He didn't break the gaze like a normal person would. In fact, he smirked for no reason in particular. I mouthed "stop that", to which he replied silently "stop what". With a huff, I turned away to study the rest of the people present at the table with us. My dad was to my left, and the man beside Seely had his same, dark hair (though his was speckled with gray), and I assumed that had to be his father. I noticed Dexter sitting on the other side of Seely's father and I offered him a smile. He smiled back and nodded towards me slightly in greeting. Simon was standing at attention on the other side of Seely, looking as if a battle was about to break out, and maybe, I thought absently, it was.

Seely looked to Simon and gestured to the seat beside him.

"Simon, really, have a seat. Take a break. Rest awhile. Have a meal. I'm sure if someone comes close enough to kill me here it was just meant to happen, and you can't stop fate."

Simon looked alarmed and opened his mouth to protest, but whatever look he was getting from Seely made him think differently of it. Slowly, he sat down in the chair Seely indicated. When he finally sat, he slouched down farther than normal, and I thought about how tired he looked. He had dark circles under his eyes and his face was haggard. This boy was very dedicated to his position, that was clear, but I couldn't help but silently curse Seely for not forcing him to take a break sooner. Simon looked younger than Seth.

Seth.

"Dad, where is—"

"So," a deep voice sizzled over my question and called my attention towards them, "this is the infamous Alyssa that my son has told me so much about."

My eyes darted to Seely, but he was carefully avoiding my gaze, for once.

"Um, yes, I guess so," I replied, lamely. I cleared my throat. "I hope he only told you good things."

Seely's father chuckled, a low, throaty sound. I looked at him more closely and saw that he was a very handsome man. He was wearing a gray, long-sleeved shirt that hugged his muscles, showing his pure strength and size. His hair that reminded me of

Seely's was cropped short all around, unlike his son's messy curls. He wore dog tags around his neck, an indication that he was in the military. Unlike my dad, his face was not riddled with laugh or smile lines. I could only imagine that he didn't smile much, and I wondered about what it must have been like for Seely growing up.

"He told me that you were kept in the dark by your father for quite a long time. He said you didn't remember anything. Or, rather, that you don't know anything about what we do here." His gaze on me was heavy, and I squirmed under the weight. "I know many things about you, Alyssa."

That sounded ominous. And again, with the 'remember'?

"No, um, my dad hasn't told me anything about this place." I glanced over at him, and he was smiling somewhat morosely at me. "But I'm sure he has a good reason. I'm sure he was doing it to protect me."

"Indeed."

Seely's father's voice was so deep, I could almost feel it. His eyes searched my face for something, and I don't know what he was looking for, but he must not have found it. He turned away from me with a little bit of what felt like disgust, and he looked at his son.

"Seely, the mission report," he barked, all the hospitality in his voice seemingly spent on our conversation. He spoke to Seely like someone might speak to an insect.

Seely straightened at the order and began to recount our day. I listened for the parts I didn't remember, like the things that happened during the four hours I was unconscious. I was a little bit awed at the way his demeanor switched so quickly, from the ease with which he'd walked to his seat to now. The difference was a little shocking, and I thought he probably had a lot of practice with this.

"We entered the Gold residence at approximately oh-six-thirty. Miss Gold was presumably still upstairs. We had explicit orders to extract her and bring her with us, but rather than ambush her after just waking up, we decided to gather Dr. Gold's things and wait for Miss Gold to make her way downstairs. We heard her come down the stairs at approximately oh-seven-hundred, and that is when we made our presence known."

I knew all of this. I was awake for this part, and I couldn't help but be grateful that they at least decided to wait until I was awake to reveal they were strangers there to take me somewhere unknown. If they had taken me from my bed, I probably would have had a heart attack.

"Of course," Seely looked at me and smiled crookedly, that ease returning back to his demeanor, "she fainted anyway."

I glared at him. He thought that was funny? Obviously. He apparently thought everything that made me uncomfortable was funny.

"Yes, okay, I fainted." My eyes narrowed even more as he seemed to think everything I said was funny. "But I would like to know what happened in those few hours I was out, if you think you can explain it." *Without making fun of me or embellishing the story.* I sent him the message silently and hoped he could see it through my stare. His smirk widened.

"Of course I can, *Miss Gold.*" *But it isn't my fault you are so easy to make fun of.*

Unfortunately, I thought I could read his thoughts as well as he could read mine.

He turned toward his father and continued the story of our day.

"After Miss Gold was unconscious," he looked at me just enough to catch my reaction. My nostrils flared as I took a breath to keep from interrupting, "We brought her to the car and proceeded to make our way to headquarters. It was all very standard. Nothing as exciting as fainting happened. Though we almost had to force-feed her as she would not admit she needed something to eat." He looked at me again, a little apologetically, "We did interrupt your breakfast, I'm sorry about that."

It didn't escape my notice that he hadn't mentioned my rude awakening. I searched his face for answers, and even though his smile stayed on his face I thought I saw his head shake to the right just a little bit. The message was clear to me, though: we are not telling our dads about the dream. I felt a little relieved about that. I really didn't want to have that conversation before I had even figured it out for myself.

I wasn't sure why, but I trusted Seely's judgment. I mean, he had been there with me when it happened. He saw the sludge that just wouldn't stop coming. He saw that there was no real explanation for any of it. And I knew he had a good reason for not letting our fathers know. I glanced at Dexter, and he was resolutely looking at Seely, his face blank. I wondered if he'd been let in on the plan, and how he felt about it either way. I couldn't decipher anything from his face.

"Lyss," my dad grabbed my hand, and I turned my face away from Seely to look at him. "I'm glad you're okay. I'm sorry I didn't tell you any of this. I thought... well, I thought it would be better if you didn't know until you had to." I grabbed his hand back, forgetting for the moment that I was supposed to be annoyed or angry with him for keeping secrets from me. He seemed so worried, and I couldn't bear to make him feel worse. I smiled at him, encouragingly.

"It's okay, Dad. I'm sure you had a good reason."

I meant what I said, but there was a little strain now in the trust I thought I always had so strongly with my dad. I couldn't help the twist in my gut as I thought about all the secrets he was probably still keeping from me. If he could keep his job and an entire world from me, there was no telling what else I didn't know. My smile faltered a little bit, but I put it back on my face and hoped that he still believed it.

"How touching," Seely's father spoke again. "However, we didn't bring you in just so your father could spill all his deep, dark secrets." I watched as his eyes darkened with those words, shooting my dad a look I didn't understand. "We have a problem, and I'm afraid it is directly related to you."

"Me?" I squeaked out, my hands turning clammy as I dropped my father's and placed mine back in my lap. "How is any of this related to me? I don't even know where we're at right now." I could feel myself getting worked up again, and I breathed into that fire inside of me, but I was barely able to control it. "I woke up this morning planning to go to school and suffer through the day with Stella and Seth and," I paused, taking another deep breath before I could continue, "I was brought here against my will. I don't know any of you in this room besides my dad. I don't know where my brother is or where he thinks I am, and I have no idea what you're talking about."

Seely's dad looked bored at my outburst, and I looked from his face to Seely's to see that he was watching his father closely as well. He seemed almost… apprehensive. I began to get the feeling that no one dared to question Mr. Evanson if they could help it. Then, I thought the problem he spoke of was something bigger that I really should be worried about.

"As I was saying," Mr. Evanson continued, as if he had barely registered that I had spoken, "we have a problem. The Undead are coming back, and they are coming back with a vengeance. They are after something." He cut his eyes to me. "They are coming towards headquarters at an alarming rate. We've already doubled the number of guards at the gates, but we are having more and more attacks. It's happening daily now."

"But how—"

"We weren't exactly sure what they're after," he continued smoothly, "but a few days ago one made it inside."

I gasped and looked at Seely. He looked a little sick. Mr. Evanson continued with his story.

"When we were finally able to corner it, it told us that it had a job to do. Seely was attempting to get more answers from it, but he failed."

I saw Seely flinch.

"Then, the creature asked for you."

It took me longer than it should have to register what he had said.

"I'm sorry… they asked for… *me*? By name?"

Seely nodded, looking at me now with somber eyes.

"Yes. They said, 'We are here for Alyssa Gold, and we won't stop until we get her.'"

My blood ran cold. I didn't know what to think or how that could possibly be true.

"But I-I… I didn't even know this place existed until today!" I jumped up, my anger erupting before I could stop it. "I wasn't in any danger at home, why would you bring me *here*?"

At the last word, my voice squeaked into a sort-of scream.

"Alyssa," Seely reached out as if he wanted to take my hand or touch my arm or something but dropped his hand back down onto the table. "You were not safe there. You weren't safe anywhere but here, inside these walls. We had to bring you somewhere where we could protect you."

I looked at Seely, incredulously. How did he know that? How did he know I wasn't safe at home?

"Did you notice anyone suspicious around you in the last couple of days?"

Not anyone but him.

"No, I…" I was going to say I hadn't seen anyone out of the ordinary, but I realized that wasn't true. I remembered the strange people I had seen at school yesterday. I'd gotten an icy feeling when they looked at me, and Stella hadn't seemed to even notice them at all.

"Actually, yes. There were these people at my school yesterday…"

Seely only nodded as I recounted my experience.

"We thought as much. We noticed there was increased Undead activity around your house, in the town and around the perimeter, and that's when the plan was formed for your extraction."

I looked at his face, trying to decide if I believed him, but all I found there was the truth. He looked as serious as I had yet to see him, his smirk almost completely gone from his face. I don't know when or how it happened, but in just *one* day I trusted this boy more than I knew I should. He annoyed me more than anyone else, but trust and annoyance don't always have anything to do with each other.

I kept his gaze, taking deep breaths as I slid back into my seat.

"Okay," I said, releasing a long breath. "I'm sorry, this is all just so much."

I looked at my dad and he smiled apologetically.

"I understand, Lyss, it's okay." He grabbed my shoulder and squeezed. "Don't take this the wrong way, but you're taking this better than I thought you would."

At that, I rolled my eyes and shoved his arm off me.

"Please continue, Mr. Evanson, I promise to listen through everything you need to tell me."

But Mr. Evanson was no longer looking at me. Instead, he was glaring at his son. I could see that Seely was uncomfortable under his father's gaze and that he was trying his best to look anywhere but his face. It was easy to see that he was working hard to ignore his father altogether, pretending that he didn't care, but I could tell just by looking at him that his jaw was clenched tightly, and his shoulders were stiff.

"I believe you and your lackey have somewhere to be, son," Mr. Evanson said.

The last word echoed through the hall, and the way he said it made it sound like some sort of curse. Seely flinched again, and I caught his gaze as he stood and began to make his way from the table.

Don't worry about me, I thought his eyes said. He smiled at me slightly.

But I'm going to, I tried to tell him. Again, I felt the need to comfort him. I suddenly had a deep disdain for Seely's dad. I couldn't stand to see him have this much power over Seely. I couldn't stand to think of how he'd treated Seely his whole life, especially behind closed doors. I decided right there that I hated that man, and if I found out that he'd done anything to hurt his son I thought I might kill him.

That sudden anger and violence that filled my chest scared me.

Seely and Simon left the room, and I could see Simon's feet dragging as Seely pulled him out into the corridor before he could fall completely asleep. Poor guy. I hoped Seely would take him somewhere to get some real rest.

I looked at Mr. Evanson again, this time without trying to hide my contempt for the man. As I suspected, he either saw none of my feelings in my eyes or he just didn't care (I suspected it was the latter), and he continued to explain what had brought me to the Association Against the Undead headquarters that day.

My head was spinning after five minutes of information, but I had promised I wouldn't interrupt. I didn't think Mr. Evanson would take very kindly to me backing up on that word.

The Undead were rising at alarming rates in the past few months. The patrols performed by the AAUD were forced to triple in the past few weeks after multiple attacks were made on the outskirts of Headquarters. They hadn't made it past the border of the forest yet, but it was getting closer and closer every time. Seely had been put in charge of assigning the guards to their posts, and, according to his father, he was hanging on to that responsibility by a thread. I had only spent about half an hour with Seely's father, but I could tell that he didn't like his son very much. I couldn't stop myself from thinking about a young Seely and everything he probably had to go through with a father who clearly tried his best not to love him. I also wondered what happened to Seely's mother, but I didn't know if Seely would be okay with me asking that question.

I still didn't fully understand my role in this whole thing, or my dad's, nor did I know if I fully believed everything I was being told or what I had seen and experienced so far. I mean, you grow up believing one thing your entire life, and then suddenly it changes. It takes a person a minute to adjust.

"You were brought here for your protection," my dad said, taking my hand. "I should have told you. But I thought sending Seely…," he paused like he was editing his thoughts. "I don't know, I just thought it would be okay."

"It was okay, Dad," I said. I squeezed his hand as a form of reassurance. "I made it here perfectly fine. I trust you. I know you would only do what you thought was best for me."

Mr. Evanson huffed from across the table, clearly uninterested in our conversation. I looked at him and his expression was purely one of annoyance.

"That's all you need to be briefed on right now. I will be retiring for the night."

With that announcement, he scraped his chair loudly over the wooden floor and stomped away. I noticed that he was very tall, maybe even taller than Seth.

Wait, I forgot I hadn't asked about Seth yet.

"Dad! Where is Seth? Is he all right?"

My dad smiled at me, and he looked relieved by the question.

"Seth is here. He's fine."

I let out my breath in relief. But... if Seth was here...

"Does he know anything about this?" I don't know why, but I whispered the question. As if I thought Seth was standing behind me and this was top secret information.

"Seth knows enough," my dad said, simply.

Well, what did that mean? Did he know about the AAUD and the Undead, but not about the plot against my life? Or vice versa?

I opened my mouth to ask him to say more, but he held up a hand to stop me.

"Lyss, I promise I'll have someone take you to see him in the morning. Tonight, all you need to know is he's fine, and all I need to know is you're both here, safe."

I didn't feel the same way. I needed to know more. Like, what exactly did Seth know? How long has he known? Did he know before I did? Was this what he was acting strange about yesterday?

I didn't say any of this to my dad, however. Instead, I nodded and gave him a small smile. He stood to his feet and so did I, suddenly eager to get back to my bed and sort through the messiness that was now my brain. My dad pulled me to his side and kissed the top of my head.

"I love you, Alyssa, and I'm glad you're here."

I wrapped my arms around his waist as we started walking back in the direction I'd come in.

"I love you, too."

I was glad to be there, walking next to him. Even if my world had flipped upside down in less than twenty-four hours, at least I was with my family. Well, one member of my family. But I was going to see Seth tomorrow, and I hung on to that knowledge.

My dad walked me to my room in comfortable silence. I had so many things I needed to ask him, but I got the feeling that it had been a long day for him too. So, I tucked my questions away in my brain for tomorrow, and I enjoyed the walk.

When we got to the door, my dad pulled me in for another hug, said goodnight, and waited for me to close the door behind me. I could hear his footsteps retreating, and I sunk against the door, letting out my breath in one big gust. What a day.

I looked around the somewhat-familiar room. There wasn't any light other than that from the lamp beside my bed. In its dim glow, I could see that I had left the bed in complete disarray after the rude awakening I had earlier. I thought of Seely and how upset he looked when he left the meeting earlier. I hoped he was okay.

I stepped away from the door about a foot or so, and I felt something grab my wrist. Before I knew it, my arm was wrenched behind my back and there was a hand over my mouth.

"Don't scream."

<h1 style="text-align:center">Chapter Eight</h1>

I DIDN'T SCREAM.

I wasn't sure I would be able to. My body froze up in an instant and my throat was already dry from earlier, raw and hurting from the sludge. I was sure, even if this intruder's hand wasn't over my mouth, any sound I made would be no more than a croak.

No, I didn't scream. What actually happened was much more dramatic.

Some instinct I didn't know I had took over, and I grabbed the wrist attached to the hand over my mouth. In what seemed like less than a second, my intruder was on the ground, my knee on his chest, his hands pinned to the floor under mine, and my shoulder tingled with the sensation leftover from his body flipping over it and to the ground.

Seeing his face, I realized I probably should have guessed who it was from the beginning. Seely was looking up at me, his eyes wide and his grin growing along with them.

"Seely, what are you *doing* here?"

My annoyance came through in my voice, and I watched with a hint of pride as his face turned pleasantly pink under the pressure I placed on his chest with my knee. We were so close, our noses almost touching. I could feel his labored breathing on my skin. The smell of cinnamon tinged in my nose and made me forget what I was supposed to be doing. I took a deep breath in... And then I froze.

What had just happened? What did I just do?

With a gasp, I stood quickly to my feet. Seely coughed when the pressure of my body was no longer crushing him.

"Dang, Gold," he pounded on his chest with his fist and coughed again. "I didn't know if you had it in you. Lucky for me you aren't armed, I guess."

He chucked, but I just stood there, horrified. What was happening to me? I had never been in a fight in my life. Punching Seth didn't really count, seeing as I never hit him hard enough to cause any damage or even leave a mark. He would never even punch me back.

I'd never flipped anyone over my shoulder like that. I had never taken any self-defense classes. That shouldn't have been able to happen, especially with the ease it did. I could still feel Seely's weight rolling over my shoulder... *How did I do that?*

I felt my breaths becoming shorter, more rapid. My chest was heating again, and there was an icy feeling crawling through my veins once more.

"Alyssa?"

I looked up to see Seely staring at me with wary eyes. I realized I had been looking at my hands blankly for far longer than is normal, huffing breaths as I stood there frozen.

"Don't worry about that, I would have done the same thing." He stepped towards me, slowly, with a hand stretched out. "It was my fault; I just didn't want your dad to know I was here." He ducked his head a little to meet my eyes. "I'm fine. Are you okay?"

I managed to shrug, and with that gesture, the caution in his eyes softened just a bit. Before I knew what happened, he grabbed my right hand that was still poised in the air and pulled me to him.

"Sorry," Seely murmured into my hair. "Usually I would ask first, but I had a feeling you needed this."

I was wrapped into a hug, which wasn't normally something I enjoyed. But I felt that I was so close to falling apart at the seams and the pressure of Seely's arms around me was the only thing keeping me together. He was right again, which was infuriating, but I didn't feel annoyed as he held me.

"I don't know what's going on with me today." My face was pressed into his shirt. Thankfully, mercifully, I wasn't crying. That was probably due more to the fact that I had cried myself out only hours before than it had to do with my own strength at that moment. But I had cried in front of Seely more in one day than I ever wanted to.

We stayed like that for a minute while my breathing slowed. I kept my face buried in Seely's chest; it smelled like that same sweet cinnamon that lived on his breath. I couldn't explain why, but just being there made me feel more like myself. At that thought, I abruptly came to my senses. I didn't know this guy, and he had definitely snuck into my room and semi-attacked me. I pushed against Seely's chest until he loosened his hold on me, and then I took a dramatic step back and crossed my arms tightly in front of me.

"What exactly are you doing here? And *why* did you think it was a good idea to ambush me like that?" I felt my eyes narrow as I glared at him.

I assessed his expression, looking for any indication that my sudden change in demeanor and proximity had wounded him in any way. If Seely noticed I was acting strange, however, he didn't show it in his expression. Leisurely, he walked over to the bed and leaned against one of the four posts that held up the canopy. Taking out his dagger, he began cleaning his nails, just like he'd done just the morning before when he ambushed me in my kitchen. I thought that the set of his jaw looked a little strange, but I brushed it off. I didn't know this boy well enough to even guess what his facial expressions could mean. But still...

I shook my head to clear it and pressed the question again, realizing that I hadn't received an answer.

"Seely, what are you doing here?"

"I want to show you something," he said, not looking up from his focus on the dagger and his hand.

I waited for him to elaborate, but he just continued what he was doing, never looking up from the dagger.

"Okkaayyyy?" I dragged the word out, emphasizing my irritation. I wasn't tired anymore (the meeting with our fathers had woken me up, not to mention being attacked in my room), but I wished for some time to think. And *geez*, who did I have to fight to get a mug of tea around here?

It seemed like the only time I had had to myself in the last fifteen hours was when I was asleep in this room earlier. I was getting frustrated with everything: what was going on at this place really? I knew my dad hadn't given me the whole story yet. Why was my dad being so cagey about where Seth was and what he was doing? That was weird. And then here was Seely. In my room. Just leaning on my bed with only the explanation of "I want to show you something" and no other elaboration. I felt my blood begin to boil and I let out a huff of air in an attempt to keep it in check. I hated feeling out of control, and my temper was something that seemed to have a mind of its own.

At my breath, Seely looked up to meet my eyes.

"If your blood gets any hotter, you'll have smoke coming out of your ears, Gold."

I only glared at him more, daring him to say something else and give me a reason to lose my temper at him.

"I want to show you something if you're interested," he continued. "But we're going to have to be sneaky about it."

I raised an eyebrow at him. I could still feel the hot blush of barely controlled anger on my cheeks, but I had to admit I was curious about where this was going.

"You want to show me something that's a secret? At this time of night? Do you ever sleep?"

Seely smirked. "Not much." He looked at me intently before he asked again, "Do you want to go with me?"

I did want to, and that feeling made my stomach flutter. I was curious about this place and the type of things they really did within the confines of these walls. I was also curious about Seely. There was something about him that intrigued me, and it wasn't just because he was completely infuriating. I couldn't stop thinking about the feeling I had earlier, that I'd seen him somewhere before. And he had asked if I remembered.

"Fine. But I need to change first."

My mouth agreed to go before my brain had completely gotten to that decision, but I knew that I wouldn't be able to stay still in my room after he left if I didn't at least see what he was talking about.

A smile spread across his face and the brightness of it confused me. It was gone before I could assess it, and he just said, "I'll wait outside."

Seely jumped up and put away his dagger into its sheath. He sauntered to the door and was out in the hallway before I could re-evaluate my decision. I let out a sigh. This time it wasn't out of anger, but out of exasperation. Seely never did or said what I expected and trying to guess what he was talking about or thinking could be a full-time job if I let it.

After I changed into a fresh pair of leggings and a sweatshirt, I slipped into my favorite running shoes. I wasn't a runner, but running shoes were the most comfortable option when it came to tennis shoes in particular. They were so light and flexible around my feet, and I knew that they would be fine for whatever thing Seely had in mind for tonight.

I wasn't sure if I should go out into the hallway to tell Seely I was ready. After all, he said this was supposed to be a sneaky thing. If I went out into the hallway dressed and looking like I was ready for something other than sleeping, I needed to be sure there wasn't anyone else besides Seely waiting for me on the other side of the door.

I pulled my hair into a low ponytail, the curls around my face already coming loose. After staring at the door for a minute, absently trying to figure out the best way to go about this, I finally decided to simply knock. I walked up and rapped the ornate wood with my knuckles, three quick times. Stepping back to allow room for the door to swing open, I waited.

Approximately three seconds later, Seely poked his head in.

"You do know doors are supposed to work the opposite way, right? You're supposed to knock when coming *in*, not when exiting."

I decided to ignore the comment that was obviously meant to goad me, and instead I said, "Are you taking me somewhere top-secret, or what?"

Seely laughed lightly and pushed the door open wider. When I could see his whole body, he gestured for me to follow him and turned to walk down the hallway. I followed silently, noticing that we didn't turn the way I had come up to my room. We turned left out the door and began walking down a part of the corridor I had yet to explore. We walked for about a minute in silence. Seely wasn't in a hurry, though I wondered why not if what he wanted to show me was so secretive. I was able to take my time and become familiar with my surroundings as we walked. The corridor got tighter and older the more we walked, and soon we turned to the right. I realized that we were now in the west wing of the mansion, which must have been older than the main part where I was staying. The floors became uneven stones rather than the smooth wooden ones that were present in my room. As we walked, I also noticed that the photos on the walls turned into paintings—portraits of young men and women who had probably once been prominent members of the AAUD, I thought.

I looked at Seely's profile in the low light. He was a little bit ahead of me, leading down the hallway, but I could make out the easy set of his jaw. He seemed at ease as we walked, and I admired the strong set of his mouth, the full lips that were set together there. His skin was pale, but I thought his cheeks might look a little flushed.

I wondered how this mission could be anything that needed to be kept secret if we were walking together in the dim light that came from small, humming sconces that were mounted in the wall periodically. Something about the glow of the lights made the walls seem like they were growing as we walked. The shadows cast in strange places, making the hallway seem like a tunnel on the verge of closing in around us. I picked up my pace just a little bit to stand next to Seely rather than slightly behind him. He glanced at me for just a second and then turned forward again, smiling slightly.

"You know, I can hold your hand if you're scared."

"Very funny."

I sneaked a look in his direction, just out of the corner of my eye, and I saw his smile widen ever so slightly. He was so infuriating, it was insane. I wondered if he did it on purpose or if it was just a talent he possessed.

"So," I began, "what is this top-secret mission we're going on at the moment? What did you want to show me?"

"You'll see when we get there."

Abruptly, Seely turned to the left, and I found myself being whirled around from his grip on my arm, steering me down an even tinier corridor. He didn't let go of me as we walked down this particular passage, and I figured it was because the stone floor was becoming even more uneven than the passage before. The only noise was our breathing, mine slightly and infuriatingly more labored than his, and the occasional slip of my shoes on the rough stone path. Seely's step didn't seem to make a sound.

"Seely?" I said his name again after several more minutes of silence. It wasn't uncomfortable, being silent with Seely, and I noted that with appreciation. Sometimes you're alone with people who make the air feel thick and layered, and like natural silence is awkward. With those people, meaningless small talk, something I've never been good at, seems like the only way to clear the fog and set everyone at ease. With Seely, the air was clear and still. Like he was the only force needed to push away the noise when he was with someone else. I thought that he probably liked the silence, the way he let it envelop us as it did.

At the sound of my voice, he stopped, bringing me to a halt with him.

"Do you have any patience at all?" He accused me with the question, but his eyes were light, and the hint of a smirk played on the corners of his lips. I gave him a scowl.

"Of course, it's just that we've been walking for so long and you haven't said anything to me about where we're going or what we're even doing. Don't look at me like that."

The smirk that threatened his face was now fully present, and I thought it looked like he was mocking me.

"I'm sorry, it's just so easy to mess with you."

I gave him another glare and said, "I would be crossing my arms right now if you weren't locked around one in a vice grip."

Seely looked at his hand on my arm as if he had forgotten it was there. He released his fingers and stepped back a step.

"Oh, sorry."

We stood for another few seconds in silence, but Seely just stared at a point on the wall behind me, not meeting my eyes. His cheeks *definitely* looked flushed now. Unfortunately, I could feel that mine were too. I didn't know why, but the air between us felt like it was vibrating with electricity.

I cleared my throat.

"Uhh, anyway, we're here," he said, taking a step back and gesturing to the stone wall behind him like it was supposed to mean something to me. I looked around him to the wall that was a dead-end and squinted, trying to see anything out of the ordinary. It just looked like a wall to me.

I pursed my lips and furrowed my brows slightly, trying to figure out what game he was playing. Why had he brought me here?

"Okay, I give up," I said, turning to him and throwing my hands up and letting them fall back down again in a signal of defeat. "Unless you brought me here to murder me, I don't know why it had to be a secret."

I heard a small sound from Seely that sounded like he was choking. I looked over at him and his face was slightly red. He covered up the sound with a cough and then chuckled lightly.

"You've got a dark sense of humor, Gold."

I thought I could see some emotion in his eyes that hadn't been there before. But then again, it could have just been a trick of the small, slightly flickering lights.

I waited for him to say something else, but he just looked at me. That same emotion I couldn't place earlier flickered in his eyes again. This time, he cleared his throat, breaking the silence.

"Come here."

Seely grabbed my hand and pulled me closer to the wall. He pulled aside a tapestry that was hanging there, sliding it over almost like a curtain. He then placed my palm against one of the stones. It was smoother than the others that surrounded it, but it was a difference that was imperceptible unless you actually touched the stone. With my left hand pressed against the surface, Seely pressed his into mine and I felt the stone move forward and click into place. I looked at Seely and felt my brows come together in confusion. He met my gaze with a smile on his face, and he leaned around me to press on the wall with both of his hands.

It was a door.

Seely stepped just inside the door and grabbed what looked like a kerosene lamp from the hook on the wall. I watched as he pulled a match from his pocket and struck it against the wall to light the lamp.

"Getting here wasn't the secret part of this little adventure," he said, a gleam coming into his eyes, whatever I'd thought I'd seen there was gone now. "What's up these stairs is the secret."

With those words, he gestured the lamp a little way down the corridor so I could see the ancient, winding staircase leading straight up.

"Does this place have a tower?" I asked.

"Follow me and find out," Seely said, smiling again.

I couldn't help the small answering smile I felt on my lips. The threat of adventure was real and irresistible. I knew Seely could see it in my face, and his own smile widened as he turned to the staircase to begin climbing.

Chapter Nine

WE WERE CLIMBING THE STAIRCASE, winding with the ancient metal, where only the sounds of our shoes on the steps existed. I could hear the whistling of the wind outside as we climbed and periodically passed small windows. The air was still, and it smelled like a musty library; I loved that smell. It reminded me of something that I couldn't quite place, but as I inhaled deeply, I had a feeling that was almost like Deja vu.

I was excited about the adventure, but I couldn't help my overactive imagination from betraying me. I began imagining ghosts and demons and other wild things lurking in the shadows of this part of the mansion, but now I had the added realization that these stories were far more plausible than I ever imagined. Every shadow in every corner turned into something else in my mind, and I tried not to make it too obvious that I was less than an inch away from Seely, just in case.

"I never said thank you, for today," I said, eager to fill the air with conversation.

Seely didn't stop climbing as he said, "Thank you for what? For kidnapping you and bringing you here against your will? I think they call that Stockholm Syndrome, Gold."

I rolled my eyes at his back.

"You're ridiculous," I said. "I *mean* thank you for watching me freak out today and not looking at me like I'm an idiot."

Seely still climbed, but his foot hesitated a little and skidded on the next step. He grabbed the small rail with his right hand to keep from tripping.

"I just…" I continued talking, not quite sure where I was going with this. "I don't usually break down like that in front of people. So, thank you for helping me stay sane, I guess."

Seely still didn't say anything, and I looked up at the back of his head. We continued climbing for a few more seconds, and I heard him say quietly, "You're welcome."

We were silent after that, those words hanging in the air between us. A few moments later we reached a landing. I was grateful to be off the staircase. My legs were burning with the strain of the climb, and I again cursed myself for not starting my running routine that I always pretended I would.

The ceiling was low here and Seely had to hunch to stand up all the way. There was about an inch gap between my head and the roof. Raising the lantern to the ceiling and searching along for something, Seely found a wooden hatch above our heads.

"Hold this," he said. He was smiling wider now, and my stomach did a little flip.

I took the lantern and held it up so he could see exactly where the latch was located on the side of the door above our heads. The small door was made of thick slabs of wood that looked like they were covered with some kind of resin to seal them from the elements. The latch was an ancient metal chain with a hook at the end, linked through a metal eye.

"Does this door go outside?" I asked.

Seely looked at me with a twinkle in his eye. He twitched his eyebrows up and back again quickly as he unlatched the door and shoved it open.

I looked through the open door and saw only stars. I had never seen that many stars all in one place, except maybe in a movie about someone drifting off into space. Thinking about where we were, I realized there hadn't been much that I could see on the way in. I knew we were in the middle of the forest, but I guessed by looking at the millions of stars over my head that we must be very far away from anything to be able to see this much of the night sky unencumbered by light pollution. The milky way was visible, with purples and blues swirling in a mist together with streaks of white. Every star was a beacon, hypnotizing me.

I felt my mouth fall open, and I wasn't sure exactly how long I gaped at the open hole in the ceiling.

"Come on," Seely said, breaking my reverie. He reached up and pulled down a small ladder, gesturing for me to climb up first. I smiled at him, and he returned it right back, this camaraderie between us coming easier the more time we spent together. I climbed the ladder as quickly as I could, and I felt the ladder shake slightly as Seely began to climb behind me.

The ladder was only a few rungs, and when I had taken two steps my whole head was outside. I focused on getting my entire body out of the hole before I let myself look around and take in the view.

It *was* a tower.

Well, it was a kind of a tower. We came up from the hidden stairwell onto the roof and in what could best be described as a turret. It was a square about the size of a small living room with walls that came up a little higher than my waist. It reminded me of pictures of castles I'd seen in movies and fairy tales. It was different, though, and I realized it must have once been used as a guard tower of some kind. I could see the whole property from up here.

The mansion stood in the middle of thick woods. The grounds themselves seemed to consist of a large square of a courtyard in the front of the building, and from this vantage point I could see that the long driveway curved to the left as it led out of the courtyard and eventually disappeared into the woods. We had come in that way a few hours earlier, though I hadn't been paying close attention. Not that I could see anything through the dark tint of the windows of the town car anyway.

I turned to see Seely looking at me. I couldn't read his expression.

"Do you like it?" he asked, his voice soft.

I looked around again as if I wasn't already sure I loved this place. I took in the woods to my left and then turned my attention back to the stars. The air was so fresh, with every breeze blowing whiffs of pine my way. I made out a few constellations I remembered from star gazing with my dad. I could see the milky way so vividly, I wanted to reach up and run my fingers through it.

"It's okay," I said, fighting a smile. He said it was easy to mess with me, but I was beginning to feel the same way about him.

I heard him chuckle under his breath and when I turned to look at him, I saw he was walking toward a bench that was against the main part of the building. He sat down and looked up at the sky. Without waiting for an invitation, I walked over and took the spot next to him on the bench.

We sat in silence for a little while, both of us settled down on the bench with our heads tipped back, staring at the sky. I was counting the stars, as many as I could, and when I got to three hundred Seely finally spoke again.

"There's a lot about this place you don't know," he began, "and I want to tell you. I really do. I'm just not sure where to start."

He paused and took a breath, and I waited in silence. I felt my body stiffen as I braced for whatever it was that he was going to tell me.

"Your dad briefed us a little bit before we came to collect you, but he didn't warn us just how unprepared you'd be to see us. I also know there are things he wants to tell you himself, but I don't know if that's the best plan." He sighed, and neither of us looked at each other. "He has something planned for us here, and I can't figure out what it is. He was acting harsher than usual at dinner." Seely let out a hard laugh. "Usually, he does a better job at hiding his hatred of me than that display tonight."

My blood was beginning to boil as he talked about his father. I really hated the way he made his son feel.

"This may be hard for you to believe, but he wasn't always like that with me. Before my mom died, he was a lot nicer. I don't think he really ever liked me, but it was more of the way he hated everyone." I didn't know if I should say something to that, but he continued. "And there's something going on with Dexter too. He's been all on board with everything my dad is deciding to do, and I don't know when that started. I know there's something wrong, I just can't put my finger on it."

I sat there in silence, soaking in what he was saying. It seemed like he was speaking more for his own benefit than for mine. It was like he had to get his thoughts out of his head, and I just happened to be the person sitting there.

I wasn't sure why Seely brought me there. I wasn't a part of the crew he was mentioning. I barely knew Dexter and I had only had one encounter with Mr. Evanson, which had already skewed my vision of him into a strong dislike, and maybe even hatred. I had the feeling that Seely just needed a friend, and that those may not be so easy to come by in this place. I *was* curious about his mother, though… I thought maybe I should wait until we'd known each other for more than twenty-four hours before I pressed the subject, though.

"You're probably wondering why I brought you up here."

I looked to my right to see Seely was looking at me again. Could he read minds? This was, what, the third time he'd known exactly what I was thinking? I nodded, still not breaking my silence.

He shrugged. "I thought you might like it. I also know how suffocating it can get in there. I thought you might want a route of escape if you ever needed it."

He winked as he said the last sentence, and I smiled. It was thoughtful of him, even if he was annoying me just a few minutes earlier. Even if he did sneak into my room and pretend to attack me.

"Thank you," I said. My voice came out smaller than I intended for it to, probably due to the lack of usage in the past moments. I cleared it before I continued. "I really appreciate it. You know, everything."

Seely didn't say anything, but he nodded and leaned forward, putting his forearms on his knees for support. I noticed his dagger at his side in a holster. Its hilt was a shining obsidian, and it glittered in the moonlight. I had a quick, startling thought that I could disarm him quickly if I wanted to. I shook my head to clear the picture of myself swiping Seely's knife and holding it to his throat. I would have to unpack whatever that was later.

"What are you thinking about?"

I jumped at the sound of his voice, and I felt my face flush. I hoped the shadows of the roof concealed the blush I felt on my cheeks.

"Nothing." I answered too quickly, and I saw Seely's eyes narrow a little as he pursed his lips. He didn't believe me, but he didn't push me either.

We turned away from each other and Seely sunk down on the bench to rest his head in order to better see the stars. I followed his lead and leaned back as well. The sky was shocking, all the blues and blacks mixed with whites.

"I always thought the sky was just black," I said, before I could stop the words from leaving my mouth. I felt Seely settle a little bit more beside me.

"I used to think so, too. But then I started coming out here. The skies are so clear this far out. You can't see stars like this anywhere else."

As if on cue, a star shot across the sky.

"How did you find this place?"

Seely sighed. "My dad can be… difficult. And he knows every nook and cranny of this place. I spent most of my childhood here trying to find a place he didn't know about, just to get a minute to breathe without him criticizing me."

He let out another long breath and I tried not to think about the intimacy of the moment as we talked about our lives under the watercolor night sky.

"Anyway," Seely continued, "I was exploring this part of the mansion one day." He smiled, remembering. "Well, I was supposed to be patrolling. But I was a twelve-year-old kid wandering the halls. I think my dad sent me over here just to get me out of the way. I found this tapestry on the wall and for some reason I decided to inspect it. I saw it move just a little bit, almost like it was being blown by wind somehow."

I turned to look at his profile in the moonlight. He was still staring up at the sky and his dark hair fell back from his forehead and I stared at the silver light that reflected off of it. I wanted to touch his hair again, and I tried to stifle that thought as quickly as it came.

"I pulled back the tapestry and ran my hand along the wall, found the stone you pushed earlier, and the rest is history." He shrugged. "As far as I know, my dad still doesn't know about this place. I'm sure he would have done something to mess it up by now if he did. Maybe he's waiting for the right moment to strike." Seely laughed then, but the sound was bitter. It was the sound of resignation. I couldn't imagine having a father like that, and as much as I had been annoyed today by the boy sitting next to me, I couldn't help but feel sorry for him.

Seely breathed in deeply once, letting it out of his mouth a second later. "Don't go feeling sorry for me now, Gold." He stood and stretched a little bit, raising his arms to the sky. Turning to me, Seely held out his hand. "Do you want to go see your brother?"

I took it without hesitation, and my heart jumped a little. A part of me noted it wasn't just because I was going to see my brother.

Chapter Ten

AS SEELY LED THE WAY BACK DOWN
the ladder, neither of us spoke. It didn't take us as
much time to go down as it did to go up, I thought.
We walked through the door that was still open at the
bottom, and Seely let me exit first before coming
through the doorway behind me. I watched as he
placed the tapestry back in front of the invisible door
that somehow knew to slide into place after we were
through it. I was going to try and memorize this trip,
knowing then that I didn't want this night to be the
last time I saw the tower.

We made our way back down the corridor we'd
come from, but this time we took a left at the end of
the hall instead of turning to the right.

We walked for a while in silence, but again I didn't mind. I knew I was going to see my brother soon, and I could feel my excitement rise with every step. Seth was okay. Seth was *here*.

Why was Seth here? What did he know about this place? My mind was spinning in circles, and I knew that even if Seely had bothered to say anything I probably wouldn't have heard it anyway. I was too lost in my own thoughts.

At the end of the hallway, we came to a stairwell and Seely swiftly jogged down the steps. I followed as best as I could, but he was *fast*, and my legs felt kind of like jelly. It made sense, seeing as he was some kind of soldier in this place, and I was completely out of shape. I was sure he trained often and in a way that kept him ready to fight at all times. He had muscles that ran tightly down his arms that proved that to me. Not that I'd been looking...

At the bottom of the stairwell was a small alcove. Directly in front of us was a door.

This door looked like what I imagine the door to a scientist's lab would look like. It was massive, made of a thick, steel-looking material. There was a keypad to the left of the door, and there was no handle. Naturally, Seely sauntered up to it, pressed several numbers into the keypad, and stepped back a little as the door slid open. *Just like a scientist's lab*, I thought to myself.

Seely turned to face me and stepped even farther back from the door.

"Ladies first, Miss Gold."

He bowed in a slightly mocking way, though almost everything he did seemed to be mocking, and gestured for me to enter the room. I rolled my eyes and followed the direction his hand was pointing, straight through the doorway. After being in the oldest part of the castle with lowlights and then on the roof in the black night, I had to blink several times as my eyes adjusted to the harsh fluorescents that flooded this room.

The door we entered opened onto a sort of platform. There were rows of tables with lab equipment to my left and people were working, scurrying everywhere with notepads and microscope slides and even some steaming containers of things I probably didn't want to know the specifics of. The air was sterile, and it smelled like bleach, as well as other chemicals I couldn't really place.

To the right side of the platform were rows of computers with even more people in white coats huddled together at different stations, seeming to compare notes about whatever it was they were looking at on their screens. Something seemed off about the scene, and it wasn't just the fact that this room existed just down the hall from what reminded me of a medieval tower. I thought for a second about why this seemed weird.

"What time is it?" I whispered to Seely. I didn't want the random people on the platform to hear me, for some reason.

"Almost midnight," he answered me in an equally hushed voice.

I almost asked him another question when I spotted a mop of curly hair and a familiar figure down the row to my right.

"Seth!" I forgot about not wanting to draw attention to myself as I practically screamed the name and ran to my brother. I felt the weight of hidden stress lift from my shoulders as I saw my brother standing there, unharmed. He was leaning over a computer when I came in, but at the sound of my voice he stood up and turned, his smile wider than usual. Without giving him the chance to speak, I ran to him and wrapped him in a hug. I felt him laugh and wrap me into an equally crushing embrace.

"You finally made it, Lyss! I heard you went all hysterical and passed out." I pulled back to glare at him and saw him look to Seely who was leaning against the door frame with his dagger out again.

Seth continued with a smile. "Were you the one who knocked her out, Evanson? I bet it was easy."

Evanson? I wondered at the ease with which my brother used a nickname with Seely. They seemed to be more familiar than they should be, especially since I didn't know anything about this stuff, these people, or this place.

I stepped back and punched him in the arm, to which he let out a satisfying yelp and rubbed the spot on his arm that took the brunt of my attack.

"No one 'knocked me out'," I said, making air quotes around the words with my hands. "I just fainted."

"The pure shock of my presence was just too much for her," Seely crooned.

I narrowed my eyes at the dark figure in the doorway. Seely wasn't looking at me. He was just wearing that same infuriating smirk and still picking at his nails with his dagger. I looked at the blade more closely, noting the black obsidian hilt and the darkness of the actual blade as well. I wondered what metal it was made from. My eyes traveled down the weapon, admiring its beauty. I felt a stare on my face and jumped out of my observation to meet Seely's gaze, his dark eyes shining.

"You see something you like, Gold? Feel free to keep staring."

He winked and I grimaced, turning away from him and back to my brother. Seth was staring at us, his face thoughtful. I cleared my throat.

"So, what are you doing here? *How* are you here?"

Seth's gaze turned hard, careful. I could practically see his brain working to come up with an explanation.

Seth was debating whether or not he should lie to me.

I felt my eyes narrow slightly and I shifted my weight to my left leg, backing up from him just a little bit. I heard footsteps approaching and knew that Seely was now standing beside me. Seth looked to him. I watched as my brother and this person who should be a practical stranger had a silent conversation. My head whipped back and forth from Seth to Seely and back again. I couldn't understand the situation. How could Seth know this person so well when I had only met him today?

"What's going on here?"

At my question, Seth snapped his attention from Seely to me. He chewed on his lip. He looked… nervous.

"Lyss, have a seat."

I was so sick of people treating me like an invalid. Yes, okay, I *had* passed out initially. But I wasn't some fragile thing that couldn't handle whatever secrets were going to be uncovered here. Seth tried to grab my arm and lead me to a seat, but I jerked out of his grip.

"Tell me," I said, my voice slipping into a flat acceptance. I could hear the undertone of anger that laced the words, and I knew Seth would also be able to.

"Lyss—"

"Gold—"

Seth and Seely both started at the same time, and I could have sworn my skin caught on fire with rage. They were being ridiculous and dragging out something that didn't need to be dragged out. I'd had enough of secrets and dramatics for one day.

"Tell. Me." I seethed the words through clenched teeth. Seely opened his mouth, but before he could say anything I continued, "And if you want to keep your tongue, I suggest you shut up." Seely laughed quietly at that, and I added, "Unless you're going to tell me what's going on, obviously."

I couldn't stand the thought that he was laughing at *me*. I knew my anger was plain on my face as I turned back to Seth. He was pursing his lips slightly and looking back and forth between us like he was watching a tennis match. I didn't understand what I saw in his face, so I just waited for him to answer me. Seth met my stare and sighed like he was not looking forward to whatever was coming next.

"Okay, Lyss. I don't want to freak you out more than I'm sure you already are, but—"

Just then, a very familiar voice sounded from down the stairs that led up to the platform Seth, Seely and I were standing on. Seth whipped his head toward the sound and when he turned to face us again, his eyes were wide.

"Uh oh."

Seely snorted a laugh.

And Stella walked on to the platform.

She was dressed in joggers and what looked like a Nirvana t-shirt, all wrapped in a stark-white lab coat. Her hair was in a messy bun on the top of her head, and, though I'd never seen her look this disheveled other than our *Harry Potter* movie marathon when we were thirteen, she looked serene, calm. She looked like she was as comfortable in this cold, unfamiliar place as she was sprawled across my couch with a gallon of buttery popcorn.

I froze, halfway between shocked and hurt. Seth was here, in this private lab, with these people... He had called Seely "Evanson". They had a private, silent conversation right in front of me, like they've known each other for years...

I stepped back once and felt the pressure of a hand on my back.

"Breathe, Gold."

I wished I had taken up their offer to sit earlier. As if he could read my mind yet again, Seely reached out to the station beside us and spun around the chair to be placed perfectly behind me. He pressed gently on my shoulders, and I plopped into the seat.

"Oh. Uh, hi Lyss!" Stella said, still frozen on the top of the stairs. She took slow steps to where Seth, Seely and I stood. I felt like I was floating; like this was a dream. "How long have you been here?"

I didn't answer. I wasn't sure what to say. My head was spinning again, and I was focusing on my breathing. If I passed out again now, I would never hear the end of it—especially from Seth and Seely. I focused on that heat in my chest. Stella studied me during her whole agonizing walk from the steps, and her eyebrows came together in what looked like confusion. I wasn't sure what expression was on my face, but I tried my hardest to keep it blank.

"You haven't told her yet?" Stella asked. She looked at Seth with an accusing glare. My vision blurred and I took in a deep breath.

"No, Stella, I was just about to." Seth let out an exasperated sigh. "Perfect timing as always," he mumbled under his breath.

They all turned to me again and I was surprised that my anger didn't flare up. I supposed I couldn't focus on not throwing up or fainting (I wasn't sure what I was feeling) and being angry at my friends all at the same time. I saw the concern on their faces.

"You're green, Gold," Seely whispered from beside me. "Breathe."

So, I did.

"Enough of the theatrics," Seely spoke again. This time he addressed the couple in front of us. "Alyssa needs to know the *truth*, and she needs to know now." He paused and I guessed he was looking at me and assessing my well-being. "She can handle it. Probably."

I looked at him then, just to glare, and found him grinning at me. He wiggled his eyebrows twice and I realized he was trying to distract me. I appreciated it, especially as my nausea dissipated and the fire inside me subsided to embers.

"Okay, you're right," Seth began. He brought his own chair around and sat closer to me, our knees almost touching. "Lyss, I know you're probably confused…" He paused, assessing me. I only nodded, hoping he would continue without making me speak. I wasn't sure I could.

"I'm assuming Seely filled you in on the AAUD a little bit." He turned to Seely. "Did you tell her anything about what we're doing here? What *she* is doing here?"

Seely shook his head. "That's your story to tell. And I know my orders."

What orders were those? Seely wasn't supposed to tell me about Seth? My mind was racing, again, and I felt my eyebrows draw together in confusion.

Seth nodded, though I thought he looked a little miffed, and turned his attention back to me.

"I work for the research department here." He gestured to Stella. "We both do, actually. Well, we're technically interns, I guess."

None of this was making any sense. I would know if either of them had jobs at a secret organization, right?

"*How* is that possible?"

My voice came out in a whisper.

Stella brought a chair over to complete the circle. Seely still stood at my side, and no one offered him a seat. I looked up at him. His face was blank, and maybe even a little bored.

"I'll be..." Seely looked up at the ceiling, thinking, "anywhere else." He shot me a wink. "Yell when you're done. Or faint. I'll come for whichever."

He sauntered away, down the stairs Stella had come up, and there was a part of me that wished he had stayed. Something about his presence was beginning to be a comfort, and I felt like he would be on my side for whatever I needed. Then again, I didn't know him, and I could have been totally wrong. I pushed those thoughts aside, turning back to the two people in front of me.

"Tell me," I said, finally finding the volume I was looking for earlier. "Tell me all of it."

"Okay, wait wait wait," I held up my hands to stop Seth from speaking. "So, you're telling me that every weekend you were with 'Grandpa'," I put air quotes around the word, "you were actually working here. And the summers you were gone to camp you were actually…"

"Here," Seth finished for me.

"That doesn't make any sense."

"I know. I know. We were trying to protect you."

I shook my head. Seth had told me all about the threat to my life.

"There are people, things, out there that have sent specific information to Dad about all the ways they want to kill you," Seth had said moments before. "We were trying to keep you from this place because it's too close to everything that wants to hurt you."

The "things" he was referring to were actually the league of Undead who had been making more and more attacks on the base. They were the ones Seely's father had been talking about earlier. When I asked why they were coming after me and not him, Seth simply said, "They just like you better, I guess."

There were a lot of holes in his story, and when he would ask me to recall specific details of the past years, my head began to swim, and I felt another headache coming on. I don't know why, but I didn't totally believe him, even though it seemed like he was telling the truth.

"Do you remember the summer house we used to go to with Mom? The one in California?"

I nodded. Of course, I remembered that. We used to go there every summer. We would even take Stella and her parents, who were also involved in the AAUD somehow.

"That's a headquarters. A lot like this one. We used to go there during the summers so we could have a beach vacation and Dad could be near to where he needed to be. In case anything happened.

That last summer was the year they sent their demands."

"'That last summer?'" I breathed the question.

"Yes. They sent a message to Dad that said they wanted you, specifically."

I sat back in my chair.

"They didn't give a reason, as far as I know, and Dad didn't know what else to do but separate us from the situation. The same week Dad received that message, Mom disappeared. So, Dad was trying to stay active in the AAUD, complete his duties as a Founder, make sure you stayed as far away from the Undead, and anything to do with them as possible, and then he was alone with us."

Seth took a deep breath before he continued.

"At the AAUD, when you turn thirteen, you're settled at a headquarters, and you begin your training. It's a hard job and a dangerous one, especially for people like us and Seely who are the Founder's children. When I turned thirteen, Dad finally told me about this place and everything there was to do with it. He brought me here when he told you he was taking me to camp, and I started learning how to defend myself. I'm not a warrior-prince like Seely, but I can hold my own." He smiled a little bit. "I found myself spending more and more time here at the lab, so when I turned sixteen, I asked for my placement to be moved here."

I was listening intently, I really was. But at the same time my mind had begun to wander. When everything you think you know comes crashing down in the span of one day, you have to take a second and re-evaluate your life a little bit.

Seth had explained to me that Stella had been a part of the AAUD since she was thirteen as well. Her family vacations in the summer were taken at one of the many stations throughout the United States. According to Seth, Stella was working with the research department in the lab here, diving deeper into the origins of the Undead. She was using it as an internship to put on her college applications, so I guess it was unfair to say that *everything* we talked about was a lie. She was still apparently planning on going to college with me next fall.

I tried to think of a time when Stella or Seth had been missing from my life, that may have been suspicious and able to be explained by this revelation, but I was coming up empty. My memory was acting up on me, and I could focus on their faces throughout the years in my mind, but not really the situations themselves.

I could feel my brain spinning. I couldn't grasp onto any of the memories that passed through my mind with any strength. I couldn't retrieve the details, and that was beginning to make me feel a little crazy. That, accompanied with the anxious fire that was filling my chest once again and the ice that had begun to make its way through my veins… I was about to lose it, and I didn't want to do that here.

I rose to my feet, vaguely aware that Seth was still speaking. I hadn't heard what he was saying, but I decided that I didn't really want to right now.

"I'm going back to my room," I said, my voice barely above a whisper.

Seth froze mid-sentence.

"Lyss, what? I'm trying to talk here," he said, his voice nonchalant. He was trying to be funny, but I could see the stress in his expression as he plastered a smile on his lips.

Seth's attempt at joking was half-hearted at best. He was scanning my face and I didn't know what he saw there, but the forced smile melted off his mouth. When his eyes met mine, they were wide and... scared? No, that couldn't be right.

"Lyss..."

Before he could finish whatever he was about to say, Seely was at my side. He took hold of my elbow and pulled me from the wide-eyed stare of my brother. I didn't answer Seth as I let Seely drag me to the door. I only stopped when I felt Seth grab my other arm and jerk me to a halt.

"Lyss, don't walk away from us. You need to hear this! You need to let us explain."

Before I could process the words, Seely was in front of me. His hand was removed from my elbow and was now gripping Seth's forearm. I could only see the profile of his face, but his jaw was set. His hair had fallen in front of his forehead, and his words were seething. I didn't need to see his eyes to know they would be burning with anger. I wondered what shade of green they would be just then,

"She owes you nothing. The only thing you should give her is the whole truth, but I know you can't do that. We *both* have our orders." His tone of voice sent a chill up my spine. "Back up, Seth."

I saw that same emotion I had recognized as fear creep into Seth's eyes again as he looked at Seely. They just stared at each other for an immeasurable moment. I watched with confusion. Was Seth really afraid of Seely? I couldn't really blame him at this moment, honestly. Seely looked like he was ready to murder someone. But why had that same emotion come into his face as he looked at me? Seth wasn't afraid of me, and he had no reason to be. That didn't make sense.

As I watched, Seth's face drained. Looking pale and resigned, he nodded to Seely and released my arm. He looked like he was about to say something to me, but Seely again grabbed my elbow and swirled me to the door and out into the dark passageway. I was grateful to be out of that room.

I was grateful for the cool air that hit my face. I was grateful for the low light emanating from the sconces on the walls rather than the harsh fluorescents that had been suffocating me in the lab. I was grateful to be away from people I loved but who I felt so hurt by. I was grateful Seely was there, leading me up the stairs, one of his hands on my back and the other still holding my elbow.

We rounded the corner and Seely stopped. As he was holding me, I stopped too.

"Are you alright?"

I didn't trust my voice just yet. And crying in front of Seely (again) was not an option. So, I just nodded weakly. I stared at his chin. I felt that if I met his eyes, I *would* start crying, and that was something I really wasn't ready to do.

I felt warm fingers under my chin, and Seely lifted my face to meet his gaze. He looked at me closely; it was almost too intense. My face burned under his stare, and I knew it had to be bright red. His dark eyes searched and searched for something, but I assumed he didn't find it as his face fell slightly into disappointment. I got the answer to my question, though, as I noted his eyes were closer to forest green in this light.

"What is it?" I whispered the question. His face hardened and he stepped back from me. I hadn't realized we were standing so close, maybe two inches from each other. My back was pressed against the hard stone of the wall, and he leaned against the wall on the other side of the landing. My heart was racing, my breath coming out in sharp huffs. Though the air was still stiff in the stairwell, I could swear I felt a cool breeze dance along my skin, leaving goosebumps along my arms in its wake. I shivered, involuntarily.

Seely arranged his face into that mocking grin.

"You're stronger than you think you are, Gold," he said. I blanched at the unexpected compliment. "You'll be fine."

He pushed away from the wall and began sauntering down the hallway.

"You coming or not?" He called back to me over his shoulder.

I started a little bit at the abrupt change in him. But I followed. I was getting used to not knowing what to expect from Seely.

He stayed in front of me the whole way back to my room and didn't say anything else.

When we got to my door, he turned around so swiftly I didn't have time to stop before I crashed into him. We were close again. Too close. *Not close enough,* a voice whispered in my head. I shook it a little bit, clearing out the intrusive thought I didn't want to hold on to.

Seely's brows furrowed slightly as he looked at me and he stepped back a little, pushing away from me with his hands on my shoulders. I saw something in his face, I thought, but before I could think about it, he swooped down and captured my hand. I watched as he lifted it to his mouth and kissed my palm, just like he had in the car. His lips were like fire on my skin, so soft and warm. His hands were rough, like the hands of someone who'd been trained in combat. If I thought my heart was racing earlier, then it was on the verge of exploding now. I tried to focus on keeping my breathing somewhere close to normal.

When he removed my hand from his mouth the sensation was like ice. Fire and ice. I felt my face flame and more goosebumps travel up my arm.

"Sleep well, Gold."

And I watched as Seely turned and walked down the corridor, away from me, without another word.

Chapter Eleven

AS SOON AS I ENTERED MY ROOM AND laid down on the bed, whatever confusion I had been feeling about the scene in the hallway dissipated. I shouldn't be tired. I wasn't, really, at least as far as my body was concerned. But my head hurt, and I couldn't make sense of a lot of the things I'd heard tonight.

What were these orders that Seely and Seth were apparently bound to? Why would Seely say that Seth wasn't going to tell me the whole truth? Why was Seth scared of me? And why did Seely just kiss my hand in the hallway?

I crawled into the bed, my thoughts racing, and I don't know how long I laid there tossing and turning until I finally fell into a fitful sleep.

A sleep that was filled with nightmares.

I was gasping, but this time I wasn't in the ground. The black dirt wasn't choking and suffocating me. I was on the ground in a clearing in the woods, looking up at the swaying pines and the bright blue sky. There was one tiny cloud making its way across the opening, and I thought it looked peaceful. Only for a moment.

I was gasping from fatigue. In my hand, I held the flower-hilted dagger. I jumped onto my feet in one smooth motion and swiped at the thing in front of me. It was coming at me with impossible speed, its skin was white and pallid. I couldn't make out its face clearly, but I could tell it was still bleeding from the cuts I had given it earlier, its black blood dropping on the ground. Good, I thought. I would make it do more than bleed from a few cuts. I would kill it if it was the last thing I did.

The thing stepped around me, careful of the proximity to my dagger. I held it ready anyway, prepared for the creature to take even one step forward into my range of motion. I could feel the strength in my muscles and the tension in my shoulders. I took a deep breath to steady myself. Rule number one when dealing with the Undead, always be alert. They were inherently crafty. And extremely fast.

An Undead… that was what I was facing. Its tall, slender form reminded me of a serpent; its movements were lithe and graceful, and if its eyes weren't so glassy it may have been beautiful.

I saw the scene as though I was watching myself from afar. I saw my hair pulled back into a tight ponytail on my head. It swished in the wind, the curls unkempt and pieces falling around my temples, just like they always did. I saw that I was wearing all black: black leggings and a black tank top with black boots. I wondered for a second at the uniform. But then, the Undead spoke.

"You're fast, girl," it hissed through clenched teeth, his icy breath touching my face. Holding my breath, I watched as its mouth curved up into a sensual smile. "But we are faster."

Before I could retort or even react, they were on me. The version of myself in the dream that stood back and watched tried to scream, tried to warn the other me, but I couldn't make a sound. I watched as three other Undead formed from thin air. They appeared out of a cloud of black dust. They surrounded me. Somehow, I was in both places: watching and fighting at the same time.

Panic. I felt such acute panic. There was no way I could fight them on my own.

"Where is he?" I whispered to myself.

He who? I wasn't sure.

"Your Beloved is not here to see you die," crooned the Undead. "How sad."

I knew he meant it was anything but sad. He was excited to kill me. He would not shed any tears for me when I inevitably lay dying on the ground, and I knew it then:

I was going to die.

"I can take care of myself," I pulled together all the false bravado I had practiced so carefully throughout the years, but I still knew he wasn't convinced. "What, are you scared, Orthan?"

The Undead, Orthan, apparently, smiled.

"You know nothing scares me, girl."

A chill went up my spine as I watched the Undead draw closer. I was alone, with only a dagger to protect me. I was good, and I could probably fight off two or three. But four? I was dangerously outnumbered, but I would go down fighting.

"Will he know you loved him, in the end?" Orthan drawled. The Undead closed in closer, cornering me. I prepared *myself to strike and dodge the teeth that I knew were coming quickly after me.*

"There will never be an end for us."

I screamed as I lunged at him, and my dagger sliced through his chest. The wound was deep and black blood began pouring out. He hissed, and I knew I only had minutes to finish the job before he healed and came after me again. I ran towards him, aiming for his head, but…

I was grabbed from behind. Cold, clammy hands held me back as I thrashed and screamed. The three other Undead had grabbed me, and I was thrown to the ground, losing hold of my dagger. I rolled for it as claws broke my skin and shredded my clothes. I was vaguely aware of the sting and the hot wetness that flowed down my face. Was it blood or tears? In either version of my dream-self I couldn't tell.

I watched as my futile attempts to retrieve the dagger were thwarted. I watched as my head was snapped back with a kick, and I heard the sickening crunch as one of the creatures stomped a foot onto my arm.

I watched as Orthan, already healing from the wounds I'd inflicted, rose from the ground, smiling. He had blood in his mouth.

I watched as he walked over to me as I screamed and fought and clawed with everything I had left in me. The other creatures held my limbs pinned to the ground and I had no hope of moving them.

I watched as Orthan bent down to my face as if to kiss me.

And then I watched as he ripped my throat out with his teeth.

I jolted awake, gasping. My hand clutched my throat and I applied pressure, trying everything to stop the bleeding… But, of course, there was no blood. It had been a dream. My throat burned, which I assumed was from the events of the day before.

But I was okay. I was safe in my bed, or at least the bed I'd been given at the AAUD.

I exhaled and then took in a couple deep breaths, desperate to slow my heart rate. A dream. It had been a dream.

I looked around frantically and tried to take deep breaths as my heart slowed. Looking around, I didn't see any of the black sludge that had accompanied my earlier nightmare. I took that as a good sign.

I could see through the window that the day was just breaking, and I sighed. Usually, when I was at home in my bed on a normal day, it took everything to even get me out of bed in time to get ready for school. I idly wished I was the person that woke up at dawn all the time.

I scooted on the bed until my back was against the headboard, and I slowly lowered my hand from my throat. My breathing had calmed but my heart was still pounding in my chest. I was covered in sweat.

"Just a dream, just a dream," I chanted to myself, my voice quiet and quivering.

But it felt so real.

So real I could still feel the icy chill of Orthan's teeth as they ripped through my skin… The thought made me shudder, and I fought to push it away. I sat silently on the bed, breathing into the heat in my chest that remained blazing. I watched the sunlight on the floor fade from orange as the sun rose outside.

Giving up on even the idea of getting more sleep, I swung my legs off the bed and padded across the floor. The surface of the floor was cold, and it cleared my head a little bit more.

I went straight to the shower and began to run water. I turned the heat all the way up, and when I ran my hand underneath the stream, my skin automatically turned red. I needed to get out of these sweaty clothes, and I thought the extremely hot water would help stop my racing brain and make sense of whatever I'd just seen. With the water steaming as I turned the showerhead on, I turned to the vanity to search for a hair tie to get my hair out of my face. Some of the strands still stuck to the sweat at my neck and temples.

When I turned to the mirror, I stopped dead in my tracks. I thought maybe the world stopped too, moving in slow motion as I stared at my reflection.

I didn't know I was screaming until I heard a pounding on my door, and I didn't know whose hands were on my face until he turned my head away from the mirror and forced me to meet his eyes.

"Look at me, Gold." It was Seely. His voice was urgent, barely controlled. "Look at me!" He screamed the last part; it was a command.

He was holding my face steady, and his eyes were wide and wild. I looked at him, following his order, but my vision was a little blurry.

"Did...," I swallowed, my throat bone dry, "Do you see it too?"

My voice was a whisper. The world felt far away, like I was looking through a long lens.

Seely's eyes were confused for a moment and his brows gathered together. He opened his mouth, probably to ask me what exactly had made me go insane, but then his eyes traveled down to my throat.

His face paled and his mouth fell open. His hair looked like midnight against his pallid skin and his eyes were so wide I could see the green.

"Oh my god."

His hand moved from the side of my face to touch the skin on my neck, and it felt like a blaze of feathers. My throat felt tender, and it burned with the contact of his fingertips. He traced the jagged, purplish scar that now existed from the bottom of my jaw directly beneath my earlobe all the way to the base of my throat.

It was a bite mark.

"Alyssa, tell me exactly what happened. I need to know everything."

I sat in a chair beside the ornate fireplace that faced my bed. My hair was still damp but drying. I didn't even bother to drag a brush through it. I knew I would regret that later when my curls were untamed and frizzy, but at that moment I couldn't think about anything else but the dream and how in the world that translated into a scar.

After Seely had succeeded in calming me down in the bathroom, he had left me to take a shower and get my breathing under control. I was in there for no more than ten minutes, but when I came out in a fresh pair of leggings and another sweatshirt, Seely was already pacing like a mad man and the fire was blazing. There was also a mug on the table between the two overstuffed chairs that faced the fireplace, which I found was filled with tea and the perfect blend of milk and sugar. I could have cried; I was so excited to have that small comfort that I'd been missing in the last couple of days.

I was sitting in that chair, sipping on my mug of tea, when Seely asked that question *again*, even though I had just told him the whole story.

Well, most of it. I left out the part about the Undead taunting me about my 'Beloved', whatever that meant. It felt… too personal? I wasn't exactly sure. I just knew I didn't want him to know that part of it.

I tried to make it a joke to avoid the seriousness of the situation. "I literally just finished telling you the entire story. Were you not listening?"

He shot me a look.

"Funny. Actually, I'm trained in the art of listening to people's stories, even when the people telling them are very bad story tellers."

I stuck my tongue out at him, but I wondered if he was being serious about his training.

"And you must be a very bad storyteller, Gold," he stopped his pacing to face me. He placed one hand on each arm of my chair and leaned forward. "Because I *know* you're leaving things out."

I stared at him for a couple more seconds, but then I broke my gaze away and looked to the fire, taking another smooth sip of my tea.

"How did you know how I liked my tea?"

I asked that question to avoid his eyes. He knew too much about me just by looking at me with those eyes, and I didn't want him to see the thing I hadn't said. I'd barely admitted it to myself.

Seely just stayed leaning in front of me. I looked down at his hand and saw that the knuckles that gripped the arms of the chair were white.

"Alyssa." I felt his warm hands under my chin, lifting my face up and forcing me to look at him. With his other hand, he took the mug from my hands and placed it on the table. Reluctantly, I met his gaze. "You need to tell me everything," he continued. "You

—*we*—don't know what might be key to figuring out what's happening with these nightmares."

I stared at him, into his eyes—mine searching his for any reason not to trust him. What I found was nothing but an endless, deep green lagoon of openness and concern… concern for me. I stared, probably too long, but long enough to see the anxiety fade into something else. I watched his face soften and his mouth part slightly. I was breathing heavily, and I felt my eyes widen at the change in the air. It felt charged and staticky between us, and I was again reminded of our moment in the car. I could almost feel his lips on my hand from last night, and I wondered what they would feel like on my lips instead. His breath sped up like mine did, and I could hear my heartbeat flutter in my ears as it began to race faster.

Someone cleared their throat from the other side of the room.

Seely didn't drop my gaze or my chin, but his features hardened again, slightly. The air between us stilled until the static was more of a quiet hum.

"Simon," he murmured. "I forgot you were there."

I couldn't move my head from Seely's grasp, but I heard Simon nervously shuffling his feet. Blushing, I realized I'd forgotten he was there too. Seely smirked at the flush on my skin, but he still didn't let me go. I kind of didn't want him to.

"Gold, you can tell me," I guessed we were back to talking about the dream now, and I fought the disappointment. "Whatever it is. I need to know every detail so I can decide what to do next."

I sighed and realized I had already decided I would tell him before I even knew it. Something was changing in me when it came to Seely, and it was both scaring me and exciting me. I didn't really understand why it was happening so quickly, but I just couldn't explain how it felt so right to me.

"Okay, so you know the whole story with the Undead and the dagger that was the same as the one in my other dream," I began. Seely nodded, waiting patiently. "And you also know that he was talking about how he was going to kill me, and I had fought him back before the others showed up. But..." I swallowed. "He also told me something else."

Seely just looked at me, staring into my eyes with that same intensity.

"He asked me about someone."

I paused too long and Seely said, "Who, Gold?" His voice was almost a whisper. "Who did he ask you about?"

"He called him my Beloved?"

As I said the words, I searched Seely's face for any sense that I had reason for feeling so self-conscious about this part of the story. His features didn't betray him, but I felt his hand tighten on my chin ever so slightly.

I continued.

"He asked me if... if I thought..." I swallowed. I felt self-conscious with Seely's eyes on me. Those eyes were practically pleading with me to continue. So, I did.

"He asked me if... someone... knew I loved them in the end."

I shifted uneasily in my seat and Seely finally dropped his hand from my face. He stood up straight and took a step away from me, closer to the fire.

"To whom was he referring? Did he say?" His voice was suddenly stiff, reserved. I didn't really know what that change meant.

I didn't want to tell him. I didn't want to say the words… some part of myself recoiled from the thought. Something about what Orthan said to me in my dream felt intimate and private, and though I was beginning to trust Seely and maybe even feel something for him, I still didn't know him.

I steeled myself, though, and decided to say the words out loud.

"No, he just called him 'my Beloved'?"

The last part turned into a question as my embarrassment reached its peak. I didn't even look at Seely, and I was grateful that he'd released me when he did. I knew my face had to be red.

"And I don't know why that sounds like a big deal because it totally probably isn't," I continued, trying to explain my reaction, "but for some reason it's absolutely mortifying to me right now."

I dared to glance at him then, and I found him looking at me. His face was softer than before, his eyes unreadable. His jaw was set, and I saw the muscle twitch.

"And did he tell you who that person was?"

I stared at him and simply shook my head. I saw his eyes flash to Simon, who I had once again forgotten was against the wall.

"Very well, then."

Seely turned away from me and I watched as he passed Simon and the two walked out the door together without another word.

I stared after them, unsure of why what I said would elicit this kind of reaction. Why did it matter to *him* what Orthan said to me? I didn't even know why it mattered so much to me.

I traced the line on my neck. I could still feel the scar, and it hadn't faded any more. It was still a jagged, slightly purple line that I couldn't explain.

My tea had gone cold, the day had officially, fully broken, and I was alone. I didn't know why my chest felt so empty at that thought.

I thought of Seth and Stella and how I wished they were here right now. And then I thought about how they had lied to me, and the cold pang of jealousy split my heart in two. I felt it breaking, and the molten lava inside began to spill into my chest. I looked out the window, yet again trying to focus on my breathing. The heat was becoming too much inside of me, and I hated myself for how weak I felt these past couple of days. I hated my family for lying to me, and I hated Seely for leaving me alone without even an encouraging word. I hated that I wished Seely was still here to hold my hand, and that made me angry at myself. That rage was so hot under my skin that it felt like ice. It bubbled under the surface, and I was a little bit worried about what I might do. I didn't understand these feelings or where they were coming from. I thought about the way Seth looked at me earlier... like he was scared of me. The thought sent a shiver through me.

Chapter Twelve

I SAT THERE FOR A WHILE, LONELY AND confused and scared. I also wished I had gotten to finish my cup of tea before it went cold, or at least that I had a new one.

The window I stared out of practically went from floor to ceiling. I realized, with a pleasant feeling of surprise, that it was a door. There must be a balcony of some sort out there. I thought about getting up to explore as I watched the birds fly past every few minutes, but I couldn't bring myself to move.

I don't know how it happened, but I must have dozed off for a few minutes because the knock on the door surprised me.

Before I could even open my mouth to invite the person in, the door opened slightly.

"Miss Gold?"

It was Simon. He sounded wary and I felt a pang of something that reminded me of a protective instinct.

"May I come in?"

His voice had the same strange lilt and accent that Seely's had, and I wondered if that meant they had been raised in the same place. Considering how close they seemed to be, I assumed they'd known each other for a long time, no matter that Simon couldn't be more than fifteen or sixteen.

"Of course!" I called, finally finding my voice. I stood up from the chair, feeling a little embarrassed that I had been sleeping, yet again. I'd been sleeping a lot since I got to this place, but with everything else happening that seemed to be worse, I didn't dwell on that fact for too long. Absently, my hand reached up to my throat to feel the scar.

Simon entered the room, and I almost tackled him when I spotted the steaming cup of tea he had in his hands.

"Seely thought you might want another cup since he knew the first was wasted," he said as he handed me the mug from his hands. I took it eagerly and took a huge sniff before the first sip. The tea was aromatic and spicy, and I wondered which variant this cup was. From the first sip, it was perfect. Yet again.

"Thank you, Simon," I said, flashing him a smile. As much as I had going on, the smile was genuine. The warmth that filled my chest was not like the fire I'd felt before. It was comfortable and safe. It cleared my head enough to hatch a little bit of a plan.

I liked Simon, and I didn't want to take advantage of him, but I thought I might be able to get some answers from him.

"Y-you're welcome, Miss Gold."

I rolled my eyes at that. Why did everyone here try and call me *Miss Gold*?

"Simon, I'm guessing that even if I ask you again to call me Alyssa instead of 'Miss Gold', you'll still refuse?"

A small smile threatened his lips.

"You would be correct."

A smile crossed my lips too as I made my way back to my chair and sat the mug on the table beside the cold one. Simon came over and took the cold mug from the table. He turned quickly back to the door as if he was eager to avoid conversation with me.

Unluckily for him, I wasn't about to let him leave without asking a few questions first.

"So, Seely has you running errands for him while he… does whatever he does all day?" Simon stopped at my words, looking like he was half braced for a fight. "I mean, what *is* he doing today?"

"Seely is… busy." Simon wasn't looking at me. Actually, he was staring at the door as though he would do anything to be there. I got the sense from him, though, that he was kind enough of a person to not try and escape from me while I was in the middle of speaking.

"Very detailed information, thank you for that, Simon." I kept my tone light, joking. But I was getting irritated. I wanted to get information from Simon, but it was proving to be harder than I thought it would be. "What time is it, anyway?" I asked, realizing I hadn't checked the clock when I woke.

"It's almost nine," Simon answered. "Seely has to report to his father every morning at eight-thirty, so he decided to send me with the tea until he could make it back here."

"Report to his father?" My nose wrinkled a little bit. I didn't like the idea of Seely having to do anything for his father, though I know that was foolish. He'd been doing that long before I got here. At least it explained why he had left the room so abruptly earlier. That somewhat made a weight lift off my chest. At least he wasn't upset with me. "What does he report to his father about?"

Simon sighed and his gaze flicked briefly to mine before he turned once again toward the door. I could tell he didn't want to answer me, but also that he didn't want to be rude.

"That's a long story. And it's also one I'm sure Seely will be happy to tell you all about later."

I blinked a few times at Simon's tone before a smile spread across my face. His voice had changed from timid and concerned to authoritative and strong in a matter of moments. To me, it seemed like he may be attempting to do his best Seely impression. He still didn't look at me, as he fully faced the door, and I could see that his knuckles were turning white from the grip he had on the mug. I wondered what kind of orders he was under when he came up here and who gave those orders. Was it Seely? I assumed it had to be, since he's the one who gave him the tea to bring me. Did he forbid Simon from speaking with me for more than a minute? I felt a flicker of that cold rage and I pushed it down before it could become anything more.

"Do you need anything else, Miss Gold?" His voice was quiet. "Seely will be finishing up with his father, and I should really get back to them."

"Actually, I do need something else," I said. Slowly, Simon turned to face me. His expression was grim, like he knew whatever I was going to ask was not going to be pleasant for him. "I need to get out of this room. I'm going with you."

His eyes widened and his face paled slightly. I almost felt bad for causing this boy distress, but that feeling dissipated as I grabbed the warm mug of tea and took a long drink. Whoever kept making tea for me knew exactly how I liked it, and I was grateful for that, especially at that moment. I wondered if it was Seely or someone else. The tea settled my nerves and warmed my insides, keeping that anger docile.

"Miss—," he cut himself off. "I don't think that's such a good idea. He won't like it."

"Who won't like it?" I challenged. "Seely or Mr. Evanson?" Simon opened his mouth to answer but I spoke before he could. "Actually, it doesn't matter. Either way, I'm going with you." I slipped on my shoes, feeling grateful that I had left them by the bed. I was pretty sure Simon would sprint away from me as soon as I turned my back if I had to go searching for them in the closet or bathroom. He looked a little horrified as he followed my actions, but his gaze slipped into resolution soon enough. I guess I looked determined enough that he didn't want to fight me on this. He nodded once and turned quickly on his heels as he made his way out the door.

I was practically jogging to keep up with him. His gait wasn't that much longer than mine, was it? Simon seemed determined to stay as far ahead of me as possible and I let him. As long as I didn't lose him down the corridor, I didn't care whether or not he wanted to talk to me. The only sound reverberating down the hall was the clomp of Simon's army boots, the softer slap of my sneakers, and me sipping at my tea. I'd swiped it from the table before running after Simon.

We passed several people along the way. Some of them nodded to Simon and acutely ignored me, while others waved tentatively or even openly stared with wide eyes. Simon even gave my old mug of tea to one of them. I wondered if all these people knew who I was—*Dr. Gold's daughter*—and then I realized it was probably part of their job descriptions (no matter where they worked in the base) to know who came and went. Especially when the new presence had a death vow hanging above their head. I shivered at that thought, remembering the dream from last night.

After about two minutes of walking in near silence, we reached a door. This door was giant, heavy, and wooden. It was so dark it was almost black, and the hinges shone a dingy gold color. Simon whirled again to face me, almost causing me to spill the remainder of my tea on him. Fortunately, for him at least, I managed to spill it all over myself instead.

"Hey!" I nearly shouted at him. "That was two good drinks right there that are now *wasted* and also all over me!"

Simon looked mortified. He cleared his throat to gather himself.

"I apologize, Miss Gold. But this is our destination."

I stopped my lame attempt at wiping off the tea that now stained the front of my sweatshirt and looked at the door again. This must be Mr. Evanson's office. I looked to Simon who, once again, was not looking at me.

"I'm going to go in and make sure everything is fine and that Seely is ready to go. You need to stay out here." I opened my mouth to protest and then shut it again. I didn't need to push my luck with Simon. He may be young, and he may seem nice, but he was also a soldier—a soldier who was blindly loyal to Seely. If I wanted him on my side, I should probably be nice to him. I set my jaw and nodded once.

I could have sworn I saw Simon's eyes widen just a little in surprise as he gave me a nod of his own and then turned to the door. He knocked twice, quickly, and then entered. The door made a booming noise as it shut behind him, and suddenly I was alone in the hallway. The people we'd passed earlier had apparently found their destinations, and the only sound I could hear was my own breathing. I listened closely, trying to hear voices from the other side of the door, but I didn't hear a thing. I frowned slightly. I didn't want to be alone here, but I guessed it was nicer to be here where I could interrogate Seely at first glance than in my room where I would absolutely get lost if I tried to go anywhere else.

I sighed.

I didn't want to have to stand out here and think about the events of the last day or so. I didn't want my mind to go there while I was alone in this hallway. The people we'd passed on the way here had evidently found their destinations outside of the corridor, because I was alone there, and the only sound was my breathing. Which was beginning to come more quickly.

Just when I thought I was about to freak out completely, I heard the doorknob rattle. Seely exited first, followed closely by Simon, and he immediately turned to see me. He was wearing a dark blue sweater paired with black jeans, with a black t-shirt peeking out from the top. His boots were scuffed and old, but I could tell they were the kind of shoes that were the most comfortable—the kind that were practically molded around your feet from wearing them so much. I tried to pretend not to notice how good he looked, especially the hair that fell over his forehead, so perfectly disheveled. His face looked a little angry, which I kind of expected from the night before, but then he looked at my shirt.

"Next time I'll make sure I specify that your mug should have a lid. Write that down for future reference, Simon."

Simon looked a little unsure about whether he was serious.

Seely smirked at me as he strolled over and leaned on the wall beside me, less than a foot away. I fought the urge to stick my tongue out at him again.

"Is this what you were so afraid to tell me?" Seely turned to Simon who was a few steps back from us. He was looking at Seely intently, trying to gauge his reaction.

Simon answered, "Yes, sir." He continued to gaze at Seely, and I wondered if Seely was ever actually harsh with him. I hadn't witnessed it myself, but I didn't understand this level of authority he seemed to have over the boy.

Seely let out a long breath. "Well, I should have known you wouldn't just stay anywhere and wait for me."

"How would you possibly know that?" I snapped, harsher than I intended. "You keep acting like you know me, but in case you forgot, we just met yesterday."

Seely's smile dropped a fraction. There was an endless moment of silence between us. I immediately felt bad about saying it, though it was the truth. I would be lying if I didn't say I felt like I'd known him for longer than a day, though I wasn't going to admit it.

"You're right, of course," Seely said at last. His voice was careful. "I don't know you."

Again, I was lost in his gaze. His eyes were extra green today. I silently prayed my face was not turning red from the sudden intensity. Seely pushed off the wall and walked to the wall across the hallway. His step was casual as he shoved his hands into the pockets of his pants.

"Your… brother told me how you like your tea, by the way. He thought you might be upset after last night and wanted to make sure I knew how to make it, as apparently it's something that calms you."

I stared at him, and I began to feel embarrassed. I felt the heat rush to my cheeks, and I looked down from Seely's face. I hadn't thought about the possibility that Seth may have told him anything about me.

"I also asked him for advice on how to keep you safe while you're here," Seely continued. "He advised me that you're not usually great at taking orders."

He was silent for a moment, and I looked up. He was looking at me too, smiling crookedly again.

"Sorry," I said. "I'm just a little…"

"On edge?" Seely offered. "Freaked out? Upset?" He let out a short laugh. "Yeah, dreams that leave you with visible scars tend to do that to a person."

I offered him a small smile and swallowed the lump that had formed in my throat. I was trying to avoid the panic that came every time I thought about my dream. Both of my dreams, actually. I prayed that it wasn't becoming a usual occurrence, but having two nightmares in two days that both did actual physical damage? My stomach knotted as I truly thought about what that could mean for any future restful nights.

"Something else you should know about me," I cleared my throat. "Don't leave me behind." Seely's eyebrows quirked up at that, and he opened his mouth to answer. I held up my hand to stop him and continued. "I understand I'm new here and I don't know a lot about what's going on—"

"Or anything about what's going on," Seely amended. I rolled my eyes.

"Or anything," I conceded. "But that doesn't mean you just get to run off without telling me anything. Like this morning? I think I could have handled knowing you had to meet with your father. But instead, you just left. And then sent Simon with some tea and apparent instructions not to talk to me unless absolutely necessary." I gestured to the boy who stood at alert beside Seely. I thought I saw a flicker of embarrassment pass across his face.

"Okay," Seely said. I turned my attention from Simon and back to Seely at that word.

"Okay?" I asked. I could hear the disbelief in my voice, and Seely's left eyebrow rose as his smirk turned into something a little more genuine.

"Okay, Gold." He shrugged. "I do have some conditions, though."

I crossed my arms in front of my chest. "And what would that be?"

"Next time, think about drinking your tea instead of wearing it."

I had forgotten about my stained shirt, and I looked down at the brown splotch. When I looked back at Seely, he was smirking again. Making fun of me. I raised my arm to deliver a solid punch to his upper arm. Right when I was about to make contact he caught my fist, bringing my arm down and stepping closer to me.

"My other condition," he said, only inches from my face, "is that you listen to me when I tell you things are dangerous." I could feel his breath on my face. It smelled like cinnamon. "I know you can take care of yourself, for the most part, but don't go running into danger just because you can. At least take me with you."

Before I knew what I was doing, I nodded.

"Good," Seely said, stepping back from me and dropping my hand. "Also, I didn't explicitly tell Simon he wasn't allowed to talk to you. I think you just intimidate him."

That time, I did punch him. Seely laughed and didn't even rub his arm, which made my anger amplify. One glance at Simon told me his face was flushed with what I assumed was embarrassment.

"Simon," Seely called to the boy. At once, he was at Seely's side awaiting orders. "I actually need you to take point in the guard change today. It's happening in about fifteen minutes, and I need to take Miss Gold here to finish our discussion."

Simon looked at Seely with something like disbelief. "S-sir? The guard change? I've never done that on my own."

Seely turned from me and took the two steps that brought him directly in front of Simon. He clapped him on the shoulder and gave it a squeeze. "I trust you. God knows you've watched me do it a thousand times. You'll be fine."

Simon's eyes were still wide as he blinked rapidly a few times. He swallowed hugely and then nodded once.

"Yes, sir."

Then he saluted at Seely before turning briskly and walking down the hall past Seely's father's door.

"Tell me the truth," I said once Simon was out of hearing range, "what are you using to blackmail him into acting like that around you?"

Seely laughed softly, his eyes closing as he rubbed his hand across his face. His curls were wild today where they fell indiscriminately over his forehead, and I liked the way his hair looked especially dark in this light. I saw the light glint slightly off a line on his arm.

"What happened there?" I had stepped forward and, as if on instinct, I reached up to touch the line that ran up his upper arm and disappeared into his shirt. There was a scar there.

"I have a lot of scars, Gold," Seely said. He stepped back, casually. Almost too casually. I let my hand fall back to my side and I tried to push down the feeling of rejection that that one step threatened to fill me with. Seely placed his smirk carefully on his face, but I felt my own stay blank. "Come with me. We have some things to discuss, and there are some other people who would like to see you."

***

"...and anyways, we wanted to tell you so bad. We really did. But we were told that this was the best thing for you, to keep you safe!" Stella was still talking after five minutes, and I had admittedly zoned out for about a minute of it.

After we left the hallway in front of Mr. Evanson's office, Seely had led me back to the lab.

"I spoke with them last night after you went to sleep," Seely told me as I hesitated outside the door. "They want to apologize and speak with you. I thought," he took a deep breath, "I thought after this morning you might need your friends."

Of course, he was right. I did need my friends. When I saw Stella, I didn't think about the dreams or the scar on my neck. I didn't think about the cold feeling of betrayal or the anger that came along with that. I just hugged her and let the normalcy of her touch drive out the bad feelings that came along with everything that had happened to me in the last couple of days.

"Apparently there was a very good reason we were supposed to keep you in the dark." It was Seth who spoke. I looked at him, but he was glaring at the new scar on my neck. "How in the world are we just glazing over that thing on your neck?"

I flinched.

"Actually, I was trying not to think about that, thank you, Seth."

Seth sighed and shook his head, sitting back in his chair.

"Not thinking about it doesn't mean it isn't real, Lyss."

Seth and Stella were sitting next to each other, their knees touching. I had already asked them if they were really dating or if that was a part of the lies too, to which they said they were, and that spending weekends and summers together brought them a lot closer. Having that knowledge now made their secret relationship make more sense, especially the fact that I had no idea how they even knew each other well enough (outside of the time I spent with each of them) to even know that they liked each other. When I hung out with Stella at home, Seth rarely joined us. Unless it was movie night, of course. It made sense now that their extra time together had blossomed into something more. That was about the only thing that made sense about any of this, so I hung onto it.

But now, Seth was asking me about the scar. Obviously, I knew we needed to talk about it. I knew that. But it was so nice to just sit and talk with my friends for a while about normal things. Well, as normal as a secret organization they'd been a part of for years without telling me can be.

"Seth's right, Gold," it was Seely who spoke next. Unlike the last time we were in the lab, he'd stuck around to join our little circle. He hadn't really spoken yet, but he was lounging back in his seat with his legs extended in front of him. He seemed relaxed. I looked to him and met his eyes, already fixed on mine. "That's one of the main reasons I brought you here." Seely leaned forward and braced his arms on his thighs. "We need their help."

"Why haven't we told our dads about it already?" I asked. I was partly deflecting the conversation, but I realized I also really wanted to know the answer. "If they're in charge, shouldn't they know about this? Shouldn't we ask them for help?"

Seely was shaking his head before I even finished asking my question. "We can't tell them about the dreams."

"So that's why you left out the story about the mud earlier?"

Seth's eyebrows jerked up just when Stella's furrowed.

"Mud?" Seth asked with flat curiosity.

"Yes," Seely said, matter of factly, "Your sister here has a very dramatic way of waking up. On the way here, she almost drowned in mud and this morning she woke with her throat scarred from, presumably, an Undead."

Seth let out a breath. Stella's hand lifted to her mouth in surprise.

"Whew," Seth breathed. "Do we know who it was?"

"Orthan."

With that one word from Seely, it was as if all the air was sucked out of the room. Stella paled and Seth's head whipped to Seely.

"Orthan? Really? Are you sure?"

"Ask her." He gestured to me as he once again leaned back in his seat. He was the only one who seemed unaffected by Orthan's name, which was either truly how he felt, or he was just pretending. "She's the one who had the dream."

Seth's eyes turned to me.

"Um, yeah, that's what he said his name was." I shifted uncomfortably in my seat and sat on my hands as I leaned forward a little bit. "I don't know why that name means anything to anyone. I've never heard it before."

Stella cut her eyes from Seth to Seely and back to me so quickly that I wasn't sure I actually saw it.

"Orthan is not just an Undead. He is *the* Undead. He's their leader, a king of sorts." Seth wiped a hand across his face. "When the threat was made on your life, it was Orthan who made it. He's been their king for a while now, but it wasn't until your tenth birthday that he set his sights directly on the AAUD. You were the trigger for some reason, and we're still not sure why." I cut my eyes to Seely, who still managed to look bored. I wondered if he would teach me how to keep my emotions off my face like he was able to do so well.

Seth continued.

"Do you know much about what he threatened to do to you?"

I shook my head. "The only thing I know is that he threatened to kill me."

"Not just kill you, Lyss," Seth was shaking his head. "Orthan wanted to use you as a sacrifice. An ancient ritual that, according to legend, can make the kind of Undead that we can't kill. The kind of Undead that not only possesses the strength and power of the Undead, but other powers as well. Usually, some kind of manipulation of natural elements, or at least that's the theory." Seth shrugged as he leaned forward, resting his forearms on his legs. "We've never actually seen one of these creatures in action before." His eyes searched my face. "From everything we know, they can seem human, blend in with people, and then strike when it's least expected. That's what Orthan wanted to use you for. So, Dad decided to keep you away."

I shivered. The thought of being used as a weapon against my will made my blood run cold.

"Where is Orthan now?" I asked, my voice quiet.

Seth shrugged.

"We don't know. Haven't seen him in…"

"About two years," Seely said. His voice was soft, controlled. I looked over at him, but he had his dagger out again, flicking it under his nails in a way that told me he was thinking about something that made him uncomfortable.

"So, Dad and everyone else just decided it was better that I didn't know about any of this at all? That I couldn't defend myself and I wouldn't be prepared for all of this when it inevitably happened?" My voice was still quiet, but I could feel my control slipping. The heat in my chest was building, and I knew it was only a matter of time before I lost it all together. I could already feel the icy rage in my veins and tried to focus on my breathing. "Dad kept me from all of this, and that's what he thought was best?"

Seth looked at Seely for a moment. I looked at Seely just in time to see his head move to the left once. *Was he shaking his head? About what?*

"Um, yes. Dad kept you from all of this. That's what he thought was best for you and for all of us." Seth looked uncomfortable now. I could feel the tension coming off Seely in waves. He was looking at Seth like he wanted to punch him.

"There's more going on here that you're not telling me," I whispered. My breathing was *not* helping. "I deserve to know."

"Lyss—"

"No!" I jumped up then, unable to control myself anymore. "I didn't get a choice in any of this. I didn't decide what was kept from me, and I didn't get to decide to be here now." I took a deep breath, trying to push down the cool fire inside me. "I deserve to know, and I choose to know. *Everything.*" I stood there for a second, my breathing coming in heavy huffs of air, and then finally took in the scene around me.

Seth had his arm in front of Stella and was braced on the chair so that he could jump in front of her at any moment. I turned my attention to Seely. He was standing with one hand extended towards me and the other… on his dagger.

"What the *hell* is going on here?" I couldn't control the anger anymore. It was seething out of me like rays of light. I felt the heat so acutely under my skin that I was freezing cold where the air touched me. "What do you think I'm *possibly* going to do?"

Seely stepped forward. "Gold," he said, his voice light. I looked at him and saw him motion to Seth with his head with a quick jerk to the right. I heard their footsteps as he retreated with both girls. My head was so foggy, so heavy. I could have sworn the lights got brighter and brighter as I stood there, breathing rapidly. My chest was on fire. There had to be a flame there.

"Look at me. Stay right here with me, Gold." Seely took a step closer to me and I heard a sound like a growl. Where was it coming from? "Easy. Look at me, Alyssa! Only at me." He called me Alyssa, which got my attention. I didn't think he'd said my actual name since we'd first met. My attention snapped fully to his eyes. "Good. Just look right here at me, Alyssa." And I did. I probably would have even if he hadn't ordered me to. I could get lost in those eyes, and I'd done that before. I wanted to now. The deep pools of jade were welcoming and warm, and they reminded me of warm arms and kisses on my forehead and… something else. Something stronger I couldn't place.

Looking at Seely felt like being at home.

My breathing slowed as I continued to stare into Seely's eyes. The lights dimmed and my brain cleared. I blinked a few times as I let out a rough breath and finally broke my gaze from Seely's. With what sounded like a sigh of relief, Seely took the two more steps that brought him directly up to me. He wrapped me in a tight hug. I was a little stunned and my arms were pinned at my sides. I could feel Seely's breath on my neck as he breathed deeply, in and out. The contact left goosebumps in its wake. His heart was racing, keeping time with mine.

He held me for an immeasurable moment. When both of our hearts were beating slowly and steadily, finally Seely stepped back and looked at me. He kept his hands on my shoulders and his eyes searched mine for something.

"What was that?" My voice was barely above a whisper. My stomach twisted as I thought about how I'd gotten to this point. "I don't understand what's happening to me, Seely."

The emotion that broke on his face looked awfully a lot like pain. As quickly as it came, though, it was erased as he rearranged his features into something that resembled his usual, casual smirk. His eyes still shone with that emotion, though.

"I'm not sure, Gold."

"They were… Seth and Stella, they were… afraid of me?" It came out as a question, but I knew the answer. I remembered the look Seth gave me last night that was magnified in his face just now, and a chill ran down my spine. "They feared me yesterday, too, I… I don't understand what's going on." My voice was relatively calm, except for a quiver, but I could feel the ice start to run in my veins again. I could feel the tears filling my eyes as a lump formed in my throat and I tried to swallow it down.

Seely looked briefly panicked.

"Hey, Gold, stay with me." He put a hand on either side of my face. His touch was rough on my skin, and it snapped my attention to him. "Everything is going to be okay."

Seely's voice was getting farther and farther away, and the walls were tilting at the oddest angle. The fluorescents were pulsing in my vision, and I smelled... berries? That was a weird detail.

"Everything is going to be okay now, Alyssa. Just breathe."

I felt a pinch in my neck, but Seely's hands held my head still so I couldn't move to see the source.

"Get ready to catch her, Evanson." Seth? Seth was back?

"Always."

Seely's voice was the last thing I heard as I slipped into a heavy blanket of sweet relief and darkness.

Chapter Thirteen

I DREAMED THAT I WAS RUNNING THROUGH A FIELD. The grass was tall, up to my waist, and my nose tickled with the breeze that swept through the open space. It was spring and the wildflowers were in full bloom. I was running, panting with the effort, when something came from behind me and wrapped me around the waist, halting my pace. I screamed, my lungs and throat burned with the effort. The stranger tightened their hold on me as they spun me around in a circle.

"Got you," the stranger said against my back. I could feel the vibration of his voice against my skin. "You really should spend more time training with me and Dex than getting stuck in that head of yours."

I laughed then, and it was so free and happy that my heart almost broke at the sound. When had I ever been that happy?

"Oh, shut up, and put me down!" My feet touched the ground but the arms around my waist didn't loosen. They just wrapped around tighter as the person behind me rested their head on my shoulder. I felt his lips on the hollow space between my neck and my shoulder, and I leaned into the touch. It was all so familiar, so natural. It felt like I had been doing this exact thing every day for my entire life.

"If you're tired of losing in races, I can think of a few other things that we might be able to do to occupy the time." His breath hit my neck and I could feel the goosebumps spread from the spot the heat of it hit my skin. It smelled like cinnamon. I flung an elbow back, hitting him squarely in the ribs. He let out a short groan and I smiled.

"Ouch, Gold. You wound me."

As quickly as I could, I grabbed the stranger's wrist and, pushing the arm away from my body just a few inches, I wedged my elbow in between his arm and my stomach to break his hold on me. Before he could make even a sound of protest, I leaned into his weight, using it to my advantage, and flipped him over my shoulder until he landed on his back on the ground in front of me with a satisfying *thunk*. The air whooshed out of him, and he began to cough.

"Dang, Gold," he fought to catch his breath, still coughing. "I didn't know you actually wanted to hurt me. We could have been having a lot more fun."

I growled at him, forgetting for a second that my hand was still holding on to his wrist. Swiftly, he flipped around, pulling me towards him with my arm and kicking my legs out from underneath me. I screamed as I fell, but I landed relatively softly on top of him. We were invisible in the high grass. The wind blew the blades gently back and forth. I could hear the cicadas kicking up their song as the sun began to set. But I didn't see any of this. The only thing I saw were a pair of eyes so dark green they could have been mistaken for black in the right light, if one wasn't paying close enough attention. Fortunately, I was only staring at his eyes. I got the feeling that it was my favorite pastime. Like I could spend every second of every day staring into his eyes and I would never spot all the differences, never get bored. I never wanted to stop looking at him.

"Hey, you know what?"

He reached up and pushed the hair that had fallen out of my braid back behind my ear. He left his hand on my face, so light on my cheek, and I leaned into the calloused skin. His hands were always so warm.

"What?"

"If you take a picture, it'll last longer."

I slapped him on his chest and tried to push away, but he wrapped his arms around me in another vice grip. I tried to wriggle out of his grasp, but only succeeded in turning over. He followed my movement, now hovering above me as I felt my hair tie digging into my back. I wriggled enough to reach up and pull it out from under me, letting it drape freely over the newly flattened grass.

"Alyssa?"

I started at the sound of my name. He never called me that unless it was something serious.

"Yes?"

"There's something I need to tell you, something I don't think you know."

His eyebrows scrunched together in a way that left a wrinkle in between them. I reached a hand up to smooth the line.

"So serious," I teased. "What is it?"

I don't know why, but I was nervous. What could it possibly be? What could he be about to tell me? The funny thing about happiness, I thought, is that the smallest thing can bring it crashing down. And in that moment, I thought I was the happiest I had ever been.

"I...," his usual easy demeanor was gone, replaced by something I thought could be nervousness. I could almost hear my heartbeat in my ears.

"I love you, Alyssa." He looked me in the eyes for a moment and then broke the connection as a faint blush crept across his cheeks. I traced that blush that ran right along that light line of freckles that had started to pop out for the year as the weather got warmer and the sun stayed out longer.

I was wrong before. *This* moment was the happiest of my life.

I didn't say anything for a minute and his eyes found mine again. The worry in them sent a pang of discomfort to my heart. Anyone else who knew him would be shocked at the man he was when he was with me. When he put down those shields and guards and that facade that was accompanied with a smirk. I loved that smirk, and I loved that teasing idiot who never let me beat him at anything, not even once. But I loved who he was when he wasn't trying to be anyone so much more.

I placed my hands on his cheeks and stared into those eyes once again. "I believe I may have had a little bit of an inkling about that, *Evanson*." I kissed his nose before he could respond.

He snorted a laugh, and I took the opportunity to push him back over. He opened his mouth to say something, probably a snarky remark to push past the emotional atmosphere, but he didn't have time to get it out before I crushed his mouth with mine. We fit perfectly, knowing exactly where to go next. He always tasted like cinnamon.

"You know I love you too," I whispered when we broke free. I was out of breath and my heart was racing, and I knew that now my cheeks had to be as red as his were. The smile he gave me was so wide and genuine, I just wanted to commit it to memory and keep it in my mind forever. His smile fell into a smirk, and the sight was beautiful.

"I know," Seely said, as he kissed me again.

I jolted awake, breathing heavily. As far as my recent dreams went, this one had been great. No one tried to kill me, and I didn't wake up throwing up mud, but I was feeling… unsettled. The fact that a dream about Seely could feel so real… I shook my head to clear my thoughts. My heart was racing, but it was slowing gradually with every breath.

I touched my lips and they felt oddly warm, maybe even a little bit swollen. I felt a warm blush creep up my neck and across my cheeks. Truthfully, I had never been kissed before. I was woefully lacking in the romance area, and I was sure my dream was a culmination of my obsessions with romance novels and movies. I knew one day my brain would have too much of that content and go over the edge. I had had dreams like that before, obviously, about epic loves and frolics through fields, but never one that felt so absolutely real.

And never one that left my heart feeling strangely hollow.

I looked around, finally realizing I was in my room. There was a fire burning steadily in the fireplace on the wall I was facing. I could see out the wall-sized window to my left that the sun had long begun to sink below the horizon. The dusk was dawning, and I could see the stars beginning to shine in the way I'd only seen them do since I'd been here. Thinking about the stars brought me uncomfortably close to thinking about Seely and dark passageways and those eyes... I shook my head again. My thoughts were getting dangerous and, I had to admit, rather annoying. I felt like my head was full of cotton or something, like I couldn't complete one single thought process. In fact, I hadn't stopped to ask myself a very important question:

What was I doing back in my bed?

The last thing I remembered was with everyone in the lab. I remembered Seely brought me there after my dream that had left me with a scar down the length of my neck. Absently, I reached up to see if I could still feel it. The line was apparently a permanent raised place on my skin now. I brushed my fingertips along the length of it. I wasn't really a vain person. I'd given up on being beautiful a long time ago. But I thrived on being at least average, on blending in and not drawing attention to myself. Stella was the beauty, Seth was the brains, and I was the constant. I was always there, silent, waiting for my time to come but secretly hoping it never would. I was comfortable being alone and I was comfortable in the role I played in the world. With a scar like this, I thought ruefully, I didn't have a hope of being as invisible as before. Maybe I would get into wearing scarves.

Again, noticing my train of thought had derailed, I fought to refocus. What had I been thinking about before? I looked around the room and noticed a glass with a note propped up against it on the nightstand. I scooted over on the enormous bed so I could reach, and I leaned over to inspect the note.

"Drink Me."

Just two words, written in a dark scrawl. I picked up the paper and flipped it over, but there was nothing else. I ran my hand over the words and noticed the deep indentations the words made in the thick stationary. I wondered who wrote it, I didn't recognize the handwriting right away.

I picked up the glass and sniffed. No smell, which I figured must mean there was water inside. I took a big gulp, grateful that the water was cold and that it seemed to clear my head a little bit.

I remembered then. Almost instantly, I remembered what had happened and why I was in my room. I touched the side of my neck where I'd felt the pinch earlier, but I couldn't feel any type of mark. I remembered Seely holding me, trying to keep me together after I'd... After I'd what? I furrowed my brows. I remembered the scene now, Seth stepping in front of Stella to protect her, then both of them running away as Seely stayed to calm me down. I remembered the look of fear in their eyes, even Seely's, but I still didn't know *why* I'd scared them. I had no idea what happened. I only knew my vision had begun to blur, my blood ran cold, and the room had started to shift.

I took another drink of the water as my hands began to shake. I wasn't sure what was going on with me the past few days. It's almost like I woke up three days ago and I was a different person, even though I didn't know it yet. Had it only been three days since the first day of school? So much had changed already, I almost couldn't believe it. I thought back to that first day. I went to school, the first day of senior year. Stella and I… we had plans. We were excited for the year and excited for the future. Seth was just doing the thing he called "cooking" and failing. My dad was working and leaving donuts for me on the kitchen counter. Now I knew that most of what I believed about the people around me had been a lie and Seth hadn't spent months out of each summer for the past four years at camp. He'd been here, training. Stella too. Their family vacations that kept her away during the summer were taken here, or at another base somewhere across the country. Either way, they'd all lied and kept secrets from me. No one told me about the AAUD because of the threat on my life.

Without really thinking about it, I reached up again to touch the scar. Orthan had threatened my life. Orthan, the same one who had attacked me in the dream last night. He was the one who ripped out my throat and left this scar as a souvenir. I still wasn't sure how something like that was possible, how a scar could appear after dreaming about it, but it didn't really matter. It was something that happened, and now I had to deal with it.

I sat the glass of water back on the nightstand and swung my legs over the side of the bed. Carefully, I placed my legs on the floor and stood up. I was not going to chance fainting again. The other thing that had started to happen in the past few days, it seemed, was that I was increasingly lightheaded and weak. I'd never fainted, to my knowledge, and in the past few days I'd lost consciousness more than I thought was probably healthy. The only time I'd felt more strength than I knew I had was when I flipped Seely over my shoulder. I smiled a little bit at the thought, and then frowned. As good as that had felt, it was yet another thing I couldn't explain. I'd not been invited to train at the AAUD when I turned thirteen. I didn't have the same skills that Seely and, presumably, Seth and the twins possessed. I shook my head again. I wondered what I'd been given to make me go to sleep. Whatever it was, it made my head feel so extremely heavy. It made it almost impossible to focus on any one detail.

"I don't know what's happening," I whispered to myself.

I'm not the kind of person who thrives on the feeling of the unknown. I like to have a plan and I like it even more when that plan is executed as well as something can be. When things happen to throw a wrench into said plans, sometimes I crumble under the pressure. I could feel myself fighting that crumble now, and maybe that was part of the weakness I'd been feeling since the morning Seely came and stole me away.

Seely.

I was facing the window-filled wall and I turned my head to face the other wall where the door led to the outside corridor. I couldn't see any indication that someone was waiting for me in the hallway, but I had a sinking feeling in my stomach that I couldn't quite place.

Sliding myself onto the cold floor, I walked around the bed, watching the shadows flicker from the light that came from the fireplace. They looked sinister and I fought back a shudder.

I got to the door and paused, listening. I don't know what I was listening for exactly... breathing? Footsteps? Hushed words? Either way, I didn't hear any of those things on the other side of the door. I felt a little stupid for even thinking someone would be posted there. I let out the breath I hadn't known I'd been holding. Tentatively, I reached my hand to the doorknob and turned it.

The door didn't open.

My brows coming together slightly, I tried again. Maybe I needed to turn it the other way? It was an old door, I'm sure it wasn't out of the ordinary for it to get stuck from time to time. I twisted the knob. Pushed. It didn't open. I turned the knob the other way again. Pushed. It didn't move an inch. I turned the knob each way one more time. I pushed and pulled, not quite ready to admit what I was beginning to understand.

I was locked in here. Someone had locked me in here.

Whatever was going on with me that caused my friends to drug me and lock me in my room, I was going to find out. Though, I wasn't sure if I wanted to know.

I took a step back from the door and huffed a breath.

"Alright," I whispered, to no one in particular, "if they want to lock me in here, I'll just have to find another way out."

I looked around my room, surveying my options. I didn't see any doors that led anywhere but the closet and the bathroom. I walked into the bathroom to search in there, but there wasn't even a window. The closet was the same. Just a room filled with clothes and shoes that magically seemed to all be my size. No way out of the room, though.

It hit me then: the balcony door! I wasn't sure how far down the drop was or whether it would actually be a feasible option for escape, but I knew, at the very least, I could get some fresh air. After learning I had been locked in, the walls seemed to be inching closer and closer by the minute. I wasn't really a claustrophobic person, at least that I could remember off the top of my head. But, then again, I had never been locked in a room with no obvious means of escape before. I was having flashbacks to the darkness and the sludge that filled my lungs. I took a deep breath, settling myself. I *would* find a way out of here. And when I did, there would be hell to pay from my brother and my friends. Including Seely, though I wasn't sure what he was. I'd only known him for a couple of days now, but somehow it seemed much longer. He'd been there to keep me from completely slipping into oblivion since he first showed up at my house, and then there was tonight's dream…

I heard a short, startled laugh escape my lips.

"Focus, idiot," I whispered to myself.

I walked to the window I'd inspected earlier. I deduced that it might be a door that led to a balcony, but I hadn't had a chance to really explore my observations closely. I walked up to the expanse of glass and peered out again. The sun had officially set now, and the cicadas were surely screaming. Though, I couldn't hear them. I thought that was a little strange, seeing as how this building seemed so old. Surely it wouldn't be soundproof. I'd learned, though, that almost anything was possible at the AAUD headquarters.

I touched the glass, noticing the cold of it. Was it cold tonight? That didn't seem likely, not in the middle of August. I felt my brows furrow together with the question. Such strange things happened in this place. I traced the right side of the window, looking for anything that might look like it could act as a latch or a door handle. I didn't find it there, but when I walked over the few steps to the left side, there was some type of lever sticking out from the side, right behind the curtain that was gathered and tied at the edge of the pane. I pulled it and it fell away from the window slightly. It was a window crank, I realized. I pulled the curtain back and tucked it behind the gear, grasping the handle with both hands. It was just like the type of crank you would use to roll down a window in a car, only this one was more ancient and bigger than one would normally be. I leaned into it, and, to my surprise, it turned without much effort.

I let out a breathless laugh. I didn't realize how much I needed the fresh air outside until I was about to get it. With every turn of the handle, the bottom panel of the window began to rise outward. I could feel the warm brush of air hit my legs. My nose tingled from the dust that was stirred up, but I could also smell fresh pine and crisp, cool air. I cranked the lever up and down and back again, until I thought there was enough room for me to fit through. I dropped to the floor and looked out the opening, not able to see much until my eyes adjusted a little. I could fit, but what worried me was the terrace outside. It looked like it was a balcony... it also looked like it hadn't been stepped on for a very long time. A thick layer of dirt coated the concrete of the floor, and the wrought iron railing was now a deep rust color. I could see flecks of white where I thought it had probably been painted that color once upon a time. The lattice seemed to be connected only by spider webs, and I tried to ignore some of the more intense cracks in the stone floor.

I looked left and right. The terrace wasn't huge, but it was dark enough out there that the shadows could be hiding anything in its corners. I shook off the thought. I was getting off track, again. It was so hard to focus, and I swore I would make Seth sorry for whatever poison he put in my body that was doing this to me. I felt the coldness begin to seep into my veins again at the thought of real fury, and I hurriedly pushed it away. Whatever that feeling meant, it evidently wasn't good. I was not going to let myself lose control again, I promised myself.

I crawled out of the opening and gingerly rose from the grime. Wiping my hands on my leggings, I looked around once again. The view up here was beautiful. I could see the back gardens that ran almost the entire expanse of the grass that led up to the line of woods behind the manor. There was a fountain in the middle of the maze-like hedges, I noticed. I made a mental note that, as soon as I got out of my room and found out why I was locked in there in the first place, I was going to explore there first.

Though there was a warm breeze blowing every now and again, I felt goosebumps rising on my arms. Somehow, I'd ended up in a t-shirt rather than the sweatshirt I remembered having on before. I silently prayed that Stella was responsible for the wardrobe change and not Seth. Or Seely. I almost shuddered as that thought brought me once again back to my dream.

I continued to walk to the edge of the terrace. This view was beautiful, but it was nothing compared to Seely's tower. I looked up at the sky again. The stars were so beautiful here. Somehow, when I was at the tower, they seemed so close I could reach out and touch them. Here, on my own terrace, the stars were more like a famous painting in a museum that I was forbidden to get too close to. I could admire them, but they didn't belong to me.

I finally reached the railing and placed both hands on it, shaking it back and forth a bit. It didn't budge, though it looked like it could crumble at any moment, and that eased my mind a bit about the structural stability of this place I was standing on. It would really suck to die falling off a crumbling balcony after being locked in my room. I stepped up to the bottom layer of the scaffolding and leaned forward, looking down at the ground below. It was a far jump, maybe twenty or thirty feet.

"Would that really kill me?" I mumbled to myself. I may not die from the fall, but I certainly wouldn't be running to confront anyone either. I stayed where I was and leaned forward a little bit more, closing my eyes. "Think, Alyssa," I whispered to myself again. "What should you do?"

My eyes were still closed as I felt something, or someone, grab my shirt from behind. I didn't even have time to scream before I was pulled backwards and fell to the ground. Someone had grabbed me, once again.

Chapter Fourteen

MY EYES BULGED AS I FELL BACKWARDS, being dragged back by my attacker. I flung my arms out to grab onto the rail, but it was already too far out of my reach. My mind raced along with my heart as I fell onto whoever had pulled me from behind.

How am I going to get out of this?

I cursed myself for being so stupid, for walking out here blindly without even examining the shadows. It had even crossed my mind that someone would be able to hide there. But how was I supposed to know someone would be waiting out here? *Why* would someone be waiting out here?

I wrestled with my assailant for a moment longer, finally able to wriggle free enough to turn a look at his face.

Two deep green eyes stared into mine.

"What. Is. Your. Problem?" I pounded Seely's chest with my fist after every word. "Why are you such a creep? What, were you just out here waiting to pounce?"

Seely's eyes were huge as he stared at me, not saying anything. I could feel his heart pounding underneath me.

"What..." I was confused. I was sure my eyebrows drew together. "What's going on? You seem scared?"

The last word came up as a question. Was Seely afraid of me too? After everything that had happened today, I didn't think I would be able to handle another person being afraid of me. And I'd seen the threat of fear on his face earlier, so I knew it was possible. I watched as his eyebrows furrowed slightly, matching mine.

"You were..." He breathed the words at me. "Weren't you thinking about jumping?"

Jumping? *Jumping?* Seely thought I was going to *jump* to my possible death?

Before I knew what was happening, I was laughing. I couldn't stop laughing at the look on his face. I felt kind of bad about it, but I just couldn't imagine that he was so worried about me jumping. It just showed how little he knew me, no matter what kinds of dreams I had. My body was shaking with laughter for a full thirty seconds before I opened my eyes and looked at Seely again. He wasn't angry or annoyed like I thought he would be. He was looking at me with what I thought was concern.

I reached up to wipe my eyes, as tears were leaking out from my burst of hysteria, but I wasn't laughing anymore. There was something wrong. I didn't understand why Seely was looking at me that way.

"What is it?" My voice was rough from the laughter, and it came out quieter than I expected. "I'm sorry, I didn't mean to laugh. I just thought you must be joking if you thought I would jump to my death, I mean… What would make you think that?"

Seely was just looking at me. I was still laying on top of him, his arms locked around me in a vice grip. The position reminded me way too much of the images in my head I was trying to shake free of. A moment passed and I thought he just wasn't going to answer me, but finally, after several heartbeats, he did.

"Do you want to tell me exactly what you were doing leaning all the way over the rail if it wasn't you trying to scout out the best place to jump then, Gold?"

I shot him an incredulous look, but I could tell he wasn't joking. I sighed before answering him.

"Not that I think I should even entertain this ridiculous question with an answer, but I was checking to see if there was a way down from here that *wouldn't* result in death. My door is locked, and I couldn't get out," I stared him down, "but I'm sure you already knew that."

Seely didn't flinch at the malice that had seeped into my tone, and he stared right back at me. His eyes were still wide, though he'd returned to his stoic facade. It was almost like his act couldn't make it all the way up to cover the emotion in his eyes.

"So, you *were* contemplating jumping?"

I rolled my eyes at him. Not only was he infuriating, he also wasn't wrong. I had thought about jumping for a second before I talked myself out of doing anything crazy. How had he known that?

"I know you better than you think, Gold," he answered my unspoken thought in a soft, almost fragile voice.

I stared at him, trying to decipher anything from his gaze. After a few more moments, I realized where we were. I realized the position we were laying in.

"Uhhh, do you think you could let me up now?" I held up my hands, away from his body. "I promise not to go near the railing."

That time, Seely rolled his eyes. "Don't be ridiculous, Gold. You would never be able to even look at that railing with any intent before I could stop you. Again."

I placed my hands on his chest, not trying to be gentle as I pushed myself up and off him. He let me go easily, to his credit, and before I'd blinked it seemed like he was standing straight up and closer to me than I thought was necessary. Seely reached out and grabbed a curl that had slipped out of my low ponytail, probably in the process of me being drugged and then brought back to my room. And caged like a wild animal.

He tucked the strand behind my ear and lingered there for a moment too long. I took a step back. Some emotion passed over his face, but it was gone before I could determine what it was. He held my gaze for a moment before breaking free from it and looking down at his hands. I let my eyes roam down the shoulders of his shirt, admiring the muscles I could see.

"I need to tell you something." He took out his dagger and began picking at his nails with it again. He was nervous. I felt my heart kick up a beat again.

"Is it about why you were lurking outside my room in the shadows of a terrace like a creep? Because I'd love to know the answer to that question." I crossed my arms in front of my chest, tightly.

I really did want to know the answer, but it was more so his shift in mood that caused me to try and change the subject. I had so many questions that didn't have answers already. I wasn't really looking forward to having even more questions regarding whatever he was trying to work up the nerve to tell me.

That was what he was doing, I realized. As he stood there with his dagger picking precariously at his nails, he was trying to work himself up to telling me whatever it was he needed to tell me. I felt goosebumps on my skin again, but this time it wasn't from the slight chill in the air.

I let out a sigh.

"Fine," I said. Seely looked up at me, finally. "You can tell me whatever you need to, but can we at least go inside? It's getting a little cold." I remembered my wardrobe change then. "By the way, *please* tell me it wasn't you who changed my clothes?"

Seely smiled a little at that, some of his signature smirk returning to his features. I felt a little bit of the weight lift from my chest at that expression. Maybe his news wouldn't be that horrible after all.

"I wish I could take the credit for that, but unfortunately Stella beat me to it. Though I wouldn't mind helping you out next time you need someone?"

I punched him in the arm, and he laughed quietly.

"Come on, Gold," he said, turning to the window. "Let's get you inside before you freeze in the sixty-degree weather."

And he's back to making fun of me, I thought. *That's a good sign.*

Seely walked over to the window and pushed down a handle on the side of it that I hadn't seen before. To my surprise, the entire window slid over to the left, creating a doorway.

"Rather than make you crawl through the dirt again, I thought I should show you how this panel actually works."

"Thank you," I said. I meant it. I planned on exploring the terrace even more in the daylight, maybe even clean it up a little bit, so I was grateful for the tip. I brushed past Seely when he gestured for me to enter the room before him, and I watched as he slid the panel back into place and cranked the window shut again. For some reason, I wasn't even embarrassed Seely had seen me mumbling to myself and crawling through the dirt. He didn't make me feel self-conscious in any way. I didn't let that thought settle yet. I would tuck it away until later for further inspection. For now, I watched Seely as he left the window and walked over to the fireplace. He picked up one of the stokers and began to poke the fire as it was dimming. He replaced the rod and walked over to the right of the fireplace where there was a stack of wood, picked up a couple of logs, and placed them on the fire. He hadn't said a word the whole time, just crouched by the fire.

I sighed, resigned to let him stew in his own thoughts until he was ready to explain them to me. Walking over to my nightstand, I picked up the glass of water and took a long drink. I immediately wished it were tea instead.

"I can call for some tea, if you'd like."

I turned to see Seely leaning against the back of one of the chairs in front of the now roaring fireplace, staring at me.

"How do you do that?" I asked him.

His left eyebrow quirked up. "Do what, exactly?"

"Read my thoughts all the time."

Seely's laugh was hard and short. I didn't get the idea that he actually found it funny at all. "Would you really like to know?" His voice was soft, and as I stared into his eyes; I could swear I saw moisture building there. That emotion I saw on his face outside once again crossed his features. What I could see in the fire light that I couldn't see on the terrace was something I thought looked a lot like pain. Without thinking, I stepped towards him and reached a hand out lamely. He was too far away for me to touch, and I let my arm drop back to my side.

"I would really like to know what's bothering you, yes," I said. My voice was stronger in here than it had been out on the terrace. "Even if it's something horrible, which you're making me think it is since I've never seen you anywhere close to a loss for words until now, I want to know. I need to know." I walked closer to him, and I watched his eyes grow more wary with every step. I stopped a few feet from him.

"Are you afraid of me too?"

The words came out of me in a broken whisper. I didn't know why, but I knew I would crumble completely if he said he was. Somehow that mattered more than either my brother or Stella being fearful of me. And they had been, I'd seen it with my own eyes. So why did it bother me so much that I now saw that same fear in Seely's face? It shouldn't matter to me, and it shouldn't matter more what he thought than my brother and the friend I'd had for years.

But it did.

Seely shook his head. "I'm not afraid of *you*, Gold. I'm afraid of the way you're going to look at me after I tell you what I have to tell you."

My breath caught in my throat. I thought what Seely had to tell me would be bad, but what could it possibly be that would make me look at him so differently that he was… afraid? My skin felt cold, despite the heat coming from the fire. I thought I saw a bead of sweat on Seely's forehead.

"Okayyyy…" I dragged the word out and then paused, giving him an opening to begin. Though, he didn't take that opportunity.

He stared at me for a moment longer as if he was hoping whatever was racing through his brain would somehow leech into my own thoughts. Obviously, that didn't happen, and after several heartbeats he turned away from me. Seely dragged a hand through his hair and down to the back of his neck. I watched as he gripped his skin so hard it turned white under his fingers. He was still turned away from me, facing the fireplace, when he stood up and started pacing back and forth.

"Seely?" I was whispering again, standing there, lamely.

"I don't even know how to start with this, Alyssa." He huffed the words at me, wringing his hand as he paced back and forth. He still didn't look at me, and we were back to him calling me Alyssa again, which I didn't know was a good sign or a bad sign.

"Is it about you locking me in here? I'm not that mad about it, I promise. You don't have to work yourself up over it."

Seely snorted a laugh. "No, it's not that. And this wasn't my decision anyway. Actually, I told them that locking you in here wasn't going to work and that it was a stupid idea. I volunteered to at least be posted outside your door, but they refused." Seely stopped his pacing and looked at me, his crooked smirk plastered on his face, though the expression didn't completely reach his eyes. "Apparently I looked a little too distressed to perform as the good soldier I'm always supposed to be."

His tone was bitter, and I didn't feel any comfort in his eyes. The way he was looking at me was scaring me more and more with each passing second.

I wondered who "they" were, and I hoped my dad wasn't involved in that decision. I hadn't seen him all day, I realized.

"Okay," I tried again, "just come out with it, Seely."

"I know, Gold, I should just come out with it. I should be able to do that. Especially with you." Seely wiped his hand across his face aggressively and he focused his eyes back on me. His dark curls were wild tonight, falling over his head in every different direction. "The thing is, Alyssa, I can't stand the fact that what I'm about to say is not only going to shatter your world, but *our* world. I can deal with my world being shattered." His voice had grown quieter. "It has been for almost two years now. I'm not worried about myself."

He turned and plopped into one of the chairs facing the fireplace.

"Seely." I said his name slowly, walking to stand in front of him. I wasn't entirely sure this wasn't still a dream. He wasn't making any sense, and my anxiety grew with every word of nonsense out of his mouth.

Seely was leaning over in the chair where he was scrunched down. His legs were splayed out, the right one bent at the knee and bouncing and the left lying almost straight out. His hand was on his face, covering his eyes. I crossed my arms. I was feeling cold again, despite the roaring fire.

"Seely," I said again. He still didn't look at me. I wanted to reach out and touch him, but my arms felt glued in their position. He dragged his hand down his face before letting it fall into his lap. When his eyes met mine, they were burning. I could see the fire reflected in them, but more than that he looked like he was burning from the inside out, being consumed by whatever he was trying to tell me. Something was extremely wrong with him. I stumbled back a step.

"What's wrong, Seely?" At my words, Seely jumped up, putting his hands on his face, and pacing back and forth a couple more times. "Why are you acting like this?" The pitch of my voice was rising. He was acting like something else had control of his brain, making him move around against his will.

"Why am I acting like this?" He let out a short laugh and dropped his hands to his side in fists. He was really scaring me now. "I'm acting like this, Alyssa, because I'm in love with you."

I froze in place. I hadn't been moving, but I could feel myself completely freeze. Even my heart seemed to be totally still.

"You... You're what?"

I wasn't sure what I was hearing. He... loved me? Seely loved me? How was that even possible? We'd known each other for about three days, and a lot of that time I'd been unconscious. I hadn't even had a conversation with Seely about anything real, at least not since he showed me the tower. You couldn't fall in love from moments like that, could you? I realized Seely still hadn't said anything after his declaration, and that I had been standing here for a few seconds too long, trying to process it.

"You don't love me, Seely, that's impossible," I said, my voice calm and measured despite the twisting of my gut. I was trying to reason it out. "You've only known me for a few days. I don't even know your middle name or where you grew up or what your favorite color is…" I trailed off, suddenly feeling very stupid as I realized how little I knew about what love was. Maybe none of those things were important? Maybe they all were?

Seely laughed again, but I didn't think it was at me.

"The thing is, Gold," he turned to face me full on, "you *do* know all of those things. You know everything about me, more than I even know about myself. And I, you. That's what makes this so hard for me to tell you, to try and explain any of this."

My head was still spinning from his first revelation, and I couldn't make sense of what he was saying to me. Maybe I hadn't heard him right.

My head was feeling heavy and thick, and I wanted to crawl into bed and go back to sleep, instead I stood frozen in place.

"Seely, that's impossible. I would definitely remember you."

He smiled at me then, though it was cold and distant, rueful.

"That's the thing, Alyssa, dear. You wouldn't remember me. That was the whole point."

"The whole point of what?" I was getting a little irritated at the cryptic sentences. "Just *tell* me, Seely. Out with it."

Seely walked up to me so fast that I staggered backwards, practically falling into the chair behind me. He didn't stop coming towards me until we were face to face. He leaned in again, just like he had that morning, with a hand on either side of the chair. I was like a prisoner to his gaze, and I knew I wasn't going to be let go until whatever he had to say was out in the open. I swallowed.

"I love you, Alyssa. That's the whole point. I love you and I... I couldn't save you." His eyes filled with moisture, though no tears leaked out. "Why did you do it? I never got an explanation. By the time I got there, I was basically cleaning up after a corpse. *Why did you do it?*" Seely took his hands from the arm rests and grabbed my upper arms. He shook me a couple of times.

"*Stop it!*" I tried to scream, but it came out as a harsh whisper. "Seely, you're scaring me. What's happening to you? What's wrong with you?"

Seely let me go, staggering back a step. He ran his hand through his hair again, the curls still falling perfectly. It seemed like even extreme distress couldn't take that away from him.

"I'm sorry, Gold, I shouldn't have grabbed you like that, I just..." He turned to the fire and placed his hands on the mantle that was placed above it. "This whole situation has basically made me certifiably insane. That's why they wouldn't let me keep watch at your door, you know? They were afraid of me barging in here and doing the very thing I'm doing now. They didn't want me telling you the truth and blowing up their whole plan. But I can't stand it." Seely still wasn't facing me, and I heard his voice tremble slightly. He cleared his throat before continuing. "Do you know what it's been like to see you these past few days, when I know you don't remember me or remember anything that happened? How hard it is to listen to the stories they feed you about what's happened throughout your life? The half-truths and the omissions are almost more than I can take. I can't get too close to you because that would be inappropriate. You don't know me, and I don't want them to think I can't be trusted around you. I can only look at you, knowing what happened and knowing what's coming. But I won't be a part of it."

Seely turned sharply toward me, and I flinched back slightly. His eyes softened at my movement, and he went to sit in the chair placed beside mine.

"I am sorry for acting like an insane person," he said after a moment. He did look sheepish at the thought, so I decided to believe him. I also decided to ignore the growing irritation I felt at the fact that he still hadn't told me anything of consequence. "I'll be good. I'll sit right here, and I'll tell you the whole story. Is that alright with you?"

I just nodded. I wasn't sure if I would be able to speak. Seely saw the gesture and probably guessed at why I didn't respond verbally. He gave me a nod of his own and slowly turned to face the fire. I kept my eyes on his face. The shadows that danced there made him look... dangerous. He *was* dangerous, I realized. Or he could be if he wanted to be, at least. I thought about how the people who followed him seemed to hang on to his every word and command. How they followed what he said almost blindly. *There's probably a good reason for that.* For the first time since I'd met him, I was afraid of Seely.

"You and I were on patrol that day," he began. I felt like I was being thrust into the middle of the story rather than the beginning. I was on patrol? That had never happened? I bit my tongue to keep from interrupting. Whatever was going on with him, I would let him finish his story before screaming for help.

Seely continued.

"We were supposed to stay at base. It was a routine patrol day, no outstanding threats against the fortress, no sightings of the Undead for miles. You and I were just... having a normal day.

"Simon was still too young to be on patrol, this is the first year he's been allowed to do so, but he came running outside to us as we stood on the patrol tower. 'An Undead sighting! About three miles out!' he said. He was panting so much that I knew he ran all the way from the fortress to the outskirts of the woods where we were. He looked so scared... I remembered thinking it was strange that my father had sent Simon out to tell us instead of one of the more skilled soldiers. Anyone who was more trained than Simon would have been able to explain the situation to us plainly and simply, without any theatrics. Simon was about to faint right there!

"You told me to go back to the house with him. You said you were going to wait for me there and check out the threat once I got back from making sure Simon was safe and breathing and I found out what exactly he was blubbering about. You said you would wait right there while I figured out what was going on. In fact, Alyssa, you promised. You

promised me you would be there when I got back."
He turned his face towards me. I could see something
like agony written all over his face.

"You promised," he said again, quieter this time.
"Anyway," he continued, turning back to the fire, "I
took Simon back to the house. He was just
stammering that something was wrong, that I
shouldn't leave you alone up there. I didn't really
know what he was talking about, but I guessed he was
just freaking out about the Undead spotting. Simon
has never been one to have nerves of steel, you know.

"When I got there, everyone was frantic. People
were running around and trying to organize a party to
go and assess the situation of the Undead spotted
only a few miles from base. I learned that it was
Orthan who was there. The same Orthan who had a
vendetta against you for whatever reason, and the
same one who had literally placed a death threat
against you. We'd kept tabs on him for the years that
followed that threat, by the way, so I'm not sure how
he got past us. He was never supposed to get so
close."

I shivered at the thought of Orthan and realized I
was touching the scar on my neck. I let my hand drop
back to my lap as the rest of me sat frozen, waiting
for Seely to continue.

"As soon as I heard that name, I ran back to our
post. I mean, I sprinted, faster than I've ever run
before. I guess I had a bad feeling, like I knew
something was going to happen to you."

A fresh layer of goosebumps spread over my skin.

"You weren't there," he whispered. The only
sound was the roaring of the fire and the heaviness
of my breathing. I wondered if Seely could hear my
heart too. "I couldn't have been gone for more than

ten minutes, but by the time I got back to the post you were gone. I walked to the edge of the forest, but everyone knows not to go into those woods alone. We're *trained* not to go into those woods alone. So, I didn't understand how you could be so inconceivably *stupid*." He spat the words at me, letting his anger overflow once again. Taking a deep breath and holding it for a few moments, Seely moved his legs until both were bent at a perfect ninety-degree angle. He gripped his thighs so tightly I could see his knuckles turn white. When I had taken two more breaths, he'd finally released them.

"I didn't believe you'd actually gone in there," he continued, "until I saw the trail of your footsteps leading through the brush and past the trees that mark our barrier. So, I followed you, obviously. I didn't have a choice. I wasn't going to let you die alone, at least. We had actually just…" He looked at me out of the corner of his eye. "Never mind. But there was no way in hell I was going to wait for backup when you were apparently walking directly towards your death. I have no idea what you were thinking, and I still don't have any idea. The only problem with that is, neither do you. So, it's not like I can just ask. You're sitting three feet away from me and I can't ask you the one question that's haunted me for almost two years now! It's the worst kind of torture."

Seely leaned forward and put his head in his hands.

"I searched for you for miles, but after about one hundred yards into the forest, I lost your trail. So, I was basically stumbling around for half an hour, trying to find any clue as to where you'd gone. Dexter caught up to me, eventually, and I know I probably should have waited for him before running blindly into the woods. But I couldn't think, Gold! The only thing I was thinking about was all the horrible things I could imagine happening to you when Orthan got his hands on you.

"About five minutes after Dex met up with me, we heard your scream. It sounded so close, but I couldn't really tell if that was just because it was so loud or if you were actually in close proximity to us. I ran in your direction without a thought, and Dex caught me just before I stepped into the clearing where Orthan and his cronies were gathered together. They were just huddled there. They had their heads together like they were whispering something top secret. I didn't see you there, or any sign that you'd been there, so I waited, and I watched. Within another minute, they'd Dissipated away, and Dex and I stepped into the clearing."

I made a mental note to ask later what it meant that the Undead "Dissipated" away. Seely's head was still in his hands, and he took in a deep, shaking breath. I was listening with rapt attention. I took in a shallow breath of my own, thinking that I couldn't remember if I'd been breathing at all the whole time.

"The first thing I saw after we walked a few feet was blood. There was blood everywhere; it was splattered in the trees and some droplets had even made their way almost to the edge of the woods where Dex and I had been hiding. I didn't notice them when we were over there, I'd been busy looking for you and watching what Orthan was doing."

Seely leaned back and his breath caught in his throat. He wouldn't look at me now.

"I knew it was your blood before I saw what they did to you. I don't really know how, but I knew you were bleeding somewhere, and I knew you were going to die. I mean, there was so much blood, Alyssa. I knew there was no way that, if you were still alive, you'd be alive for long if I didn't find you. So Dex and I searched the entire clearing. We went through the trees, and we searched as far into the forest as we dared, being split up. After about thirty minutes, I was completely frantic. Dex was trying to keep me calm, like he knew we would never find you if I lost it before then.

"That was when I heard it. There was a rumbling happening under our feet. It was like an earthquake, but I'd never felt anything quite like it. There was a pool of blood in the middle of the clearing, where I guessed the attack happened, and it opened like a cavern. I hadn't thought to look there because I didn't see you. Now I know that, whatever ritual they performed, they'd buried you and spilled your blood over the grave. You crawled out, right in front of my eyes, pale and… Undead."

I shook my head, and I knew then that he was crazy.

"That's where you got the scar," Seely gestured to me without turning his gaze at all. "I can't explain why it popped up after your dream because it should have been healed when your transformation was complete, but I'm assuming whatever happened in your dream is really what happened to you before I got there."

I hadn't realized I'd been touching my neck again until that moment, but I jerked my arm down and gripped the arm of the chair.

"Seely, maybe we should talk to someone," I tried. My voice was calm and careful, kind of the way you speak to a toddler you're trying to rationalize with.

"My dad? Seth? I'm sure they could help you make sense about all of this."

Seely barked another cold laugh. I flinched at the sound. There was no humor in it, and I felt fresh fear creeping up my spine.

"This is one reason they didn't want me to tell you." He turned to look at me, finally. His eyes were shining with moisture. Tears, I thought, though none escaped down his face. "And why would you believe me? It's a crazy story. You shouldn't be here right now, at all. Let alone… mostly alive? We're not really sure." He shrugged.

Mostly alive? My heart was pounding again, and it made me feel completely alive.

"You know, I didn't know what had happened in that clearing until your dream." He was quiet now. "When you told me, I… it was all I could do not to storm out into those woods and confront Orthan myself. We have tabs on him and his whereabouts, I could probably find him. That's all I want to *do* is find him. He should be suffering for what he did to you." Seely took what looked to be a steadying breath. "I should have been there."

"Seely, how does it make sense that if an Undead wanted to kill me, I'm still here? You also said I *was* Undead. I'm clearly alive and breathing, with a heartbeat and everything?" The last part turned up into a question. "And another thing, I would definitely remember this happening to me!"

"But you did remember, Gold. You dreamed it."

If that were true… But no. My recent dreams couldn't be true. I thought about the dream from tonight and shook my head to clear it away. But then I remembered the dream that had me coughing up black sludge that looked an awful lot like mud, and the dream of Orthan that left me with a very real scar.

Seely was crazy. My dreams were not true, and I needed to get out of that room before I started to believe him.

Chapter Fifteen

I STOOD TO MY FEET AND SEELY LOOKED AT ME, dully, pushing his hair off his forehead where it threatened to fall into his eyes. He guessed what I was thinking almost immediately, just like he always did.

"What are you expecting to do, Gold? They're under strict orders not to let you out, no matter how much you kick and scream. And I can almost promise you, you won't be able to get that door open. They put a lock on it. Strong enough for Undead and humans," he waved his hand absently through the air towards the door, "just to be safe."

I didn't believe him.

"What are you talking about, Seely? Who in the world would try to keep me in here?"

I moved to go to the door and Seely stood from his chair, directly in front of me and so close. I could smell cinnamon and almost feel his heart beating out of his chest. I could see the pattern of wool on his sweater, so detailed it almost made me itchy.

"I'm not lying to you, Alyssa," Seely said. He held up a hand in a stopping position. It didn't escape my notice that his other hand rested on the hilt of the dagger at his side where it was sheathed to his belt against dark jeans. His eyes were so wide, I thought I could see the whole world reflected in them. There was something else reflected there, too.

"Are you…" I paused, the question getting stuck in my throat. "Seely, are you… afraid of me?"

When I got the last sentence out, a giggle that sounded a lot like hysteria escaped my lips. I placed a hand over my mouth, but it was no use. After the first laugh escaped, more and more came. I placed my hands over my face, shaking with laughter.

No, it wasn't laughter.

Seely's arms were around me before I could even realize I'd gone from laughing to crying. The sobs were wracking my body now. My ribs ached from the effort I was taking to hold on to any piece of sanity at all. My head was hurting already as I struggled to keep the tears from flowing. I wasn't sure why I cared about Seely seeing any other vulnerable part of me. He was the one talking crazy.

But through the sobs, my mind was working.

Some part of me was starting to believe Seely's story.

I pulled back from him as my sobs quieted, though the tears still flowed.

"Tell me," I said, looking into his eyes. His eyebrows pulled together. "Tell me how any of this could be possible. How could I not remember you or this place? How could I not remember turning into... into...?" Another sob broke through my chest.

"Right, um," Seely looked uncomfortable for a second. "You were told that you were kept from the AAUD because of the threat to your life, right? Well, that wasn't true. When you turned thirteen, you came here to train, just like everyone else. Your dad thought it would be better for you to learn how to fight if it came down to it. He figured it made more sense that you be able to defend yourself than it would for you to be a sitting duck, if Orthan ever decided to make good on his death promise. Which makes a lot more sense than the lie they fed you today." He paused. "That's why I had to walk away yesterday, in the lab. I didn't know what they were going to tell you and I didn't want to sit there while they filled your head with things that held back who you really are. You are a *warrior*, Gold."

I blinked at his words. My tears had slowed, and I was breathing deeply as I tried to keep them at bay.

"So, how do I remember a completely different life than you're describing to me?" I knew my life couldn't have been a lie. I remembered Seth and his cooking, my dad and his morning donuts, Stella coming over every afternoon...

"Do you really remember anything other than the day before I came and got you? Do you remember anything concrete? Think about it. Can you name any of your teachers in high school? Classmates other than Stella and your brother?"

I shook my head, slowly. The answer was no, no matter how much I wanted to deny it. I couldn't remember any of those things. I could remember bits and pieces of a life: summers with my dad and Seth, hanging out with the girls almost every day, and even going to school through the years. But I couldn't remember anything that had happened recently that was concrete enough to hold on to. I remembered I'd even thought about this a couple of days ago, about how everything I tried to remember was like water slipping through my fingers.

I could feel myself begin to fade out of reality again. He was making sense, which made everything else that I thought I knew stop making sense. Seely gripped my arms as if he could feel my body about to give out and betray me.

"Stay with me, Gold. There's more you need to know," he said, as he held me up. "They kept you sedated most of the time so they could run their tests, from what I understand. You were kept hidden away for almost two years while they experimented on you and attempted to figure out what was wrong. I'm not sure if you were awake at all from the time I left you in that lab until a couple days before I came for you. They didn't tell me, or wouldn't tell me, is a more accurate way to describe it. I had an idea of where you were, or really what the circumstances would be if I *did* find you, but it was all but impossible to get through security. My dad kept me plenty busy, and of course no one would tell me exactly where they were keeping you. Of course, they wouldn't tell me. They knew I would come get you."

I didn't want to know any more, but I let Seely lead me to the chair I had just come from. I sank into it with an unsophisticated thud. My head rocked back a little with the jolt, but I held Seely's gaze. It was the only thing keeping me in place at that moment.

"Your family loves you, and I believe that, but I can't say that I think what they did to you the past two years is moral or right. They planned that school day to draw Orthan and his crew out of the shadows. They were guessing he would be able to sense you if you were awake and moving, which I guess turned out to be true. That school was crawling with Undead that day. I guess I understand why they would want to do it, we need to know exactly what happened to you and what Orthan wants with you to understand Orthan's next move. Orthan wanted you for a purpose, and that purpose was not simply to turn you into an Undead. Not that your family knows that, at least not as far as I know. If anyone else knew that about you, I don't think you would have lived this long." He placed a hand on my chest, right above my heart. "You have a heartbeat, Gold. That's something we've yet to understand." His hand moved to cradle my neck and up to my cheek. "You're warm. You live and breathe and eat. We don't completely know what Orthan did to you and what his plan is for you, but we're pretty sure you were made to be the type of Undead that Seth was talking about earlier—the kind that is stronger than the usual Undead in that they have powers, but is also closer to human than the others?" He shrugged. "That's a possibility. We don't even know for sure that those Undead exist. But what we *do* know, Gold, is that you're something other than human."

I wasn't crying anymore, though I wasn't feeling particularly calm. My family used me as *bait?* I thought back to that school day and I remembered the creatures with silver-white hair and black eyes that reminded me too much of Orthan and the feeling of his teeth sinking into my throat. I remembered Stella and Seth acting so strange, and when I asked them, they swore nothing was going on. I thought about our movie night… they were babysitting me, I realized. They were just making sure no Undead came to steal me away, and that if they did, they could protect me. Or maybe just capture them. At that point, I wasn't so sure what their intentions were. But Seely's words made me feel safe. He would have come for me right away if he knew where I was this whole time. I didn't really know what was going through my brain at that moment, but I believed every word. I felt a strange sensation buzzing in my chest.

I believed him fully now, about all of it, and I wasn't sure if I should be more afraid or comforted by that realization.

"I carried you all the way back here," Seely reached out and gently touched the scar on my neck with his fingertips. "By the time I got you here, your scar looked just like this. It was perfectly healed, except for a faint purple line. Actually, it was even less noticeable than it is now, for whatever reason. Another mystery, I guess.

"I knew, then, that you had to be Undead. But when I took you to the lab, you were breathing!" His brows furrowed together as he continued to stare at the scar. "Your heart was pumping, and you had some color. Your wounds, however, were completely healed."

Seely dropped slowly to the floor in front of me, balancing in a crouch. His hands were resting on my knees.

"I didn't tell them what happened in the clearing and neither did Dex. I was afraid that if they knew you had been made into something even close to an Undead, they would have killed you on the spot. I told them I found you in the clearing and you had passed out and I didn't know what happened to you, which wasn't totally a lie." Seely gave me a crooked grin that looked a little more genuine than the last one. It slipped away almost as soon as it appeared, though, as the severity of this conversation came crashing back down on him. "Even though we knew Orthan wanted you, we didn't really know much more than that. We knew there was something he needed from you, specifically, but none of our leads have panned out, even now. I didn't have anything to tell them when I brought you in that didn't include the possibility of us being killed, so I pretended I didn't have my own theories.

"They made me leave you there. They said they would find out what was wrong with you, and they would fix it, but I prayed they wouldn't find out the root cause of your condition. I would have burned the place to the ground if they hurt you in any way, though now I know they did at least a little bit of that." He winced. "I'm sorry I didn't just take you away from there, Gold. I should have taken you and ran far away. You would have woken up confused and angry and Undead, but you would have been safe without being poked and prodded constantly. Without being sedated and locked away for years." He lifted one of his hands from my knee and dragged it across his face again.

"When I brought you to the lab, they kicked me out almost as soon as I got you on the table. Your dad told me they would come and get me as soon as you woke up—as soon as they had any answers."

Seely looked down at his hands.

"They never came to get me," he whispered. "I waited outside the lab for almost twenty-four hours before anyone came out that door and noticed I was still there. When they saw me, it was almost like they forgot they'd made me a promise. Your dad came out then and told me that you were gone. He told me you'd woken up, but they'd made sure you didn't remember anything, that it was too dangerous for you to remember anything about the AAUD and Orthan and anything related to it. Which I guess included me.

"He told me you were going away until they could figure out what was happening with you and how to fix it. He said it wasn't safe for me to see you. He said you wouldn't remember me anyway, so it's not like you'd be missing me.

"Your dad thought it would be in everyone's best interest if you relocated and started over somewhere. So, you went with him and Seth to Pleasantville, USA. They completely messed with your memories, and you've been living in limbo for two years. While I stay here, with my good-for-nothing father, training for a position in a world that means nothing without you, and wishing you'd waited just ten more minutes before running into those woods."

Seely looked up to me then. His eyes were no longer just shining with moisture, there were tears flowing freely down his face as he stared into my eyes. I felt the tears falling down my own as I looked at him too.

Seely was facing me, away from the fire and he was still positioned in a crouch with his hands resting on my knees. I couldn't see the green of his eyes in this light, with the shadows from the firelight and the hair on his forehead hiding the color, and for some reason that's all I wanted to see in that moment. I reached out and touched the curls that fell onto his forehead. His hair was always so dark, especially in the dim light of the evening that had been passing us by as we talked. The locks were soft and thick in my hand, and I relished in the feeling of it.

I pushed his hair back and ran my hand down his face to caress his cheek. I watched as his eyes grew wider and his lips parted. I was suddenly reminded of my dream. Of his lips on mine and the way our bodies fit perfectly together…

I can't really explain what came over me as I stared into his eyes for a longer moment than I meant to, but the next thing I knew I was kissing him.

We were closer than I'd gauged, and I slammed into Seely with enough force that the air was knocked out of him a little bit. He rocked back with my weight and lost his balance, tumbling backwards as I accidentally tackled him. For a moment, his lips met mine with fervor. I remembered my dream, and the feeling of familiarity was almost overwhelming. I belonged here somehow. Maybe not in this place, but definitely with Seely's arms around me and his lips capturing my own.

Almost at once, I felt him freeze under me. He gripped my forearms and pushed me away. The movement was gentle enough that I didn't feel the sting of rejection right away. As I leaned back a little, I looked into his eyes once more and fully realized what I'd done. I knew my face had to be blood red and I prayed the fire would be enough to keep Seely from seeing it. I was already mortified enough.

I jerked back into a seated position on the ground, but Seely grabbed by hand before I could move away completely.

"I- I'm so sorry. I don't know what that was."

Seely didn't look angry or annoyed with me. He just looked thoughtful, maybe even a little sad.

"You know, Gold," Seely said, the swagger returning to his voice, though I thought I detected a slight quiver, "I anticipated a lot of different reactions from you. Screaming, crying, denial. Even physical violence." He smiled at me, and my chest warmed with its sincerity. "But I never anticipated this. Though, I must say, I'm not complaining in the least. Feel free to jump me anytime."

Seely let out a laugh and I joined in with a breathless one of my own.

"I had a dream tonight, before I went out on the balcony," I whispered after we'd both quieted. I still felt embarrassed, but that was dissipating a bit. "It was about us, running through a field and..." I blushed then. "You told me you loved me."

Seely was still smiling, and he nodded at that. He didn't show any sign of embarrassment or fear at the story.

"If you recall about five minutes ago, I told you the same thing, Gold. I'm not embarrassed about it."

My chest felt fuzzy, and the emotion was strange and familiar all at once. I didn't know how any of this had happened. One minute, I was thinking Seely was clinically insane, and the next I was attacking him with kisses and thinking about how much I liked the way I felt when he told me he loved me. A part of me believed him because a part of myself felt *right* when he told me those things. A part of me that hadn't felt right as long as I could remember. Though, I was learning tonight that my memories couldn't be trusted.

"Was that real, then?" I asked him. "My dream?"

Seely nodded.

"It sounds like it. That was the night before your accident." His eyes darted to mine for a second but dropped to where my hand was still placed in his. He wrapped his tighter around mine. "Have you had any other dreams? About the past?"

At first, I shook my head, but then I realized he wasn't looking at me.

"No," I answered. "I've told you about all of them. It's just been those three, at least that I can remember. Which, apparently, I can't." I sighed and Seely looked up to meet my eyes. "I feel so… weird. Confused. Like, how is my life not my life? And how can I feel like I've known you my whole life yet not at all?" I shook my head again as I looked down at my hand in Seely's. "I still have so many questions."

"So do I," answered a voice from across the room.

In a heartbeat, Seely and I were standing, facing the door, our backs to the fireplace. Seely stood in front of me with his arm out in a protective stance. We stared at the figure by the door that I swore hadn't been there the minute before.

"Father," Seely practically growled the word, "what are you doing here?"

Chapter Sixteen

MR. EVANSON STOOD AGAINST THE WALL, just staring at us. His face was impassive, but there was something bubbling just under the surface. His jaw was set in a way that couldn't hide the anger he was feeling under the facade. I wasn't sure how long he'd been in here or how much he'd heard. I didn't hear anyone come in while I was talking with Seely, but I guessed he could have snuck in while we were deep in conversation. Or when we were kissing. I suppressed a shudder at that and sent up a silent prayer that he somehow hadn't seen that part. I couldn't help the blush that crept across my cheeks, though being caught kissing would be a lot easier to explain.

Seely stood stalk-straight with his arm out in front of me. At some point, he'd taken out his dagger from its sheath. I felt a chill roll through me as I realized what that meant.

Seely thought his dad heard what I was. He also thought we might have to fight our way out of this. It didn't escape my notice that he was willing to use a dagger against his own father if that was what he needed to do. I wasn't sure if that made me feel better or worse.

"So, Seely, it seems like there's a lot you and I need to talk about," Mr. Evanson smiled without any humor, sending another chill down my spine. His deep, gravelly voice felt like it was grating on my nerve endings. "Oh, and let's not forget Miss Gold, here." His gaze moved over me with distaste before sliding back to his son. "I knew you were going to pull something like this. I told Gold we should lock her up again and put her back under, that it was a bad decision to let her out at all. Whatever bond you two share, which is very inconvenient for me by the way, I knew it would come back to bite me. I should have taken care of either one or both of you when I had the chance."

I didn't really like the sound of "taken care of". I was pretty sure it didn't mean sending us off to a nice vacation somewhere. It didn't mean we would be able to stay together. I realized then that being with Seely was what I wanted more than anything right now.

"I knew you two would be the downfall of what I've built here, but I didn't know exactly how. And now I hear that she's one of them? An Undead?" He laughed. "As if I didn't already know this. There's nothing that goes on regarding the AAUD or my sons that I don't know about. Who do you think sent

Simon out to get you that day? Do you think this wasn't a part of my plan? Nothing catches me off guard, and you should know that by now, Son." Mr. Evanson stepped away from the wall and Seely pressed farther into me, raising his dagger towards his father. Mr. Evanson just smiled at his son like this was all a game. Maybe it was to him.

My blood ran even colder than before as the realization of his words hit me. He had planted me there that day. He had planned for Seely to leave me. He probably knew exactly how I came to wander through those woods, though I couldn't remember it. He'd known this whole time. Did my father know? Seth had been talking about the type of Undead that I *could* be earlier, but that didn't mean they knew. Maybe they were suspicious, but they couldn't have *known*... right?

"Seely, don't hurt yourself. Especially for garbage like this. Let me take care of it, whatever spell she's put on you. Who knows the kinds of things she's put into your mind! You can never tell with these creatures." He gestured his hand to me like I was a fly he was trying to shoo away. "They like to play with the emotions of humans. You don't love her, Son. You're being controlled by her." I knew he was lying, and I knew Seely also wouldn't buy this story. At least, I hoped he wouldn't. Obviously, I hadn't been controlling him. I didn't even know who I was at this point. My brain was filled only with the false narrative planted there by the people I thought were there to protect me, and Seely's story from tonight.

Mr. Evanson took another step toward me. His face was red, sweat beading around his temples. Though I didn't know him, I knew better than to think he was scared of *me*. Something else was going on. "That's why I made sure she was taken away from you. I know you can't see it now, but it was the best thing for you. What can come of this… relationship? Are you planning on becoming a filthy abomination along with her? If you think I'd ever let that happen to someone with my blood, you're sadly mistaken. Whatever our friend Orthan has planned, the first step had to do with this one becoming one of them." He gestured to me again, without looking at me or even really acknowledging me, veins popping out of his neck. The way he was talking about me like I wasn't even there was making me wonder if I was invisible.

"It was going to happen eventually, Son, I just… moved the process along a little bit." It didn't escape my notice that he'd come two steps closer through the course of his speech. He was trying to distract us.

"Don't take another step, or I won't have a choice about what I do next." Seely spoke to his father, his voice strong and sure. The words came through his teeth. He stepped a little to the side, which, I noticed, positioned himself perfectly in front of me and in an even more protective position. That same warmth bloomed in me just as an almost-familiar icy heat began to race through my veins. The edges of my vision blurred as I watched the scene unfolding before me, father against son. I started taking deep breaths.

Mr. Evanson laughed, and it sent another chill up my spine.

"Don't strain yourself, boy. You won't win against me. I've been killing both weaklings and Undead for nearly forty years" He pointed to me while keeping his eyes on his son. "If challenging me is something you want to do, though, make sure it's for a noble cause. I'll find you another whore, but I'll be taking this one. She's of greater use to me than she is to you."

The air went completely still at those words. It seemed to me like time itself froze. I couldn't hear the fire or either man in front of me. Out of the corner of my eye I saw Seely turn towards me and say something, but I couldn't hear the words. I only saw Mr. Evanson as he smirked at me, his face surprising me with how much it looked like Seely. I took a step towards him.

"Try it."

The sound of my own voice brought me back to reality. Nothing had changed in the room, but I felt different than I had a few moments before. I felt stronger and surer of myself and my body. Suddenly I was waiting for him to come to me. I *wanted* to fight, and I knew I would win if it came down to it. I felt myself smile.

Mr. Evanson's eyes widened slightly, but other than that he showed no indication that he heard me. He was just standing there, across the room, staring at us. His jaw was set and, before I even knew what was happening, he lifted his hand and flung something at us. I stopped the knife as it flew less than an inch from my face. My hand gripped around the blade, and I felt a shock of pain before I realized what had just happened. A nervous laugh escaped my lips, and I turned my eyes to Seely. His face was white with shock or dread, or something like it, and I realized exactly how close the knife had come to going directly through my eye and into my skull.

Mr. Evanson had thrown a knife at my head.

He had *thrown* a knife at my head.

He'd tried to kill me.

If I had been anything other than what I was, if I had been fully human, I would be bleeding out on the floor right now. My head whipped from Seely to his father, who I thought had taken a step back, towards the door. Once again, my vision blurred around the edges. It was like tunnel vision, and all I could see through my blind rage was Mr. Evanson's face.

I was going to kill him.

"You tried to kill me," I hissed. I literally *hissed* the words at him. Something was happening to me, and some part of me, maybe the human part, was frightened, but the only thing I cared about then was seeing Seely's father lying dead on the ground.

"You tried to kill me, and you failed." I heard myself laugh, but I sounded far away. "You had one chance, Mr. Evanson. I won't give you another one." I felt myself raise my arm to strike back at the man who just attempted to kill me. I felt no regret or hesitation or shame as I drew my arm back and tensed my muscles to strike.

"Stop!"

Seely grabbed my arm and jerked it down before I could let go of the knife. I screamed a pathetic protest at the action. How could anyone come in between me and my kill? I drew the knife to his neck and pressed it in until a thin line of blood formed, and a drop trickled down his neck.

"Gold," Seely said, his words choked, "Gold, look at me. Put the knife down." I heard him, but it sounded like he was in a tunnel. Like *I* was in a tunnel. It reminded me of the dream I had of Orthan when I both lived through his attack and watched it from afar. I was in my body at that moment, obviously, but it was also like I was watching the scene play out from across the room. I could see my stance as I braced myself against Seely. I could see the curve of muscles in my arm that I don't remember toning as I both held myself back and pushed harder into Seely's throat. I saw him reach up and wrap his hand around mine. His strength was nothing against me, and I could tell the gesture was one of coaxing rather than a prayer of overpowering me. Even as I held a knife to his throat, Seely looked at me calmly and without fear. I met his eyes, his pupils dilated so wide that I could barely see the green around them. *He's scared*, I realized. *Scared of me or for me?*

I felt my heart begin to slow and my blood stop its icy trek under my skin. My vision came back to normal as I stared at him. Slowly, so extremely slowly, the green of his eyes appeared again around the black. Seely was the only thing keeping me grounded amidst the rage I didn't know how to control. I found myself suddenly wishing I could remember the lost years I spent with him.

"If you kill him right now, with only me as a witness, they'll have everything they need to label you a monster." I let him lower my arm down to my side and take the knife from my hand. My fingers were limp as I felt the blood rushing back to them. I hadn't realized I was holding the knife so tightly.

"If my dad knows what you are," Seely continued, "then it's a safe bet there are others who know as well." His voice was soft and soothing, and I could tell he was trying to soften the blow of the implication that my dad knew about me. My brother. Stella. I felt a lump forming in my throat and I pushed it down. I had to hold it together here.

Seely smiled a little and said, "I don't know if your family knows, Gold. I know that's what you're worrying about. If they do know, though, it won't be hard to convince them you're just an Undead monster if they find out you killed one of the AAUD commanders." At that, Seely looked over my head to glare at his father, who I had forgotten all about. Seely had just finished telling me that I was a warrior, but I didn't know what kind of warrior turned their back on their enemy while actively trying to kill their… whatever Seely was.

I turned around quickly, bracing myself. I remembered the dagger that Seely had given me was on the bedside table and I couldn't stop my eyes from going to it. Mr. Evanson followed my gaze and laughed. My eyes snapped back to him.

"Do you know what that blade is good for, *girl?*" He said the word "girl" like he didn't think it accurately described me anymore. I thought he probably wanted to call me something like "trash" or maybe "whore" again. Ice began to fill my veins.

I could only watch as he walked the few steps that brought him to the dagger. He was closer than I was, and I didn't dare move in his direction. I didn't trust my temper or whatever it was that gave me tunnel, killing vision, and I knew Seely was right. Whatever happened in this room was going to be used against me, and I needed to make sure Mr. Evanson didn't have any more power over me than he did when he first walked in.

He held the knife in one hand and gently pressed onto the end of the blade with the pointer finger on his other hand. I could feel the confusion plainly on my face when I watched a drop of blood fall from that place on his finger and all the way down the blade to the hilt.

"This dagger is good for killing the one thing that should have never existed in the first place." He pointed the weapon at me. "Undead. Just like you." His voice turned thoughtful. "Though, I suppose we don't exactly know what you are yet. There's a reason Orthan wants you and had to wait until you were Changed to get what he needs. We just haven't figured out what that is yet."

"So, you're going to kill me before you get your answers?" I snorted a laugh. I couldn't help but goad him. "That seems like a brilliant plan. I don't think I'll really be that useful to Orthan if I'm dead."

"You're already dead, girl." Mr. Evanson's voice was softer than before, and it scared me more than I wanted to admit. "But you're also right. You're of no use to me dead." He pulled the dagger back from where it had been pointing at me moments before. I watched, still not fully understanding, as he turned the blade on himself. "You have too many friends here, and I need your family on my side before I can complete what needs to be done. Sometimes you have to take matters into your own hands.

I watched as Mr. Evanson plunged the blade of my dagger into his stomach, and I think I screamed.

Chapter Seventeen

"NO!"

It was Seely's voice I heard shout the word. The blood was rushing so fast through my body that I could hear it in my ears. I wasn't quite processing what was playing out before me. Everything seemed to be going in slow motion again, though this time it wasn't because of whatever unknowns were running through my mind, but from the shock of what I was seeing.

Mr. Evanson had stabbed himself in the torso with my dagger. He grunted as it entered easily through his skin, his face going white with pain. Blood began pumping out almost immediately. I didn't know how *purple* fresh blood looked when it came out of someone. And the smell… it was a warm metallic that reminded me a little of cooked salmon. He staggered back a couple of steps until he hit his back to the wall, then he sank to the ground with a groan, blood still flowing freely down his hand and dying his shirt a shocking color of red.

"Alyssa," he said, looking up at me with a smile, "I can't believe you did this to me. I only came in here to protect my son, and you tried to kill me?"

I stared at him blankly, hoping my mouth wasn't gaping like I knew it probably was. I couldn't believe what was happening, that anyone could be that insane, that he would try and kill himself…

It clicked for me then.

"You… you're going to tell them *I* did this? That I stabbed you?"

He smiled then, and his mouth was filled with blood.

"But you did stab me. And whose word will they believe? Mine or yours?"

"They're my family. Of course, they would believe me." I shook my head. His plan would never work, there was no way my dad or Seth or Stella would believe anything he had to say if my word went against his. There was no way.

"You're not their daughter or their sister or their friend," Mr. Evanson said, "you're one of *them*. You're Undead, Miss Gold." He coughed as he struggled to raise himself up higher on the wall. "You're Undead, and you won't exist to them in any way that matters once they see just how much of a monster you truly are." He tilted his head a bit, raising his ear towards the door. "And that should be happening any minute now."

I watched, my face and body frozen in pure horror and shock, as Mr. Evanson gave me one last smile. I watched the right side of his face rise higher than the left and his nose crinkle slightly, just like his son's.

Everything seemed to happen in slow motion.

The door slammed open, and his smile faded. As if on cue, the color drained from his face altogether and he slumped forward as though he was trying to reach the person standing in the doorway. I realized it was a soldier, one of the boys that had stood in my kitchen with Seely just days before.

"Help, she—she… she's an Undead. She tried to kill me. Detain her."

With those words, Mr. Evanson fell over into a crumpled mess on the floor, whether from his injury or more theatrics, I didn't know. I could see his shoulders rising and falling faintly, meaning he wasn't dead. Yet.

Seely was still at my side, his dagger in his left hand. I watched as both of his arms raised in a surrendering position as he turned his attention to the man standing in the doorway. He looked about the same age as we were.

"Geordan." Seely took a step forward, his arms still raised. "Let me explain. Let *us* explain."

The boy, Geordan, looked from Mr. Evanson to Seely with wide eyes, clearly not knowing what to believe and trying to think of what the next right move would be. He held a gun at his side, and I watched, with horror, as he raised it towards us. Seely and I were standing so close together that I couldn't tell if the gun was pointed more at him or at me, but Geordan's eyes were fixed on Seely.

"I have to take her, Seely, it was an order."

"No." Seely's word was final, its authority almost ringing through the air between us and Geordan.

I watched as Geordan turned his gaze to me, his hands shaking. I heard more footsteps pounding down the hallway, and I knew we were about to be ambushed by a whole slew of soldiers. Well, Seely would be. I figured I was going to be dead or unconscious in the next minute or so.

What happened next seemed to also happen in slow motion. Geordan still had his gun aimed at my head and I watched as his hand tightened in preparation to pull the trigger. I had a fleeting thought that the bullet probably wouldn't kill me if I were an Undead. I guessed he was trying to stun me so his soldier buddies could take me to wherever they could keep me sedated and docile again. Would I lose these memories too? I knew I'd lost so much already, but the thought of losing these few days with Seely and everything I'd learned almost sent me over the edge.

Suddenly, I felt Seely shift beside me. He raised his hand with the dagger, and I knew he was going to throw it. Geordan saw it too, and the gun that was trained on my head shifted ever so slightly. I knew it was now pointing directly at Seely.

A bullet that would stun me would kill him instantly.

Geordan pulled the trigger as I screamed and threw myself in front of Seely. He didn't even have a chance to let go of his dagger.

We disappeared in a cloud of icy, inky dust.

Coming to, I realized I was no longer in the base.

I opened my eyes to a canopy of trees and moonlight that barely leaked through the leaves above me. I was vaguely aware that my shoulder was sore, and I rolled over to my side, heaving a cough. Whatever kind of dust surrounded Seely and me as we escaped was lodged in my lungs now.

Seely.

Coughing again, I sat up abruptly. Too abruptly, apparently, as I almost fell over from the dizziness of the blood rushing from my head. I'd been through too much trauma in the past few days, and I also realized I had no idea how long I'd been lying there on the ground.

"Seely," I croaked out the name. Coughing against the scratch of the dust, I tried again, louder this time. "Seely? Where are you?"

Had I jumped in front of him in time? Did he even disappear with me? Was I out here all alone while Seely was bleeding out back at the base? *He's probably dead by now.* I cursed the voice in the back of my mind that always jumped to the worst conclusions. He wasn't dead. He couldn't be dead. He—

"I'm over here, Gold. I can practically hear your mind whirring over there." He coughed from somewhere to my right. "I'm okay."

I jumped to my feet and ran in the direction of his voice. I had landed in a clearing, while Seely had apparently been deposited in the high grass and trees that stood just outside the clearing. I couldn't see him from where I had been laying, but when I stood, I could see a mass of dark clothing slowly turning to its side, with a cough.

He was a clump of darkness. His hair, with only touches of light hitting it in places where it was able to break through the trees, was like a void of black.

He was wearing the dark colors that came with his soldier's uniform, black boots, and a black sheath at his side for the dagger I saw lying a few yards away from him.

I knelt beside him and took his head in my hands, turning it from side to side to assess any damage. His nose was bleeding, which I guessed must have happened when we landed. He was coated in a layer of black dust, making the skin that shone through look even paler than usual. I wiped at the coating with my thumbs, but it didn't budge much.

"We need to find water or something to get you cleaned up."

"I think we need to work on your Dissipating, Gold. At least the landing part. I think I cracked a rib."

Huh, so that's what Dissipating meant.

He sat up straighter as I dropped my hands from his face and rocked back into a sitting position. Seely rubbed his side and winced as he took in a breath. "No, I definitely cracked a rib." He shrugged. "It could have been worse." He gave me a smile and winced again, touching his bloody nose. "You broke my nose, too? My beautiful face? You'll never want to look at me when I'm standing here like Owen Wilson." He gave me a softer smile that time, probably trying to minimize the pain that came along with moving his face at all. I leaned forward again and touched his nose, gingerly.

"I don't think it's broken. It's already stopped bleeding."

I smiled a little. He was okay. We were okay. We'd escaped, and no one got shot and now we would... Now what?

My smile fell almost as soon as it appeared.

We escaped the AAUD and Seely's father, yes, but what exactly what were we going to do now? Where were we?

"Seely, do you know where we are?"

He looked at me with a little bit of concern at my abrupt change in demeanor, but then he moved his gaze to the trees around us.

"I'm not sure," he said, a little quieter than before. His brows furrowed together slightly. "The trees look similar to the ones surrounding the AAUD, so I don't think we're far… But I think we're pretty deep into the forest. Which… isn't great."

"Why isn't that great?"

Seely sat up completely now, still holding his side. I got to my knees, hovering over him as he propped himself up on a tree. He was breathing fast, shallow breaths.

"Seely—"

"I'm fine, Gold. Just need to rest for a minute." I waddled over on my knees anyway, and I reached out uselessly. I had no idea what to do, or even what I could possibly do at all, but I wanted to help. I *needed* to help.

Seely reached out with his other hand and grabbed mine.

"Maybe you should take some deep breaths, too." He squeezed my hand and I looked at his dirty face. "I'm fine."

I nodded, though I wasn't sure I believed anything he was telling me. He was alive and breathing, but he wasn't fine. I decided to pick that battle after he'd told me what he'd deduced about our situation.

"Tell me, why is being so far in the forest a bad thing?"

"Sit down and take a breath. And then I'll tell you."

I did what he said, though it made me grind my teeth a little to comply so easily. I may not know who I was, but I knew I didn't like being told what to do.

"Thank you," Seely said.

"For what?"

"For listening to me. You never do that."

Me not listening to him had apparently gotten us into this mess in the first place, so I bit my tongue again. I could comply, and in this instance I would. I wasn't going to wander off in the woods alone to die again, that was for sure.

Seely smirked at me, which I pointedly ignored, as I sat still, breathing deeply, and waited for him to begin. After about five breaths from me, he finally spoke.

"Being deep in the forest that surrounds our AAUD headquarters is a bad thing," Seely paused to wince at the breath he had to take in to speak. My hands fluttered uselessly, and he waved me off. "Geez, Mom, I'm fine. Take it easy."

I glared at him for that, but I needed to hear the story, so I didn't say anything as I leaned back again in my seat.

"It's a bad thing because we attract a lot of Undead and Others with our presence. There are a lot of AAUD soldiers at base, if you can imagine that since we were nearly murdered by a whole slew of them just now, so there are a lot of Undead and Others who live in these woods, waiting for a stray soldier they can slaughter or turn or hold for ransom. The other problem is," he took a deep breath before he continued, "people who come and scout these woods have rarely ever come back. That means, we don't know a lot about the layout or the scope, and we definitely don't know how to get out without being attacked or killed. Technically, the AAUD owns these lands. That's a legality that allowed our grandfathers to create a reserve of land and keep the humans from wandering in and getting lost or eaten or Created.

"When those idiots thought they'd eradicated the Undead completely, they simply left the Others in these woods to live out the rest of their days. The Undead are the real threat to all humans at all times, while the Others stay in their woods and generally don't come out. The problem now is not only that the Undead are *not* gone, but—"

"We're also in their territory."

Seely nodded.

"I've been in worse situations before. Mostly with you." He smiled, but there was a little pain behind that statement. "We'll be fine."

I nodded. I wanted to believe him, but I couldn't help but think practically. We were in the middle of a forest surrounded by *things* that wanted to kill us. I also had no idea what he meant by "Others", though I was a little too afraid to ask just then. I thought I would probably know if we came across them, and that was enough knowledge about them for me at that moment.

The only safe haven we knew of was the AAUD, but that was the last place we could run to right now. Seely said he didn't know the scope of the forest, yet they owned the land. There had to be a record of it somewhere. I looked up at him and noticed him smiling at me.

"Just out with it, Gold. Tell me what you're thinking."

I was still shocked at how well he knew me. It was strange to be looked at like that by a person I'd only remembered knowing for a few days. I'm not saying it wasn't nice, just that it was strange.

I cleared my throat.

"Well, I was thinking that you're hurt, and we don't really know where we're at. I was also thinking how it's strange that you can own a piece of land without knowing the scope of that land. Which means your father, and maybe mine, must be hiding something from you. Which made me also think that they probably know more about this land than we do. Which means we should probably get moving before they come to find *us*, don't you think?"

Seely blinked at me.

"You think my father has been hiding from me that he knows what these woods are all about? That he has a detailed map?"

"Maybe not detailed, but he definitely has a map. He knows more than we do, at the very least."

Seely seemed to consider that for a moment.

"Considering what just happened, that checks out. I didn't put much past him before, but knowing now that he was going to *kill* you, or at the very least impale you with a knife in the head…" He shook his head. "Yeah, you're probably right about his knowing more than he ever told me. What I can't figure out, then," he took in another shaky breath, "is what happened to all the soldiers we've sent out trying to get a grasp of this place."

"The Others and Undead might not just be stories," I said. "That could all be true."

I didn't say it, but the thought passed through my mind that Seely's father might have known exactly what happened to those soldiers. He probably sent them directly to their death. I knew I didn't have to say it because Seely already knew these things about his dad, better than I did. If I had gotten to that conclusion, I was sure he'd beaten me there. I wanted to ask him what he thought, but instead I just pursed my lips and reached out to touch his face again.

"Do you think you can get up and walk a little way? We need to find water."

Seely leaned his face into my hand and looked at me. I could see that he was in pain, both physical and something deeper. He nodded.

"I'm fine, I told you this already, Gold." He smiled at me as I rolled my eyes and stood. I held out my hand to him.

"Let's go, then. I think I can hear a river or a brook or something. It can't be that far away."

Seely nodded and gripped my hand. I could tell he held his breath as he rose, and I sent a silent prayer that his injuries weren't too severe. Maybe I knew how to take care of these kinds of things before, I was sure AAUD soldiers had to go through some kind of training, but that girl was gone. At least for now. I wondered if I would ever get her back.

I felt a little bit better once Seely was standing, even when he took a step and swayed. I held tight to him, and he steadied.

"I'm fine, Gold, I promise. We'll work on your landing skills later."

"Just shut up and lean on me."

He nodded and wrapped an arm around me as I wrapped mine around his waist to support his weight. We walked, slowly, deeper into the forest.

"I really hope this water isn't far away, Gold," Seely rasped, already breathing heavily. "I could really use a drink."

Unfortunately for us, the brook was very far away. I wasn't sure how long we had walked, but it had to have been at least a mile or two before Seely asked for a rest.

I wasn't feeling tired at all, though I knew I was basically carrying his full weight on my shoulders, and I wondered if that was because of previous training or simply the enhanced abilities of the Undead. Maybe a mixture of both.

I tried to be gentle, but I ended up letting Seely fall into an unceremonious lump on the ground, his head hitting the side of a tree.

"Oh my god, Seely, I'm so sorry. Are you—"

"If you ask me if I'm okay again, Gold," Seely rasped, "I might just have to tell you the truth."

I knelt beside him and felt his head. He was burning up, with a thin sheen of sweat covering his forehead. The questions I'd been avoiding began bubbling up my throat. I couldn't avoid the fact that Seely was hurt and only getting worse the longer we had to walk. He could die here, and I would not let that happen.

"Let me see your rib, lift up your shirt."

Seely just looked at me, his eyes a little glazed. He didn't make a move to lift his shirt, so I did.

"Fine."

I grabbed the hem of his shirt and pulled it loose from the holster that was still around his waist. We'd remembered to grab his dagger when we'd begun our trek through the forest, so it was securely placed by his side. Seely still held the side of his body as I tried to pull up his shirt to look. I tugged at it lightly, but his hand only tightened around his side.

"Seely," I began, looking him in the eyes, "you have to let me see. Maybe it isn't so bad. Just let me look."

I tugged at the shirt again, but he still held tight to his side. I was getting frustrated, but even more than that I could feel my concern growing. What could be so bad that Seely didn't even want me to look? What did he know that I didn't know? What was he keeping from me?

"Seely." I could feel my panic rising and I took a deep breath to keep it at bay. "Let me see."

He was staring at me, looking tired and grimy and half dead, but very determined.

"I'm stronger than you," I said. "Don't make me prove it."

His lips quirked a little at that, but he held fast.

"I'm fine, Gold. I just need to rest a minute. Don't worry about my side."

"You not wanting me to see it makes me want to see it even more, you know that right?"

"Of course, I know that," his smile was more genuine now. "I also know you're not stronger than me."

I shook my head but answered his smile with my own. At the same time, I placed my other hand over the one that held his side.

"I have to see, I'm sorry."

Seely looked at me intently, his eyes watery and glazed. He sighed and let me remove his hand. When I lifted his hem, I wished he hadn't allowed me to look at all.

Seely's rib wasn't broken.

Actually, he'd been shot.

Chapter Eighteen

"OH MY GOD."

I whispered the words, my mind not quite comprehending what I was seeing. Seely had been *shot*? But how?

"How—"

"It must have been sometime between you jumping in between me and Geordan and the others showing up at the door. I guess they shot first and asked questions later." He shrugged. "We must not have Dissipated fast enough to avoid the bullets all together."

I resisted the urge to punch him.

"How could you not tell me? We've been trekking for miles in what is basically a jungle—"

"A bit of an exaggeration."

"...and you're over here bleeding from a bullet wound. You could die, Seely."

"That's probably another exaggeration." He grunted, straightening up on the tree and pulling his shirt back down. "I've had worse, Gold. I'm still breathing, and I can keep going until we find this mythical brook you seem to be able to hear. Though I have to say I'm not convinced."

I was still looking at his side where the wound was, but at those words I whipped my gaze to his face.

"Wait, you can't hear anything at all?"

When we first started walking, I could hear the faint tinkling of moving water. Now that we'd been walking in the direction of the noise, it sounded like the water should be right here. It was almost roaring to my ears.

My Undead ears.

"Is that something that... people," I almost choked on the word, "like me can do?"

Seely smiled at my obvious confusion.

"If you're asking me if Undead have superhuman hearing, the answer would be yes. But, like I told you before, I don't really know what you are. I guess we can reason that you must have the Undead hearing abilities. Or you're just insane." He shrugged again. "Either way, this was all wishful thinking on my part."

"Seely, you're an idiot."

I leaned forward again and lifted his shirt, and this time he didn't stop me.

The wound wasn't deep, more of a graze than an actual bullet wound. The gash was deeply red with bruises already forming around it. There was also a strange, spidering pattern going out from the wound in a grotesque, veiny scene. He may be breathing and staggering along, but he was not okay. I knew he couldn't go on for much longer, and I knew I needed to find help soon. I at least needed to find some water.

"What are you thinking about?"

Seely's voice was quiet, and when I looked at him, I saw that his eyes were even glossier than before, and his head was resting limply against the tree.

I moved in closer to him, brushing the hair from his forehead and feeling the sweat and heat coming from his skin.

"I'm thinking first about how you're stupid for not telling me you were this hurt. I'm thinking second that you're not going to make it much farther without water and medicine, and I'm thinking third that…" I looked from Seely to the trees beyond us. There was water so close, I could feel it. I could definitely hear it, but I could also taste it in the air. I knew it had to be just beyond that next ridge.

"I'm thinking that you're not going to like this, but I'm about to carry you to that water. It can't be more than half a mile away. Do you feel that, in the air? The rise in humidity? We're so close."

Seely laughed.

"You're not carrying me, Gold, I'm…"

He fell forward with those words, slumped almost completely to the ground before I caught him.

"If you tell me you're fine one more time, I'm going to kill you before that bullet wound can."

"How romantic."

Seely's eyes were getting more and more glassy, even in the short time I held his face in my hands. I saw him trying to close his eyes and I shook him awake.

"Stay with me, Seely. You can't go to sleep now, not yet."

If he went to sleep, I had the sinking feeling that he would never wake up again. And if he never woke up again, before we even had a chance…

I pushed the thoughts from my head before I could begin to panic. At the same time, I stood and hauled Seely to his feet. He groaned but opened his eyes more than he had before.

"Can you walk, or do I need to pick you up? I don't know much, or anything, about who or what I am either, but I know I can carry you." I grabbed his chin as his head lolled a little to the side. "Hey. Look at me, Seely. Can you walk?"

He didn't answer, just nodded, but I slung his arm over my shoulders and wrapped both arms around him. I lifted until he was barely supporting any of his weight at all, and I began walking. His weight was like nothing to me. Obviously, I could tell it was there, but it was like carrying a small bag of groceries or a couple of books. I could go for a while this way, though I hoped I was right, and the brook would be just over the next hill. Seely didn't have a lot of time.

We walked forward, step by step, and I thought about what was going to happen next.

So, say we find water in just a few paces. Then what? Will it be magical water that heals bullet wounds and keeps people from dying from their injuries? I could believe in a lot of things after the past few days, but that seemed way too good to be true. Even if we found water soon, I wasn't sure I would be enough to save Seely. I could feel my thoughts spiraling down that hole of what-ifs, and I turned all my concentration on listening to Seely's ragged breathing. As long as he was breathing, we were still okay. As long as he was breathing… As long as he was breathing.

Suddenly, there was a break in the trees. I couldn't hear anything but the stream that I knew lay beyond the next tree line. I picked up the pace, basically dragging Seely as I half staggered, half sprinted towards the sound.

We broke through the trees and what I saw was nothing short of an oasis. A pool of crystal-clear water sat in front of us, bubbling from an invisible spring somewhere underneath the mass of the pond. It was way better than a brook. A freshness filled my senses, cool and refreshing, almost like taking a big drink of water when you wake up thirsty at three in the morning.

"Seely! It's here. We made it."

I sounded out of breath, though I didn't feel tired. I figured it was because of the relief I felt at finally reaching some sort of haven.

It didn't escape my notice, however, that Seely didn't answer me. I realized then that he had gone completely limp around me. As it turned out, I was carrying him, just like I promised I would.

"Seely? *Seely*."

The distress was clear in my voice as I walked forward a few more steps, directly into the water. I didn't care about the feeling of the mud and icy water seeping into my boots and wetting the hem of my leggings. I didn't care about anything at that moment.

I lowered Seely into the icy water, praying over and over again that he would open his eyes.

"Please, please, please. Please don't be dead. Please don't do this to me."

His mouth was slack, and his eyes were closed. His face was devoid of color. He *looked* dead, though

I could hear the slight flutter of his heart. A *very* slight flutter.

I held him in the water and used the hem of my shirt to wipe away the dust and blood that remained on his face. I felt tears falling down my face as I looked around frantically.

There was absolutely nothing I could do. We were sitting in an oasis, but water wasn't a miracle worker. I lifted Seely's shirt to look at the wound and it had only gotten worse. The maze of veins leading away from the bullet wound were snaking their way all the way up to his neck now. They looked so odd and technical and…

I realized with a start that it wasn't the wound from the bullet that was going to kill him. The bullet was laced with some kind of poison.

"No," I said. The word came out as a broken sob.

I was crying now, tears flowing freely as I hugged Seely tightly. He was so cold, his breath slow, his heartbeat growing fainter by the minute. We needed a miracle, and I knew we weren't going to get it.

I would kill them. I would go back to that base and burn it and everyone in it to the ground. I would make them wish they never brought me back to the AAUD, never used me as bait, and that they had killed me ten times over when they had the chance these past couple of years.

They would pay for this. All of them.

When I was done with them, the AAUD would be nothing but a memory of an organization that existed once upon a time.

I sat there, holding Seely and crying, utterly giving up any hope of saving him, so I didn't hear them come up behind us. I didn't know they were there until I heard the sound of a gun cocking right behind my head.

I snapped my head up. I was still holding Seely, and he was still breathing, but I knew it was only a matter of time.

"What do you want to do with them?" A male voice said.

"That one doesn't look like he has much time. Maybe we should just kill them now?" It was a female who spoke that time.

"Please," I said, my voice quiet. "You have to help him."

There was silence behind me, then. I didn't know how many people were there, what they looked like, or what they wanted. I just knew I had one chance and I had to take it.

"Do it."

A woman's voice was the last thing I heard before something blasted the back of my head and the world went black.

"Who do you think they are?"

"I don't know. The boy is wearing an AAUD uniform, but he was also shot by one of their bullets. I'm not sure who they are or what they did to deserve that. They must be rogues."

"So, Father is really going to like them."

"Exactly."

There was a rush of hushed laughter as the girls continued speaking. I squeezed my eyes shut once before opening them to the dim light of whatever room I was in. There was a light directly above me, but it was shut off. There was a glow in the room that

I thought may be coming from some sort of fireplace. It had the movement of fire, at least.

The ceiling was made up of wooden slats, and I thought I was in a cabin or something like it. The air felt a little damp, almost like a cave, though it was very warm in the room. I thought I could smell coffee somewhere in the air. I didn't have any memory of how I got there, but I did remember the assault, whatever it was.

And Seely.

I sat up quickly, and this time I didn't sway. I did wince, though, as I felt a sharp pain in the back of my head. They had hit me with something, I guessed. Something hard enough to knock me out so they could drag me to this cabin. But what was strong enough to knock out an Undead with one blow? And who? Maybe it was just that whatever I was, was weaker than your run-of-the-mill Undead.

The back of my head was tender as I pressed on it. I turned slightly to the right and saw two young girls staring at me with wide eyes. They were sitting in wicker chairs, just a couple feet from the bed I was on. I swung my legs over the side to sit up fully, and the girls flinched just a little bit. I could touch them if I reached my arm out far enough.

"Um, hi," I said.

They continued to stare at me, looking like they'd just seen a ghost.

"Uh, I'm Alyssa. Can you tell me what happened to the boy I came here with? Where is he?"

They looked at each other, and it reminded me of Stella and me and our silent communication. I felt a pang of sadness twist my stomach. I would worry about that *after* I knew if Seely was okay. He was the one who'd been shot, not me or Stella. For all I knew, she was safely back at the AAUD, in the lab, figuring out a way to kill me. I was oddly comforted by that.

The girls in front of me turned away from each other and back to me. They couldn't have been more than twelve or thirteen, and while they looked similar, I didn't think they were twins. They both had the same strawberry-blonde hair and mousy features, with deep-set eyes that were dark blue in this light, but the girl on the right had lost some of the baby fat that seemed to still round the other's features. I thought she was probably older.

"Can you take me to him? Please?"

"We can't take you to him, yet. Not without Katrine." The one I thought was older spoke to me first. She seemed more confident and surer of herself than she looked in the beginning. She held her head high, nose pointed slightly to the ceiling like she was trying to exert her limited power. I got the feeling she wasn't really scared of me, just scared of doing or saying the wrong thing in general. I could understand that.

"Katrine?" I asked.

"She should be here any minute. She probably knows you're awake by now." The one on the left spoke to me then. I wondered how Katrine would know anything about me being awake, but I decided that probably wasn't the most important thing I needed to find out just then.

"Um, right. But Seely, is he…," I almost choked on the words. Swallowing down the tears that threatened to spill over, I said, "Is he alive?"

Rather than answer my question, the girls just looked at each other again. I was getting annoyed, verging on angry, the heat already building in my chest, and I didn't want to lose control in front of these girls. Whatever had happened, I didn't think it was their fault.

Almost against my will, I reached out and grabbed the arm of the older girl. Her chair was the closest to the bed, her arm just within my reach as I sat on the edge of it.

"You don't have to tell me anything about who you are or where I am," I said, "but please answer the question." My voice came out harsher than I intended it to, and the girl looked down at her arm where my hand grasped it. Her eyes were wide again. She was afraid of me.

I jerked my hand back and leaned back on the headboard of the bed.

"I'm sorry."

The words were whispers, and I felt exhausted. He was dead, I knew it. She would have answered me by now if he wasn't. Seely was dead, he was dead, he was—

"He's not dead." It was the younger girl who spoke that time. "He's okay. He's right next door. Max is watching him."

I let out a breath I didn't know I had been holding and leaned my head back on the wall. The relief I felt was short-lived as I jumped from the pain as my head met the solidness of the headboard. I forgot about the injury I'd received in coming to this place. I reached my hand up again and pressed it to the wound gently. It hurt, but the pain was lessening the longer I was awake.

"What did you guys do to me?"

"Max told us to tell you he's sorry about that," the older one told me. "It was Katrine's call. They were out on a hunt, and they came across you both at the pond. Max shot you so we could bring you back here.

I'm Sammy, by the way, and this is Lilah." Sammy held out her hand for a handshake.

The way she said that, so nonchalant, I wasn't sure I heard it right.

"I'm sorry… you said he—he what? He *shot me?*"

My voice went up in pitch at the end of the question. How and why would they shoot me? They couldn't know I was Undead, right? *How* would they know that when they'd only seen me crying in the water with Seely? The only explanation I could come up with was that they had intended to kill me. So why did they bring us back here and apparently nurse Seely back to health?

"He said he was sorry about that. They had to get you back here and apparently you weren't very stable when they came across you." The younger one, Lilah, was the one who said that to me. Her sister, Sammy, only nodded. "Katrine will explain everything when she gets back, just wait a minute.

But I couldn't wait even another second. These people, whoever they were, had not only kidnapped us and brought us here, but they'd kidnapped me to do it. As much as I wanted to believe these girls and I thought they seemed like they had good intentions, I couldn't just sit there and take their words for it that Seely was okay.

I swung my legs off the side of the bed and stood. Again, my head didn't rush, and I didn't sway. I realized I was feeling stronger with every passing day. I fleetingly wondered whether or not that was because of the lack of sedation since Seely had come and gotten me three days ago. Four days ago? I realized I didn't know how long I'd been out. Or if any time had passed when Seely and I Dissipated out of the AAUD. I had no idea how any of this worked.

The girls looked a little scared, maybe even nervous, as I stood there. I looked at them, trying to be open and take away any fear they may have. I didn't want them to fear me, and their faces reminded me of the way Seth and the twins had looked at me the last time I'd seen them. Was that just yesterday?

"I have to see him," I said, finally. "I'm not going to hurt you. Please just tell me which way to go."

At the same time, the girls pointed to the door on the wall to my left.

"Turn right and it's the next door," Sammy said, her voice quiet.

"Thank you," I said, smiling at them. I thought their faces warmed a little at that gesture, and that made me feel better.

I turned to the door and twisted the knob, pulling it open to a narrow hallway. Directly in front of me was a wall with a portrait of a lake or a pond with a meadow surrounding it. In normal circumstances, I may have stood there for a minute or two and contemplated the colors and brush strokes. These, however, were not normal circumstances, and I knew Seely was just a little way down the hallway.

Turning to my right, I saw the door I assumed Sammy was talking about. It wasn't guarded, and I couldn't see any light coming from under it. There may have been some firelight, but that was all. I could hear breathing—two people were breathing on the other side of the door.

Okay, so there were two people breathing. I prayed that one of them was Seely, but either way I might have to fight my way in there. The back of my head throbbed dully, though I was able to pretty much tune it out. The fact that I had been shot in the back of the head and was still breathing? I would have to unpack that later. I needed to see Seely, now.

I turned the knob, and, to my surprise, it opened with a soft click. I could hear one of the people inside hitch their breath a little. So, they'd heard me entering. Good.

I pushed the door open wider and stepped into the dimly lit room. Just as I'd thought, there was no electrical light on in the house, only the fireplace blazed. It was almost uncomfortably warm, and I wondered why that was. I turned my attention from the fireplace to the small bed that sat in the far-right corner of the room. There was a human lying there, that was for sure. I could smell the faint salty scent of sweat and something else that made my stomach twist. Sickness, I thought. He smelled like sickness. I looked back at the fireplace, realizing he must be going through some kind of fever. That was why they had the fire roaring so high, I guessed, to combat the chills that often accompany a fever.

I walked over to the person on the bed. His dark curls fell over his face, but the closer I got I knew it was him, without a doubt.

He smelled like cinnamon.

I made it across the room in two long strides, then, and I reached my hand out to move his hair from his forehead. Seely was lying on his stomach with his arms and legs sprawled out over the small bed. He looked peaceful, sleeping there, looking beautiful, and breathing. I only really cared that he was breathing.

I touched his forehead and noticed it was damp with sweat. His skin was warm, but not burning with fever. It just felt warm like it would be if it were warmed by a fire, which it definitely was. The room was sweltering.

"Who left the fire like this?"

I realized I'd wondered the question aloud when I heard a soft gasp come from the far-left corner of the room.

Chapter Nineteen

I TURNED AROUND SO QUICKLY, I ALMOST took Seely with me. Thankfully, he remained on the bed and asleep.

"Who are you?"

The boy stood in the corner of the room, right where the door swung open upon entrance. I hadn't seen him as he hid in the shadows, and I cursed myself for being so stupid. I knew I heard two sets of heartbeats, two people breathing, and yet I forgot everything about stealth as soon as I entered and saw that Seely was alive. I could easily be dead by now, I thought. A little fatalist, maybe, but not far off. I mean, I *had* just been shot in the back of the head, and I still wasn't sure if they even knew what I was or if they just got lucky and didn't end up killing me. Then again, I'd lived through being shot in the head so maybe it would take a little more to kill me.

I didn't want to worry about that then. Instead, I just stared at the boy standing in the corner. He was shadowed where he stood, but I could see flickers of his person. He had the same light hair as the girls that I'd awoken to in my room just minutes ago, and I thought maybe they were siblings.

"What's your name?"

He hadn't answered my first question, so I tried again with that one. He just stared at me like I was a ghost. And maybe I was. His name came back into my memory just then.

"Max?" I saw the look of recognition on his face, and I knew I was right. This was the boy who the girls said shot me in the head. To his credit, I guess, they did say he was sorry.

"Max, I'm not angry with you for shooting me. The girls told me you were sorry, that you were just following orders, and I understand that. Sometimes we have to follow orders that we don't totally agree with."

Max stepped forward slightly, though I couldn't tell if I was coaxing him out with my words, or if he was getting ready to run. I didn't know whether either one of them were good.

I could see, though, as he stepped more into the light, that he looked to be about my age. Probably somewhere between seventeen and nineteen. He had one of those faces that could either be fifteen or twenty-five, and I couldn't tell in such low light.

Maybe I didn't get the super sight along with the super hearing. That sucked, but that was my luck.

I tried to speak to Max again.

"I just came here to make sure Seely was okay." I gestured to the shape on the bed behind me. I kept silent tabs on the sound of his breathing and the steady rhythm of his heart. "And now I see that he's fine. So, um, that's great." I looked around at the tiny room. There was nothing but the bed, occupied by Seely, the fireplace that continued to blaze bright and hot, and I wiped my palms on my leggings as they started sweating. There was a small chair that sat a few feet from the bed. There was a basin of water beside Seely's bed with a washcloth laying over the side. I assumed it had been used to help regulate his temperature to get his temperature under control. That thought made my stomach twist slightly. How bad had his injury really been?

"Can you tell me what happened?"

Max just continued to stare at me from across the room. I stepped forward, reaching an arm out in a gesture that I thought was welcoming and inviting, but at my move he slammed his back to the wall behind him.

"Please," he rasped, "don't hurt me."

I could see his fear plainly on his face. I could feel it. I could *taste* it. It hit me like a knife in all my senses, and I was taken aback by it. I froze my steps right where I was.

"I'm not going to hurt you."

I tried to make my voice as calm and soothing as possible, but it didn't matter. With every passing second, Max's heart raced faster and faster. I was starting to become a little worried about his health at that point. Surely hearts weren't supposed to go that fast?

"Max, I need you to slow your heart down. Please just take a couple of deep breaths." I stepped backwards until the backs of my legs brushed against the bed where Seely still slept. I could tell he was still out from the steadiness of his heart and his breathing. I was grateful for that. I didn't want to have to divide my attention between the boy in the corner and Seely if he woke up.

I thought I heard his heart slow a little, but it wasn't enough. I knew he was close to passing out or screaming, or both, neither of which I really wanted to happen. I didn't know who would come to check on us if Max did decide to scream for help, but I also didn't want to potentially be shot again, even if it didn't kill me. The back of my head pulsed with the faint pain when I thought about it. I may not have been angry with the boy standing in front of me, but I was definitely annoyed at the entire situation.

And who was this Katrine that the girls were talking about? How did she know I was Undead at first glance, if she even did? Why would she give the order to shoot me when she didn't know who I was?

I thought about what it might have looked like, me sitting in the water with Seely. His face was covered with blood and dirt, and he was barely breathing by the time they snuck up behind us. I was a sobbing, blubbering mess just sitting there helpless, begging for someone, anyone to save him.

I shook my head to clear it of my reverie. It didn't matter how we got here, all that mattered was that we were here, now. Max was still staring at me like I was a hideous creature.

Well, I guess I was now that I thought about it. I wasn't human, at least. I couldn't blame him for being afraid of me, I just wished he would answer just one question.

"Can you tell me where I am, Max?"

Max continued to stare at me. I watched as he cut his eyes from me to Seely sleeping behind me, and then over to his right, in the direction of the door. I sighed. It didn't seem like he was going to tell me anything.

In the blink of an eye, Max darted for the door. I was a little stunned, and I watched him wrench open the door and attempt to run out.

The only problem with his plan was that there was a woman standing in the doorway that he unceremoniously crashed into.

The two figures fell to the ground with a huff of air and a grunt, though I couldn't tell which noise came from who.

I was still frozen in front of Seely, who drew out a long snore, but didn't move otherwise. How in the world was he sleeping through all of this? Maybe he was always a heavy sleeper and that was just another thing I couldn't remember. My face flushed a little bit at the thought that I might know any intimate detail about him, and I pushed it away.

The woman that Max had crashed into was currently trying to untangle her legs from his. She was wearing leggings with a shirt that had two long flaps, one on the front and another on the back. Her skin was a honey brown and her hair fell into waves almost as dark as Seely's. I also noticed she had a nose ring that was glittering on the left side of her face.

From what I could see of her face in this light, she was a beautiful woman. She had full lips that were shaded a deep red, and I could see the white teeth housed behind them. Her nose was strong and sharp, but it fit her face perfectly.

She also looked at Max, not with anger or frustration at what he'd done by running into her and knocking her down, but with fondness and understanding and something that I might even describe as love.

Something twisted in my stomach, and I wasn't sure what to do with the feeling. I wasn't sure where it was coming from.

"Max, this is why we don't run in the hallway, remember?"

The woman laughed.

"I'm so s-sorry, Katrine. I didn't mean to—"

"I know, Max, relax. Go and find your sisters. I need their help with dinner now that our guest is awake, it seems."

So, this was Katrine. Interesting.

My gaze turned more critically towards her as she finally rose from the ground. This was the woman who had ordered Max to shoot me in the head, and I wasn't going to forget that or let my guard down any time soon. I felt my eyes narrow ever so slightly as I watched Katrine walk through the door. I shifted so I was closer to Seely, shielding his head from any bullets that may come its way.

You never knew around here, apparently.

Katrine took two more steps before stopping about three feet away from me. She held out her hands with the palms facing towards me, obviously trying to show she was unarmed and didn't mean to harm me. I didn't really believe her, but my body relaxed a bit even as I moved closer to Seely. My hand was brushing his hair now as I stood over him. He still didn't stir, but I could hear that he was breathing deeply, and his heart was pumping healthily.

"Hi. Alyssa, right?" She asked me the question, but I didn't venture an answer. "Okay, that's fine. You don't have to answer me. I'm Katrine Sanders and this is my home." She gestured to the door where Max had officially escaped and, I guessed, ran down the hallway to get his sisters. "Max and the girls are not my biological children, but I do claim them as my own. If we're all here together, we might as well be a family, right?" She laughed, and the sound was full of some secret I wasn't privy to. "We have our own stories that you can know if you choose to listen to them later, but right now we need to talk about why exactly you're here."

"You shot me."

It was the first thing I said to her, and it wasn't an answer to any question she asked. It wasn't even a question itself, just a statement of fact. It was the thing mostly on my mind, and I had apparently lost all willpower when it came to sifting carefully through my thoughts and choosing what to say. The shock of finding myself in a strange place with strange people apparently made me bold and impulsive.

Katrine only smiled at me, and I thought she looked a little sheepish. I thought maybe she should at least look sorrier.

"Technically, I didn't shoot you. But I did give the order. I'm sorry about that, I know it can't be too comfortable to receive that kind of wound."

Not comfortable? I reached up and felt the bullet wound on the back of my head. Actually, I thought it had felt larger when I first woke up. I could have sworn it was smaller now, and the skin wasn't as tender now as it had been even minutes before. Weird, but I was beginning to expect that by now.

"You should be feeling better by now, right?" I snapped my attention back to her as she spoke again and dropped my hand from my head. "Whatever sedation they gave you at the AAUD seems to also slow your Undead processes, but I think it's gradually wearing off." She gestured to Seely. "Your blood was clean enough to save your boyfriend, anyway."

I followed to where she gestured and where Seely slept so soundly. I had wondered why or how he slept so soundly, through yelling and Max tackling Katrine and... oh my god, what had she said?

"My... blood?" I looked from Seely's sleeping face to Katrine's carefully blank one. "What exactly do you mean by that?"

I worked hard to keep my voice even, but I knew I wasn't fooling her. My mind was taking me to places I wasn't sure I wanted to go, and I could feel how easy it would be to fall into a spiral, and I thought it would probably be a good idea to at least wait for that until I heard Katrine's answer. Whatever it may be.

Katrine looked from me to Seely and back again with what I thought might be pity, and I felt a flame brewing underneath my skin. I couldn't lose it here and now, but if she looked at me like I was a lost puppy for much longer I might just have to retaliate for the shot to my head.

I crossed my arms and felt my face meld into a glare. "Are you going to answer the question? Or should I ask a different one?"

Katrine smiled a little at that. "You didn't answer mine either, remember?"

She was right about that, though I wasn't going to admit it. I wasn't worried about what was fair here.

"That's different. I'm at your mercy and I don't know who you are. What if I tell you my name and you use it to, I don't know, blackmail me? Hold me for ransom?"

She chuckled quietly and I felt that anger flare again.

"From what we could tell, you guys were running away from the AAUD, and you were completely alone. From the state he was in when we found you, it doesn't seem like anyone you left wants to find you. And knowing what you are? I'm guessing you were more of an experiment to them than anything they would really value. I don't think we would get much for you if we turned you over." She was still smiling, perfectly sweet and carefully cautious, but I could feel that she was trying to get under my skin. I didn't really know why, maybe she was trying to push me to see what I could do? Maybe she wanted a reason to get rid of me? Either way, I wasn't going to give her the satisfaction of any of it. Little did she know, Mr. Evanson would probably pay her extremely well to hand me over to him. Well, if she thought I was worth nothing to the AAUD, I definitely wasn't going to correct her. With my heart beginning to race and my blood pumping icy heat through my body, I smiled at her.

"You're probably right," was all I said.

We stood there for a moment, not speaking, just assessing each other. We were like lionesses protecting our pride and waiting to see who would back down first. Whom the other could devour first.

Finally, Katrine cleared her throat. I felt a little smugness at making her squirm, even just a little bit, but I kept the smile off my face.

"Maybe we could go into the next room and talk?" She gestured to Seely again and I thought I would like very much if she would leave him out of this, out of her brain, and out of whatever she was talking to me about. I didn't like the way I knew he was at her mercy too and the people who answered to her if I left him in here alone.

On the other hand, I needed answers. And the logical part of my brain pointed out that, if they wanted us dead, they would have killed us instead of giving us places to rest and recover. I pushed aside the knowledge that they had been the ones to inflict my injury in the first place. They *had* saved Seely. He would be okay for a few minutes, surely.

And if he wasn't, no one was going to walk out of here.

I nodded at Katrine, and she motioned to the door with her right arm. I just stared at her for a second because she truly had to be crazy if she thought I was going to walk away with my back to her, especially after she shot me. Or at least made the call for someone else, Max, to shoot me. I didn't really think that qualifier mattered.

She sighed after a few seconds and nodded. "I see. Of course. Just follow me."

I waited until she had taken a few steps and was about to walk out the door before I made a move to follow her. There was another man in the hallway. He had the same blonde hair as the girls and Max, though this guy wasn't scared of me at all. In fact, he smiled so widely at me, I thought maybe there was something on my face or in my teeth that was funny. He seemed almost too excited to see me, and I had a feeling there was some joke I wasn't in on. I quickly ran a tongue over my teeth and stared at the man as I passed him. When I turned to my left to walk down the hallway, I saw that Katrine had stopped and was waiting for something.

"Sean," she called out to the man, "could you shut the door please? Our guest still needs his rest, and I don't want to disturb him."

The man was already closing the door before she'd finished the sentence, ahead of her thoughts.

"Of course, Kat. I also called for some tea from Bernard to be brought into the sitting room. I thought you may need some refreshments," he looked at me, then, "but I'm not sure… I mean, I don't know what you eat?"

I didn't understand where he was going for a moment, and then I remembered what I was.

"I'm not sure, honestly." I shrugged. "As far as I know, I just eat normal food."

The man nodded, his features smoothing from where they'd gone tight with worry about my diet. He took a couple of steps down the hallway to bring himself closer to me and he thrust out his hand.

"I'm Sean. Very nice to meet you, Miss…" He looked around me to Katrine, obviously waiting for her to tell him my name. I remembered I hadn't given it to them.

"You can just call me Alyssa," I said.

Sean nodded, his hand still out. "Alyssa, then. We're happy to have you here."

I don't know why, but I took his hand. I felt nothing but warmth and welcoming coming from him, and I trusted him more than Katrine almost immediately. There was something about Sean that screamed openness at me, whereas Katrine basically had the words "I have too many secrets, don't even ask" tattooed across her forehead.

I heard Katrine clear her throat behind me.

"This way please, then, Alyssa. We'll be more comfortable in here."

I followed her down the hallway just a few more steps, noticing the cabin wasn't that large from what I could see. We reached the end of the corridor in just a few feet and turned to walk through an opening on the right. I had yet to see any windows, so I wasn't sure what time of day it was. The corridor was dark, but without a way to see outside it could have been any time.

We entered a sitting room that seemed to double as a library. There were shelves along three of the four walls, the only bare wall being the one with the door. The shelves were lined with worn and weathered books of every shape and size. They seemed to be strewn along the built-ins without rhyme or reason, but I was a reader too and I knew that anyone who had this many books most likely knew exactly where to find the specific book they were looking for. I smiled a little at that, that sense of normalcy.

The only furniture in the room were two sofas that faced each other in the middle of the space, both overstuffed and too large for the size of the room with a small table in between. There was barely any room around the sides to walk around, and it didn't even look like my legs would fit between the table and the couch to sit. I thought you would probably have a hard time getting to a book on the lower shelves that were close to the ground and hidden behind the backs of the couches. The books were basically furniture themselves, there were so many of them. Though the room was cluttered and small, it felt homier and more comfortable than cramped.

Katrine sat on one of the couches as I watched Sean pull out a door that had been flush to the wall before. He looked at Katrine and gave her a brief nod before sliding the door from one side to the other, effectively shutting us in.

I turned to Katrine, and she was pouring some tea I hadn't noticed into two cups already splashed with milk and sugar.

"So," she said, setting the teapot down and placing a small spoon on each saucer, "do you want to tell me what happened to bring you here or would you like me to tell you the conclusions I've drawn myself?"

She picked up one of the saucers and handed it to me, and I took it without much hesitation. I was unsure about Katrine, but… it was tea. And I *was* thirsty. And I also figured that she could have killed me already if she really wanted to. What choice did I have but to choose to trust her while I was stuck in an unknown place with nowhere else to go?

I stirred the tea and took a sip. It wasn't as good as the cups I'd gotten from Seely, but it was good enough.

"I think you have some things to answer, too. Like, why did you shoot me in the head? How could you possibly know I wouldn't die from a wound like that? And what were you talking about, giving Seely my blood?"

"That's a lot of questions, Alyssa. I also haven't forgotten that you didn't actually answer any of *my* questions yet, either. You didn't even tell me your name, you told Sean." She smiled as she took a sip of her own tea.

"That's true," I conceded, "but the way I see it, your information is just going to give me some peace of mind while my information could be a matter of life or death."

I took another sip of tea, letting the warmth fill my chest. I welcomed this warmth, as opposed to the fire that sometimes threatened to explode out of me.

"I'll tell you my story if you answer my questions," I said.

I'd offered that up before I meant to. Again, I cursed myself for not thinking through my decisions. Was it really a good idea to give this woman information that could get both me and Seely killed? What if she didn't really know anything about the AAUD and she only needed some information from me to destroy the whole compound with my family in it? I wouldn't be sad to see Mr. Evanson go, truthfully.

But I couldn't see another way. I needed to know where I was and who these people were, and I needed to know what happened to us. I needed answers that only Katrine could give me, so I would offer her all I had, which was my own story.

I watched Katrine's face as she pursed her lips a little, contemplating my offer.

"Okay, Alyssa," she said after a moment. "I'll answer your questions if you then answer mine. Deal?"

"Deal."

Katrine took another sip of her tea, and she smiled a little as she sat the cup and saucer back down on the table between us.

Gesturing to me with her hand, she said, "What's your first question?"

I thought about what I really wanted to know the most, and I settled on what she meant by Seely being healed by my blood.

"You told me that you... healed Seely. With my blood." I squirmed a little bit under the pressure of the question. "What exactly did you mean by that?"

"That question kind of bleeds into another one I believe you asked: how did I know what you were? If you don't mind, I'll combine those together and kill two birds with one stone, so to speak." She smiled a little wider at me and then leaned back into the high back of the couch, getting comfortable.

"I guessed at what you were because, when we found you and the boy, you were… glowing. Like a fire. Though, it was strange because the water around you had begun to freeze."

I thought about that… hadn't I noticed how cold the water was, even though it was sitting in the middle of the late summer sun? I also thought about how I'd felt in the lab back at the AAUD: like there was light coming out of me. Could that really be true?

"I didn't know for one hundred percent certain, but I made an educated guess and took a calculated risk. I've only heard stories about creatures like you, though. I haven't ever seen one in real life." She took another sip from her tea.

"So, you didn't know what I was, and you still shot me in the head? That doesn't really make me feel any better about being trapped here." I tried to ignore the qualifier of whatever I was. I didn't want to think about the reason I'd been turned into this thing.

Katrine held up a finger.

"First, you're not trapped. We're mutually sharing information my family and I take care of your friend who is recovering in that room there." She jerked her head in the direction of Seely's room and held up a second finger, like she was counting the reasons. As if I couldn't understand the words that were coming out of her mouth.

"Second, I didn't shoot you. I gave the order. Which I understand is not that much different, but it's also not the same."

I frowned at her. It wasn't different.

"Semantics," I mumbled.

"Don't you want to know more about how I made that educated guess about what kind of creature you are, Alyssa?"

I frowned deeper.

"Didn't you just tell me? Because I was… glowing? Or on fire or ice or whatever?"

Katrine nodded.

"Yes, but that's not normal for an Undead. I've seen plenty of them, but never one like you. Most of you don't have special abilities other than the occasional Dissipating and super-human senses." Her brows creased slightly. "Shouldn't you know that, especially since you're one of them?"

I felt my face fall. I should know that, I guess, because I *was* one of them. The fact of the matter was that I didn't know anything. All I knew was what other people told me. I was an Undead, and that was a fact I couldn't just ignore any longer. I mean, I'd been shot in the head and lived, which wasn't something that a normal human could do. I had been able to basically carry Seely for miles without getting tired or even registering much weight on his part. These people had apparently given my blood to help heal him…

"I don't know much of anything, if I'm being honest," I said, my voice quiet and barely steady. I focused on the growing hum of warmth in my chest that wasn't from the tea, breathing into the feeling. "According to Seely, I woke up three days ago—or maybe it's four now?" My brows furrowed. "I'm actually not sure how long I've been here. But anyway, I woke up a few days ago and I thought I knew who I was, but it turns out I didn't."

Katrine just listened intently, nodding as I spoke. She looked interested in what I had to say, maybe even a little concerned. It was oddly comforting, though I still felt myself wanting to shrink under her gaze.

"I suspected as much, especially when you didn't even attempt to fight back when we found you at the pond. If you knew what you could do you probably would have blasted us all." She laughed and it seemed genuine, though I wasn't really sure what was funny. "You may find that funnier later," she said, clearing her throat.

"I wasn't for certain what kind of creature you were, but the only kinds of things I'd heard of that could have powers like yours are Undead. There are legends of a specific group of Undead who are… gifted, to say the least. I have many books about them, I'll have Sean put them together for you, if you want."

I didn't doubt she had books about every subject imaginable. I wondered, though, if Seely had any idea about these types of Undead. I wondered if he suspected that I may be one, and if so, why he hadn't told me anything about it.

"As for giving your blood to… Seely, was it?" Her voice sounded a little smug, and I realized I'd given her new information by saying Seely's name earlier. I silently cursed myself. I needed to be more careful with the information I let slip around these people. I still didn't know who they were or if I could trust them at all. Katrine smiled a smile that let me know she was amused that I thought I was really keeping secrets from her. "His wounds were severe, at least when we got to you both. He was minutes if not seconds away from death, and I know you didn't know what you were doing, but icing the water wasn't really helping him heal." She looked like she was contemplating something for a second. "Though actually, now that I think about it, the cold did slow his heart rate which may have given him enough time for us to get him back here and get him some of your blood.

"I don't know how much you truly know about the Undead. You say it's nothing at all or at least not much, but I'm not sure how much I can trust you just yet." Her mouth twitched in a semblance of a smile. "I know you were probably thinking the same of me. But this is my home and I have to keep my family safe no matter what. Whether or not you believe you're dangerous, you're still one of them."

The tone and finality of those words sent a chill down my spine. I was both a little afraid of her authority and the fact that she was right. Maybe I was wary of her, but she also had every right to be afraid of me. Looking at the bare facts, she probably had an even bigger reason to fear me than I did her. If I really needed or wanted to, I could probably fight her and win.

"Anyway, about your blood," Katrine continued, oblivious to the thoughts racing through my head. "The Undead have a property in their blood that allows them to heal humans. I'm not sure what the science is behind it, but I do know that I've yet to see a wound Undead blood can't fix, barring missing limbs or organs, of course. I haven't seen it replace biological material, just speed up and enhance the healing process.

"After we, um," she looked like she was searching for the right words, "collected you and were able to bring you back here, we retrieved about a pint of blood from you to give to your…" She looked at me with a little more scrutiny then, maybe even a little judgement. "Who is he to you, anyway?"

I stiffened.

"I don't think that information is super relevant to this conversation right now, is it?"

Katrine's lips pursed together in a line. It looked like she may be trying to hold in a smile, but her lips formed into a grimace.

"I suppose it isn't, Alyssa."

The truth was, I didn't know the answer to her question. I knew what Seely told me and who we were to each other, and I knew the feeling I got when I thought about him. I thought I believed I loved him before, and I wanted to believe he loved me now.

But the truth was I *didn't* know any of those things. I didn't even know who I was if I was being really honest with myself. And yes, he'd told me he loved me and used the present tense, but did he really love the girl I was now? Could I just trust that and accept it? I didn't think so.

So, I didn't want to answer her question for more reasons than just not trusting her in general.

"The important thing in all of this is that you and Seely are both here, safe, and on the mend. If we wanted to kill you, it would have been very easy to do while you were incapacitated." She reached for her tea again and took a small sip. Her face scrunched slightly, probably meaning it had gone cold in the duration of our conversation. "I also wouldn't have set my children up at posts by your bedside if I truly thought you were going to hurt us. Though, they are very capable of taking care of themselves." She smiled sweetly and I could tell how much she cared for and admired her children with just that expression. I assumed she and Sean were together, and I wondered at who their biological mother was.

I pushed that thought away quickly, though, because it wasn't really that important. What *was* important was what she'd said.

She was right. Seely and I were here, apparently safe, and I was fine despite my gunshot wound while Seely was apparently on the mend thanks to my blood. I still shuddered a little bit at that thought. Did they inject it into him, or did they make him drink it?

Wait, wasn't *I* supposed to drink it?

Nope, I wasn't going there yet. There wasn't time for the spiral I knew would accompany that thought if I let it sink deeper. And I felt fine for now. I was a little thirsty and lightheaded, but not hungry. Definitely not looking for any kind of blood at the moment.

"Alyssa," Katrine said my name slowly, letting the sound linger between us. It was like she was testing it out on her tongue, like maybe it didn't sound right to her or something.

"Yes?"

My voice was wary now, concerned at why she was acting so strange all of the sudden. Either way, I was not expecting the next thing that came out of her mouth.

"Would you like to talk about your mother?"

Chapter Twenty

"WHAT DO YOU KNOW ABOUT MY MOTHER?"

I didn't know what I'd been expecting her to say, but it wasn't that.

Who was this woman? I didn't know her, and I didn't think I'd ever seen her before. Even though my memory was definitely not reliable. Still, how did she know anything about my mother?

"I know you don't know who I am. In fact, we've never met before. Your mother and I started to grow apart around the time she and your father got together. We were childhood best friends. Inseparable." Her lips tightened and her smile turned a little bitter. "But you know, sometimes boyfriends

265

come between friendships. Especially when that boyfriend was a Gold, also a founder of the AAUD. I had my own business there, at the base, but there are a lot of secrets that come with being tied to a Founder. Sometimes best friends can't come before information, on either side." Some emotion passed across her face, but I wasn't sure if it was discomfort or regret. I didn't know her well enough to decide.

Katrine rang a bell that was sitting by the tea tray on the table between us. Within a few seconds, the door to the sitting room slid open and a short, older man sauntered through.

"Bernard, we're done with the tea. I trust the girls are helping with dinner?" She looked at me for a moment. "Our cook has been ill for a few days so we're helping out with some of the chores," Katrine qualified.

Bernard walked briskly, with a purpose. He made his way towards us and picked up the tray from the table that held the tea and our used cups.

"Of course, Katrine. Dinner is ready whenever you are." His eyes darted to me for a second and then back to Katrine. "And, uh... the other... *guest* is awake." He pointed at me. "He's asking for her. I'm afraid he might end up attacking Sean if we don't let him see that she's okay soon, ma'am."

Katrine sighed.

"You two are particularly violent, aren't you?" Her voice was playful, though she wasn't wrong. It seemed like we were both always ready to fight someone. My lips quirked up a little at that thought. Almost as quickly, I felt the blood drain from my face.

Seely was awake! And... presumably, okay? I jumped up from the couch where I sat. I would find out for myself.

"I'll go to him now. We don't need this to come to a brawl with Sean stuck in the middle."

I stepped between the couch and the coffee table to make my way to the door, but an arm reached out to stop me.

"Wait, Alyssa."

I looked at Katrine, incredulously.

"You're okay with your husband being attacked by my… by Seely?"

She pretended not to notice the hesitation, but I saw her lips purse and her eyes narrow slightly. I wondered what she was thinking about, especially when her expression made her look a little miffed.

"I'm definitely not okay with your Seely hurting Sean. I'm only asking you to let me come with you before you burst through the door and make his confusion worse." She was still gripping my arm, but I let her. "Just let me help you explain that you're not in danger, and then you can have your privacy, okay?"

She was probably right, I thought. If I came bursting through the door alone, who knew what Seely would think. I needed Katrine's calming and sure voice to ease the tension of the situation first, especially since she seemed to know a lot more about this whole situation than I did.

I nodded, and I felt her grip loosen a little. She let out a deep sigh and gave me a small smile.

"Thank you. Now let's go help the boys."

At those words, we heard a crash against what sounded like a body against a wall or a door, accompanied by a couple of loud grunts.

Katrine and I looked at each other for a second, and together we scooted through the small study and ran through the door and down the hall to the room where I'd seen Seely sleeping earlier.

Katrine got to the door first, her long shirt swaying around her trousers with the abruptness of her stop. She turned the knob and yanked the door open, and Sean toppled out with it.

"Sean!" Katrine bent down to help him up. I noticed his lip was bleeding and I wondered if Seely had hit him. The thought that he would actually punch someone he thought was holding me captive sent a warmth flooding through my chest.

I snapped out of it pretty quickly when I saw that raven-black mop of hair burst through the door with a rage that was barely contained. He stalked toward Katrine and Sean, looking murderous. His eyes were glazed and unseeing, and I was suddenly afraid of what he would do if he got his hands on them.

Luckily, the corridor was so small that I was standing between them and him before he could take another step. I wondered if that was part of my Undead abilities, or if I'd always been agile. I wouldn't know the answer either way, apparently.

"Hey, Seely, *stop*," I placed a hand on his chest and looked him square in the eyes. His pupils were dilated so large I could barely see the outline of green surrounding them. The color was so dark normally, but now…

I gasped as I looked at them. They looked like someone else's eyes.

Like Orthan's.

"What's wrong with him, Katrine?"

My voice was almost a whisper. Seely had stilled under my touch, but he was too still. His chest heaved slowly up and down, and his eyes bore into mine, unseeing. Had Seely been turned into an Undead and they just didn't think to tell me? I felt the heat flooding my chest and the ice beginning to run through my veins. I wasn't going to be able to stop myself from what happened next if someone didn't tell me what was going on right now.

I was looking at Seely, but I heard Katrine and Sean stand up from where they'd been on the floor.

"It's the blood," Katrine said.

I chanced a glance in her direction at that.

"My blood?"

She nodded.

"Sometimes it can have an effect on humans like this, especially when they've been through a trauma and needed quite a bit of blood for healing." I saw Katrine glance at Seely with a little bit of a grimace, and I looked back at him as well. His eyes had not left my face, and our eyes met again as soon as I turned. "He'll be okay, Alyssa. Just take him back into the room and try to talk to him. He'll come out of the stupor eventually, I just don't know when that may be." She paused for a second as Seely and I continued to stare at each other.

"I'll have dinner brought to the door in about twenty minutes. I won't have Bernard knock, just in case that could set Seely off again. He'll just leave it outside for you both when you're ready."

I only nodded as I pushed on Seely gently, willing him through the open doorway. To my surprise, he obeyed, stepping backward as I stepped forward until we were through the threshold and in the still-too-hot room.

As quickly as we entered the room, either Katrine or Sean slammed the door, maybe both of them at once with the force that occurred, shut behind us. Maybe it was both of them. I didn't know, but I heard their footsteps retreating rather quickly down the small hallway.

I waited until I heard another door shut somewhere in the house before I moved again.

Seely was still staring at me with those wild eyes. I took stock of the rest of him, running my hand through his hair to push it off of his forehead. His skin was covered in a thin layer of sweat, probably the remnants of his fever. I pressed the back of my hand onto his forehead, though, and I didn't feel that he was actively feverish. I knew *I* felt like sweating, though. After I got Seely sorted out I was going to extinguish that stupid fire.

I still had one hand on Seely's chest, and I pushed him towards the bed, not letting my gaze leave his. I thought maybe I could see more green around the pupils now, but I wasn't sure in the dim light.

We reached the bed in a few steps, and I kept moving until Seely's legs hit the side of it. I moved my hand from his chest and placed both of them on his shoulders, pushing him into a seated position. He was weirdly compliant in this state. It was a little creepy not to see his eyes light up as he teased me, or his lips pulled into a smirk or a smile.

"Maybe it wouldn't be so bad if you were stuck like this for a little while," I said to him, trying to make a joke. He just looked at me with that same stare, his eyes wide and wild and… blank. I shivered. "Actually, I take that back. I can't even joke about that. You're really creeping me out right now, Seely."

As I expected, he just continued to stare. I wondered where all that rage had gone that had him charging at and attacking Sean just minutes before. I wanted to smile at the thought that it had to do with him seeing me, but I really didn't know if he could see anything. Just the possibility that I could have that effect on anyone made my heart feel full and happy, even in the wake of the information I'd begun to get from Katrine as we sat in the study.

I was close to sweating in this room. The heat was almost unbearable, and my mind was swimming with the thickness of the air. I turned away from Seely and looked to the blazing fireplace. I needed to put that fire out or I was going to go insane.

I picked up a poker that was placed on a hook beside the hearth. Meticulously I began to spread out the embers. The fire wasn't as wild now as it had been before Katrine found me in here when Seely was sleeping peacefully. I turned to look at him where he sat on the bed, just staring at me blankly. He wasn't sleeping peacefully now. I would have much preferred either sleep or anger than what I was getting from him right now.

"I'm not really sure what to do about it, but you've got a bit of a staring problem right now, my friend."

I turned my attention back to the fire, trying to smother the flames as much as I could with the ashes that were already present. Of course, Seely said nothing the entire time. I wiped my hands on my pants as I placed the poker back on the hook. Turning back to Seely, I sighed.

"Well, here we are. Alive. And safe, I guess." I walked over and sat next to him on the bed. He didn't turn to look at me this time, he just continued to stare at the slowly dimming embers in the hearth.

"That was Katrine and Sean. This is their house, apparently, and Sean is the one you just tried to kill." I patted his leg lightly. "I don't think they'll hold that against you, though. Katrine told me this happens sometimes when a human is healed by Undead blood."

I looked at him as he continued to stare at the fire. My eyes narrowed a little.

"You almost got yourself killed out there because you didn't tell me that you were hurt. You got *shot*, you idiot! Why would you not tell me that?"

Seely didn't answer, but I didn't really need him to. The frustration that I'd felt since I thought he was going to die was spilling over and I needed to get it out. I kept my voice low, though, just in case anyone might be listening to our conversation.

"You got mad at me for going into the woods alone and getting turned into an Undead, which, I'll admit, was a very stupid thing to do. But then you told me you cracked a rib, but you were fine, when actually you were shot and were totally and completely not fine. You almost *died*, Seely! You were dying. You would have died if Katrine and her family didn't find us when they did."

I was silent for a moment. The fire still crackled.

"Katrine said they had to give you about a pint of my blood. Did they make you drink it, or did they inject you with it?"

No answer, but I thought I saw his fingers twitch a little.

"I also have a question about me. You know, the Undead thing. I know I can eat regular food because I have been, but am I also supposed to eat, or drink, blood?"

The silence after that question stretched out for longer than I wanted it to. I wasn't uncomfortable, but I was worried. I shouldn't be missing him when he was right beside me, but the silence and the staring and the creepiness of it all was too much.

"I don't really know how to navigate any of this, and I don't know who we are to each other." My voice was quieter now, and I could feel the lump forming in my throat. I swallowed hard to push it down before the tears started to spill over. "I do know that I like you, and when I look at you, I want to believe that everything you've told me is true. I want to believe that you're mine and I'm yours and that all of this will be okay because we can go through it together."

I turned towards him now.

"I need you to snap out of it, Seely. We have work to do and people to run from. Or maybe we'll take them down, I don't know. But the point is I need you to help me figure it out. I can't do it without you."

His eyes still showed me nothing, no sign that he was in there at all. I sighed, both in frustration and defeat, as I tried to keep my own panic from taking over my mind. Katrine had told me this was only temporary and that Seely would be fine. She said he would break out of this stupor in just a little time, but what if she didn't know that for certain? She could have just been telling me that to keep me calm. To keep me from killing her. Which I might do if anything done to him was irreparable.

I reached out and took his hand that rested on the bed between us. I held it between both of my own and spread out the fingers, flipping it over and back again, examining the details of it.

Seely had a lot of calluses. I figured it was from his training. His nails were short and neat, though the skin around them was frayed and red in some places. I wondered if he chewed on his nails when he got nervous. Then, I wondered if that was an answer I would know before all of this.

I wrapped his hand in mine and placed them back down together on the bed. I looked up into his face then and noticed he'd moved to look at me again.

"You have no idea how creepy you look right now," I whispered as a semi-hysterical giggle escaped my lips.

I let go of his hand and tucked my legs up under myself on the bed, so I was resting on my knees, facing Seely completely. I wanted to look at him, really look at him, and I realized this was a perfect opportunity. If he had to be zombified and I had to sit and wait to see if he would ever even come out of it, I might as well make up for lost time and memories.

I placed a hand on either side of his face and adjusted it, so he was looking at me directly. His eyes were still black and glazed over, but at least they were looking at mine.

"Okay, stay right there." I dropped my hands, and his head didn't move. "Thanks," I muttered.

Tentatively, I lifted my hand back to Seely's cheek. His skin was pale and a little sallow, but I thought it had the kind of tone that could get pretty tan in the summer. I wondered why he was so pale.

I ran my fingertips down his cheek gently, feeling the stubble that had begun to grow there. It was a shadow on his cheek, poking my fingers in something like a rough caress. I liked the feel of it on my fingers, and I flattened my palm against it.

I noticed the faint outline of freckles covering his nose and I raised my other hand to trace them gently with my pointer finger. I liked the way they made him look more human. I liked the way I thought I wanted to memorize those constellations on his face, map out the fate that lies in the stars there, and live my life by that.

I smiled a little and moved my finger up to his eyebrows. They were full and just as dark as his hair. They were in a neat pattern naturally, but I traced the hairs down to where they strayed from the arch. There was a little scar there, above his left eye, that I hadn't seen before. It was small and crescent shaped. Did he crash his bike and crack his head open when he was a little boy? Did something get thrown at him hard enough to leave a scar? I frowned. Did I know any of this before and would he get bored of trying to remind me of all the memories I'd lost?

"I hope not," I said aloud.

At my words, I felt a hand wrap around the one I'd placed on Seely's face. I snapped my attention back to his eyes, eyes that were now more green than black, though his pupils were still dilated larger than normal.

"Uh, hey," I breathed, lamely. I couldn't even understand the feeling of relief I felt as a weight lifted off my chest. Seely was okay.

"Hello, Gold." Seely smiled. His voice was hoarse, and I remembered he had been sleeping for a long time, after having been brought back from the brink of death. He probably needed some water.

I opened my mouth to ask if he needed just that, but he interrupted me.

"What exactly are you doing, Gold?"

His lips quirked up in the semblance of that signature smirk, and my heart thumped louder than before.

"Um… what do you mean?"

His smirk widened and he interlocked his fingers through mine as he brought them both down onto the bed.

"I mean, why are you tracing my face like that? I know I was in a bit of a stupor, but I could still feel what was going on."

I blushed, but Seely only continued to smirk at me.

"I mean, I don't mind it. I just wasn't expecting it."

I felt my blush deepen. He felt everything? I was getting close to mortified at that thought.

"Hey, Gold, I'm just teasing." He reached up with his other hand to touch my face now. "You forget that in another life we were basically soulmates. I know it's weird for you and that you've had all of this… *stuff*, for lack of a better word, thrown on you in a really short period of time. You can do anything you want to me, any time." All the sincerity was gone out of his voice when he reached the end of that speech, wagging his eyebrows up and down like an idiot.

I yanked my hand from his and punched him on his shoulder. He winced a little and I remembered what I was.

"Oh god, I'm so sorry! Did I hurt you?"

Seely rubbed the place where I hit him, but he smiled.

"That serum is *definitely* wearing off, Gold. You're going to have to pull your punches with me from now on, I'm afraid."

I laughed and the sound was breathless. I was going to have to unpack whatever else the serum my family had used on me was suppressing later. But for now, I needed to tell Seely everything I knew about this place and these people.

"Could you hear me at all while you were zombified?"

One of his eyebrows went up. "Zombified?"

I rolled my eyes. "You know what I mean."

He smiled at that. "I couldn't at first. The first thing I remember, really, is you staring at my nose like you were trying to read a book printed there or something."

I tried to ignore that, but I felt myself blush anyway. He was dangerously close to what I'd really been thinking.

"I was just looking at your freckles," I said. My voice was soft, embarrassed. I could feel my skin blazing and I cursed myself internally.

Seely raised a hand to touch his nose, absently.

"My freckles?" He smiled in a way that made me think he wanted to say something else but was holding his tongue.

"Yes, your freckles. What about it? I like them."

Seely smiled wider at that with all his teeth showing that time. They were so white, I wondered if they were something he took particular care of. A small dimple appeared on his cheek, and I reached out to touch it before I knew what I was doing. I couldn't even stop myself, I just had to touch him.

My fingers met his skin and his smile faltered, taking the dimple with it.

"You have a dimple too?" I sighed. "Are you just perfect, or what?"

Seely laughed, then, and it was a real laugh. He leaned forward, clutching his stomach, and closing his eyes. The dimple came back.

Rather than feeling embarrassed, I smiled. I was laughing then too, and I fell back onto the bed, my head resting on the bundle of blankets that had been tangled by Seely in his sleep. I reached up to wipe a tear from my eye and saw Seely looking at me. He'd stopped laughing, but there was still a smile on his face. He had dark circles under his eyes that I hadn't noticed before and I sat up again to get a closer look.

"You're a lot nicer when you don't know the full extent of what an idiot I really am," Seely said, smiling at me as I reached a finger up to trace the bruise-like crescents under his eyes. "But, if I'm being honest, I like it better when you're mean to me."

I narrowed my eyes at him, but I also felt the smile spread across my face.

"Right now, I'm just happy you're alive," I said, tracing my fingers down his face once more. "But don't worry, I definitely know how big of an idiot you are."

I flicked him lightly on the nose and got up from the bed. I remembered we were promised dinner, and then I remembered Seely probably needed something to eat. I noticed, with a start, that I didn't really feel hungry. I was just *very* thirsty. I didn't know if I wanted to know what that meant or not.

Was it the effects of the serum still exiting my system? I had eaten when Seely picked me up a few days ago, but… had I eaten since then? I swallowed. The answer was no, I hadn't. I should be wasting away by now, but instead I felt perfectly fine. My stomach twisted as I thought about what it could mean if I didn't need to eat food.

Of what I might eventually have to eat instead.

I walked over to the door and opened it just a crack. Sure enough, there was a cart sitting in the hallway with a covered tray that contained what I assumed was food. There was also a teapot and I prayed it was still hot. Maybe I didn't need it to survive, but I needed that tea for my ever-thinning sanity in the wake of every revelation that seemed to jump out at me.

I turned and looked at Seely where he was still sitting on the bed. He raised an eyebrow at me with a question.

"What are you…?"

Without letting him finish, I opened the door wider and wheeled the cart through the opening.

"Dinner is served, Mr. Evanson." I winced as I thought of Seely's father.

"Too soon," Seely said, chuckling softly, his mind obviously going in the same direction as mine. "I am curious what you've magically brought me to eat, though."

Coming out of the fog of my thoughts that surrounded the AAUD and everything we had to face sooner rather than later, I gave Seely a smile that I hoped reached my eyes. I pulled the lid off the tray to reveal two peanut butter and jelly sandwiches, a side of fries, and a large pitcher of milk. I wrinkled my nose a little at them. I guess it was good I wasn't hungry since I hated peanut butter.

"Bon Appetit, I guess?"

I shrugged as Seely laughed and walked over to the tray.

He picked up a sandwich and took the biggest bite I'd ever seen.

"Delicious," he said through the mush in his mouth. Crumbs fell out of his mouth and onto his shirt as I pretended to be disgusted.

Really, all I wanted to do was kiss him again.

Chapter Twenty-One

"DID YOU KNOW THAT I REALLY HATE PEANUT BUTTER?"

Seely and I sat on the floor on top of a blanket in front of the still-dying fire. I realized, much to my dismay, that there was no window in this room to bring a breeze in, so we were sitting on the ground in an attempt to get away from the swirling, heated air that continued to rise.

"I did know that, actually," Seely said, looking at me with a grin. His hair was stuck to his forehead in places where it met with his sweat. "About three years ago I dared you to eat a spoonful of it and you ended up puking your guts up in the mess hall." Seely laughed like that could have possibly been funny as he eased himself back to rest on his forearms. "Your brother was so mad at me for that, but he got over it I think."

My heart twisted a little bit at the mention of my brother. It made me think about my dad and Stella and… Seely's dad trying to frame me for murder. I laid back on the blanket and grabbed one of the pillows we'd thrown off the bed to put behind my head for support.

"Do you think they believe I did it?"

Seely was quiet for a moment, and I thought maybe he didn't know what I was talking about. I propped myself up on an elbow and looked over at him. He still had crumbs on his shirt from the sandwiches and there was also a small wet spot from when he'd basically guzzled the milk a few minutes earlier. I thought people weren't capable of drinking milk that quickly, but I guess Seely was excluded from that statistic.

Seely looked up at me with a strange expression on his face. I didn't know that I wanted to know exactly what he was thinking, but I thought he would probably tell me anyway. I needed to know the truth and look through all my options before we decided what our next move would be.

"Go on, just tell me."

"I'm not afraid of hurting your feelings, Gold, I'm just not sure how to say what I want to say."

I tilted my head to the left, confused.

"What do you mean by that? Just tell me what you want to say."

"Fine." Seely brushed away the remainder of the crumbs from his shirt and sat up farther, leaning his forearms on his thighs where they were crossed underneath him. He looked me in the eyes directly, and I braced myself for whatever it was he was hesitating to tell me.

"My father is the leader of the AAUD in every way that matters. Yes, your father is supposed to be a co-founder of sorts, but he's spent too much time both mourning over the loss of your mother and then you." He watched me carefully as he continued, but I felt my face remain blank. I hoped he couldn't see the panic that was probably beginning to arise in my eyes. "He's lost the ear of the army and he hasn't been to visit any other base since your… accident. No one blames him for that, I mean that's half of his family that was either gone or seriously altered. But it's just the truth, that's what happened.

"Your brother and Stella also pulled back to help him with you, constantly staying with you and, apparently, keeping you sedated and out of harm's way." He let out a deep breath and I thought he looked angry.

"I already told you I didn't know where you were, and I didn't. Because I would have been there every day too. I'm trying not to hold a grudge against them for what they did to you, I'm trying to tell myself it's because they were trying to protect you and the AAUD and everyone involved, but I have to say I kind of want to inject each and every one of them with that godforsaken serum and see how they like waking up with no memories and no knowledge of what had happened to them or how much time had passed." His nostrils flared menacingly as I watched. He looked absolutely infuriated, and part of me wondered if I should be feeling scared rather than excited about his obvious disdain for what was done to me. He cleared his throat before continuing. "But I'm also a little grateful they left me behind. I was able to stay as close to my father as he would allow and follow him on missions when he thought I wouldn't be too much of a nuisance to him.

"The point I'm trying to make is that I saw him take over the bit of control your father had in the AAUD little by little in the past year and a half."

I continued to stare at him, though now I was more confused than worried.

"Okay, but what does this have to do with whether or not my family is going to believe him?"

I sat up from my elbows and Seely took my hand, using his other to lift my chin and hold it there so I didn't have a choice but to stare at him.

"I don't have an answer for you as to whether or not your family is going to believe my father or if they'll stick by you. I wish I could give you some peace of mind, but I really don't know what's going to happen with that." He brought his thumb to my bottom lip and pulled it gently, distracting me a little bit. "The point I'm trying to make is that it won't matter whether your family believes you're innocent or not. My dad owns the AAUD at this point, and that means he decides their direction. He decides who they take action against and who they don't. If he's decided we're targets and he wants us dead or captured, we might as well already be."

He dropped his hand from my face, but I was frozen in place. He was right. I knew he was right. And I was a fool for thinking there was any other way out of this than to fight through it.

"Okay," I said, slowly. "So, we have to fight back." Seely just stared at me like I hadn't spoken. "Right?"

Seely stared at me for another long moment. I wondered if I'd said something wrong… But we had to fight, right? We couldn't just sit back and let Seely's dad hunt us until we were eventually caught and killed.

There was also the small matter of Orthan and of me being some kind of Undead, and of everything that entailed. We still didn't know why I wasn't like a normal Undead, though there were theories, and we didn't know why Orthan wanted me or what he needed me to Change for. Now that I thought about it, we really didn't know anything.

The only thing I did know was that we couldn't continue to sit here and hide in Katrine's home. We had to take matters into our own hands, and the only way I knew we could do that was to face it and fight. I felt that same ice flowing through my veins, and as it reached my heart, I felt it turn into fire.

It felt like power.

"You're glowing, Gold." Seely smirked at me. "Quite literally."

I looked at my arms in a little bit of a panic, and sure enough there was a gold sheen glimmering off my skin. It felt cold in the warm room, and I looked back up at Seely with what I knew had to be wild eyes. He was just smirking at me still and he raised one of my hands to his lips, kissing the inside of my palm.

"You're beautiful, Alyssa." My breath caught in my throat, and I was sure my heart was going to crash through my chest at any moment. The chill of my skin turned warm, and I watched as the gold tinge slowly faded and dulled.

Seely brought my hand back down with his and smiled at me.

"Of course, we'll fight them. What else can we do? You and I can't lose." I felt a twinge in my heart at that statement because I knew it was a lie. We could lose, and we probably would.

"Either way," Seely continued, placing his hand under my chin, and inching closer to me, "we'll be together. And we'll figure this out."

I nodded, pretending not to notice how close we were, or the feel of his hot breath on my face. It smelled like peanut butter, and I didn't even care. Seely bent closer to me, and I tilted my face up in preparation of being kissed. My heart began racing again.

To my disappointment, he gave me a peck on the bridge of my nose and pushed back to stand. A little stunned, I blinked twice before looking up to see his outstretched hand waiting to pull me to my feet. He smiled at me still, but there was something hiding in his eyes. He ducked his head a little and those black curls fell over his eyebrows, somewhat concealing that emotion in their shadows. The movement also made his eyes look even more sunken, and though a lot of color had come back from the meal he'd just devoured, I remembered just how much trauma his body had been through in the last day or so.

I tried not to seem hurt or confused that I'd clearly been expecting a different kind of kiss as I offered him a small smile and let him pull me to my feet.

I could feel myself falling deeper with every moment I spent with Seely, but maybe he missed the girl he'd lost more than the thing that stood before him now. I forced myself to maintain a smile, even as my throat closed with panic.

"We need to talk to your friend, Katrine," Seely said, pulling me to the door. I let myself be taken across the room, but I snorted at his comment.

"She's definitely not my friend, though she did say she knew my mother."

Seely stopped and turned to look at me, both his eyebrows pulled up nearly to his hairline.

"Wait, *what?*"

I shrugged. "I don't really know what to believe when it comes to her. Honestly, I hadn't thought much about it until now. When she told me about it, I was only really worried about you."

Seely's face melted into a careful calm, and I realized I may have revealed too much about myself in that statement, especially considering his sort of rejection just now.

I swallowed and Seely cleared his throat before simply turning towards the door again.

"That's something else we can ask her about, then," he said. His voice was gruffer than before, and I wondered what emotion lay behind it. He was full of mixed signals and secrets, and, as much as I hated to admit it, I wanted to know every single one of them.

I let Seely drag me down the hallway and to the door to the sitting room. I didn't know if Katrine or Sean would be in there now, but I thought it would be a good place to start looking. I pulled my arm and Seely to a stop. He turned and looked at me with a question in his eyes, but I just gestured to the door in front of us.

"This is where Katrine and I sat and talked before," I told him in a whisper. I wasn't sure why, I guess I just didn't want to be caught out in the hallway before we were ready. "I don't even know what time it is right now, but if they're awake I have a feeling they'll be in there."

Seely only nodded and lifted his hand from my arm to knock on the door with three short raps. We waited a moment, and Seely looked back at me. I wanted to reach out and grab his hand, but where I had been confident enough to do it before, I didn't even want to try if there was a risk, I would feel that sting of rejection.

Before I had taken another deep breath, we heard a soft voice from inside the room.

"Come in."

Chapter Twenty-Two

BEFORE I REALLY KNEW HOW IT HAD happened, Seely and I were seated in the too-small study, nestled together on one of the couches that was too large for the room. I'd been in here earlier so I'd expected the over-crowded, almost manic-inducing, space, but I watched Seely out of the corner of my eye as his eyes darted back and forth, taking in as much as he could about his surroundings. I could tell his Undead blood-induced stupor was almost completely worn off from the way his instincts had begun to kick back in. He was on high alert, his back straight and his feet rested on the floor as if he was preparing to run at any moment.

I, on the other hand, leaned back into the overstuffed loveseat with my feet tucked under me, my hands wrapped around a steaming mug of tea. I was so glad Katrine didn't bring out the teacups again. I just could never make the perfect cup in those little things. I inhaled the steam of my cup and took a small sip. The liquid was the perfect blend of creamy and sweet, and I sighed quietly as its warmth hit the center of my chest. I felt someone staring at me and I turned to see Seely's eyes fixed on me.

"Can I help you?" I asked, taking another long sip of my tea.

"Is there a reason you're so relaxed?" His eyes darted from mine, around the room, and back again. "I can't even focus in here. Who needs this many books? And who are these people anyway?"

I shrugged and Seely practically groaned.

"For someone who wants to take on the AAUD, your fighting instincts seem to be a little skewed."

I scowled at him over my mug but resisted the urge to hit him again. I'd hurt him last time and, though I didn't mean to, it scared me. I had realized just how much I didn't know about who I was or *what* I was, and that was enough to terrify me into holding in my rage. It wasn't easy to do, as my knuckles tightened around the mug, and I knew my knuckles had to be turning white at that point.

"You, uh, might want to take it easy on that mug before it shatters."

I focused my eyes away from the wall where they'd drifted and back to his face. One of his eyebrows was pulled up a little and he looked sort of concerned about what exactly was going through my head at that moment. He also looked like he was getting ready to make fun of me if and when my mug actually did explode.

I only glared at him and took another long drink of my tea.

He opened his mouth as if he wanted to say something else, but I guess the look on my face made him think otherwise. He closed his mouth again and turned away from me, facing in the direction of the couch across from us. I thought I saw the side of his mouth twitch with a smile.

Seely and I sat close together on the couch, but it didn't escape my notice that he was careful not to touch me. The way he angled his body kept us about two inches apart, and I didn't think it was an accident.

Hadn't he just kissed my hand and called me beautiful? But then he'd faked me out with that weird kiss before he dragged me out here to confront our captives, or hosts, we weren't completely sure yet. He'd said in another life we were practically soulmates, but he was very right about that being another life. One I didn't know anything about. I didn't even know if I was even the same girl from back then in any way that mattered.

I wasn't sure of anything, and every step I took brought me closer and closer to that helpless feeling that always seems to accompany me when I don't know the exact right thing to do next. I didn't even have an idea of what to do next. An *inkling* of an idea.

And I knew I shouldn't care that much about whatever Seely and I were to each other. I knew I should be worrying about my family and myself and what they might be thinking of me or planning to do to me. What they could be planning to do with both of us, actually, I amended in my brain. Seely was just as much of a fugitive as I was, and he'd even been shot for it. But Seely wasn't Undead. There was a chance they would take him back in one piece and that he would be okay at the end of this. Myself on the other hand…

I didn't want to believe that Seth or my dad could possibly do something to harm me, but if they believed all Undead were evil and irreparably changed, they might just do anything to save themselves and their organization. Especially if they thought getting rid of me might be for the greater good of all, if it thwarted whatever Orthan was planning. We needed to figure that plan out as soon as we could, I realized. It could be the difference between life and death for either or both of us.

Staring at Seely's profile, I knew I should care more about those things than about the distance between us on the couch, but I didn't. I also knew I didn't have a real reason to feel self-conscious, but I did. It was like as soon as Seely told me what we'd been before, I started to notice every little thing he did that could be construed in any way that might mean he didn't love me the way he loved the person I used to be.

It sounded so stupid, even in my own head, but I couldn't help but think it. My palms were sweating.

"I can basically hear you thinking over there, Gold," Seely said, lolling his head over to look at me. I blinked rapidly a few times. "And if you stare at me any harder, you're going to catch me on fire." He pointed at my eyes. "I can see it in there. It happens when you're angry. Or thinking yourself into a hole deep enough to get angry or upset about something that began from practically nothing."

I narrowed my eyebrows at him, and he only smiled wider.

"It's nice to see that hasn't changed, at least."

My breath caught in my throat. So, did that mean other things *had* changed?

Shut up, Alyssa, I said to myself. *Of course, other things have changed.*

I felt my face fall and I saw the concern on Seely's face as he leaned closer to me.

"What—"

"I found it!" Katrine burst through the door before Seely could finish whatever he was going to say. I didn't know if that was a good thing or a bad thing. I was being stupid and sensitive, and I didn't know if I wanted to know how Seely felt about that.

Katrine breezed into the room and sat on the couch across from us. She'd changed into a different flowing tunic in the same style as the last one, but this one was midnight blue, patterned with hundreds of tiny silver stars. It reminded me of that night on the roof with Seely. I immediately turned my attention to her, taking a drink of my tea while it was still hot. I felt Seely's stare on my face and I hoped he thought the flush on my cheeks was from the warmth of the tea.

I cleared my throat.

"You found, uh, what exactly?"

She held up a small leather box with a tarnished gold clasp on the front. It looked worn and old, but I could tell it had once been something beautiful. The gold details embossed on the leather swirled in an intricate pattern that looked like vines and flowers. I looked at it curiously as Katrine waved it back and forth a little as a small smile spread across her face.

"I told you I knew your mom, Alyssa," she sat the box down on the table in front of me, "and this box is full of proof of that."

She sat on the other couch with a huff and curled her feet under her legs. Sitting like that she looked like a teenager rather than a woman in her forties, which is what I assumed she must be if she had really been that close to my mother.

Katrine held out her hand and gestured to the box.

"Go ahead. Open it."

I looked at her and she nodded encouragingly. I didn't know why, but I felt nervous. I took another sip of my tea, but the warmth only succeeded in burning my throat rather than bringing me any comfort. Setting it down on the table, I tentatively touched the top of the box. Sure enough, it was leather, and it felt old. I thought if I wasn't too careful with it, I could easily watch it disintegrate beneath my fingers.

"It was my grandmother's, so it's old, but it won't break. It's okay to handle it."

Katrine's voice was encouraging, but I knew my eyes had to be wide as I picked up the box and carefully undid the top. I flipped the lid open on my lap and I looked down at my mother in a picture that sat on top. She was staring back at me, her eyes crinkled in the widest smile I'd ever seen. I felt the lump in my throat growing larger and I reached for my tea to take a quick gulp. My hand was shaking slightly, and not even tea could succeed in calming my nerves.

I'd never seen this picture of my mother. Actually, I hadn't seen that many pictures of her ever. I remembered that we didn't have that many pictures of her lying around the house, and when I tried to think of the last specific picture I'd seen of her, I came up empty. I couldn't trust my memory, so maybe we didn't have any pictures of her in our house? When was the last time I'd seen her face in anything but a memory?

My face was feeling hotter and hotter while my blood ran cold. I was fighting back the tears that threatened to overflow as I picked up the picture on top and brought it close to my face for a better look.

She looked like me, but she had something magnetic about her person. Even in a still shot, I wanted to be near her. I ached for the person I didn't know and would never know, and I knew a lot of that had to do with her being my mother, but it was also just her. Her eyes looked like they knew things about the world you didn't know but would want to, and her smile was infectious. Oddly enough, though, I only felt like crying.

"That was the last summer we spent together at the AAUD base." Katrine's voice was quiet, and I looked up to see her looking at me with what I thought was compassion. "There are… several very important things in there. I think you should take some time to go through everything while you're here." She cleared her throat, as if she was also trying to clear the now heavy air. "I told you we were best friends for most of our lives, Alyssa, and I meant that. It's all in that box and you can look through all of it and see those memories for yourself." I dropped my gaze back to the picture in my hand, back to the girl who stared back at me like everything in her life was perfect. How was I going to go through this whole box when I couldn't even make it past the first picture?

"What we need to talk about right now, though," Katrine continued in that same soft voice, "is what you kids are planning on doing now. You can stay here for as long as you need, but you're going to have to decide where you're going next. You're new to being an Undead, Alyssa, and I know you Dissipated from the AAUD, but you didn't go that far."

I looked up at her again, confused.

"That was my biggest question." It was Seely who spoke now. He'd been so quiet next to me I hadn't even wondered what he was thinking. "How is it that you and your family live in these woods? How have you survived amid all the Undead and the Others?"

Katrine's smile seemed to get stuck, it turned sour right before my eyes.

"I don't think that's something we need to get into right now, Seely." I felt a chill run up my spine at the sudden change in her tone. "I promise I have no ill will toward either of you and I will do whatever I can to help you, but I will not compromise my family to satiate your curiosity. Our living here is our business, and I suspect you will find out more than you wish to if you dig for those answers." She still smiled, but I could feel the dare in her voice. "You might find out those answers anyway. Do not ask me questions about my family and I won't ask you any about yours."

I brought my eyebrows together at that last statement and turned to look at Seely. He had the same confused expression on his face, and I could tell he had no idea what she was getting at. After a few heartbeats, Seely leaned back, smoothing out his expression.

"Very well. As long as you help us, I suppose I can refrain from asking any questions." His voice was stiff, and I could tell he was barely controlling some emotion under the surface of his skin.

Katrine only nodded, but I thought she looked a little… relieved? But that didn't make much sense.

"So," Katrine said, letting out a breath of air in a huff, "what are you guys planning to do next?"

Seely and I looked at each other. He quirked an eyebrow at me at the same time I pursed my lips at him.

"Oh, so you have no idea." Katrine laughed quietly. "That's fine, we can work that out."

I was still looking at Seely, and I could swear we both had the same thought at the same time. I could see the light come on behind his eyes and I watched his confused expression melt into that perfect smirk. I couldn't help it, I smiled right back and nodded at him.

"We don't really have a full plan," I began.

"But we know we're going back." Seely finished the thought.

Katrine's eyebrows went up and reminded me of Seely's for a second.

"You're going back?" She asked. "To do what exactly?"

"We need to figure out what the Undead want with me," I answered her. "And we can't just wait here until Mr. Evanson brings the whole AAUD Guard down on top of us. You said it yourself that we're not very far away from the AAUD headquarters. How long do we really think we could wait here until they find us?"

Katrine looked troubled, but she didn't disagree with me right away. There was something like sadness or concern in her face, but she seemed to fight to keep her expression carefully blank otherwise.

"Do you really think you can just waltz into the AAUD and, what?" Katrine questioned. "Fight your way through? With what skills? With what army?"

My heart sank a little. Though I'd obviously known that was a problem, I managed to push it out of my brain. It was foolish, but I thought if I made the decision to go back and fight then maybe everything else would just work out.

"I know I knew how to fight… before."

I saw Seely nod out of the corner of my eye.

"Before your family erased your memories?" Katrine asked. Another knife to the heart.

"Um, yes. But I don't think they did that on purpose, for the record."

"Okay, so, before your family 'accidentally'," she put air quotes around the word, "erased your memories and used you as bait for the Undead who turned you, you *think* you could fight. Is that the plan I'm hearing?"

I swallowed. "Well, that's not really a *plan*, that's just… what I have to work with at the moment." I reached out and grabbed Seely's arm tightly. "Seely can fight for sure!"

Katrine raised an eyebrow. "The same Seely who got shot and almost died before we found you?"

"Hey, I would have been fine." Seely said, his voice gruff with barely contained rage.

"No, you would have been dead." Katrine held up her hands in a surrendering position at the tone of his voice and the murderous expression on his face. "I'm just trying to help. Poking holes in your plan might save your lives, and I think that would be a pretty big help for you right now."

"Okay," I sighed, "I appreciate all the hole-poking, but what would really be helpful is some practical advice. What do you suggest we do? We can't stay here forever. Probably not even any more than a few days. Who knows? They may already have people out here searching for us. If they find us here, not only are we sitting ducks, but your family would also be in danger. I don't want that. We don't want that. But we're kind of in a tough place right now."

I closed the box on my lap and closed the latch, setting it back on the table and leaning forward to look more closely into Katrine's eyes. She looked calm, though calculating, and something tightened in her features. I prayed we could truly trust her.

"So, if you're saying we're unprepared, I'm not disagreeing with you. I'm just saying we need to figure out an actual plan." I paused for a second, thinking. "Here's what I'm proposing: we stay here for three days. No more, but maybe even less if we find it necessary. In those three days, we'll train and prepare as much as we can. I wish we had more time, but it seems like whenever I'm in a situation where I need to use whatever skills I've forgotten, they come out." I pointed a thumb at Seely. "You can ask him; I've flipped him on his back twice in the past few days."

"That's true."

I could hear the smile in Seely's voice, and I lost the fight of a small smile of my own as it spread across my face.

"I know I can do it. And if I can't, I don't really have another option." I turned to Seely, then. "Our plan should be to sneak into headquarters, gather any information we can about Orthan and what he's planning to do with me, anything we can possibly get on your father," I swallowed before I said the next part, "and I need to talk to Seth. Or my dad. Or Stella. Or all of the above. I need to know if they're on our side, or if they ever could be."

Seely opened his mouth in what I knew was going to be a protest, but I held up a hand to stop him.

"We can't do this alone, Seely. We need other people on our side, or your father is going to capture and murder us both without blinking an eye, especially if what you told me about him owning the ear of the guard is how most of them feel." I looked at him for a moment. "What do you think?"

He stared at me for a couple of heartbeats, but it may as well have been an hour.

He thought I was stupid. I knew it. I should have never opened my mouth. Like I knew anything about strategy or stealth or training—

"I think you're the smartest person I've ever known, Gold. I would definitely be dead without you, and I will gladly die for you." He shrugged. "Or with you. Whichever comes first." He smirked at me, and I felt that warmth saturate my heart. I was becoming accustomed to that feeling when it came to how Seely looked at me. "I need to see Dex and Simon, too. Surely, they'll help us out, though I have been surprised before."

I felt my own smile spread across my face as we continued to stare at each other. The emotion in Seely's eyes was something that I was pretty sure was mirrored in my own. To be honest, I kind of forgot there was anyone else in the room.

Katrine cleared her throat.

"Well, that's adorable and everything, but I have to tell you I still think this is a suicide mission." I turned to look at her. I didn't see condescension or pity on her face, only concern. I wondered if I could really trust anything she said. I didn't know this woman, though she had pictures of my mother and stories that I didn't have a way to confirm. I realized, though, that I didn't really have a choice. Seely and I were going to have to trust that she would at least not kill us in our sleep. My mind wandered back to the rooms we'd woken up in, and I wondered if the doors had locks.

I looked back at Seely, but he was just staring at Katrine with a quizzical expression.

"Do I," he began. "I mean, have we…" He shook his head. "You look so familiar to me."

Katrine seemed slightly taken aback by the question, but I didn't see anything suspicious in her gaze. She looked like a woman who'd been asked an offhand question, which she was.

"I'm afraid we don't know each other at all, Seely. An easy mistake." She shrugged, her nonchalance perfectly practiced, just like someone else I knew. Maybe even a little too practiced.

Seely looked skeptical as he pursed his lips and leaned back into the couch, but he didn't say anything else.

There were a couple of beats of awkward silence before anyone spoke again. I could almost hear each individual's brains working overtime, trying to figure out what to say next, probably thinking through my half-baked plan and trying to determine how long it would take us to be caught and killed.

If I had to bet, I wouldn't bet on myself. Maybe Seely. I thought he would be fine, even if we got caught. He wasn't an Undead, after all, and they would probably just hold him to keep me from doing anything crazy.

I didn't even know if three days would be enough time to train or prepare in any meaningful way. I didn't even know where that number came from, I just felt the need to say something when Katrine asked me. Seely had said it was a good idea, but he could just be saying that to help me out in front of a stranger. I hoped I didn't look like I had no idea what I was talking about, even though that was absolutely the case. I hoped I wouldn't be the reason we were killed.

"So, you'll stay here for a few days, prepare yourselves as best you can, and return to the belly of the beast in the hopes that your friends and family won't want to kill you and will actually help you on your quest?"

She looked at us for a beat, like she was waiting for an answer. I just stared back, but Seely nodded next to me.

"That seems to be the gist of it, yes," I answered as confidently as I could, and I hope it came across that way.

Katrine looked from Seely, to me, and then back again. She set her lips in a tight line, but only nodded.

"I told you I would do everything to help you, and I will. You can stay here as long as you'd like, and Sean and I will do what we can." Katrine stood, then, and I did too. I took it as our cue to go back to our rooms for bed. It was well past two in the morning at that point, according to a small clock on the shelf, and though Seely and I had slept for hours, we were both exhausted. Our sleep wasn't the restful kind, it was the kind that we needed for healing and our minds and bodies were both equally exhausted from it. At least, I was. I assumed if I was finally tired then Seely had to be running on fumes. I assumed that whatever I was, I didn't get tired often. Since the serum had begun to wear off, I was feeling stronger and more awake, and I thought I could probably go for days without sleeping.

Unfortunately for us, in a few days, if everything went according to plan, we would be back at the AAUD.

"Thank you, Katrine," I said, trying to show the gratitude plainly on my face. "Really."

I smiled at her, and she returned it right back to me.

Without answering me, she bent down and picked up the box from the table. She held it out to me as if she was gesturing to me to grab it.

"Take it," she said. "These were my memories, but I don't need pictures for that. I want you to have it. Look through it. Every piece in there is important to me, and I'm sure it will be for you too." She shrugged a little as she continued to hand out the box to me.

I looked at her for a second, and I knew my face had to be blank with surprise. I thought about pretending to refuse the gesture, maybe that was the polite thing to do, but I *wanted* to take it. I wanted to explore the contents and the pictures and glean absolutely anything and everything I could about my mother.

So, I reached out after just a second of hesitation and took the box from Katrine.

I held the box close to my chest and nodded towards Katrine. I didn't trust my voice at that moment.

She nodded back at me, like she understood exactly, and I was grateful for her at that moment.

"Well," she said, scooting around the table until she was almost to the door, "I think it's time we all go to bed. Tomorrow, the hard work starts, apparently." She turned from the door to smile back at us. "Well, for you, anyway."

Seely and I followed her out without another word to either her or each other. There was a hum that surrounded us that I thought was coming from the anticipation of what was to come in the next few days, and also a spark of electricity in the air that I couldn't place. I didn't know whether I was the only one who could feel it or not.

Katrine led us down the hall a couple of steps and stopped just in front of my door. The cottage was so small that Seely's door was within a few more steps. I wondered where Katrine and her family slept and I hoped we weren't taking their space, but when I opened my mouth to ask, she turned around so quickly I was startled into silence.

She held up her hand with her finger pointing first at me and then at Seely. There was something stern in her gaze that caused the words I was going to say to lodge in my throat.

"Under my roof, you'll stay in your own rooms. Understood?"

I thought if I had known my mom for long enough this was probably a glimpse of what it would be like.

I also thought, if a hole opened up and swallowed me whole just then, it wouldn't be the worst thing that could happen.

I felt my face flame as my eyes widened. Out of the corner of my eye, I thought I saw Seely turn toward me and then back again, but it was so quick I could have been imagining it.

"Of course," I told her. My voice came out just a little louder than a whisper, and a little like a question. I was so confused about where this was coming from. Why would she care so much?

She looked satisfied as she opened my door for me and waited until I was inside before closing it again.

"Sweet dreams, Alyssa," she said as the door closed with a click.

I still felt the flush on my cheeks as I scrubbed my face with water from a small pail that was sitting on the bedside table, and finally crawled into the warm bed.

Chapter Twenty-Three

THE NIGHT WAS UNEVENTFUL, BUT I DID get a few hours of sleep. It took forever to feel fatigued enough to sleep, and when I woke up the cool blue light of the early morning was streaming through small slits that I realized were windows at the top of the wall. They looked like the kinds of windows you might see in a basement.

I sat up with a start as the realization sank in. This cabin wasn't a cabin at all. This was a bunker. We had to be underground.

My skin tingled as I thought about the last time I was underground, at least to my knowledge. I didn't remember crawling through the dirt and coming up again after I was Made into something else, but Seely described it in enough detail to make me feel glad to have forgotten it.

I got out of the warm bed and shivered as my feet touched the cold concrete floor. It smelled musty in there, as though this door had been shut for a long time before I got here. The walls of the room were yellowing like they hadn't had fresh coat of paint in twenty years, and they were completely bare, except for the small, rectangular window at the top of one wall. I could see a little bit of sunlight peeking through, which was my only indication of the time of day.

I was so hot the night before, both from the fire in Seely's room and the embarrassment of Katrine's implication, that I'd tossed my leggings and sweatshirt over one of the small chairs in the room before I went to bed the night before. All I had on were the thin shorts and oversized t-shirt that I assumed Katrine had left for me, and I wondered if they were hers or one of the girls'. I could probably squeeze into Sammy's clothes if I needed to, but I felt a twinge in my gut that was the guilt of imposing on this family. I shimmied out of my shorts and shoved my legs back through the leggings. They were dirty, but definitely warmer and less revealing than the shorts. I preferred to be more covered than I was in the shorts and shirt I had on, and I quickly brought the sweatshirt over my head. The air was chilly in my room, and I wished I hadn't let the embers of the fire burn all the way out.

The night before, though, I hadn't even been thinking that far ahead. I was thrown off by Katrine's comment about me and Seely.

Stay in our own rooms? Of course, we would. Why would she even say that? It wasn't like she knew us or anything about us. She may have known my mother, but she wasn't my mother. The more I thought about it, the more annoyed I became at her.

Before I could stew for too long, there was a light knock at the door. I froze where I was standing in the middle of the room. I had just taken the ponytail holder out from the bottom of my braid, and I worked my fingers through the plait as I took the few steps that brought me to the door.

Opening it, I was surprised to find that it wasn't Katrine or Sean waiting for me. It wasn't even Sammy. Lilah looked at me through the crack in the door, her eyes wide and gleaming, ocean-blue, and beautiful.

"Katrine sent me to get you." The girl held up a small bundle that was in her hands. It looked like a towel and maybe some clothes. Oh, I hoped it was a change of clothes other than shorts. "If you'll follow me?"

"To where, exactly?"

"Oh, to the washroom. Katrine thought you might want to freshen up after yesterday. She told me you guys got caught up talking about so many things that she forgot to show you where it is." She just stared at me, blinking for a second. Her expression was blank, and I didn't sense any fear there. If anything, I only saw apathy in her features. I didn't know if she wanted me to say anything or if she was just waiting for me to follow her, but I nodded and opened the door most of the way so I could squeeze out of it and into the hallway to stand beside her.

"Of course, thank you," I finally said. "Lead the way."

Lilah walked me down the hallway and, rather than turning to the right where I'd sat in the sitting room several times yesterday, she led me to the left, sliding another door open and revealing a different corridor I hadn't seen before. This hallway was smaller than the other, and it seemed to get even smaller as we walked several feet. It could have been a trick of the light or a growing panic that accompanied me whenever I was in an enclosed space. *Maybe I'm claustrophobic.*

We walked past a few doors that remained closed, and Lilah informed me that these were the family's quarters. The rooms Seely and I had taken over were apparently spares that were usually used for storage if need be. "Katrine likes to have that wing of the house to herself. She's usually in her study reading and… doing whatever," she shrugged. "She doesn't like to be disturbed."

We walked a little farther down the hallway and reached another door on the left. Lilah didn't hesitate to open it, and inside was a rather large bathroom, with a tub and shower on the opposite wall from where we stood at the door. To the left, there was a large vanity that almost spanned the entire wall. There were two sinks, and the counter was cluttered with so many different things: hairbrushes and hair ties, toothpaste splotches, and a couple of makeup bags that were overflowing.

I smiled at the sight. It was comforting to see something… normal. That clutter meant normal people lived here and that maybe, though the jury was still out, these people weren't going to kill us.

Lilah set the pile she held on to a stool by the tub.

"Here are a couple of towels and a change of clothes. They're Sammy's, so they should fit you fine."

She looked at me for a second before showing me how to turn the water on and off and control the temperature, then she left me without another word to clean up. I barely waited for her to shut the door behind her before I tore off my dirty clothes and stepped into the water that was already steaming.

It couldn't have been more than ten minutes since waking up in my room that I was standing under a steady, if not fairly weak, stream of warm water. It cleared my head and loosened my muscles, making it easier to think. I stood directly under the hot water, letting the stream run down my face. The tub was one of those old-fashioned claw foot ones that you always see in Victorian movies: bright white with a little brass foot on each bottom corner. But the only thing I really cared about was that it was clean and didn't seem to be running out of hot water as I stood there.

What exactly was I going to do to "train" today? I realized it was my own bright idea, but also, I didn't have a clue where to even begin with that. I guessed Seely would be able to help me but thinking of Seely brought back other memories and thoughts and fears that I didn't really want to face at the same time I was facing mortal danger.

So much for relaxing.

I turned over the ancient knob, just as Lilah showed me, to stop the water. I couldn't have been in the shower for more than five minutes, but I felt so much better. The grime of yesterday had been worse than I anticipated, and I'd scrubbed my skin enough that it shone red in the lights of the vanity as I stood there after my shower.

The clothes Lilah had left for me were leggings and a rather close-fitting tank top, which automatically made me feel self-conscious. I would ask Katrine where I could wash my clothes as soon as I got the chance. I missed my sweatshirt.

I picked one of the brushes from the sink and began yanking it through my hair. I couldn't be bothered to worry about preserving my curls when I didn't even know if I would be able to save myself, or Seely, from what seemed like could be our inevitable end.

"Stop thinking like that, Alyssa," I said aloud to myself. "You'll survive. You'll be okay. You both will." I let out a deep breath and put the brush back down on the counter. I placed my palms on the counter and leaned forward until I was as close as I could get to the mirror, the edge of the vanity pressing into my stomach.

My hair hung in loose waves around my face. It was still wet, but not dripping, though the water from the ends that touched my shirt left dark shapes in the gray material. I looked at myself as close as I dared, taking in my eyes and the slight dark circles that surrounded them. Seely had said my eyes glowed when I began to feel that fire in my chest, but right now they looked brown and boring, just like always. Even my hair looked brown instead of red when it was wet. Brown, dull, and boring. I knew it was probably petty and irresponsible to even be thinking about things like this when I needed to get out there and start preparing myself for what was coming.

I knew it was stupid, but there was something about my reflection that made me pretty positive I was going to fail. How could I win? How could I survive this? I looked like a child with my hair wet and my skin flushed from the hot water. I felt like a child. This was a fool's mission, but I was trying to remind myself to stay positive. It wasn't really working.

There was a knock on the door, and I jumped back from the mirror. My reverie shattered, I shook my head back and forth a couple of times to completely snap back to reality.

"Coming!" I called, hanging my towel on the hook by the door. I grabbed a hair tie from the counter and hoped one of the girls wouldn't be too annoyed to let me borrow it. I'd left mine in the room when Lilah came to get me, and I needed to get my hair off my neck. It was starting to suffocate me a little. Opening the door, I expected to see Lilah or Katrine, maybe even Sammy or Max, but instead Sean stood in the hall. Seely was behind him, still wearing his dirty clothes from yesterday, with a towel and what looked to be a change of clothes in his hands. His hair, though it always looked infuriatingly gorgeous, was a mess on the top of his head. Even though he was doing his best to wear his usual smirk, he had bluish circles underneath his eyes, giving away just how much the past days had taken a toll on him. I looked away quickly before he could catch me staring.

"Oh!" I said, a little startled. "I'm sorry, I was just finishing up." Suddenly feeling a little self-conscious, I pulled my hair into my hands and around to one side. I began to braid as I stood there, just to keep my mind and hands busy. I stole a glance at Seely and saw that he seemed to also be studiously avoiding my eyes, staring down at the towel in his hands that seemed to be absolutely fascinating.

I tried to ignore the way that made me feel, but I couldn't shake the tightness that crept up my throat. Was he being weird because he was embarrassed about what Katrine said last night? Was he worried about training and our mission and everything that was to come in the next few days?

Or had he just realized I wasn't the same girl he loved before, and he didn't like who I was now as much?

In my mind, all those things were possible. And I wanted to ask him, I wanted to know, but not with Sean standing right there, and not with my wet hair in a lopsided braid. I would ask him later, for sure.

Definitely later.

"Oh, not a problem, Miss—Alyssa." Sean smiled at me, and I noticed his eyes were the same color as Lilah's. "I was just bringing Seely here to get washed up before you get started today." He turned to Seely, who was still looking at his towel, and then gestured to the door. "The bathroom is right through here. You should find everything you need in there. Would you like me to show you how to control the shower or anything?"

Seely smiled at Sean, the picture of politeness.

"I think I got it. Thanks for the clothes by the way." He held up the bundle in his hand and Sean just nodded. Finally, Seely turned to me. He met my gaze, but his eyes were guarded. I could feel that mine were too, and I wished I could read his mind. "I'll meet you out back when I'm done and we can get started, okay?"

That was it? No good morning or anything?

He's not your boyfriend anymore, Alyssa, I told myself. *He doesn't necessarily owe you a good morning.* Of course, I was right. I didn't know what we were, but whatever it was, Seely didn't owe me anything. Maybe the weirdness was all in my head. I thought that was entirely possible.

I smiled what I hoped looked like an easy smile and nodded. "Absolutely." Turning my attention to

Sean, I said, "I'm assuming someone will show me where exactly that is?"

Sean smiled back at me, and I didn't see anything false about his expression. His honey-blonde hair and his ruddy skin exuded warmth, and I thought he was just a warm person all around. I wanted to like him, and I wanted to let my guard down a little and trust him, but that's what made him so dangerous. If anyone in this cabin wanted to harm us, Sean had a pretty good shot of doing it.

"Of course. I was just dropping Seely off here and I'll take you to the clearing now. If you'll follow me?"

Sean turned and began walking down the hallway, and I followed quickly behind. When I passed Seely, I looked at him and our eyes met. He looked away quickly, and I thought I saw a blush pass across his face.

So, I wasn't making it up? Whatever, I knew he had to come and face me sooner rather than later. I would ask him when we were alone outside. I hoped the shower would clear his head like it did mine.

Sean led me back down the corridor I'd walked through with Lilah.

"That door right there," he pointed to the next door on the right from the bathroom, "leads to the kitchen. Our cook has been ill for a few days, but she seems to be on the mend. If you need anything, you can call for one of us or Bernard and Cook should be able to get it for you." He looked at me from the corner of his eye. "Though, I'm not sure we would be able to get any… blood. At least not human."

At his words, I seemed to choke on the air.

Sean turned to me, looking a little sheepish.

"I apologize if that was forward, it's just that I don't believe we've ever had an Undead here before. I don't think I've ever been this close to one before, actually. At least not civilly. Though, you don't seem like the Undead we were always taught about."

We were still walking, and I cleared my throat before I spoke.

"If I'm being honest, I don't know what I eat. I think I can eat food. At least, I've done it before. But I haven't really been hungry in a few days, so maybe I just need food… less often than humans do? I'm not sure." I shrugged. "So, my only request would probably be plenty of mugs of hot tea. I seem to be pretty thirsty lately."

Sean chuckled lightly, like we were discussing the weather and not me possibly drinking blood. "I think we can do that for you, Alyssa."

We reached the end of the corridor and entered the now familiar hallway with the door to the study in front of us. The door was opened slightly, and I could see Katrine sitting on one of the sofas, sipping something out of a mug with her eyes closed.

"Let's keep going this way," Sean said, pulling my attention to him. His voice was barely above a whisper. "We try not to disturb her in the mornings."

I nodded and continued to follow him, now toward mine and Seely's room. Katrine seemed to be treated like royalty around here, which was a little weird. I wondered why they acted like she was their boss rather than their mother or their wife. Except, then I remembered that I didn't know the extent of any of their relationships. I could tell the girls and Max were related at least—that was obvious from their features. Sean too had the blonde hair and blue eyes and that warmth that seemed to follow every one of them around. Well, except for Max. But, in his defense, we didn't get to know each other under the best circumstances.

We'd reached the end of the hallway at that point, past the door to Seely's room, and Sean stood directly in front of the wall. He lifted his right arm and placed his hand on the wall, dragging it down in a line almost in the middle.

"It always takes me a second to find it." He chuckled as he brought his arm back up in that same line. That time, he stopped about midway up and brought his fingers into a fist. "Got it!"

With those words, Sean pressed into the wall and a door that I hadn't seen swung inwardly, revealing a set of dark stairs. As the door opened, lights shone one by one up the stairs. There weren't a lot of stairs so we couldn't be that far underground, but it was enough to make my stomach lurch.

Sean traipsed nimbly up the stairs and I followed, keeping pace with him effortlessly. I wasn't feeling tired at all, actually, and I thought maybe there could be some perks about this whole "Undead" thing.

We reached another door at the top of the staircase, and this one was large and iron, with a huge bar that went across the entire length of the door and disappeared into the stone wall surrounding it. Sean reached out and grabbed some type of handle that protruded from the bar. Straining, he brought the handle down towards his chest and then pushed from the side of it over to the left. His face became red, and he was placing all his weight on the bar, but it didn't move. Sean stopped straining for a moment and let out a huff of breath.

"Sometimes when there's been a storm the handle gets stuck, and it rained pretty hard just a couple of days ago." He wiped a hand across his forehead as I remembered the storm clouds that were rolling by as I first stepped out of the car in front of the AAUD. "This might take just a moment."

Sean took a deep breath and prepared to push the door again, but I got an idea. My right hand flexed open and then closed again as I thought about whether or not I thought I might be able to push that door open by myself.

"Um, Sean?" I asked, my voice not coming out as confident as I'd hoped it would. I cleared my throat and tried again. "Could I try something?"

Sean looked at me, his brow furrowing slightly.

"Can I?" I asked again, reaching for the door handle. Sean stepped aside, still looking a little confused, but he let me take his place in front of the door. I grabbed the bar and turned it up first, just like Sean had done. It felt as smooth as spreading soft butter over a warm piece of bread, and I wondered if this was the easy part. Sean had done the same thing just now. I was feeling a little nervous because I knew I was going to look stupid if this didn't work. But I felt a tingle in my veins that made me want to try.

I pushed on the bar, softly at first, and it moved microscopically, with a scraping sound. I leaned into it, flexed my muscles more tightly, and, with a scream of protest, metal scraped against metal as the bar slid across the length of the door and into its place in the wall.

I released the handle and stepped back. My hands were coated red with rust and before I thought about it, I wiped them on my pants, staining the black leggings with red streaks. I didn't really care. I could feel my face break out into a beaming smile.

"I did it."

I turned to Sean, still smiling, and he was beaming right back at me. His expression seemed genuine, and I felt a little shy under his approving gaze.

"It usually takes a few of us together to get that thing open when it's stuck like that," Sean said, stepping up to the door next to me. He pulled down the smaller handle that was attached to the door and pressed against it. The iron gave way and the door swung open, revealing a small clearing flooded with the light of the morning. I covered my eyes with my fingers for a second. The light was blinding after spending so much time in the cabin, and I needed a moment for my eyes to adjust.

Cabin. Bunker. Whatever it was.

"This clearing isn't very large," Sean said, "but it should be large enough for you and Seely to prepare."

My eyes were pretty much adjusted, and I removed my hand, blinking at the scene before me.

The clearing was so green, with little white and yellow wildflowers growing in clumps spread out in a way that almost looked strategized. The open space was probably about the size of two of the cramped studies from downstairs, and the wide-open space was something I didn't know I'd missed. The trees around the clearing were dense and thick, and I could tell it would be dark within that parameter no matter how bright the light was shining in the clearing.

The best thing about the clearing, by far, was the view of the sky. I looked up as far as I could without being blinded and took a deep breath of the fresh air. Either I hadn't realized how cramped and stuffy it was down in the cabin, or I just didn't want to let myself go there. My stomach twisted slightly as I thought about going back down those steps and shutting the door in a few hours. I didn't want to panic about that just yet though. I wanted to enjoy this moment of fresh air and sunlight as long as I could.

"Katrine and I weren't sure what you may need to practice out here, and we have limited supplies of ammo and weapons here, as you might imagine."

I turned toward Sean, then. He was standing in the dark doorway still and I was completely in the sun of the clearing.

"I spoke with Seely this morning, and he told me you lost something that may be similar to this." Sean reached out with something from behind his back. A dagger.

This dagger wasn't the same as the one I'd lost at the AAUD. It was a galvanized steel with a hilt that looked like obsidian. It was completely black, and it looked extra menacing. I missed my dagger and the weight and feeling of it, of feeling powerful in some respect, but I was drawn to this new dagger by some appeal that I couldn't quite place. I reached out to where Sean held the blade towards me and took it by the shining handle. I held it out from me and moved it from side to side, watching it glimmer in the sunlight. It was beautiful, there was no doubt. There was something familiar about it, but I couldn't quite place it in my mind.

"It's beautiful." I said. My voice sounded a little awed, and I guess I really was. I still didn't fully trust these people, but Sean had just handed me a weapon and was about to turn his back on me to walk back through the open doorway. He had to have known I was stronger than he was, especially after my display with the door, and he probably also figured I could kill him with little more than the flick of a wrist if I really wanted to.

Either this was part of their elaborate ploy to make me comfortable and trick me into letting down my guard so they could eventually kill me, or Sean and Katrine were genuinely nice people who wanted to help us for whatever reason.

I wanted to believe the second one. I wanted to believe that people could be good and nice and want to help other people—or Undead—like me and Seely out of the kindness of their hearts. But I couldn't help but think that Seely's own father had just tried to kill us, and my family and closest friends had apparently been keeping me sedated and asleep for nearly two years now. So, I guess it wasn't too much of a stretch to imagine that those who had no real reason to be kind to me would betray me when the ones who were supposed to support and protect me had already done it.

I looked up from the dagger and saw Sean looking at me with a glimmer in his eyes. "It looks like it fits you," he said. "I know it doesn't replace the one you lost, but it will do for now."

I smiled, and I had the biggest urge to throw my arms around him in a hug. He seemed like an open book and the type of person I would be happy to stay around for a while. Sean reminded me of my dad, at least the memories of my dad that weren't tainted with lies and deceit. My heart ached with the thoughts of my family, and I pushed them away as I brought my attention back to the dagger in my hands. My eyes were pricking with tears that threatened to fill them, but I couldn't let that happen right now. I didn't want to show all my cards to these people, even though I couldn't deny anymore that I was beginning to trust them.

Sean smiled at me once more from the doorway before turning slightly away and dragging the creaking door with him.

"As soon as your boy is ready, I'll lead him back up to you. Hopefully you've released the door enough, or it'll take the both of us." He chuckled softly as he closed the door and left me outside all alone. It met the wall with a decided thud, and I didn't hear the scrape of metal that I was expecting to accompany the metal arm on the door. I guessed Sean decided not to try his luck with that latch again until he could use my help. That made me smile a little, but it faded as quickly as it had come when I turned and faced the empty clearing.

I had absolutely no idea what I was doing. Or even where to start. This was hopeless and *I* was hopeless and… what was I thinking with this plan?

I looked at the dagger in my right hand. It was still glinting in the sunlight, but its darkness that had initially looked powerful and exciting to me was beginning to look more ominous.

It felt heavy in my hand as I gripped it tighter, moving my wrist back and forth. My palms were beginning to sweat, and I prayed it wouldn't cause me to drop the blade. I wasn't sure what I planned to do next, but I raised the dagger up higher. I brought the blade above my head and back down again. I didn't put my strength into it, but the dagger made a whooshing sound as it came back down towards the ground.

I pulled my arm back again and jabbed forward once as if striking an invisible being in the air. Moving my muscles like this, I felt my blood begin to warm and my limbs stretch in a way that was almost uncomfortable. I'd been idle for too long.

But it felt good to be moving like this. The ache in my muscles was sending signals through my brain of familiarity, though I couldn't place those feelings with memories. According to Seely, I used to fight like this all the time. Before.

So, I continued with the pattern for a few sets. Up. Down. Back. Strike. Over and over. I switched to my left arm instead, just to see if I could. Whatever training I'd had before, I felt almost as confident in my motion with my left as I had with the right. I heard a surprised, breathless laugh escape my lips as I completed another jab.

I stopped for a second to catch my breath, and I realized I wasn't tired. I wiped a hand across my brow and there was no layer of sweat there. I know I didn't have memories of doing this stuff before, but I thought it was probably strange to have not broken a sweat in doing this for minutes on end.

The muscles in my arms were tingling, but even then, I felt like I could keep going this way for forever.

"Weird," I said. My breathing had already evened out.

"Not the word I was going to use," a voice said behind me.

I whirled around, feeling the blood rush to my cheeks. I pulled the dagger back, prepared to strike if I needed to.

Seely stood behind me, his hair darker than ever as it hung damply over his forehead. The stubble of yesterday was gone, and he was wearing a tight-fitting tee and loose joggers. It looked like someone had loaned him their clothes, just like they'd done for me. I looked down to see that his feet were bare, which made my eyebrow quirk up a little in a question.

"My shoes are still wet from the pond, and no one here has any that will fit me." I looked back up to meet his gaze as he spoke. "So, we work with what we've got." Seely shrugged, his nonchalance back in full force. He had his sheath strapped to his side with the hilt of his dagger sticking out from the cover.

It was made of obsidian.

"Hey," I said, letting down my guard a little and loosening my stance as I walked a couple steps closer to him. I held up the weapon.

"Sean gave me this dagger to practice with, you know, since your dad took mine and stabbed himself with it."

"Naturally."

"And I thought it looked familiar, but I couldn't figure out why." I stood directly in front of him as I handed him the blade. "It looks just like yours, Seely. Isn't that a weird coincidence?"

Seely took the dagger from me and looked at it closely. I watched as his dark eyes squinted in concentration, his eyebrows knitting closer together. I noticed the twitch in his jaw as he clenched his teeth together.

"What are you thinking?" I asked him. I tilted my head to one side, suddenly a little concerned. Maybe I should have kept it to myself, but I thought it was interesting. And strange.

Seely shook his head and broke his gaze from the dagger, turning back to me. His face broke into a crooked grin, but his eyes looked troubled. "I'm thinking that it *is* a weird coincidence," he flipped the dagger, so he was holding the blade and the handle was out towards me. I grabbed it. "But I'm also thinking that we have some work to do, and we can worry about this later if we need to."

He continued to smile, and I nodded at him.

"You're right. We do have a lot of work to do."

Silence fell after those words, and it was uncomfortable for the first time. When I'd been with Seely in the AAUD headquarters, when he showed me his tower, before I knew about anything happening between us, the silence wasn't awkward. But now the air was filled with things we wanted to say but couldn't, or wouldn't, bring up the words for fear of upsetting the precarious balance on which our relationship stood. Seely went from calling me beautiful to avoiding my eyes, and I went from wanting to kiss him to... well I guess that feeling never really went away. But it was layered with the frustration that I couldn't help but feel like there were things he didn't tell me even when he wanted to.

He doesn't owe you anything, that voice told me again. *You also don't tell him everything you want to say, don't forget that.* It was still right.

"So," I started, trying to break the silence. "I'm not really sure where to begin with any of this." I turned and walked back farther into the clearing, putting space between us, and also trying to think about what to do next. I hated the feeling that I had to map out every move around Seely. Why was everything easier before I knew anything about our past life together?

"That's okay, Gold, I'm here to help." I couldn't hear Seely's footsteps through the springy grass, his bare feet concealing much of the noise, but I could sense him walking closer to me. I was still facing away from him, and he reached out to touch my shoulder.

"This works better if you look at me," he said, and I could hear the smirk in his voice. Everything was funny to him, and if it wasn't so infuriating it would be another thing to add to the list of reasons why his very presence had the ability to make my heart race, and my breathing quicken.

I turned around, but again I forgot I wasn't totally human anymore. It was almost like I thought about turning around and then before I'd decided to, I was facing back towards the cabin and looking right at Seely's eyes. They widened slightly. I stared into them, and my movement caused him to lose balance a little bit as his hand fell from my shoulder. He stumbled over one step, and I reached out and steadied him with one hand on each arm.

"I'm sorry, I…" I dropped my hands and stepped back once. "I never know when something strange is going to happen, I'm trying to get used to it." I wrung my hands together. "I'm sorry," I said again.

"Don't apologize to me, Gold. Any abilities you find out you have can only help us if we figure out how to use them to our advantage. I welcome any creepy, Undead traits you may have."

He smirked at me again and I rolled my eyes. He knew how to automatically help me feel better.

"Gee thanks, I'll be sure to let you know about any 'creepy' Undead ability developments."

"Good." Seely unsheathed his dagger as he walked a few paces away from me. "Now, I saw some of your moves just a minute ago." He pursed his lips as he flipped the dagger over a couple of times in his left hand. I flushed what I knew had to be a bright red. Seely looked up at me, finally holding his dagger steadily. "Show me."

I blanched a little at that. "Sh-show you? Like… just start slicing through the air again?"

He nodded. "That's a good start, yes."

I held up the dagger in my hand and looked closely at it. I could almost see my reflection in the handle. I really didn't want to do this, but I knew I didn't have the option of being shy or nervous. We were in a limited time frame.

"Go on, then, Gold. I'm not going to laugh at you."

"I didn't think you were."

My voice came out snappier than I thought, but Seely just smiled. I let out a breath as I worked myself up to it, and then attempted to clear my mind as I repeated the sequence I'd been working on when I was by myself. I tried not to think about Seely watching me probably make a fool of myself, I only focused on the movement and the stretch of my muscles as I pushed myself.

Up. Down. Back. Jab. Again.

After a few of these, I stopped. My breath had quickened, but again I wasn't tired at all. The muscles in my arm felt warm and primed and ready to continue, but I wanted to hear what Seely had to say.

I looked up at him, not really knowing what to expect. He was staring at me, his eyes wide and his lips pulled into a small smile. He still held the dagger in his left hand, but he was almost completely still. I straightened myself from the jabbing position I'd stopped in.

"Um… yeah," I started, lamely. "So, that was it."

"Interesting."

Seely brought his dagger up and began picking at his nails, just as he'd done the first time I saw him in my kitchen.

"Interesting? That's it?" I snorted as he kept cleaning his nails, and he finally looked up. That same small smile played on his lips. "Gee thanks for the compliment."

"You're getting angry?" It was more of a question and less of an observation.

"I'm getting annoyed." I flicked my messy braid over my shoulder and crossed my arms in front of me with the dagger sticking straight up.

"I don't mean to annoy you, Gold, I'm just…" He took a step towards me and let his hands fall to his side. "I'm not really sure what to say about that."

I knew I looked like an idiot, but I wished he would just come out and say it. I could feel the inside of my chest heating up as a flush blazed across my cheeks. I was moving from annoyed to angry, and if Seely wasn't careful he was going to be on the receiving end of any number of those "creepy, Undead abilities", as he put it.

"Okay, simmer down. I didn't mean to make you mad."

"I'm not mad." Though I had to admit my voice came out a little seething. "Yet. You'll know when I'm mad."

"I can already tell when you're mad, Gold. And now it's a little easier when your eyes glow like that."

Shoot. I'd forgotten about that.

"Okay, so maybe I'm mad. But just tell me what you're thinking and get it over with, Seely."

He smiled a little wider at my admission. "Okay, but what I'm thinking is… You just keep impressing me, Gold. At literally every turn when I think you can't get any more surprising, you do. You should really start believing in yourself, but I guess if you can't I can do it for you."

I wondered if my mouth fell open. That was not what I was expecting him to say.

"Are you being serious?"

Seely stepped closer so we were only a few inches away.

"Dead serious." The right side of his mouth quirked up. "No offense." I punched him in the arm, extra lightly that time. He still rubbed his arm where I'd made contact, though. "I know you don't remember your life before you woke up the other day, but it's clear that your body remembers. What you were just doing? That's a sequence we used to do at training every day. You remembered that, and you executed it perfectly."

I couldn't help the smile that spread across my face at his words.

"Really?" I asked, and Seely nodded. "Well, that's... good, right? That means we're not starting completely from scratch?" I smiled wider now. "Maybe we won't die in the first five minutes."

"Oh, we'll last at least ten," he said, his smirk still on his face.

Seely reached out and grabbed my arm, dragging his fingers down it and leaving a trail of goosebumps in their wake. I took in a short breath and let my arm drop as Seely grabbed my hand in his. I still wasn't used to his touch, and a part of me hoped I would never be.

He stepped in again, our noses almost touching. In spite of myself, I leaned into him, breathing deeply. How did he still smell like him when he was wearing someone else's clothes and had used someone else's soap and shampoo? Either way, I took another breath through my nose.

"Which is very good news, of course."

Without warning, Seely pulled my arm into him and grabbed my other wrist that held the dagger, causing it to fall to the ground. With a quick kick and a swipe of his leg, I was on the ground, and he was hovering over me with a knife to my throat.

"The bad news is, you're out of practice, and easily distracted."

The air was knocked out of me, and I breathed heavily as I squirmed to get out of his grasp.

"You may be stronger than I am now, Gold, but you're out of practice." He pushed off the ground to stand up, leaving me on my back on the ground. "We still have a lot of work to do in three days."

He held out his hand to me and I felt a little embarrassment mixed with a little hope. He was right, I was out of practice. But I'd done this before, and I thought with a little practice I could do it again. And I *was* stronger.

I reached up and clasped my hand in Seely's.

"You realize I've done that to you twice?" I said as a reply. It lessened my embarrassment slightly.

He pulled me to my feet. "So, I have one more to go until we're even."

Seely bent down to pick up my dagger and tossed it lightly to me. I caught it without even looking. Seely smiled so widely at me, his dimple appeared.

"Let's get to work."

Chapter Twenty-Four

"AGAIN, ALYSSA, COME ON."

I was breathing heavily as I swung my body around and brought my foot up into a kick that Seely deflected with his forearm. I brought my leg down and planted my feet, using my toes for balance. With a grunt I thrust my arm forward, palm up towards Seely's face. He told me not to pull my punches, not even for him, and so I didn't.

He dodged it at the last second and bent down to the ground to swipe his leg across the ground to knock my feet out from under me. I dodged his leg the first time, but I wasn't expecting him to come back around and he caught my feet easily with the second swipe of his leg. I landed on my back with a huff as the air rushed out of my lungs.

"Good," Seely said. He appeared over me, beaming from ear to ear, as sweat dripped from his temples down the sides of his face. His hair was stuck to his forehead.

I'd discovered that, even as an Undead, I could still sweat. I had better stamina and I didn't get as tired as I probably would have before, but as I lay on the ground I was practically wheezing as I felt the sweat matting my hair to the nape of my neck and running down my back. I knew I had to look like a drowned rat, while Seely's glistening skin made him look closer to Edward Cullen in sunlight.

"Good?" I rasped. "How was that good? You get me every time."

Seely reached down and held out his hand. I took it and he helped me haul myself up. My ponytail was coming loose from its hair tie, and I reached up to take it out the rest of the way. I ran my hands through my hair from the roots. My scalp was sore from wearing my hair back tightly repeatedly these past few days.

"Yes, but I'm amazing." He dodged my punch again, knowing it was coming. "I also know your fighting style and it's pretty easy for me to guess your next move."

We walked over to the iron door and Seely turned the handle to pull it open. He let me enter first and I pulled the bar on the door with him to help to close it completely. My hair was still down, and the strands were sticking to the tops of my arms where they met with the sweat there.

"I probably know you better than anyone, Gold. If we have to face anyone at the AAUD and we're forced to fight them, I doubt they would be able to guess your moves."

What he said made a little sense, but I didn't like the idea that I was predictable in any way. Predictability couldn't be a good thing when it came to fighting, right?

Seely's door was the first to the left and he opened it as I didn't hesitate to walk through the threshold and collapse on the pile of pillows on the floor. I'd discovered that Seely did not appreciate having more than one pillow, so he threw the others on the floor every night before he went to sleep. His room was, for some reason overrun with pillows. I'd taken to making this my seating area whenever Seely and I sat in his room and spoke about things, which happened every night since the first one we'd spent at the cabin.

Seely sat beside me on the pillows, presumably trying to save his bed from the sweat and the grime of our day spent practicing the different ways to kill each other. I sank down farther into the pillows, lying on my stomach and hugging the cushion under my chest close and tight.

"What are you thinking about, Gold? Come on, out with it."

I wanted to roll my eyes at him again. He could never just let me stew in peace. Well, at least not any more than five minutes. Seely always wanted to know what I was thinking, and I loved that about him just as much as I was annoyed by it.

Still, I sighed at his question.

I was obviously thinking about what we had to do tomorrow. I was thinking about how these three days had flown by too fast and how I felt like I wasn't ready or prepared. I was thinking about what it would be like to have to face everyone at the AAUD, including my family. I was wondering what might happen if my family didn't want to help me and instead tried to capture me or harm me. If I had to fight Seth? My dad? Stella? I didn't want to think about that. I didn't want to fight them, but I would if I had to. And I was definitely already worrying about it.

Also, as much as I thought I would be able to look my family in the eyes if they hated me and still somehow find the will to fight my way out of the situation, I didn't really know how I would react in the moment.

"Hey," Seely picked up the piece of my hair that had fallen over my eyes and tucked it behind my ear. I looked up at him from where my face was buried in the pillow I held to my chest. Only one of my eyes was exposed. "It'll be okay, Gold. Don't stress about the 'what-ifs', just think about what you know you have to do. We might not even meet anyone the whole time we're there." He shrugged, his favorite gesture. "We could be in and out before anyone even notices. If we do get caught, though, we know how to fight." He looked at me more closely, forcing my gaze to stay locked with his. "*You* know how to fight, Gold. You'll be fine. We'll both be fine."

I voiced one of my concerns. "And if our family and friends don't want to help us?"

"I don't know if you remember, but my family already tried to kill me once." Seely smiled at his joke, but I didn't really find it that comforting. "And if everyone else tries to do the same, well…" he looked like he was actually thinking about it for a second, "well we survived it once, we can survive it again, right?"

I rolled my eyes at that and stifled a groan at the reasoning of that statement. It wasn't that he was wrong, he was just seeing everything too much in black and white for my comfort. I liked to look at things from all angles and to follow every string of a situation to see where it could possibly lead. But I could also see where both of those lines of thinking on their own could get you into more trouble than you were prepared for, so maybe it was good we were on the same team.

"Sure, Seely. That's definitely all we have to worry about. Logically, if we survived the first attack, which you barely did, by the way," I narrowed my eyes at him as I said that "we have nothing to worry about and we'll be able to survive the next one if and when it comes."

Seely brought his brows together slightly as he looked at me. "I'm sensing some sarcasm there."

"Of course not. Why would you ever think that?" I leaned up so he could see my whole face and batted my eyes at him innocently before letting out a sigh and turning over on my back. I brought the pillow that was underneath me along as I rolled over, and I put it over my face. I fought the urge to scream. The excess anxious energy I was feeling about what we had to do had been building steadily as the days passed. While we were training, it was easy to channel my fear and anger about everything that had happened in less than a week into every punch and jab and swipe I took at Seely. But it was times like these where I felt that heat filling my chest and I had to actively push away that ice that flowed through my veins before it was able to explode in whatever display would occur that time. The main problem with that was that we never knew exactly what was going to happen when that power manifested itself.

Seely and I had had a couple of conversations about whether or not we should explore that power that was constantly contained under the surface of my skin. We decided, after I showed more than a little hesitation, that we should wait and use those powers when I was able to actually harness and use them in a way that would help us in a fight, rather than harm us.

Actually, Seely had wanted to explore them more. On that first day, he'd tried to get me to attempt to Dissipate on command. After many failed attempts that included me standing in the clearing with my eyes closed and fists clenched, the best I could do was conjure a small cloud of dust that circled my feet that did no more than make my shoes dirty.

I decided after that that if I couldn't figure out how to access those things inside of me on command, I would just keep them safely tucked away for later. My biggest fear, if I was being honest, wasn't that they would come out in the middle of a fight, and I wouldn't know what to do with them. I was afraid that I wouldn't be able to control them, and I would end up hurting someone I cared about without meaning to. It had almost happened as I held Seely in that pond when he was dying. I'd almost killed him from hypothermia before he could die from the gunshot wound. I hadn't voiced that particular concern out loud, but I had a feeling Seely could guess at the root of my hesitation.

I felt a hand cover mine and tug gently. I squeezed the pillow tighter to my face, digging my fingers into the rough fabric on the back. I never understood decorative pillows anyway, they definitely weren't comfortable.

"Gold, come on." Seely tugged on my hand again. "Talk to me."

Feeling a little like a child, I shook my head where it lay under the pillow. Seely laughed and I lifted the cushion slightly to peek one eye out and look at him. He was sitting back on the floor with one leg down and the other up and bent at the knee. He rested his forearm on the leg that was bent. He met my gaze as I looked up at him and tilted his head to the side slightly. The small smile that was always there played on his lips, but his eyes were wide and serious.

"I need you to talk to me, Alyssa." Woah, *Alyssa*. The use of my full name took me aback. He was definitely serious. "We're about to walk into what could be certain death, and I need you to keep your head as clear as possible. I'll have your back through this no matter what, but I also need you to have mine." He bent his head down a little farther and tugged on my hand again. That time, I let him take it. The pillow that was over my face fell to the side and I grabbed it with my other hand and moved it farther away from me.

"Nice to see you, again." That smirk appeared as though it was just waiting for me to show my face. "Now, talk."

I sighed. Seely was right. He was infuriatingly right, actually. We were a team on this, and a team needed to be on the same page if that team was going to be successful.

"Okay, if you really want to know, I'm just… worried."

His right eyebrow ticked up. "About?"

"Did you really just ask me what I'm worried about?"

"I meant something specific. Pick one of the things you're specifically worried about and let's talk about it."

I sighed again. "Okay, Mom."

Seely chuckled softly and I sat up further on the wall, propping my back up against a couple of the pillows. I waited a moment, fully expecting Seely to say something to prompt me again, but he didn't. He just waited for me to speak.

"Okay, fine. The first thing I'm worried about is that I'm going to get us killed in a fight. Either I won't be able to fight the way I need to and I'm going to leave you out there alone and, in a lurch, or something weird is going to happen and I'll shoot lasers out of my eyes or catch the whole room on fire and that wouldn't be very helpful if I don't know how to use it."

"That might not be super helpful, but it would definitely be pretty cool."

I sighed again.

"It might be cool until you're dead and I'm left there, alone, having killed you."

Seely didn't have anything to say to that, and after a moment passed, I looked over at him. He was staring at his shoes, which had dried by the second day of training. He looked like he was thinking about something particularly unpleasant.

"What?" I asked him. "Don't you think about things like that?"

"Of course, I think about things like that, Gold." His voice was quiet, and I wished I'd kept my mouth shut. "I think about the what-ifs, just like everyone else. But when you're about to go into battle, you can't have your head full of what-ifs. You have to focus on what's right in front of you and what's happening in the then and now. If you don't, *that's* when people die." He looked at me. "That's when you lose the people you love."

I looked back at him and swallowed. The implications of his word choice were not lost on me, but I tried not to let it settle in my brain in any meaningful way.

"You're right. I'm sorry."

Seely shrugged. "Don't be sorry, Gold. You have valid reasons to be afraid, and I asked you to voice them. I'm glad you told me. I just need you to try your hardest to keep your mind clear." Seely cleared his throat. "I won't be losing you again."

Seely turned away from me after those words, and I stared at his profile. Since that first night in the cabin when I'd sat with Seely as he ate peanut butter sandwiches and he kissed my hand and called me beautiful, he hadn't given any other real indication that he was still interested in me romantically.

We trained, we ate (or Seely ate. I was never really hungry, though I tried a few pieces of food every now and then), and we slept. I may be an Undead now, but I was grossly out of shape from years kept frozen in time. That counterbalanced any superhuman stamina I may have. Apparently, spending almost two years basically comatose was not that great for maintaining muscle tone. Seely never seemed to be quite as tired as I was at the end of the day.

But when Seely said stuff like that... my heart didn't hesitate to flutter, skip a beat, and all that other corny stuff you watch in movies and read about in books. Of course, we hadn't talked about any of this. I didn't think this was something that fell into the realm of keeping my mind focused and clear for the fight ahead. But actually, wouldn't that mean I *should* ask him? Shouldn't we talk about everything? Clear the air and have everything out in the open before we left the comfort of this bunker and faced the enemy? Our friends and family?

"Seely, I…" He turned to me.

"Yes?"

I looked into his eyes. They were greener in the low light of the room, somehow, almost glowing.

"I was just wondering—"

A knock on the door had me practically jumping up to put some distance between us. Ever since Katrine had made the comment about Seely and I staying in our own rooms as if we were animals who couldn't control themselves, I felt very self-conscious about doing anything around her that could be construed in any illicit way. Usually when Katrine was around, I kept my distance from Seely and stayed busy with whatever Lilah and Sammy had in store for me. Max usually glared at me from the corner of whatever room we were in, which was almost equally disconcerting.

It wasn't that I didn't want to be close to Seely. And it wasn't that I didn't think about kissing him just about twenty-four-seven, because I did, believe me. It was that I didn't know anything about that part of myself. Before I'd known the dream about me and Seely was real and I'd kissed him in my room at the AAUD, I really thought I had never kissed anyone before. Anything beyond that… My palms began to sweat just at the thought of it. Thinking about doing anything physical with Seely made me nervous, of course, but, more than that, I didn't know if I'd crossed that threshold before than it was the thought of crossing it now.

"Gold, I don't think Katrine will think you were ravishing me in here just because the door was closed and there are pillows on the ground."

I snapped my head back to him, and he was smirking up at me from where he remained on the ground. I reached down and picked up one of the said pillows and chucked it at his head with as much force as I could manage.

"Shut. Up." I hissed as Seely caught the pillow effortlessly before it smashed into his face. I turned to the door and tried to make my voice sound nonchalant. "Come in!" Unfortunately, I'd overcompensated and definitely sounded like I was being held against my will there rather than someone who was just sitting there innocently. Which I totally was. I don't know, there was just something about the way Katrine looked at me and Seely that made me want to make her proud of me, and I was so worried about what she would think of me sitting in here, just the two of us, by ourselves.

"Everybody decent?"

A head poked in from the crack of the opened door, and it wasn't Katrine, but the blood rushed to my face anyway at those words. Sean opened the door wider and strode in. Seely laughed as he rose from the ground.

"Of course, Sean." Seely stepped forward slightly and Sean clapped him on the shoulder. They'd gone from Seely trying to kill him to being the best of friends in a matter of days, and it was kind of amazing to me. I thought of the way Katrine was friendly one second and side-eyed me like she wasn't sure whether or not to crush me the next. I didn't think we were ever going to get there, especially considering Seely and I were leaving in the morning.

"I know, I'm just giving you a hard time." He looked at me, then. "Katrine wants us to all sit down to dinner in a little less than an hour. We know you're leaving in the morning, and we'd like to give you a proper send-off." He gave me a small smile. "What do you think about that?"

I realized, with a little bit of a start, that he was solely asking me for my opinion. At least, that's what it seemed like was happening. He still had his hand on Seely's shoulder, but he was looking at me like I might be the only problem with the dinner arrangement. Had I made myself seem that difficult? Did I put off some kind of energy that made him assume I would be the issue in this situation?

"Of course," I answered, a little too quickly. The words came out in a huff, rushed and falling over each other slightly. "You've done so much for us already. We would love to get to say goodbye, and to get a chance to thank you all for your help." I arranged my features in what I hoped was a convincing, easy smile. Though, out of the corner of my eye, I saw Seely trying to hold in a laugh, which told me I probably looked more like I was in pain than anything.

Sean just smiled wider at my words, though. "Great!" He exclaimed, taking his hand from Seely's shoulder to clap it together with his other one. "You two should get freshened up, and we'll meet you in the dining room in about", he glanced at the watch on his wrist, "forty-five minutes?"

I maintained my smile and nodded. Seely didn't say anything, but I could feel him watching me. Sean headed for the door and turned back to us one last time. For a second, I thought I saw some emotion flash across his face, but I couldn't quite place it and it was gone as quickly as it had come.

"It's been so nice to get to know you both," he said, his voice quieter than before. "I hope you remember that I mean that."

With that, he disappeared through the door and closed it behind him. It shut with an audible click and... something about that sound made my stomach drop. Ice-cold dread began to make its way up my veins, and I had no idea where it came from.

I waited until I heard Sean's footsteps retreating from the door before I turned to Seely.

"Did that feel... weird to you?"

Seely studied me for a second. "I mean... I think *you're* definitely acting weird," he shoved my shoulder playfully. "But no, I don't think Sean inviting us to dinner is weird, if that's what you're asking."

"Hmm..."

That dread still filled my veins and caused my hands to threaten to shake. But that could be residual dread from the task at hand. I shook my head. Seely was probably right.

"Okay. I don't know, I just had a weird feeling."

I turned away from Seely to the door. I was going to go to my room and grab a change of clothes before heading to the shower to get ready for dinner, but Seely grabbed my arm before I could effectively brush past him.

"Wait," he said, and I turned to meet his eyes. "If you have a weird feeling, we shouldn't ignore it. Just because I want to trust Sean because I like him doesn't necessarily mean we should." My heart thumped louder with those words. "We'll be cautious tonight." He pressed something into my hand, and I grabbed it tightly, without looking. It was my obsidian dagger. "We'll take the daggers, be on alert, and if anyone tries anything we'll fight our way out." Seely winked at me and dropped my arm to let me leave, but I just continued to stare at him for a moment.

After a few seconds, his smile fell and he stepped closer to me, searching my eyes. I stepped forward too, no longer caring whether or not Seely still loved this version of me like he did the one that had died almost two years ago. I wasn't worried about Katrine or Sean or anyone else that may come in and judge me. I wasn't really worried about anything as I reached out and grabbed the back of his neck to pull his face to mine in a crushing kiss.

Unfortunately, I underestimated my own strength again.

"Ouch," Seely mumbled into my lips.

"Oh, oops," I said, stepping back a little. "I'm sorry, I didn't mean to attack you like that. And I definitely didn't mean to crush you. Did you chip a tooth?"

Seely rubbed his lips back and forth as a laugh escaped his lips. He reached out and grabbed my arm, pulling me closer to him. He took his other hand from his mouth and placed it at the small of my back, tugging me forward even more so that my hands now rested on his chest, the dagger sticking out from under my palm and flat against his shirt. His shirt was still damp from sweat that hadn't dried, and I didn't even care.

"Are you kissing me because we might die tomorrow, or because you just want to kiss me?"

I pulled my eyebrows together. "Does it matter why?"

"It matters to me."

His eyes were wide and searching. Meanwhile, my mind was racing.

It matters to him because... It must matter to him because he doesn't want me to get my hopes up. He doesn't want to have to tell me I'm not the same girl he loved before. Yeah, we might die tomorrow, and that was a good enough reason in itself to get in one last kiss.

But I knew that wasn't what this was. I'd been falling for Seely before I even knew about our history, probably from the first time I saw him leaning in my kitchen doorway with that stupid dagger. I was definitely feeling it when he showed me the tower and again when I jumped in front of him in an attempt to save him from a bullet.

And when he was dying in my arms, I knew no amount of time with him could ever be enough. I knew then that, whoever I was now, I loved him.

My feelings weren't the problem, in fact they weren't even a question. I knew that I loved him. I wasn't exactly sure when those feelings of the past week had turned into something tangible, but they had. I guess they probably developed so quickly because, even though I couldn't remember our time together before, some part of me definitely did.

I loved him. The problem was, I didn't know how he felt about me.

I knew how he felt about the old me. He'd told me as much when he revealed everything to me back at the AAUD. I thought I knew he felt something for me now, but honestly through all the mixed signals I wasn't sure. And wouldn't it make sense for Seely to look at the face of the girl he loved once with that same expression, even if I wasn't her anymore? Even if he didn't feel the same way about the girl I was now?

So, the problem I found myself in at that moment was whether or not I should be truthful and risk everything right before I was about to go into a battle for both of our lives or tell a white lie to save the both of us from embarrassment and distraction.

"Isn't the fact that we might not be alive tomorrow enough reason for a kiss?" I smiled a small smile, and I hoped it looked natural.

Something flashed in Seely's eyes for a second, but all I could place was a slight hardening of his eyes. They were so green today, so beautiful. Those green eyes focused solely on my mouth.

"Of course, that's a good enough reason," he said, and he didn't waste any time before bringing his lips back to mine. I stood still at first, letting him set the pressure so I wouldn't accidentally break his teeth or bust his lip, which was apparently a real probability, but after a second it wasn't enough to just feel him. I needed him closer.

I dropped the dagger and it fell to the ground with a muffled thud as it landed halfway on a pillow. I trailed both of my hands up from where they were placed on his chest until they were tangled in his hair. It was so soft and smooth, and I realized just how much I was always wanting to touch it.

His lips tasted like salt from the sweat that was still stuck to his body, and I couldn't get enough of it. I opened my mouth to breathe in more of him and Seely's chest rumbled beneath mine as he let out a low growl in the back of his throat. I didn't know how long we'd stood there, but it felt like we were an infinite collision of tongues and teeth and breaths that continued to quicken.

I hadn't realized we were moving until I felt the sensation of falling. I landed on top of Seely on the bed with a gasp. We looked at each other, breathing heavily, hearts racing. Seely's eyes were wild, his pupils dilated so large I could barely see a ring of green around them. My hands were still twisted in his hair, so I untangled one of them and brought it up to his face. Using the tip of my finger just like I'd done when he was in his zombie state, I traced his eyebrows first, smoothing out the hairs that had been pushed out of place. I then brought that finger down to trace the bridge of his nose, the harsh plane of that feature was covered in freckles, even more now than when we'd arrived a few days ago. Spending long days in the sun had tanned his skin and made freckles appear on his nose and his forehead and along his arms.

"You're just so…"

I paused, biting my lip. I hadn't meant to say that out loud, and I didn't want to finish the sentence. I looked from his nose and moved my hand to push back his hair from his eyes.

"I'm so what?" Seely's eyes were glistening from some emotion I could only guess at. I shook my head. I felt Seely's laugh vibrate his body and he reached up with one of his hands that had been resting on my back to touch my face softly. I leaned into his touch and continued to stare into his eyes. Without another word, Seely raised up into a seated position, bringing me with him. I removed my hands from his hair and clasped my arms around his neck to keep my balance. I moved my legs until they were around him and I was raised slightly, staring down into his face.

Seely slid his hand up from my cheek and into my hair, the strands wild and curled to the roots from the moisture that was now dried there. He pulled me to him once again and our lips met in a kiss that was neither passionate nor obligatory, but it felt to me like this is what we were born to do. Without thinking, really, and without breaking the kiss, I lifted the hem of his shirt from where it lay on the hem of his waistband. I felt Seely freeze as I tried to bring it up higher.

"Alyssa," he mumbled against my mouth before pulling away to look at me, "what exactly are you doing?"

I probably should have been embarrassed, and maybe I would be later, but the flush that flashed across my face had nothing to do with embarrassment.

"I'm not doing anything," I said, tugging on his shirt again. "I swear."

I felt the grin spread across my face, and I saw the answering one flash on Seely's.

"You are dangerous, Gold." He said, but he lifted his arms so I could lift the shirt the rest of the way over his head. I tossed it to the ground and admired the way his curls fell in an effortlessly beautiful pattern across his forehead.

"And you're gorgeous," I said, with a shrug. "That's what I was going to say earlier, but I guess I just needed you to be half-naked first."

I noticed faint pink lines snaking across his shoulders, and I felt my eyebrows pull together. They were scars, I realized. They covered his shoulders, and I could feel them down his back as I traced the welts with my hands.

"Your dad?" I whispered. Somehow, I knew the answer was yes before he even answered.

Seely nodded, smiling a little. "Tough love, Gold."

I swallowed the lump that rose in my throat. I would kill Mr. Evanson for that, I swore to myself then and there. But I knew if Seely wanted to talk about it then, he would have. So, I just bent down and kissed the tops of his shoulders, first the left and then the right. I would save that conversation for later.

Because there *would* be a later.

"Still gorgeous," I whispered into his skin.

Seely laughed a little breathlessly, burying his head in the crook between my shoulder and my neck. Then, the next thing I knew, I was being tackled. Well, not really tackled, Seely just turned over, so I was underneath him on the bed with my hair sprawled out widely on the bed. I gasped at the sudden movement, and then I was reminded of the dream I had of Seely and me in the field. My cheeks heated with the realization that that was a dream of a memory of another life, but this was real. Seely was real. Here. Looking at me like he could love me too.

"Your turn, then, Gold."

His words broke through my thoughts, and I snapped my attention back to him.

"My what? My turn? For what?"

My stomach dropped slightly.

Seely pulled on the hem of my shirt and wiggled his eyebrows suggestively. I placed my arms over my chest protectively.

"Are you insane?"

"So only you get a feast for the eyes?" He gestured to his body, and I laughed at the sarcasm in his voice. If only he knew how much I was actually enjoying seeing the bare planes of his body. The tan line on his shoulders and the new freckles down his arms highlighted the paleness of his skin from before to the way he'd browned up now. Rather than admit that I appreciated his shirt being off a little too much, I slapped him lightly on his chest with my open palm.

"I'm serious," I said. "It's one thing for someone to walk in and find you shirtless, but me? I would never live that down or get over it, and it would become the thing I cringe about every night before I fall asleep." Seely blinked at me, his lips clearly fighting a smirk. "Is that funny or something?"

I was growing annoyed with the way he was just staring at me, but I was also fighting to keep my voice steady and level. I was afraid of someone coming in, but I was also afraid of taking this any further in general. I could see myself losing complete control right here and now, and that terrified me. It also terrified me to think about the prospect of someone seeing my body with no buffer in between. My hands became clammy at that thought.

Seely still had his hand on the hem of my shirt, playing with it lightly between his fingers. They brushed the skin of my stomach and left a patch of goosebumps in their wake. I felt my face blaze like it was on fire, and I fought against the burning that was growing in my chest. I had to get out of here, to go and get showered and dressed and make my way to dinner like a good girl, or I was going to let him do whatever he wanted and worry about the heartache and other consequences later.

I reached down and grabbed his hand, bringing it up to my mouth. I kissed it gently before intertwining his fingers with mine.

"We need to get ready for dinner."

Seely looked down at me with that same soft smile.

"Of course, Gold, no means no. *I* can control myself." The implication of his words was that I was the one who couldn't control myself in this scenario. I opened my mouth to protest but Seely had pressed his lips to mine again before I could retort. As he probably knew it would, everything but him and the whispers of lips against lips faded away. If we continued on that way for long, I thought, I could probably forget my own name.

Finally, Seely broke away, practically gasping for air. I realized I felt fine, and honestly, I could probably keep going this way for a while longer. Maybe I didn't need to breathe as an Undead… interesting. I tucked away that theory for another day as Seely dragged himself up and off the bed, grabbing a bundle of clothes from inside one of the small drawers in the table beside the bed.

"After tomorrow, we can discuss the terms for who can be naked, how much, and when. Until then, I'm going to take a shower and get ready before Katrine has any reason to gripe."

"My being naked in front of you is something that's only going to happen in your dreams, Seely," I said.

He smiled and bent to kiss me on the bridge of the nose, just as he'd done the other night. "You're right, that's often in my dreams." I reached for a pillow to throw at him, but they were all on the ground, just out of reach. "Though, you shouldn't worry that much about it." He reached the door and opened it just enough to slip out. I realized he was still shirtless, and I hoped no one looked too much into that. "It's nothing I haven't seen before."

With a wink, he was gone, the door shut, and his soft laughter faded quickly down the corridor.

I could only stare at the door he'd left through, my mouth falling open with an audible pop.

Yup. I was going to be cringing about this later.

Chapter Twenty-Five

ABOUT THIRTY MINUTES LATER, I STOOD in the hallway right outside the door that led to the dining room. I could hear voices filtering from the room and through the crack of the door where it didn't quite reach the floor. The light that filtered through that crack flickered and changed every few seconds, letting me know that we were relying on firelight and candles rather than electricity tonight. Katrine and Sean had explained to us one day that they tried their best to conserve the energy harnessed during the daytime by solar panels, and when they didn't need to use their electric lights, they simply didn't.

I smoothed the skirt of the dress Sammy had laid out for me, wiping my sweaty palms against the soft fabric. I knew we were getting a sendoff tonight, but I didn't know it was going to be something even remotely close to formal dining. I took a deep breath.

The dress Sammy had thrust at me while I was walking to the shower (after carefully waiting until I heard Seely re-enter his room and shut the door, I might add) was a deep crimson color. It was long and form-fitting, with capped sleeves that fell to the sides of my shoulders. According to Sammy, this is how it was supposed to look.

I felt self-conscious in this borrowed outfit, and I also couldn't shake that unease I'd begun to feel earlier when Sean left Seely's room.

Right before we'd…

I shook my head back and forth a couple of times, clearing those thoughts away. Right before we'd almost done absolutely nothing. I wasn't really going to let myself get too carried away. At least, that's what I told myself.

Seely and I had had our moment, and I had to admit I enjoyed every bit of it. But it also scared me just how close I got to giving him everything… And then he'd made that comment.

It's nothing I haven't seen before.

I cringed a little internally. Had he been referring to me specifically? Maybe he was talking about someone else he'd been with. I hated that I didn't remember, and he did. It was such a disadvantage to not know your past, especially when the person you spent a good chunk of it with seemed to remember every detail.

I sighed. Here I was, standing outside the dining room of a family I wanted to trust but couldn't seem to let my guard down. I could hear slightly muted voices and laughter from behind the door. I lifted my hand to turn the knob and then let it fall back to my side. Letting out a shaky breath, I tried to focus on calming my nerves.

Seely had an uncanny ability to be at home wherever he found himself, even in an underground bunker with strangers. I, on the other hand, could never seem to stop my mind from racing toward the inevitable worst. What if they were lying, what if they tried to kill us, what if Seely was just with me because of who I used to be and not who I am now, what if, what if, what if…

I still had the same twisting feeling in my gut that had settled there since Sean had left Seely and I alone earlier, and I wasn't sure if I should trust it or ignore it. When I'd told Seely, he didn't really seem too concerned, but told me we would be armed and ready just in case we needed to be. I felt the side of my thigh for the sheath that held my dagger. It was still strapped firmly to my leg, and I breathed in and out, slowly. This was okay. I was okay.

After three breaths, my heart was pounding less loudly than before, and I had steeled myself to enter the room in front of me.

I reached for the handle a second time, and this time I forced myself to turn the knob and push the door inward. Stepping through the doorway, the first thing that hit me was the smell. The long table that filled the entire room was laid with so much food, almost anything I could ask for at a farewell dinner. There was roast chicken and potatoes and apple pie and everything in between, and the smell of all these foods somehow intermingled into something particularly mouthwatering. I thought this would normally be the time when my stomach would growl, but as I waited for it nothing came. As an Undead, I guessed that I didn't need food to survive anymore, which meant I was never really hungry. Tonight, though, I was going to feast with the best of them, even if my stomach exploded.

My mouth was so dry. It had been getting worse and worse every day I'd been here, but tonight it was hard to focus on much else. I wondered if it was a weird side-effect from the serum. Or maybe it was just another weird Undead thing, though Seely said he'd never heard of that. I didn't know, and I tried to push it out of my mind as I pushed open the door to the dining room.

"Alyssa!" Sammy and Lilah squealed and ran up to me at the same time. I held out my arms and brought them both in for a tight squeeze. I never had sisters, only Seth, but the girls reminded me of my memories of Stella. Though, I remembered that I couldn't necessarily trust those memories, especially considering Stella was a part of the group who actively kept me asleep for years. Along with my dad and brother. My family.

Nope, I thought, *not tonight*.

I forced myself to smile as widely and believably as possible. I was going to enjoy this night, no matter what problems I had to face tomorrow.

"Hi guys!" I said, and I hoped my cheeriness didn't feel false or forced.

"You look so beautiful, Alyssa," Sammy said, stepping back to look at me again. Turning to Lilah she said, "I told you redheads can wear red!"

Lilah flushed slightly and glared at her sister. I smiled. This was exactly the type of conversation I would have with Stella. Maybe I had before.

My smile turned into a frown as I thought about that.

"I didn't say they *couldn't* wear red," she said, her tone a little seething, "I just thought the green dress would look even better." She turned to look at me then and smiled. I didn't sense anything off about that smile, and it made my lips turn up again in response. I'd really taken to these girls in the past few days. They were so open and honest with me and everyone else around them, almost to a fault, and I appreciated it. It reminded me of one of the qualities I liked most about Seely.

"Your hair is more of a dark auburn than *red*, red, anyway," Sammy said. "I knew you would look great in that color, and I was right." I smiled and Sammy turned her gaze from my eyes to something behind me. "I think someone else thinks you look good too." The girls looked at each other then and giggled. I felt my smile fall and brows furrow together before that someone walked up behind me.

"I love your hair like this."

I felt a hand reach out and pull gently on one of my curls that I'd let fall loose tonight. I usually left my hair up in some way, but tonight the curls were wild and untamed. I smiled at the compliment and then turned to face Seely.

He was wearing a suit, all black, a shade that was almost a perfect match to his hair. He wasn't wearing a tie, and instead his shirt was open a little at the top. My eyes lingered there at the undone buttons, and heat flashed over my cheeks as I thought about what had happened in his room not even an hour earlier.

"Would you like to share with the class?" Seely dipped his head down a little lower to catch my gaze, and I flushed an even deeper red. Between my cheeks, my hair, and the dress, I knew I had to look like some kind of flame. Or a lobster.

"I don't know what you're talking about." Looking away, I wiped my hands down my dress again. It was becoming a nervous tick at this point. A finger was under my chin, lifting my head to meet a piercing gaze that consisted of black eyes I knew were green underneath the shadow of the dimly lit room, a mouth of full lips that were twisted to the side in a way that seemed like there was some kind of sarcastic remark just around the corner, and curls of dark hair that fell over a forehead and onto eyebrows that looked perfectly scruffy. I held back a sigh. Seely was too perfect, and I knew he couldn't see in me what I saw in him. Today had been fun, but I also knew it had to be more about us leaving tomorrow and possibly not leaving the AAUD alive than it was about any real feelings.

I mean, the feelings were real to me, but I wasn't expecting anything from Seely. He was mourning for the girl he lost, and I would let him use me as long as he needed to.

"Is this about what I said before I left earlier?" Seely still had his fingers under my chin, making it impossible to drop my head unless I pulled his hand from my face.

"What do you mean? I don't even remember what you said earlier." I felt my blush betray me.

His right eyebrow quirked up.

"Oh, you don't?"

I shook my head.

"Interesting."

His smile widened and he opened his mouth to say something else, but just then Katrine called to us from the other side of the table.

"Alyssa, Seely. Your seats are over here." She pointed to two chairs at the opposite end of the table from her and Sean. I looked over at Katrine and she was lounging in her chair, her dark hair pulled up into a low, tight bun. In this light, her honey-brown skin seemed to glow. The simple gold nose ring she'd worn earlier had been exchanged for a larger one that contained a few jewels. I couldn't really tell in this light, but I thought they looked like emeralds.

She looked more beautiful than I had ever seen her, but her eyes were shadowed, and they looked swollen. Had she been crying? Without looking at either of us, she simply pointed in the direction of our chairs again and grabbed a glass of what looked like wine, taking a long drink.

Seely had dropped his hand from my face when we both turned to look at Katrine, and when I turned back to him, he only shrugged. I felt my brows pull together as I looked into his eyes, trying to see if we were on the same page.

Seely stared right back at me and mouthed, "Yes, it's suspicious."

I almost smiled at the fact that, yet again, he'd read my mind, but the whole situation was too weird. Seely grabbed my hand, interlocking our fingers together, as he dragged me in the direction of our designated chairs before Katrine could be pushed any further over the edge. My heart fluttered a little at his touch.

We stopped at the seat that was at the head of the table and Seely motioned for me to take it. I hesitated for a moment, that same stone of dread settling in my stomach, but really, what could happen from choosing a chair? With that thought, I took my seat, and Seely took the chair directly to my left, facing the door.

I looked around and noticed that Sean wasn't in the room yet. The girls and Max had taken three of the seats to my right, with their backs to the door, and Katrine faced me from the other end in her seat at the head of the table. I watched her and her bleary eyes. She continued to take drinks from her wine, and I noticed the bottle sitting directly in front of her on the table. I wondered how long she'd been drinking tonight, and I thought it must have been a while for her eyes to already look that bloodshot.

I looked over to Seely with a question on my face. He turned to me at the same time, and I could see the confusion and suspicion finally, officially, written plainly on his face.

"So, Katrine," Seely said, clearing his throat and turning toward her at the end of the table to break the silence that was beginning to grow awkward, "where is Sean right now?"

Katrine rolled her eyes all the way over to Seely, and the way she did it made me think they weighed about ten pounds apiece in their sockets.

"He's taking care of a couple of things." Another gulp of wine. "He'll be here soon."

"Ah," Seely said. "I see." He cut a glance at me from the corner of his eye. I realized I could read his mind pretty plainly as well. Something was wrong here. I didn't know if it was anything sinister, it could just be that Katrine and Sean got into a fight and they were both taking it hard. It didn't have to have anything to do with us. But the air in the room seemed to thicken with my every thought and I felt the ice begin to flow through my veins. My chest was hot, and I focused on that heat, breathing it in and out. It felt like control, like power, like—

"Gold," Seely whispered, grabbing my hand and squeezing it under the table. "Your eyes are beginning to glow, and we should probably try to reel that in."

He was right. I didn't know how to control any of the powers that manifested at random times, and I didn't want to risk setting the place on fire. Or freezing it. I still wasn't really sure what I could do yet.

I nodded and breathed in deeply, but instead of focusing on stoking the fire in my chest I focused on mixing the ice with the fire and creating a balance within my body. Seely still held my hand under the table, and I knew I'd accomplished my goal of reigning that light in when he squeezed my hand one more time before letting it go and sitting up straight in his chair.

I faced straight forward, looking at Katrine, who was staring at me with those bleary eyes. I caught her gaze, and I couldn't look away.

"Is everything okay, Katrine?" The question came out less forceful than I wanted it to.

She just continued to stare at me. After an uncomfortable moment, when I was officially squirming in my seat, Katrine reached out a hand and gestured toward the food.

"We may as well eat while we wait for Sean." She smiled, but it wasn't warm. I felt a little bad for her. I could tell she was going through something that she didn't want to talk about at dinner. I also felt bad that I was part of the reason she had to be present at this dinner anyway. After all, it was a sendoff for me and Seely, and any other night she and Sean probably could have had it out in peace, or whatever it was they had going on tonight.

The girls and Max didn't hesitate to grab their plates and begin piling them with pieces of steaming chicken and sides of corn and green beans and potatoes and everything in between. I watched them fill their plates and my stomach churned. The way they began to scarf their food down was making me feel suddenly nauseous.

"This is a dinner for you and Seely, Alyssa," Katrine said to me. I looked from the kids eating to my right and back to her face at the other end of the table. "Eat something."

It didn't feel like a request, and rather than push her off the edge, I grabbed my plate and reached for the closest thing to me: potatoes. Perfect.

Seely was silent beside me, but he did the same. He grabbed a piece of chicken and began picking at it with his fingers. I watched him as we both took a bite of the food on our plates at the same time.

The salty, garlicky flavor filled my mouth, and I fought the urge to sigh. It was good, like… *good, good.* The whole time we'd been here, I'd barely eaten anything, but the most extravagant thing I'd seen anyone eat was finger sandwiches. I remembered Sean had told me their cook had been sick, so maybe this was their cook at their highest capacity. Though, when I thought about that aspect of the situation, I realized I hadn't seen anyone besides the family and Bernard here at all. But I didn't know very much about this place. For all I knew, there could be another floor below with quarters for some invisible employees of the house. There could be a whole underground theme park beneath my feet—I had no idea.

I pushed those thoughts aside as I took another bite of potatoes. The flavor was still delicious, but the food settled like a rock in my stomach. I tried not to think about that either. I knew I was an Undead, but if I didn't need human food to survive, I didn't want to think about what I might need to consume in its place. I could deal with being an Undead, mostly because I didn't feel much different than I remember feeling as a human. You know, besides the glowing thing.

But if I had to drink human blood, I wouldn't be able to ignore that part of myself anymore, and I definitely wasn't ready to face it.

I looked over at Seely for a distraction from my thoughts. He took another bite and coughed a little. Reaching out for his drink, he coughed louder and then took a huge gulp of water. He sat the cup back down and cleared his throat, pounding his fist on his chest. I fought the urge to roll my eyes. He was making a bit of a scene, but it was the only noise in the room besides chewing and the crackling of the fire, so I kind of welcomed it.

"What time are you planning on leaving for the AAUD?" Katrine asked the question to no one in particular, though she was looking directly at me when I turned to her.

"Um, we were thinking first light." I reached out for my cup and took a drink of water. I wished it was tea. My insides felt strangely cold in this room, though the fire should have been keeping everything overly warm.

"Where are you planning to go after you've completed your mission? Assuming you don't die, that is."

The flatness of her voice was disconcerting. I didn't know what could have happened between when I'd seen her yesterday and tonight to make her turn into a completely different person. She scared me enough, though, that I wasn't about to come right out and ask.

"We aren't really sure about the logistics of that yet," Seely answered. "We're hoping Alyssa's family and our friends will be on our side." He shrugged. This was the part of the plan we hadn't been able to figure all the way out, which scared me to death, but Seely hadn't acted like it was a big deal.

I was still watching Katrine and she was watching me. I watched her turn her eyes slowly over again until her attention was on Seely.

"So, you weren't planning on coming back here?"

I shot my eyes over to Seely and he did the same to me.

We'd thought about it, sure, but...

"No, sorry," he said, matter-of-factly. "Whatever happens at the AAUD, we can't really risk staying in this forest any longer. I don't know how we've gone this long without an attack, anyway..." Seely's eyebrows drew together slightly. I knew he was thinking about the Others and the Undead that supposedly ran these woods, and my mind went there too. I hadn't really thought about why these things hadn't even attempted to harm us while we'd been here. We spent hours on end outside in the clearing practicing and training... wouldn't something have come to at least try and fight us if they were so prevalent that trained AAUD soldiers sent into the forest often never came out again?

That unease in the pit of my stomach began to lurch again. Something was wrong here, and I couldn't figure out what. I was feeling so cold.

"Right," Katrine laughed a short and hard laugh. "I forget the things you two don't know."

My heart sank at her words.

"I'm sorry?" I whispered. "What are you talking about?"

Katrine regarded me with a sense of cold distaste.

"Did you look through that box, Alyssa? Or were you too busy having romantic trysts with this one?" She tipped her glass towards Seely as she said that, and I felt the heat rush to my cheeks. I turned my head to the children, but they didn't seem to be paying attention. "Well?" She sat down her glass and let out a harsh laugh. "Actually, the fact that you're here right now has already given me my answer."

I turned my attention back to Katrine and opened my mouth to answer her, but Seely spoke before I could.

"First of all," he said, all sarcasm and easiness gone from his tone, "as a going away party, this interrogation portion sucks. Second, what we do is none of your business. And if we'd had a 'tryst'," he put air quotes around the word, "it's pretty weird for you to be so invested in it." Seely leaned forward a little bit, and the way his eyes darkened was a little scary.

"And the last thing," his voice was low and menacing at this point, "if everyone is so worried about all the secrets we don't know, maybe one of you should just open your mouth and tell us." He smiled then, showing all of his teeth, but it wasn't a happy one. It was a smile that promised he was barely holding back his anger, and someone better explain what was going on, and they'd better do it quickly and carefully.

Katrine laughed again, and when I looked over, she was taking another sip of her wine.

"Everything you need to know is in that box I gave to you, Alyssa." She sat down her drink and looked up at me. "I know you didn't look in it because you would be long gone by now. You *should* be long gone by now." I felt so cold… and I was only getting colder.

"What are you talking about?"

"I made a promise to your mother, and I tried to keep it. But sometimes life happens and people with more power have something they can hold over your head." I looked over at Seely, but he wasn't looking at me now. He was staring at Katrine.

"I tried to warn you. I did. I tried to get you out of here before it was too late, but even if you walked out of this room right now and tried to make a run for it, you wouldn't make it a mile." I didn't understand what I was hearing, but only one person came to mind that could be involved with whatever Katrine was rambling about.

"Does Mr. Evanson have anything to do with this?"

I don't know why that suddenly came to my mind, but as I said it everything clicked together.

Katrine only smiled and brought her finger up to press against the tip of her nose. "Winner, winner, Alyssa. You got there. I just wish you'd figured it out yesterday. Or the day before." I reached for the dagger on my thigh and Katrine shot me a sympathetic look. "A dagger isn't going to save you." Her eyes were hooded, and she reached for her glass of wine. It was about half full and she downed the entire glass in two gulps. "I'm sorry, I really am."

"What…" I couldn't think of what I wanted to say. The words were racing through my brain. "Why?" was all that came out.

"He has some leverage to hold over my head. Something I didn't think even he could stand to lose, but I guess I overestimated the amount of care he has for anyone, even his family."

"His family?"

I looked at Seely and his eyes were narrowed, his brows pulled closely together in concentration. As far as I knew, Seely was his only family.

"What family does he have that you would care anything about?"

"Think about it, Alyssa. You're a smart girl." Katrine smiled sadly and she poured herself another glass of wine, almost all the way up to the brim. The sight of the blood red liquid made my stomach twist strangely.

I did think about it. I thought about the dark hair and eyes and the way she always looked like she had a secret she wasn't ready to tell. I thought about how invested she was in making sure Seely and I stayed apart and the obsidian dagger she and Sean had given me that was identical to his...

"No."

It was Seely who spoke, beating me to it. I looked over to him and I felt my eyes filling up with tears. I didn't really know where they were coming from, but I knew this realization was going to shatter some piece of Seely and I wanted to protect him from it.

"Saying no doesn't make it untrue, Seely." Katrine smiled a little, not meeting Seely's eyes. "Your father has found the one thing he can threaten that I will do anything to keep safe. The one thing I won't let him have. You." Katrine looked at me, then. "It's your fault, you know," she said, quietly, pointing at me with one finger. "You're the reason all of this is happening.

If you had left my son alone, none of this would have happened."

My head was spinning and there were so many things I didn't understand. How was she Seely's mom? How was she *here*? Why did she live in a bunker in the woods with an entirely different family? Didn't Seely think she was dead?

But before I could ask any of these questions, the door to the dining room flew open and a tall figure walked in with Sean at his tail.

Mr. Evanson stood in the doorway, smirking in a way that reminded me a little bit of Seely, and I wanted to puke at the thought.

Chapter Twenty-Six

"I HOPE WE'RE NOT INTERRUPTING," MR. EVANSON SAID, his deep voice somehow crooning and condescending at the same time. He was thinking he'd won, and that was an obvious fact that was written all across his face. He certainly didn't look like a man who had just stabbed himself in the stomach a few days ago. How was he here? And how did he seem so… healthy? And fine? I felt completely frozen. I couldn't even feel that fire in my chest that was usually sitting right under the surface. All my limbs were getting heavy.

Something was wrong, and it was more than the fact that Seely's parents were both in the room.

"Not at all," Katrine said, pushing away from the table, causing her chair to scrape loudly across the floor. I was a little bit awed at the change I saw in her. It made more sense now that I knew the root cause of this change, and the sentiment of some people bringing out the worst in others crossed my mind. "We were just having dinner. Waiting for you two to join us." She gestured towards Max, Sammy, and Lilah, who I admit I'd forgotten were even still there. "Children, go to your rooms."

Sammy turned to me, her eyes wide and quickly filling with tears.

"Alyssa?"

I didn't know what she was asking me, or why. I didn't have the answers for any of this. I felt my face become stone. I didn't know what was going to happen, I didn't know if they were involved in any way, but I wasn't going to let anyone in this room see how scared I truly was.

"Samantha. Now."

Sammy jumped a little at the harsh words. Without taking her eyes off of my face, she got up from her seat. She only turned away from me to grab Lilah and run out the door. I watched as Max stopped and leaned in closely to Sean.

"No, it'll be okay. If we need your help after, we'll let you know." Sean reached out and ruffled his son's hair that was the same shade as his own. "You know how messy these things can get, especially when they try to fight."

I waited for the fire to light in me at those words. I was counting on that heat in my chest that always seemed to rise up when I was in danger or just nervous in general.

But I only felt ice in my veins. This wasn't the icy heat that I'd given up trying to control, no, this was… just ice, settling heavy in my arms and legs. I felt my head begin to loll. I was so tired.

"What did you do to her?" The voice was distant, but I knew it was Seely's. I watched, as if through a tunnel, as he stalked over to me. His hair had fallen over his eyes and his eyes were a burning shade of green. They looked like they were on fire. His lips were moist from the little meal he'd eaten, and I couldn't stop myself from reaching out to touch them.

"Beautiful." I said, though I wasn't sure at first if it was in my head or out loud.

"Shh, Gold, it'll be okay." I felt Seely's hands on my face and they were so rough and warm. Too warm. They burned my icy skin where he touched me. I struggled in his grip, and he moved his hands to my waist to keep me steady without having to touch my bare skin. "You're so cold." His voice was barely a whisper.

Before I really knew what had happened, Seely had unsheathed my dagger and thrown it directly at his father. He moved to dodge it, but he was only able to deflect it with his forearm. I watched as a line of deep red blood dripped from the gash the blade made there.

Then a really strange thing happened.

I was suddenly ravenous.

The blood that leaked from the wound on Mr. Evanson's arm looked better to me than anything spread out on the table before me. It dripped from the gash, almost as if in slow motion. I thought that if I tasted it, I would never be satisfied with anything else. I knew that if I got that one taste, it would never be enough. I wanted to drink and drink until I'd drained him.

He wasn't a person to me anymore. He didn't have a face. He was only an exquisite meal that was ripe and ready for the taking.

"I think she's hungry," Mr. Evanson said, chuckling.

Seely grabbed my face to bring my attention back to him, and I heard a sound that was less than human escape from my lips. I *growled* at him.

It wasn't like the growl that had escaped Seely earlier during our "tryst", as Katrine had put it. This was a growl that sent chills up my own spine, and the small part of my brain that was still human, that part that was trying to fight this, was scared of me. Of whatever this creature was that was coming out of me. I knew that if I were able to move in that moment, I probably would have hurt him.

"What did you do to her?"

The anger in Seely's voice rivaled the terror caused by my own. I focused on his face in front of me, and his eyes were wild, wide and pitch black.

His question went unanswered by everyone else in the room.

"She hasn't fed at all since she woke, has she?" It was Mr. Evanson who spoke, and I thought he sounded a bit awed.

"Not that we know of," Sean said, "but you should probably ask your son. It sounded like something was happening in his room earlier. She may be taking advantage of him without his knowledge."

Seely growled then, and I mean really growled. I thought it might be something funny if I wasn't sure this is where we were both going to die. I hoped that they would at least let Seely live. I hoped that he wouldn't do anything stupid, like get himself killed for me. I wanted to remind him that I'd already died once and it was okay to let me do it again, but I was using what little self-control I still had over my body and my mind to keep my mouth clamped shut. I was afraid of what might come out if I let myself go.

"What. Are. You. Talking. About."

Each word came out in a low snarl, clipped and precise. I could see the anger bubbling underneath the surface of his features.

"What I'm talking about, Son, is that your little girlfriend here is something quite special. She's an Undead, but not just any Undead. We've had our suspicions about that, obviously, but now we know for sure. Our friend Orthan has special plans for her."

Mr. Evanson stepped closer to us, but Seely didn't take his hands or his eyes off of me. His father took a seat and settled into the chair directly to my right. He reached out and grabbed a chicken leg before continuing his story.

"You know how the Change usually occurs, right? The human subject has to be drained of all their blood, pumped with just enough Undead blood right before their heart stops, and then buried." He took a bite of the chicken. "It's a messy process, usually. It's also pretty hard to accomplish, as far as I understand. It usually takes Undead practice before they're able to successfully make another.

"There is a legend of Undead who are closer to humans. They can pass as human, in fact. They are also stronger than the usual of the species, probably something to do with them having one foot in either side of the door between human and monster. They're easier to kill in general, but they're equipped with safety precautions against that. These usually manifest in some kind of power." He took a bite of the chicken. "Has she shown any symptoms of extra abilities of any kind?"

Seely didn't say anything, but I saw him stiffen. I knew his father saw it too.

"That's what I thought," Mr. Evanson said with a little chuckle. "Anyway, Orthan heard that, in order to make one of these Undead you needed to leave the human subject with a little of their human blood left in their body before you fill them with Undead blood, but not just any blood, the blood of one of these special Undead. That's what he did with her, and I guess it worked." He laughed again.

"Why her?" Seely's voice was soft, low. "He could have picked anyone. Why her?"

"Now that is an interesting part of the story," Mr. Evanson said, wiping his fingers on a napkin. "Let's just say his first test subject, and the Undead whose blood he used to Create her, is close to Alyssa's heart. Orthan's too if the rumors are to be believed. In order to make one of what she is, apparently, you have to use the blood from one who is already Made into the same type of Undead."

Seely's eyes furrowed, and I felt the same way. His father was speaking in riddles now, and I couldn't deal with that right now. My chest was aching. My stomach felt like stone. My limbs were heavy. I couldn't even feel my fingers now.

"Seely," I whispered. It came out as a pathetic whimper.

Seely lifted his hands as though he was going to touch my face again, but I guessed he remembered how he'd burned me the last time and he let them fall back down onto my legs.

"What's wrong with her? What can I do?"

And I could see in his face that he wasn't going to leave here alive if that was what it took to save me.

No, I wanted to say. *Don't*. But my mouth wouldn't move. Everything was so heavy. Seely was so far away.

"You see, there's something that happens with an Undead after they run out of human blood. They die. Some simply fade away, while others, like our girl here, freeze up, dry out, and just keel over one day. It happens rather quickly after a certain point, especially when one doesn't know how to recognize the signs.

"Gold may have kept her sedated, but he also kept her fully pumped with blood. It's a little different than ingesting it, it doesn't last as long, but it keeps the subject alive. And it worked well for you for a while, didn't it, Alyssa?"

My dad knew? He *knew*. This whole time, he knew what I was. He knew exactly what he was doing by keeping me down. He knew exactly what he was doing by keeping Seely away from me. He *knew*.

And I had been feeling so thirsty the last few days. It was insatiable and only getting worse, but nothing else had really been bothering me. Was my body trying to tell me that I needed blood?

If I had any sense of myself in that moment, I might have known I was crying before I felt the searing tears fall onto my skin.

"Yes, yes, it's a very emotional moment for us all. But especially you, Seely."

Seely turned away from me for the first time to face his father.

"For me? Why?"

"Because this is where you choose. Either you stay here with your mother, never leaving, never seeing the light of day again, but living what could be a long, healthy, albeit boring, life with your mother, or you attempt to stop me from what I have to do next, and I'm forced to kill you."

"Klein, that wasn't a part of the deal." It was Katrine's voice I heard, I thought. My eyes searched the room for her, and I found her shocked expression to my left, right in front of the fireplace. I thought the way the fire haloed her figure made her look like some kind of deity, a goddess. I should have guessed she was Seely's mother from the beginning, they were both so beautiful.

"You promised you wouldn't harm him if I kept them here long enough for you to get everything ready. I did that."

"And from what I understand, you also attempted to warn them of this little plan before I could even arrive, is that not also correct?" Mr. Evanson snapped at her. She didn't reply, but we all knew it was true, and there was no use in denying it. "That's what I thought," he continued. "So, as far as I'm concerned, our contract is null and void. I'm here to take the girl, and if our idiot son gets in the way, I will have no choice but to kill him."

Mr. Evanson shrugged as if he thought that would only be a minor inconvenience, and I thought that was probably exactly how he felt.

Katrine was silent after that, and I knew what was going to happen next. Seely was going to fight his father and Sean, and he was probably going to die. He was going to die to save me, and I could barely even hold my head up.

Seely, no, I screamed in my mind. *Please don't do it. Let him take me. I'll find you.*

Seely looked at me as if he thought I'd said something, but he shook his head as he stood up. He took one of my freezing hands in his and bent down to plant a kiss of fire on my palm.

Too soon, he dropped it and turned to his father, unsheathing his dagger.

"This is the wrong choice, Son," Mr. Evanson said, shaking his head. He didn't sound upset or nervous, though, he just sounded… disappointed. As if he'd caught him smoking or sneaking out. "You forget who taught you to even hold a dagger."

Seely flipped the blade in his hand.

"How could I ever forget, Father? I have plenty of scars to prove it."

I thought about the scars Seely was referring to, the ones I'd kissed earlier, but where there should have been a shock of anger there was only nothingness and a sensation of floating. That would have scared me even more if I'd been able to feel anything at all.

"You won't win."

"And you won't take her."

That smirk I loved spread across Seely's face as he positioned himself directly in front of his father, ready to strike.

Before he could even attempt it, a flash of black darted from the side and stuck itself into Mr. Evanson's side. He let out a roar as Katrine let out a scream of her own and hurled herself at him.

"GO!" She screamed at Seely as he stared, frozen, at the wrestling pair on the ground. Katrine got her hand on the knife and pressed it in deeper, causing another roar of pain and frustration to erupt from Seely's father. "I said go, NOW—"

Mr. Evanson got the upper hand then, and I watched in my near comatose state as he pinned her to the ground, his hand around her throat. I couldn't help. I felt useless. I saw Sean standing stock still by the door. His expression was blank, and I realized I'd gotten this entire situation completely wrong to begin with. Katrine wasn't here of her own free will, she was being held here. She and Sean weren't together, and it was clear with whom his loyalties lay. Sean had been working with Mr. Evanson this whole time… And Katrine had been kept here from Seely. For how long? Most of his life, as far as I knew.

Katrine made a swift hit to Mr. Evanson's nose, palm up, and it landed with a sickening crunch. She scrambled up from underneath him a little and threw something at Seely. It was a small pouch.

"Take her and go, *now*, Seely! You won't have another chance."

Seely unfroze, no longer hesitating. He sheathed his dagger and reached down to pick me up in one swoop. My skin was burned from where he touched it.

Sean stood by the door, looking as though he might try and stop us.

"Sean, please, let them—"

Her sentence cut off in a strangled gurgle. Mr. Evanson stood behind Katrine with his arms wrapped around her body. My borrowed dagger stuck out from her chest, right at her heart. I watched as the dark purple fabric of her dress grew even deeper as the blood flowed out of the wound, and I heard Seely take in a sharp breath. His father pushed the dagger in deeper and I saw the light leave Katrine's eyes as she collapsed to the ground. Her eyes didn't shut as she lay there, unseeing. Sean stumbled forward a step, clearly torn about something, and Seely didn't hesitate to run through the door with me in his arms.

We made our way down the hallway and to the secret door by our rooms. Seely was able to open it easily, but we both knew the next door was going to slow us down.

"I don't know what to do, Alyssa." Seely's voice was low, panicked. We had seconds, if that, and I knew it was going to take longer than that to steady me and for him to push the door open using his strength alone. He looked at me and I at him, with bleary eyes that I was trying my best to keep open.

"Can we help?"

Seely whipped us around, and it was Sammy and Lilah, there with two bags stuffed full of something.

"We didn't know what was going on, we promise," Alyssa stammered. "Sometimes people come here, and they don't ever leave, but we like you. We want you to make it."

The girls pushed past us and grabbed the handle of the door at the same time. They pushed together, and I was amazed to see the handle slide firmly into place. On the other side of the door. Katrine wasn't kidding when she said they could take care of themselves.

"Go," Sammy said, pushing the door all the way open and throwing the packs into my arms. I clutched at them, holding on as tight as I could. I thought I gave them a smile, but I wasn't sure. I didn't feel like I was really there anymore.

"Take care of her, Seely, okay? We'll stall them."

I couldn't tell if it had been Lilah or Sammy who said those words, but without saying anything else I heard them return through the door and close it completely, sliding the metal arm into place with a finality that would have chilled my skin if it weren't already frozen.

I felt Seely lean down a little and kiss the top of my head before we dove headfirst into the darkness of the forest ahead.

Chapter Twenty-Seven

I DREAMED THAT I WAS FLOATING IN A SHALLOW POOL. The air was warm on my skin, and I only knew I was in water from the way I was floating on my back and the feeling of the cool liquid on my arms. I ran my hands through the water, though it felt strangely thick, almost like it was turning into gel or something close to solid between my fingers. I relished in the feeling of nothingness, of floating, though I couldn't remember how I got there. Or how to open my eyes.

But now that I was thinking about it, I didn't really even want to open my eyes. I was savoring the cool of the strangely tangible water that surrounded me, and the air was so warm on my face. I didn't remember how I'd gotten to this place, but I had a vague idea that something traumatic had happened to bring me to this moment. I didn't want to feel the pain of whatever that thing was. I just wanted to stay here in this mixture of cool and warmth.

I felt something hot drip onto my face, at the corner of my mouth. At first it was only one drop, but then several began to flow. It was like a steady stream of a summer's rain, purely concentrated on my mouth. That was definitely strange.

"Come on, Alyssa. You have to drink. Please."

The voice was familiar, but it sounded far away, like I was on one end of the tunnel, and it was on the other.

I moved my head slightly, trying to get away from the drops on my face, but something grabbed my chin and held me steady.

"I'm giving you the choice right now, but I will force you to drink if you won't do it on your own." More drops hit my face. "You're not dying on me, Gold."

A single drop of the warm liquid seeped into my mouth, though my lips remained closed, and my eyes snapped open before I ever decided to let them.

The taste in my mouth was like an explosion of everything warm and delicious. It was fresh-baked cookies and the perfect mug of tea. It was fresh French fries and pepperoni pizza. I needed more.

My eyes weren't focusing on anything as I licked my lips, but I thought I saw the tops of trees, maybe even a moon up there somewhere. Before I could try to make sense of my surroundings, something solid rested gently on my mouth. The liquid that had all my senses honed exclusively on it seemed to be coming from whatever it was. I grabbed on tightly, digging my fingers in, and I took a deep draft.

"Good. Drink as much as you need." I was reveling in the sensation that came with each drink, and my chest began to hum. The warmth that gathered there was spreading through my veins and limbs, making its way to my toes and my fingertips. The taste was so sweet, so savory, so... desirable. I never wanted to stop drinking.

A hand came down on my shoulder, and I heard a growl escape the lips of someone nearby.

"Okay so maybe you shouldn't take as much as you want. I'm about to pass out over here, Alyssa." There was a short laugh, but it sounded panicked. That pricked my attention. This voice sounded familiar, but I couldn't focus my mind enough to piece together where exactly I'd heard it before.

"Alyssa. Stop." It was that same voice again, but the panic this time was not even a little bit concealed as I continued to drink. The hand on my shoulder squeezed, but I barely felt it. I was lost in the bliss of the warmth and the sweetness and the smell of the thing I drank from that reminded me of...

Cinnamon.

Seely.

With a gasp, I threw the thing from my mouth and opened my eyes, blinking into the night. My gaze bounced all around me, from tree to tree, while I tried my hardest to focus. When my vision became less blurry, I realized I was staring at the dense forest that surrounded the bunker. The bunker that contained Katrine and Sean and Sammy and Lilah and Max. The bunker where Mr. Evanson had just... Oh *god*.

"Seely, Katrine is your mother?" I blurted the question out without even thinking about it.

I don't know why those were the first words out of my mouth, but they were. I guess that was the most pressing question on my mind at that moment. I realized then that I didn't see Seely. But he had to be there, I'd just been drinking his blood, right?

Oh my god, I'd just been drinking his blood. And a lot of it, too.

"Seely?" My voice sounded panicked even though it was hushed.

"I'm here."

His voice came from my left, and it was weak and soft. I snapped my head in that direction to find him, but I couldn't see anything right away. The grass was high, and I realized we were sitting in the middle of the only clearing in the midst of brambles and roots that twisted and gnarled through the ground. I couldn't see him lying there on the ground until he raised a hand in a wave. I heard a giggle escape my lips as I crawled over to him.

"I like that sound much better than the growl." Seely shuddered as I lay next to him. "I have to admit, Gold, I was a little scared of you there for a minute. I had to lay down and catch my breath," he said, taking a deep breath as if to drive home his point. "I think you took most of my blood"

I cringed. So that growl had come from me. And I had definitely taken more of Seely's blood than I should.

"I'm sorry. I think I was going to kill you."

He only shrugged. "Eh, I'm getting used to people trying to kill me. Better me than you any day."

I punched him lightly.

"Don't say things like that, Seely." I turned to my side and saw him staring up at the sky. I traced his profile with my eyes. His lips parted, breathing deeply.

His nose was sharp and pointed, yet soft somehow, and those freckles were looking as beautiful as ever. His hair had fallen back from his forehead, and I liked the way I could see every part of his face. His skin was so pale, though, since I'd chugged down more of his blood than I should. I nuzzled my face into his shoulder. "I'm sorry."

I didn't say what for. We both knew.

"At least now I know what happened to my mom," he said quietly. "She holed up in a bunker only a few miles away from me with a new family, handed us over to my dad, and then my dad killed her."

I wanted to say that we didn't know whether or not she was dead. That she could still be alive and until we saw a body, we could still have hope. But I knew that wasn't going to be helpful in this situation. I knew that no matter what I said, this fact remained true: Seely's father was trying to capture me, for whatever reason. And he'd almost succeeded.

"We can't stay here," I whispered. I was feeling strong and renewed after taking Seely's blood, but I also knew I'd taken too much and that he needed to rest for a while before he could continue on.

"I know." Seely sighed and squeezed his arm underneath me to wrap me closer into him. "Do you think the girls are okay?"

I'd tried not to think about what exactly the girls were going to do to stall Mr. Evanson and Sean, and I really didn't want to think about the possible consequences if they were found to have helped me and Seely escape. I had to believe that their father would protect them, but I didn't know how deeply his loyalties ran with Seely's father.

"I have to believe that they're okay. Who knows? Maybe they're still stalling, and we have all the time in the world." I stretched out dramatically to stress my point. "Maybe we can just stay right here forever and never have to go back to the AAUD at all. Problem solved."

Obviously, neither of us believed that, but we lay together in silence for an immeasurable moment. I was counting Seely's breaths, making sure they were steady. I wasn't sure what he was thinking about, but his hand was making small circles on the small of my back.

"Seely?" I said, after a moment. My anxiety had begun to rise, and we needed to make a plan, and quickly.

"Hmm?" He sounded sleepy.

"We need to decide what we're doing next."

He didn't answer, and I stayed still for a moment. Maybe he was thinking?

When the moment stretched too long, I raised up on my elbow to look at his face.

"You probably shouldn't go to sleep right now; not until we know you're okay."

As I looked at him, I saw that his mouth had gone slack, and it really looked like he was sleeping, except… I listened, and I couldn't hear his breathing anymore.

"No no no no no."

This couldn't be happening.

"Seely?" My voice was a whisper.

I touched his face, and his skin was so cold.

He was a corpse.

My heart was pounding, my mind was racing just as quickly.

"Seely *no*. Wake up, *please!*" I was sobbing, and I felt like I couldn't breathe any more than Seely was.

Every attempt at a breath ended up lodged in my throat. I was choking on the air.

My tears were like waterfalls, overflowing from my eyes with such force that I didn't know where this amount of water could possibly be coming from.

Then, I came to my senses. My blood.

Katrine had used it to heal Seely before, why wouldn't it work now? But then I thought about what Mr. Evanson had said about how I was Made. Orthan had taken most of my blood, almost all of it, before giving his to me. It turned me into an Undead.

Would the same happen to Seely? Had I taken just enough blood? Too much? I couldn't think about that. I couldn't run through the what ifs when I knew that he was definitely going to die if I did nothing.

Seely's dagger was strapped to his side, and I tore it out of the sheath. I sat directly over him, with one leg on either side of his body. Taking the dagger in my right hand, I cut into the wrist of my left arm, deep enough so the blood flowed freely from the wound. I didn't even feel the pain, only the determination of saving him.

I hovered my arm over his face at first, just letting the droplets fall just as Seely had done for me. He didn't move at all. I couldn't let my mind go where it was going. He wasn't dead.

I threw the dagger onto the ground and forced Seely's mouth open with my right hand. I let the blood drip directly into it, though he didn't make a move to swallow any of it.

"Please, please, please," I prayed. "Please don't."

I kept my arm over his mouth, the blood dripping from the wound until the blood had pooled so much into Seely's mouth that it began to drip out the sides. He hadn't swallowed it because he couldn't swallow it.

Because I was too late.

Because I'd killed him.

I was sobbing again, my tears soaking his black shirt. He looked perfect, even in death. Even with the blood that dripped from his mouth and ran down his neck, staining his pale skin. His eyes were so green in the moonlight, gazing unseeingly at the night sky.

I placed my hands on either side of his face and brought my forehead to his. My tears flowed down his face and mine, but I knew he wouldn't protest. *Couldn't* protest.

How had this happened? How could this be happening? I'd lost *years* with Seely, and I hadn't even known it. Until I did. And I wanted those years back. I wanted the years I'd lost and the years he and I deserved to live together. Whatever I was, whatever we were together, we deserved that time with each other.

I sat up and stared down at him for a moment longer. I felt the tension building in my chest. That heat only grew hotter until I couldn't take it anymore. I threw my head back and let out a scream that tore my throat to pieces. It was a scream that caused every bird in every tree nearby to scatter. It was a scream that shook the ground and opened a chasm in the ground to my right. I knew I was glowing this time because I could see it. My skin radiated with what looked like moonlight, and I could only gaze at it when I quieted.

I looked to the chasm that had opened from my wail, and I had a strange thought.

Bury him.

The voice didn't sound quite like mine, but I knew it had to be if it was in my head.

Bury him.

I rose from the ground, stepping carefully over Seely's body, and walked over to the hole I'd just made in the ground. It was deep, but not too deep. I could see the bottom. And the earth around it was soft and had already moved into mounds around the hole as though this air bubble in the Earth had risen up and displaced the dirt that was on top of it.

I couldn't do it.

Could I?

Was there a chance for Seely to come back?

Was this selfish of me?

Yes, I decided. Yes, to every question. None of it really mattered, though, except the second one. If there was a chance for Seely to come back, I would do anything. I took a little solace in the fact that I truly believed if the situation were reversed, he would also throw me into a hole in the ground and pray I came back as an Undead.

I turned back to him so quickly that I almost tripped over his feet. I picked him up underneath his shoulders and dragged him to the edge of the chasm. I laid him on the ground just before reaching the opening. Carefully, I placed his feet in first and then I moved his upper body, so he was resting somewhat comfortably at the bottom of the hole. It wasn't quite six feet deep, I didn't think, but it was deep enough. Though, I thought, he wouldn't be able to complain either way. He was dead.

My tears were still flowing steadily as I pushed the dirt into the opening with my hands, mixing with the loose dirt and making mud where they met the ground.

I put everything I had into that chasm. I clawed and scraped the dirt until my fingers were bleeding. I cried until I had no tears left. I sent silent prayers that I hoped would be heard and answered.

When I was done, there was nothing on the ground but a smoothed space of dirt. I grabbed Seely's dagger from the ground and sliced through my hand, letting my blood, Seely's blood, drip onto the freshly packed dirt. The final ingredient in the Undead recipe, according to what I remembered Seely telling me. I'd done everything I could, and now all I could do was wait and see if it was enough.

I realized that the roots and brambles of the forest encircled the make-shift grave like some kind of crown.

Sitting on the ground directly beside the place where Seely was buried, I folded myself into as tight of a ball as I could manage. My dress was torn and stained with mud and blood. My hands were coated with dirt, and I knew it had to be all over my face at that point, too. I didn't care.

I squeezed my legs to my chest, trying to physically keep myself together.

How long did it take to know whether or not someone was going to turn into an Undead? It didn't really matter. I was going to sit here until either Seely came crawling out of that dirt, someone came to kill me, or I starved.

I didn't know how long I'd been sitting there when I heard something rustling in the woods behind me. Without knowing how it had happened, I was standing. I reached down beside me where Seely's dagger still laid on the ground, gripping it tightly in my hand and crouching down in preparation to attack whoever was about to come through those woods. My heart was still pounding from everything that had happened, quickening with every passing second. I wondered about whether or not I should call out and force the person in the woods to step out into the clearing, but I thought better of it. Maybe they hadn't noticed me here somehow.

"I can hear your heart racing from a mile out, young one."

The voice that reached me was low, and I thought it somehow sounded old. It also reminded me of a hiss as it sent chills up my arms. I knew that voice, but I couldn't place where I'd heard it before.

"You should know better than to be in these woods all alone. But then again, I hear they've kept you in the dark for so long you've forgotten who you are, Alyssa Gold."

The voice was still coming from the shadows, but it was also still pricking at my recognition. I *knew* that voice. I wracked my brain for answers but came up empty.

"It's easy to be brave in the shadows," I called out, a little impressed with myself at the bravado I was emanating. "Step out here and so we can actually talk."

There was nothing for a moment, not even a breath or a step from the woods. Then I heard a low chuckle.

"As you wish."

The figure that stepped into the clearing shocked me. His inky hair and pitch-black eyes gleamed in the moonlight that shone into the clearing, and I felt my body stiffen. I was ready to run, in spite of myself.

There was something about the presence in front of me; an electricity filled the air where he stood, giving me a metallic taste in my mouth, and causing my hair to stand up on the back of my neck. I didn't know who it was, but I could never forget that musky, intimidatingly dark scent that made its way to me through on the breeze.

That was why the voice had sounded so familiar and unfamiliar all at the same time: because I'd only heard it in a dream. I didn't remember the day he killed me except for through the filter of my subconscious, but there was no mistaking that face. I would never forget the way it had looked when he'd come forward and ripped my throat open.

I don't know who I was expecting, but it wasn't him.

The scar on my neck that I'd all but forgotten about began to tingle slightly, and I fought the urge to reach up and touch it.

His eyes went directly to it, narrowing slightly.

Orthan.

"You have a scar?" He sounded confused, but I didn't say anything. I just sat there, frozen, staring at him. He continued on anyway. "That's interesting. That shouldn't happen. Your body healed perfectly after the Change, as all Undead do. I wonder…" He placed a finger to his chin as he looked up at the sky in contemplation. He paced back and forth slightly, and I followed every movement with Seely's dagger.

Orthan paused and looked at me again. "I am surprised, though, that your Beloved is not here with you. I'd come to the conclusion that he was all but a shadow to you." He tilted his head to the side, confused. "But then… I can smell him here. It's a spicy scent, almost like cloves or… cinnamon." Orthan continued to stare at me, his eyes narrowing slightly. "Did he leave you out here alone?"

I didn't answer him. I just stared, holding my dagger up, ready to strike when the time came.

Orthan nodded. "I see. You're not ready to talk." A slow, menacing smile spread across his face. "But you will be."

Maybe I should say something, I thought to myself. Maybe I should tell him to get a life and leave me to what I had left. Maybe I should tell him that he'd taken enough from me, and he couldn't have anything else.

Maybe I should have, but I didn't. The truth is, I didn't have anything else left inside of me. I'd poured everything I had into that hole with Seely, and if he didn't come out again, I wasn't sure that I wanted to even try and go on. I didn't have anyone or anything without him, and whether or not that's healthy, it was the truth.

Everyone else had lied to me and kept me asleep and hidden and erased my life without even bothering to ask my permission. I wasn't sure if they did that on purpose, but it happened. And I wanted to know the answer, I really did. I wanted to know if my family still thought I was me even though I was irreparably different. I wanted them to accept me and hold me and love me like I thought I remembered them doing.

But sometimes we don't get what we want. Sometimes we don't get to say goodbye to the people we love, and sometimes they're gone before we even realize they've left. Sometimes we don't get a say in what happens to us and we don't get a second chance, and that's something we have to accept as a fact of life and move on the best we can, hoping for a better future while carrying a past that has scarred us into something nearly unrecognizable.

But sometimes… sometimes we get a chance to do all those things, all at once.

As Orthan stood a few paces from me, just staring, and I stood with Seely's dagger pointed towards him, staring back, the ground began to crumble under my feet. A gust of wind blew through the clearing and swept my hair in front of my face, the strands twisting through my vision. I felt another crack in the earth and I whipped around to the hole where Seely lay.

The dirt was moving, shifting, changing, right before my eyes.

"Oh," Orthan breathed. "This is going to be fun." He chuckled again. "You have more to do before I'm ready for you, Alyssa, but I think I'll be seeing you both soon."

I turned to him just in time to see a smile of pure delight on his face before he disappeared into black dust.

I would have to deal with that later. And Mr. Evanson. And my family. And the consequences of what was happening right now in the clearing, but for that moment all I could do was watch as the dirt swirled and twisted and turned to a black sludge, just like I'd choked on in the town car on that first day with Seely and Dexter.

The earth cracked once more, and a hand broke through the surface, reaching for the stars through the black of the night.

A. H. NANCE

is a twenty-something woman living in Oklahoma. She teaches ninth-grade English and has always been in love with books, especially Young Adult fiction and romance. She's been writing stories since before she can remember, but this is her first completed novel. Stay tuned for more.

Follow Abby on Instagram using @abbywritesfiction, and on Twitter using @abbywritesbooks.

You can also keep up with her on her website: abbywritesfiction.com.